No Greater Love

By

Doris Christian

Tate Publishing, LLC.

*I*n Dedication:

To all those who dare to dream . . . have faith to believe . . .

And never give up . . .

To Thomas,
the new man in
my life ~
With hugs & kisses
Doris Christian

Synopsis of 'No Greater Love.'

Bitter, jealous, unforgiving . . . that is what best described twenty-three year old Kara Westin. That is, until a tragedy nearly claims her life. After being pulled to safety by a stranger, Kara's life takes a new and unexpected turn which helps bring healing to estranged family relationships and pumps energy into her stagnate love-life.

When a new job takes her to Atlanta, Kara comes face to face with Lorenzo Carlyle, the man who saved her life months before. Due to a picture she sees in Lorenzo's home, Kara is soon on a journey to find the truth about a diamond necklace, the exact replica handed down by her own grandmother. Before long, Kara finds that power, wealth and greed are connected to the rare necklace, which soon entangles her life with Lorenzo.

Although trying to spare her family from more heartache, Kara uncovers more shocking news in her grandmother's recently discovered diaries. When Lorenzo falls in love with Kara he vows to protect her from those willing to kill for the necklace. Yet, when his promise fails, it is Kara's renewed faith in God that helps her survive against impossible odds.

This Christian romantic fiction is sure to capture the heart of the woman reader of any age. From Michigan to the hills of Scotland, 'No Greater Love' is filled with suspense, mystery and emotion. It gives insight to the truth of God's promises. He is our refuge and strength . . . our high tower . . . our shelter in time of storm. Those who call upon the name of Jesus will find comfort in all seasons . . . and will most assuredly find . . . 'No Greater Love.'

Other Books
by Doris Christian

'For Everything There's A Season'
'When the Heart Whispers'
'Matters of the Heart'

Prologue of:
'When the Heart Whispers' series

Although she lost her mother on the day of her birth, the beautiful baby, Laura O'Brian, was soon entangled in the heart-strings of the large O'Brien family. From them, Laura learns the meaning of love, devotion and hard work. Most importantly, she learns to have a deep Christian faith.

On her twenty-first birthday, Laura's dream comes true when her family presents her with a ticket to Ireland. Finally, she would see the many places she'd only heard about.

It was during Laura's two-week vacation that she meets handsome sea Captain Marty Kavanagh. Within a few months, the love-at-first-sight relationship takes the young couple down the wedding aisle. When their sons, Tom and Eric are born a few years later, their family is complete.

At age twenty-nine, Laura's life of bliss quickly ends when Marty is tragically killed in a boating accident. Although her strong faith is tested, Laura carries on. Finally, five years later she returns home to America and her family.

Knowing her boys need a father, Laura begins dating after arriving in Chicago. Soon she meets Frank Webster. It isn't long before the man's charm convinces Laura he could be the one she's waited nearly six years for.

With the sudden death of her Uncle Walt, Laura is shocked to learn she is the sole benefactor to his estate, including a guest ranch in Montana. Despite strong rejections from her cousin, Samantha, Laura agrees to marry Frank. Weeks later, the Webster family leaves Chicago for the uncertainties of the West.

Amid the majestic splendor of the Mission Mountains in Northwest Montana, Laura's devoted faith becomes her only solace when her life is thrust headlong into a world of abuse and deception, at the hands of her new husband.

With challenges at every turn, Laura finds help and friendship from Kelly and Kara Westin, twenty-year-old twin sisters who arrive at her door looking for a summer job. And when the Webster family meets Dr. Levi North, they have no way of knowing the important role he'll play in each of their lives.

When the twin sisters decide to stay on at the ranch for another summer to work, Kelly soon finds she is the object of attention from Ned, a young deputy sheriff. Seemingly overlooked by the opposite sex, Kara remains supportive of her sister's love life. That is, until Kelly meets handsome millionaire Jock Beaumont.

Chapter One

The gray, overcast morning only added to the gloom hanging over Kara Westin as she stood at her apartment window. Outside she saw the barren trees with only a scattering of bright colored leaves hanging persistently against the cold autumn wind.

Absentmindedly, she folded her arms and stuffed her hands into the sleeves of the tattered-blue sweater she wore. Feeling the warmth of the aging pull-over, her mind darted back to her sixteenth birthday when she'd received it as a gift from her parents. She remembered her father's arms around her, hugging her like he often did. *Oh Dad, how did life get so messed up? If only you were still here to talk to, this wouldn't have happened between me and Kelly. You would have insisted we smooth things out long before now. The holidays are coming and I have no family to be with, not even Mother,* Kara thought. *It's your own fault. This could have been settled if you weren't so stubborn!* she reminded herself.

Leaving the window, she plopped down on her sofa and retrieved the "TV Guide" from her coffee table, brushing aside the self accusations. Deep down, she knew her pride was the real reason she hadn't answered Kelly's letters; that, along with a tinge of jealously. *Your twin sister married a millionaire and you don't even have a serious boyfriend,* an inner voice taunted.

Dropping the magazine back to its place, Kara flung her long blond hair over her shoulder and bolted off the sofa. "I need a diversion, a make-over," she blurted, remembering the television show from last night.

Going to her bathroom, Kara studied her image in the mirror deciding what changes might improve her ebbing self-esteem. Leaning close, she saw big blue eyes, long dark lashes, and creamy well-toned skin. Her small round face was categorized as pretty, certainly not beautiful, at least not without make-up. Yet, Kara was well aware that her model-like figure caught the eyes of women as well as men.

"New hairdo, different make-up, new *style* . . . that's what you need," Kara told the image looking back at her.

No matter what you do, you can't run away from the truth, she reminded herself. Remembering the last conversation with her sister, Kara had to accept the blame. *I accused Kelly of being a gold-digger, of marrying Jock for his money. I even threw her letters in the garbage . . . unopened. But I can't help how I feel!* she thought stubbornly, turning from the mirror.

When memories of her last conversation with Kelly refused to subside, Kara searched for a distraction. "I do have *one* friend left in the world, but I won't burden him with my woes," she whispered, grabbing her address book. A moment later she heard the familiar voice.

"Hello Ned, this is Kara. Did I catch you at a bad time?" she greeted.

"Not at all," Ned replied, sounding surprised. "How are you, Kara? How are things in Michigan?"

"Things are going okay, how about you?"

"Can't complain . . . doesn't do much good anyhow," Ned answered jokingly. "What's up? You don't sound too cheerful."

"Oh, it's just the autumn blues," she declared, letting out a deep sigh. "Summer's ending, wintry cold is just ahead, so I thought a good conversation might lift my spirits, and you came to mind. So Ned, what's new in your life?" she asked.

"Quite a lot, actually," Ned told her. "I bought a business and its doing real good."

"What kind of business?"

"Selling and constructing log homes," Ned replied.

"They *do* seem popular in Montana, from what I remember," Kara remarked. "How did *that* happen?" she had to know, feeling pleased he was getting on with his life since Kelly dumped him.

"I heard of an established contractor who was retiring due to ill health; I had a little money to go along with a bank loan, so I bought his business," Ned informed Kara. "It's nice being my own boss."

For the next several minutes, Kara learned all she could about Ned's new venture. It was obvious he didn't miss his job as sheriff's deputy, yet, Kara sensed an underlying tone of sadness in his voice.

"Kara, how's Kelly doing?" he suddenly asked, surprising her.

"I don't really know. We don't talk anymore," Kara had to admit. "From what I hear, she and Jock are doing fine. With all that money, who wouldn't?"

"Money can't buy happiness, Kara," Ned quickly replied. "So why *aren't* you two talking? She's your sister."

"We had some words and I missed her wedding," Kara said. "She wrote me later, but I didn't respond."

There was silence. "Why didn't you tell me this before?" Ned finally asked. "What happened? You two were inseparable."

"I accused her of being a gold-digger and for breaking your heart," Kara blurted out. "She wasn't *fair* to you, Ned. You loved her and I felt she chose Jock over you because of his money. I know I shouldn't have said those things to her, but you were *so* devoted to her after her accident."

"Oh, Kara, Kelly had her own battles, and I could see she didn't love me anymore," Ned answered sadly. "Perhaps she never did. Yes, I admit it still hurts, but marrying me out of gratitude *or* obligation would have been worse."

"How can you be so . . . *gracious?*" Kara then asked. "Don't you feel even a *little* resentment toward her *or* Jock?"

"No, I don't. Life is too short to hold a grudge, besides I'd only be hurting myself," Ned replied. "You're wrong for cutting yourself off from your sister, Kara, and my advice is for you to get it settled. We *have* to forgive one another and besides, she's the only sister you have. I'm sure Kelly is sick about this. *Promise* me you'll call her."

As she listened, Kara knew Ned was right. Yet, how could she just pick up the phone and call Kelly after five long months? "I promise I'll *think* about it," Kara finally said. "I appreciate what you're saying, Ned. But, I'm afraid things will *never* be the same between Kelly and me."

"Swallow your pride, Kara. Admit you were wrong. I don't think for a minute Kelly married Jock for his money, nor should you," Ned scolded. When Kara didn't comment, he added. "Tell your mother hello for me, okay?"

"Yeah, I will," Kara answered, not daring to mention *that* relationship was also strained. "I better go, Ned, I have things to do, but it was good talking to you. Take care of yourself."

"You too, and Kara, *please* settle things with Kelly," he urged again as the call ended.

For a moment, Kara sat staring at the receiver she held. She had called Ned in hopes of feeling better, but now found herself in deeper gloom. *I've got to get over this, but I sure won't do it sitting in this place,* she thought.

Leaving the sofa she headed for her bedroom. *I'll get dressed and go find someone or some* thing *to get my mind off my troubles!* Kara vowed.

. . .

Although the sun was shining, a cold wind greeted Kara as she stepped from her year old Mustang. After pulling the collar of her leather jacket up around her ears, she headed for the familiar entrance a short distance away. Not only was this upscale lounge / restaurant her place of employment, but she found solace here for her loneliness.

After moving to Ann Arbor, Michigan six months earlier to attend college, Kara soon realized her desire for higher learning had lost its appeal. Within weeks of her twenty-third birthday, she had quit and found a job as hostess. She discovered early on if she wore a smile and figure flattering clothes, she, too, would receive generous tips from the male customers.

"Hey Kara," a male voice called out as she entered the door. "You miss this place so much you gotta come on your day off?"

"Yeah, where else can a girl get a free cup of coffee?" Kara yelled back, waving at the young busboy across the room. She had to smile at the kid's enthusiasm and wondered at his happy-go-lucky attitude. Certainly *she* couldn't find reason to be so upbeat everyday. Before seating herself at a corner table, Kara removed her coat and smoothed her wind-blown hair.

Although the dining room was nearly empty, it would soon be filled with dinner guests. Business men, couples, and even singles patronized this popular eatery. Slowly, Kara was learning bits of information about the regular customers. It was hard not to be inquisitive about people, especially if one's own life held no special excitement.

"Hey Kara, Josie just called in sick, so if you want to work tonight, you got it," her boss informed her as he sat down at the table. "I know you rarely work Saturday night, so maybe you have other plans."

"No plans, but I'm not dressed for work. I guess I *do* have time to run home and change," Kara replied, glancing at her watch. "Thanks Rob, I can always use the money."

With a nod and smile, her boss left the table and disappeared through the double doors leading to the kitchen. Hurriedly, Kara retrieved her coat, grabbed her purse and headed for the door.

Suddenly, a deafening noise was heard from behind and her body was propelled through the air like a rag doll. Slamming against a hard surface, she was knocked unconscious before she could feel the intense heat from the fire.

. . .

The sound of a siren and urgent yells slowly brought Kara to. She heard a voice, masculine and tender. "Kara, you're going to be okay. Can you open your eyes for me?" he asked. Still unsure whether this was real or a bad dream, Kara waited. Soon, pain in her body brought a new awareness.

She heard someone moan . . . it was her. "We need help over here!" the man yelled.

"It'll be okay. You're going to be just fine, and I'll be right here with you," that same voice told her.

Moments later she was moved, lifted into an ambulance. Pain now gripped her body. It was hard to breathe. Finally, she was swept away to that place of blessed calm.

Being slightly aware of someone nearby, Kara drifted in and out of a drugged sleep. It was Wednesday afternoon when she finally opened her eyes.

"Are you feeling better?" someone asked, startling her. Leaving his chair, a man approached Kara's bedside; a look of concern was on his face. "Don't be alarmed, Miss Westin. I had to stay with you . . . at least till you woke up."

"I've seen you before," Kara whispered. "What happened? Why am I here?" she asked, looking around the sterile white room.

"There was an explosion . . . at the restaurant," the man informed her. "I was nearby and when the wall collapsed on you, I pulled you out." Laying her head back against the pillow, Kara closed her eyes as she fought to retrieve memories. Slowly they came.

"Rob . . . how is he? And the others?" she then asked, opening her eyes. "*Please* tell me."

Before any information was forthcoming, another man entered the room. A look of weariness showed on his rather pudgy face. When he saw the other man at Kara's bedside, they only nodded to each other.

"Hello Miss Westin, I'm Dr. Hudson. I've been treating your injuries since you came in. How are you feeling?" he asked, looking at her.

"Very sore," Kara admitted, feeling pain throughout her body. "What injuries do I have?"

"You have some broken ribs, a punctured lung, lacerations to your back and lower extremities, to name the major ones," the doctor quickly replied. "You'll be stiff and sore for several days, but you're going to be fine. We tried to locate your family, but were unsuccessful I'm afraid. Do you have anyone nearby?" he asked, glancing through her chart. "You can go home tomorrow, but only if you have someone to stay with for a few days."

For the first time, Kara thought about Kelly and her mom. Suddenly she remembered her talk with Ned, and his urging to call Kelly. *Would this be cause enough? Certainly it would be reason to call Mother,* she decided.

"Yes, my mother lives in Romeo," Kara revealed. "I'm sure I can go stay with her."

"Good, if you want to call her, I'll write your discharge orders," Dr. Hudson informed Kara before leaving the room.

"Will that be hard for you?" the stranger asked. "I mean, to call your mother?"

"Why do you ask?" Kara snapped feeling perturbed at his remark.

"I sense your reluctance. Perhaps you're not comfortable with it."

"Who *are* you? What is your name?"

"My name is Lorenzo," he said softly. "I don't mean to upset you, Miss Westin, but sometimes I sense things about people."

"Well, this time you're wrong," Kara fired back as a sharp pain tore through her side. Closing her eyes, she leaned her head back and waited for the pain to subside. "I *am* indebted to you for digging me out of that mess, but I don't need you any longer, thank you," she said sternly.

"As you wish," Lorenzo replied. "I do trust things will work out for you." Refusing to open her eyes, Kara waited until the man's footsteps sounded in the hallway.

What nerve! And why is he hanging around here? Doesn't he have a job? Kara thought bitterly. *You're being a bit hard on someone who probably saved your life, aren't you?*

Now, after everything that happened, she felt even more depressed. Not only was her body aching from head to toe, but she had to ask for help. And, now she felt guilty for being so hard on Lorenzo, her hero.

For a moment, Kara wondered if news of this incident reached Romeo. *Surely it did, if people were hurt,* she decided, reaching for the telephone near her bed. *I hope Rob and the others got out okay,* she thought, realizing no one had answered her questions about them.

Reluctantly, Kara dialed her mother's number. She was ready to hang up when someone finally answered. "Westin residence," a woman greeted.

"Hello, is Emma Westin there?" Kara asked.

"No, I'm sorry she isn't, she's at work," the female replied. "I'm her sister, may I help you with something?"

"Oh . . . is this Gina? Gina Culp?" Kara asked, knowing it *had* to be her aunt, since her mother had no other sister.

"Well, yes, this is Gina Culp. May I ask whose calling?"

"This is Kara, Aunt Gina. I can't believe it's really you!"

"Kara . . . oh my dear . . . it's so *good* to hear from you," she cheered excitedly. "Where . . . where *are* you?"

"Actually, I'm in the hospital," Kara answered, hearing Gina's sudden gasp. "I'm okay, really, but I'm afraid the doctor won't release me unless I have some place to stay for a few days. I have some broken ribs," she quickly informed her aunt.

"Oh my goodness, what *happened?*" Gina blurted.

"There was an explosion, where I work," Kara said, "I don't remember much about it."

"Kara, *you* were in that horrible accident that killed those four people?"

"Killed four people? No, it *couldn't* be the same place," Kara protested, feeling sure it wasn't. "This happened at the—"

"Blue Lagoon," Gina said, finishing Kara's sentence. "It's been on the news for days!"

A sudden chill swept through Kara's body and she felt sick. "Did . . . did they give any names?" she finally asked.

"Yes, just this morning," Gina told her niece. "Let me grab the paper and I'll read you the article." A shroud of disbelief covered Kara while she waited. "Okay, this is what it says:

'Investigation continues into the cause of the explosion Saturday, at the Blue Lagoon lounge and restaurant that claimed four lives and injured several others. Those killed were: Robert McKee, owner; Chip Newberry, busboy; Carl Phillips, cook; and Sally Rice, assistant manager. All victims were apparently in the kitchen area when the explosion took place, preventing any chance of escape. The preliminary investigation points to a faulty valve on the gas grill that was recently installed.

Those injured were taken to local hospitals with a variety of complaints. Some were treated and released while others remain hospitalized with more serious injuries including burns, broken bones and head trauma. Since the eatery was nearly vacant of customers, it is thought most of the injured were walking by outside when the explosion happened and they were hit by debris.'

"Were *you* inside, Kara?" Gina quickly asked. Still reeling from what she just heard, Kara couldn't speak. Instead, silent tears rolled down her cheeks as she thought about her friends, all dead. "I'm sorry, dear. This is obviously a great shock. How *horrible* for you," Gina added.

"I can't believe it . . . I was sitting with Rob, talking. Just seconds before. If I hadn't headed for the door, I'd be dead too," Kara uttered in disbelief.

Suddenly, she realized how close she'd come to dying, along with the others. Despair seeped into her already weakened body. *Life is too short to hold a grudge . . . that's what Ned told me. He's right. We never know when our time is up,* Kara thought, wiping her tears.

"Dear, is there *anything* I can do for you? Anyone I can call?" Gina then asked.

"Just tell Mother I called, and that I'll call her tonight," Kara replied. "I can't wait to see you, Aunt Gina."

"Me too, sweetheart. It's been far too long . . . and Kara, I'm so thankful you survived that accident. It's obvious God was with you."

"Yeah, it seems so," Kara could barely say. As she ended the call, she was overcome with emotion. Not only did she mourn the death of her friends and fellow workers, but for the first time she truly regretted the way she'd acted all these past months.

How would Mother and Kelly feel if I had died in that accident? Terrible, I'm sure. Likewise, how would I feel if they were to die? Kara wondered sadly. *I must do something, this was just too close.*

Closing her eyes, Kara rehearsed what she'd say to Kelly. But, no matter what she came up with, it sounded awkward and self-serving. *Why not just apologize? Admit you were wrong,* her thoughts argued. *If Ned can forgive Kelly, surely I can,* she decided.

. . .

The two sisters glanced at the kitchen clock one more time as they finished up the supper dishes. After hearing that Kara called, Emma felt giddy with anticipation of her calling again tonight. "Oh Gina, I've prayed so hard for this day," Emma told her sister. "I know Kelly has too. Now it seems we're finally getting our answer," she added, hanging her dishtowel over the small wooden rack.

"The poor dear has obviously been through a lot the past few days," Gina replied, dabbing hand lotion from a tube into her palm. "I hated being the one to break the news about her coworkers; it was a horrible shock."

"Undoubtedly," Emma replied, shaking her head. "To think she was that close to being a casualty is even more frightening. But, God is faithful, Gina. He honors our prayers for protection," she added as they headed for the living room. "And I pray daily for my family."

Soon after the two were seated the telephone rang, bringing a surge of joy to Emma as she went to answer. "Hello," she greeted on the second ring.

"Hello Mother, this is Kara."

"Hello, my dear. It's so *good* to hear your voice," Emma replied, feeling tears already gathering behind her eyes. "Gina told me what happened, and I'm so *very* sorry about your friends. Thank God you're alive! How *are* you?"

"I'm sore with some broken ribs and cuts here and there, but I'm going home, tomorrow," Kara told her. "However, the Doc doesn't want me staying alone. Would it be okay if I came there for awhile?"

"Oh, of course, sweetheart," Emma replied, "we'd *love* having you here. Are you able to drive or may we come and get you?"

"Well, come to think of it, I'm not sure *where* my car is," Kara said. "It was parked outside the restaurant. Perhaps I don't have one anymore. In that case, Mother, I'll have to let you know."

For the next few minutes, Emma listened intently as Kara told her about the stranger who pulled her from the rubble. "He sounds like an angel, dear," Emma finally remarked. "Being at your side all that time is quite unusual, wouldn't you say?"

"Do you *really* think that, Mother?" Kara blurted.

"It's not so surprising . . . you *do* remember what happened to Kelly, Ned and Abby, don't you? Our sweet little Abby saw the angels that day out on the lake. She said they talked to her, too, and I believe it."

"Yes, I remember, how *is* Abby?" Kara asked then, surprising Emma.

"She's wonderful, just as sweet as ever and we still play checkers every chance we get," Emma answered, smiling at the thought. "She asks about her Aunt Kara quite often as a matter of fact. She misses you, dear, as we *all* do." For a moment only silence was on the line, then . . .

"I miss everyone, too," Kara whispered in an unsteady voice.

"It'll be wonderful having you home, sweetheart. Gina is anxiously awaiting those late night talks you two used to have whenever she came for a visit. Remember that?"

"I remember. You and Kelly could never stay up past ten-thirty, but we laughed and talked till the wee hours," Kara replied with a slight chuckle.

"But now you can sleep in as long as you want," Emma offered, "no more dragging yourself out of bed to catch the school bus."

"Yes, things have definitely changed since those days, but I'm not sure I dare laugh with these sore ribs," Kara confessed. "I'll call you tomorrow, Mother, after I get news of my car, and if you'll need to drive me."

As the call ended, Emma felt as though she was two feet off the ground. "Oh sister, what a relief I feel. I do believe the time has come for our family to reconcile. Thank you, Lord!" Emma cheered, raising her hands as she looked upward.

"I'm so happy to hear that," Gina replied. "It would be a mighty sad Christmas around here if they didn't. And, speaking of Christmas, do you and Charles have plans? At least any you can talk about?" she asked with her mischievous grin.

"Nothing unusual," Emma responded, "Kelly and Jock invited Jared and Samantha to come for Christmas. And Jock mentioned a surprise for Kelly, but as yet we haven't had a chance to discuss it. As far as Charles and I are concerned, just being together is enough," she admitted happily. "He's a wonderful friend."

"Friend?" Gina bellowed. "I've never seen a *friend* look at someone quite like that before! He simply *swoons* when he sees you, and don't tell me you haven't noticed."

"Well, maybe he's a *little* interested in being more, but as yet he hasn't said anything," Emma replied, admitting only to herself that she had grown *quite* fond of the man. "*Whatever* is meant to be, I'm sure will happen in due season," she added, retrieving her knitting from a nearby basket.

For the next while, Gina thumbed through the new "Ideals" magazine and Emma counted stitches in the intricate cable design on Abby's pink and white sweater she'd be receiving for Christmas.

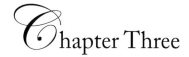

Chapter Three

As Kara finished her bowl of oatmeal and toast the next morning, she was surprised when Lorenzo appeared in her doorway. "Hello, Miss Westin," he greeted. "I understand you're going home today."

"I'm going to Romeo to stay with my mother for a few days," Kara replied, studying the man's face. "I'm surprised to see you, after the way I acted. I'm sorry, Lorenzo, for the way I spoke to you last time. Thank you for helping me, for saving my life, if that's the case," she said, wondering if in fact she *was* talking to an angel. "By the way, who *are* you? I mean *really?*"

"Just someone who saw a need and acted upon it," he told her. "I'm no one special."

"On the contrary, it's one thing to help someone in need, but quite *another* to stay at their bedside for days after," Kara refuted. "And now you're here again to check on me. Why, Lorenzo?"

"Let's just say I felt obliged to follow this through, until you recovered," he replied. Slowly he moved toward Kara's bedside, but stopped several feet away. "As I said before, I sense things about people and I feel there is great sorrow in your life, not only because of your friends dying in the fire, but other things, too. Am I wrong?"

At hearing his statement, Kara could only stare at the man; this stranger who somehow felt responsible for her. Whose sudden appearance might well make her feel uneasy, but didn't. "Are you angelic? Were you sent to help me, to save my life?" Kara asked, peering into his eyes in hopes of perhaps seeing some divine entity.

For a moment, as their eyes met, Kara tried hard to read what she saw. Was it confidence, compassion? Then, pulling her eyes free, she studied his face. *Neatly trimmed beard, dark eyelashes and brows, jet black hair . . . quite handsome I'd say,* Kara decided.

"Some may call me your angel, Miss Westin, but I assure you I'm not angelic," he answered softly. "I'm just grateful I was given the opportunity to help you, it is most rewarding."

"I still don't know who you are," Kara argued. "But I've seen you before. In the restaurant, always alone. Don't you have family? Or a job?"

"I have no family, at least not here," he told Kara, "and my business allows me all the time I need to do what I choose."

"Must be nice," Kara remarked somewhat sarcastically, finding the man's explanation quite evasive. "So all you do is follow women until they become damsels in distress and then you help them out of life threatening situations, is that it?"

"I'm sorry, but I have an appointment I need to keep. If you'll please excuse me," Lorenzo said, curtly nodding his head. "Have a good life, Kara; just remember, things aren't always what they seem."

With that, the man turned and left Kara staring after him. "What a strange duck! Good riddance," she mumbled shaking her head. Yet, she felt strangely alone, as though she'd lost someone important in her life. *It's the medication, or this place. I'll be glad to leave and forget about Lorenzo, whoever he may be,* she thought assuredly.

Later that morning, Kara had further disappointment when she talked to the fire chief. "I'm sorry, Miss, but your car was burned up, I'm afraid. There was extensive damage to vehicles parked nearby," he told her over the phone. "I'm sure the insurance adjuster will be calling you."

"I'm leaving the hospital today, they'll have to call me in Romeo," Kara replied. As she gave the man her mother's telephone number, Kara could only shake her head at this additional bad news. "Sir, would you happen to know when the funerals are scheduled for the victims?" she asked in haste.

"Yes, I believe the last one is being held this morning," he informed her. "Good luck, Miss. I do hope things work out for you."

After the phone call, Kara painfully inched her way to the window and looked outside to the dreary, cloud-filled sky. Hot tears burned her eyes as she thought about those who died and the families they'd left behind.

Her body ached. She carried bruises and dozens of sutures that closed gaping lacerations she'd received, but none of this compared to the hurt she felt inside. In one brief moment, five days earlier, her life changed. People died and she had become vividly aware of her own mortality. Now, as a veil lifted, Kara saw her life from a different view.

I have wallowed in my solitude; I felt contempt and jealousy at

Kelly's good fortune, I even shut out my own mother, Kara lamented, turning from the window. *I was ungrateful to Lorenzo who saved my life!* "You're right, Ned. Life *is* too short for all this," she whispered.

. . .

Back at his apartment Lorenzo pondered the surprising turn of events. *Saving Miss Westin's life has certainly changed my course of action. Now it should be easier to achieve my mission. Use every opportunity, that's what Mother always says. By any means possible we accomplish our goals. Honor and duty is my lineage, yet, Kara is a beautiful woman, and feisty. I would be wise to watch myself with her. If she wasn't a commoner I might end up falling for that lovely young woman,* he thought.

. . .

It was well past three o'clock that afternoon when Emma, Kara and Gina arrived in Romeo. During the drive from Ann Arbor, Gina had talked non-stop causing Kara and her mother to share a grin at the woman's excited chatter.

"I had no *intentions* of selling my restaurant, but with that kind of offer, how *could* I refuse?" Gina remarked as they pulled into the driveway. "Plus, I decided it was time to come and spend time with my sister, after all, we're not getting any younger, you know?" she went on, leaning forward to pat Emma's shoulder from the back seat.

"My, you make us sound *matronly,*" Emma laughed, "but it has been grand having you here," she added, bringing her ten-year-old Buick to a stop near the back porch. "And, there's no reason why we can't live together from now on."

"I doubt *Charles* would agree with that," Gina snickered as she opened her car door.

"Charles? Who might *that* be?" Kara asked, finding her aunt's babble most enlightening.

"You know Charles, dear. He's the chef on Jock's boat," Emma replied. "We've become quite good friends."

"Yeah, just like Cinderella and the Prince were good *friends,*" Gina teased. "Cinderella here won't admit it, but her prince is bending every *which* way to show how much he likes her."

"Mother, is this *true?*" Kara asked, realizing much had happened since she'd disconnected herself from her family.

"He's a sweet man, but I wouldn't say he's trying to impress me," Emma responded, pulling the keys from the ignition. "Welcome home, dear," she said, patting Kara's hand and smiling. "It's so good to have you here."

Studying her mother's face, Kara did notice a certain glow. Could it be her visit, or *was* Charles responsible? "Thank you, Mother. It's good to be here," Kara replied truthfully, returning Emma's smile.

"Well, are we going to sit here all day, or are we going to get this poor girl in the house and fix her something to eat?" Gina spouted as she climbed out of the car.

With a mutual chuckle at Gina's abruptness, Emma and Kara also exited the vehicle.

As she started up the back steps, Kara felt the stiffness in her body, bringing a sudden reminder of what happened. *It's good to be alive . . . things might have turned out much differently,* she thought, wondering why *she* had survived when others had not.

. . .

The delicious smell of Emma's homemade vegetable beef soup greeted them as the three women entered the kitchen after their long drive.

"Umm . . . I've been waiting all day for this," Gina remarked, lifting the lid from the crock pot. "No one makes soup *quite* like my sister," she added, licking her lips. "Maybe I'll open another restaurant and serve only Emma's delicious soup!"

"I'm afraid there isn't much call these days for just soup," Emma replied, helping Kara into the living room.

"Well, we can throw in some of your apple pie, you *know* everyone loves that," Gina boasted, tying an apron around her slender waist.

Although four years separated Emma and Gina, no one could guess Emma was older. Both had creamy-smooth-complexion and broad smiles. While Emma was fair and blue eyed, Gina had reddish-brown hair and brown eyes. Having dealt with the harsh winters in Alaska for the past fifteen years, not to mention the rough-edged men who patronized her restaurant, Gina had developed a crass exterior. Those close to her knew the other side. They realized her boldness was a cover up for the heartache she felt over losing her husband and their only child in an avalanche, five years earlier.

In no time, Emma had Kara settled on the sofa. "If you need anything, my dear, let us know," she told her daughter before heading for the kitchen.

It was hard to contain her happiness at having Kara home, yet, a cloud of uncertainty hung over her.

Two days . . . will that be enough time to prepare her for Kelly's visit? And what will she think? Dear God, please help us get this situation settled, Emma hurriedly prayed, feeling grateful for the recent progress.

In no time the meal was ready. Baking powder biscuits were browned just right when Emma retrieved them from the oven. Three bowls were then filled with the tantalizing soup.

"Smells fit for a king," Gina cheered as she poured coffee. Soon the women were seated at the table. Reaching out, Emma patted Kara's hand.

"I'm so thankful to God for watching over you," she said, seeing the now vivid bruises on Kara's face.

"I'm grateful, too, Mother. When I heard about the others, I realized I was given a new lease on life and I know there are things I must do," Kara replied. "I'm glad to be here."

With a lump growing in her throat, Emma offered a heartfelt prayer for those who had lost loved ones in the fire. "And, Dear Lord, bless that man who pulled Kara from the rubble," she quickly added before ending her prayer. "I just realized, for the second time one of my girls has been snatched from the brink of death, but you, my dear sister, have suffered far more than I can imagine."

As her eyes suddenly filled with tears, Gina reached out and clasped Emma's hand. "I only pray you'll never taste such sorrow," she whispered.

The bright morning sun filled Kara's bedroom, coaxing her awake. As she cleared her mind of sleep, she remembered what day it was. *One week . . . just one week ago it happened. Life changed for all of us, and here I am, alive. I still can't believe the others are gone,* she mourned, remembering each one.

During the past two days, Kara felt her body responding, not only to the rest she was getting, but also the loving care she was receiving from her mother and Aunt Gina. Making sure she lacked for nothing, they attended to her every need.

Lately, Kara sensed a change in her mother. "How are you feeling?" Emma asked later that morning, setting a plate of French toast on the table.

"Still sore, but getting better," Kara had to admit. "Mother, is there something bothering you?"

"Well . . . yes, I guess there is," Emma replied, retrieving the coffee pot from the stove. "Kelly's coming this afternoon, and I'm wondering what your feelings are about that."

For a moment, Kara wasn't sure how she *did* feel. First she felt a wave of excitement, then apprehension. Although she knew she had to apology to Kelly and wanted to restore their relationship, she wasn't sure this was the best time. *Life is too short, Kara. You must get this settled,* she told herself.

"I'm okay with it, Mother, really. I *do* need to talk to Kelly, the time has come," Kara told Emma, adding cream to her now full coffee cup.

"Thank you, dear. You don't know how *pleased* I am to hear you say that," Emma responded, letting out a sigh.

. . .

Excitement surged through Kelly as she got dressed that morning. The sun was shining, but had its brilliance not been pouring through the window of the luxurious Beaumont home, the room would still be aglow with Kelly's beaming happiness.

"It's a miracle, and now Kara's actually staying at Mother's!" Kelly cheered while putting on her new burgundy pant suit.

"I'm so happy for you, sweetheart," Jock told her as he sat watching. "I know how long you've waited for this day."

"I can't tell you how *grateful* I am, not only to see my sister, but that she survived that horrible explosion," Kelly said, shaking her head. "It might have ended much differently. God is so good!"

"Promise you won't be *too* disappointed if she isn't as receptive as you would like," Jock cautioned. "After all, she's there due to her accident and not by choice."

"I know, but at least Mother and I have this opportunity to talk to her," Kelly replied, sitting down at her dressing table. "It's been so hard, not having my sister in our lives. I've hated it, especially for Mother's sake."

"Is Abby going with you?" Jock then asked.

"No. She decided to attend her classmate's birthday party instead," Kelly answered, feeling somewhat relieved. "I'm afraid she'd be bored with such grownup conversation."

Finally, pleased with her hair and make-up, Kelly turned and looked at her husband. "Jock, I love you so much," she said softly. "I know these past months haven't been easy for you, either. I've been hard to live with at times, but you've been so patient."

"Because I know how depressed you've been over Kara," he replied. Leaving his chair by the window, Jock slowly walked over to his wife and bent down to kiss her cheek. "It's good to see that smile back on your face," he then whispered, his face lingering near hers.

"Thank you, are you sure you won't come with me?" Kelly asked, fingering the tiny gold earrings she had just put on. "You know how much Aunt Gina loves talking to you."

"I'll pass, besides, I have an important business meeting today. But you stay as long as you like," Jock told her as he left the room.

For the next few minutes, Kelly sat looking out the bedroom window. Although they'd soon mark their sixth month anniversary, she still marveled at her good fortune. Not only was Jock a caring and generous man, but everyday he made her feel special. *I haven't been nearly as giving or attentive to you, my sweet man. Perhaps too many adjustments,* she decided, feeling her prosthetic leg.

But now, finally, Kelly was one with her fake leg. No longer did she think of it as a curse or a foreign appendage that had viciously attached itself to her body, but rather, an apparatus helping her to look and walk nearly normal. *Now, if I can get my sister back, life will be perfect,* Kelly thought, feeling elated at the prospect.

. . .

As the day wore on, Kara rehearsed in her mind what she'd say to her twin sister. A strange nervousness refused to leave and deep in her gut she carried the burden of guilt. Yet, she couldn't deny that nagging voice of envy that still whispered in the back of her mind. *Kelly has everything! Look what you have . . . nothing. Even your new car is gone!*

Taking a deep breath, Kara pushed those thoughts aside. *But I'm alive! Rob and the others are not. And, Kelly's my only sister! What is wrong with me?* Grabbing a nearby throw pillow, Kara buried her face. *What kind of person am I?*

"Are you all right, dear?" Emma asked a moment later, startling her. "You look upset."

"Oh . . . no, I'm fine," Kara lied, trying to smile. "I just have a lot on my mind. You know, my car, finding a new job." Suddenly, she realized she *did* have important matters to think about. *Certainly more concerns than my millionaire sister has,* Kara quickly decided.

"Kelly should be arriving any minute," Emma said, glancing at her watch. "She's very excited about seeing you. We've *both* looked forward to this day, and prayed it would happen. Of course, we never wanted tragedy to bring it about," she then added.

"God works in mysterious ways, isn't that right, Mother?" Kara asked, somewhat sarcastically. "So maybe this is how it *had* to be."

Before Emma could remark, the front door opened. Stepping inside, Kelly stopped and for an instant she glanced at Emma, then to Kara. Their eyes met. The house was eerily quiet and in the next moment Kelly's eyes welled with tears. "Hello, Kara," she then whispered. "It's good to see you."

In that moment, nothing else mattered. Not the money, not Kelly's fancy home or handsome husband, nor the angry words that caused their estrangement; only the feeling of relief Kara now felt. As though someone was pushing her to her feet, she got up from the sofa. "It's good to see you too, Kelly," she managed to say, holding out her hand.

In the next instant each had flung their arms around the other, hugging amid their tears and words of apology.

. . .

The afternoon quickly passed with so much to catch up on. Due to the fact Kara no longer had a place of employment, or a car to even look for a new job, Kelly offered her assistance. "Come and stay with us, Kara," she urged as the four ate supper. "Jock may even know of a job."

"That's a splendid idea," Emma and Aunt Gina cheered in unison.

"What about your apartment?" Emma then asked.

"I can't keep it without an income," Kara admitted, lowering her eyes to the table. "I'll have to go get my things."

"We can help. Whenever you're ready, we'll make a day of it and I'll treat us all to lunch somewhere special," Kelly quickly offered. "When you feel up to it, you can move in with us, besides, the holidays are just around the corner and we'd *love* having you."

"Thank you, everyone," Kara said, glancing at those at the table. "I don't deserve your kindness, not after the way I've acted. Please forgive me for being so pigheaded," she begged, taking hold of Kelly's hand. "I was being childish and I'm sorry."

For Kelly, just having her sister beside her was enough to overlook the months of heartache she'd endured. All the sleepless nights, wondering about Kara and if she'd ever see her again, were suddenly forgotten.

"It's all behind us now," Kelly said smiling, taking hold of Kara's hand. "For everyone, life has suddenly gotten better."

. . .

For Jock, meeting other entrepreneurs was always a pleasure. Now, after meeting Lorenzo Carlyle, Jock realized their association would benefit them both financially.

"I look forward to working with you," Jock said, shaking Lorenzo's hand. "With your company researching new computer chips and ours doing the manufacturing, it should increase productivity ten-fold," he added. "And, more business means more money for everyone."

"I assure you, this is a giant step in achieving *my* goals," Lorenzo replied.

"Since you're part of our *business* family now, you'll have to drop by our home and meet the rest of my family," Jock offered. "Especially during the holidays. We're having a big get-together at Christmas so come for dinner, there's always room for more around our table. If you have a wife or girlfriend, bring her along."

"Thank you, Jock. If I do drop by, I'll be alone; I haven't anyone special in my life," Lorenzo confessed.

. . .

It was late when Kelly headed for home. The full moon hung like a silver globe against the velvety black sky, and seeing it brought memories of another night months before. *Poor Ned. That night was hard for both of us,* Kelly thought, remembering how he turned and walked away, and out of her life. *I do hope you're happy . . . with someone. Please make it so, dear Lord. He's such a good man!*

As she drove toward Grosse Pointe, Kelly's mind filled with plans for the future. She wanted to help Kara anyway she could; she planned to spend time with Aunt Gina before the woman took off on some new adventure, and then, there were plans that she alone was privy to. Laying her hand on her belly, Kelly gently massaged it. *I know I'm pregnant, but for right now, it's our secret, little one,* she decided, smiling to herself.

. . .

Later that night, as Kara crawled into bed, she felt happy for the first time in months. Despite her still sore ribs and the lacerations not yet healed, she had contentment on the inside. *I really did misjudge my sister, and now she's willing to help me despite everything,* Kara thought, remembering Kelly's generous offer.

Pulling the covers up over her, Kara closed her eyes and let out a sigh of relief. *I'm lucky Kelly is so generous. I doubt I'd be so forgiving if the tables were turned,* she had to admit.

Chapter Five

Two Months Later

It was December twenty-third. The house smelled of fresh baked pies and peppermint candy. The glow of Christmas lights brought cozy warmth to the stately Beaumont mansion.

As Kelly added the newly made White Divinity to the over-flowing platter of homemade 'goodies', she felt elated. Not only was she pleased with the array of holiday treats she saw, but recent memories made her smile.

What a hoot having Kara, Mom and Aunt Gina here helping with all this. It'll be quite a Holiday gathering with our announcements, Kelly thought, imagining everyone's surprise. "I've kept *two* secrets," she muttered softly, feeling pleased with herself. Then, after finishing the platter, Kelly carried it into the dining room and sat it on the food hutch.

This was Kelly's first time at hosting a major celebration since marrying Jock. Because it was for friends and family, and not for Beaumont Company Clients, she felt relaxed. The meal was left in the capable hands of Charles, Jock's chef from his yacht and Sylvia Beal, their devoted housekeeper.

"I'll go get ready, Sylvia," Kelly told the woman. "Mother and Aunt Gina are upstairs with Abby and Kara is out doing some last minute shopping. Are things going okay in here?"

"Yes, very well," Sylvia replied, "Charles went to get Pierre since his car is in the shop, but they'll be here soon."

"And Jock will arrive soon with Samantha and Jared, so I'll hurry," Kelly said, glancing at the grandfather's clock across the room. Just then it chimed, announcing the half hour. *Five-thirty . . . it won't be long now.*

As she headed for the master bedroom, Kelly passed by the Christmas tree in the great room, smelling the fragrance only real trees can bring. Hundreds of twinkling lights and beautiful ornaments adorned the ceiling-high tree while a mound of presents surrounded it. All the festive sights and smells suddenly made Kelly think of other Christmas', from her childhood.

Far less elaborate, yet, filled with the same anticipation. *I miss you, Dad. It'll never be the same without you,* Kelly thought, recalling the lively spirit he brought to every occasion. *Whether we were Christmas caroling, shooting off fireworks, or dyeing Easter eggs, you made it fun for all of us. But, life goes on, and now we have wonderful memories. Mother is getting on with her life, just as you'd want her to,* she thought, thinking of all the changes.

As she reached the bedroom, Kelly stopped at the doorway and looked around. "I'm so blessed, thank you Lord," she whispered.

Inside the master bedroom were two walk-in closets. The larger one was filled with Kelly's clothes, for every occasion. Whether formal, casual or in between, she had dozens of styles and colors to choose from, yet, Jock continued to buy her more. Nearly every week, he'd come home with a new outfit for her. *What a wonderful husband! And now he'll be buying yet another style for me to wear,* Kelly thought, realizing how hard it was getting to conceal her secret.

Hurriedly, Kelly removed her emerald-green pant suit from her closet and laid it on the bed, feeling its soft silky material. Tonight she'd also wear the heart-shaped diamond earrings Jock gave her as a wedding gift. *I'd better get with it, or I won't be ready,* she decided, heading for the shower.

· · ·

Light snow was falling by the time all the luggage and passengers were loaded in Jock's Lincoln SUV. With Samantha and Jared arriving from New York and the five members of the North family coming from Montana, they were all happy to finally arrive on this wintry afternoon.

As they drove from the airport, everyone was excited about the days ahead. "Kelly thinks it's only you and Samantha arriving," Jock told Jared who sat beside him in the passenger's seat. "She'll be thrilled to see everyone from Morning Star here too."

"Yes, it was *quite* a feat doing this without her knowing," Samantha replied from the back seat. "But, with everyone's help, it worked."

In the far rear of the vehicle sat Eric and Tom. Between them, their eight-month-old baby-sister, Shelby Fay North, sat in her car seat. In the middle seat were Levi and Laura, joined by Samantha Blake.

"How's Kelly doing?" Levi asked. "Has she fully recovered from the skiing accident?"

"She's doing great," Jock replied. "It's a miracle she survived the fall off that mountain, *and* has no lasting affects. Only her leg, of course, but she's gotten quite use to her prostheses," he informed everyone. "We couldn't be happier."

"And how's Abby and Ryan?" Jared then asked.

"Abby is still a bundle of energy and such a joy! Ryan is doing great. He's come a long way since you two saved his life in Austria last year," Jock replied. "He's excited about seeing both of you again . . . oh, by the way, he has a young lady in his life. They met in our Atlanta office on one of his trips. And, he promised to bring her by so we can meet her," Jock added.

"How's Kara doing?" Samantha then asked. "I'm sure glad she and Kelly patched things up."

"That's another answer to prayer," Jock replied. "Kara's been staying with us and we're thrilled to have her. I found a place for her in one of our offices so she'll be starting work after New Years. Unfortunately, she'll have to go to Atlanta for training, but then she'll be back to this area."

"Twas a grand day for all of us when Kelly and Kara arrived at the ranch," Laura spoke up. "Out of the blue these lovely twin sisters show up at the door. What a blessin' they were right from the start."

"And you thought those twenty-year-olds only came to work on Morning Star for the summer," Samantha remarked. "Instead, it was much more."

"Yes, from what I hear, it became their home too," Jock said as he drove. "Kelly said it was hard work, yet, quite thrilling and adventurous with the Rocky Mountains in your backyard. They each said how much they loved working with those underprivileged kids the second year."

"And here we are," Jared remarked, patting Jock's shoulder. "Unfortunately it was tragedy that brought you and Kelly together, but it turned out well after all."

"Yeah, life *is* full of surprises," Jock replied. "Now, we have all of you here celebrating Christmas with us. What more could we ask? And I *do* appreciate you helping me surprise Kelly. You *could* be in sunny Arizona instead of wintry Michigan, but I hope the warm welcome makes up for it," Jock said, pulling into the driveway.

"Wow! That's a *big* house!" Eric exclaimed in his usual exuberance.

"This is *lovely,* and look at *all* those lights," Samantha raved. Not only did brilliant colored lights frame the huge house and every window, but they covered every tree and bush in the front and back yards. Everyone cheered their amazement at the lovely sight.

"Thanks, Ryan helped me with some, but I hired professionals for most of it," Jock confessed. "Those trees were certainly out of *our* reach," he added, driving inside the garage and parking next to his Mercedes. "Here we are. I can't *wait* to see Kelly's face when she sees all of you. I'll keep her busy while Sylvia, our housekeeper, shows you upstairs. When everyone is set, we'll spring our surprise," Jock said excitedly as he exited the vehicle.

Opening the door leading into the kitchen, he saw Sylvia at the sink; the delicious aroma of roast beef and the sweet spice of apple and pumpkin pies filled his senses. "Sylvia, we need to get our guests upstairs without Kelly seeing them. Do you know where she is?" he asked quietly.

"She's getting dressed, sir. But I'm sure she'll be out any minute now," Sylvia replied. "I can go check if you'd like."

"No, I'll go keep her in the bedroom for a few minutes while you show our guests upstairs. When Kelly's ready, I'll go get them," Jock informed his housekeeper as he quickly motioned for the others to come in.

With that, Jock hurried away while everyone else followed Sylvia through the kitchen, past the great room and up the wide-curved stairway.

"Darling, are you here?" Jock called out, entering the bedroom.

"Yes, in here," Kelly returned, "in my dressing room."

"Sweetheart, are you okay?" Jock asked as he approached and saw Kelly holding her head.

"Yes, I think so. I felt nauseated for a few minutes," she admitted, "but I'm better now. If you'll please bring me my pantsuit, then you can rejoin our guests."

"Do you want to lie down?" Jock asked, now feeling concerned. "Our guests wouldn't mind, besides, I had Sylvia show them upstairs. I'm sure they'll need time to freshen up. As soon as Pierre and Charles arrive, we'll get their luggage in," Jock assured Kelly, retrieving her pantsuit from the bed.

"I don't need to lie down, but I'll take my time since they're upstairs," Kelly told her husband. "I can't wait to see them!"

"And they can't wait to see *you*," Jock told her, bending down to kiss her. "I love you, my darling," he whispered, touching his cheek to hers.

"I love you more," Kelly replied softly as she smiled. Winking at his wife, Jock turned and left, feeling overjoyed for having Kelly as his own.

. . .

"Samantha! Jared!" Abby cheered, seeing the couple arrive upstairs. "You're really here!" With excitement, the child ran down the hall and flew into their arms. "I'm so glad you came. We're going to have lots of fun!" Then she noticed the others.

"Sweetheart, these are friends from Montana to surprise Kelly, so we're being very quiet," Samantha told Abby, putting her finger to her lips. She then introduced each one. With a smile, Abby extended her hand and welcomed everyone in her usual grown-up manner.

"Wow, Mom will be *so* happy! I'll get Grandma Em," Abby announced. Soon, everyone had met Emma and her sister Gina. Then, amid praise at such eloquence, the guests were shown to their rooms.

Within minutes, Pierre and Charles arrived and helped Jock with the arms full of suitcases. "Pierre, thank you. It's good seeing you again," Jared told Jock's yacht captain, shaking his hand.

Just as the jovial greetings were completed, Emma and Charles saw each other. Although trying to be discrete, the smile and wink Charles aimed at the woman didn't go unnoticed.

My, do I see a budding romance here? Samantha thought when seeing the couple. *This visit just might prove more interesting than we expected!*

Chapter Six

As she left the bedroom, Kelly felt elated to be seeing Jared and Samantha again. Then she thought about the big announcements later that evening. *Jock will be the most surprised and I can't wait to see his face!*

"Well, it was certainly worth the wait," Jock said with a wolf whistle. "You look luscious, my darling." As he met Kelly in the doorway of the great room, Jock gave her a lingering kiss. "Have you any idea how blessed I feel?" he whispered. "And it's all because of you, my sweet Kelly."

"And with you, I feel like a Princess everyday," Kelly whispered back. "I have a surprise for you, my sweet Prince," she couldn't help saying. "One I believe you'll like, but right now I'm ready to see Sam and Jared."

"When will this surprise be arriving?" Jock asked, looking puzzled.

"Soon, but let's get this party underway, okay?" Kelly said, grinning.

"As you wish, my Princess," he replied, giving her a sweeping bow. "I'll go get them, but why don't you sit in front of the fire and relax."

After he escorted Kelly to her favorite chair and made sure she was comfortable, Jock hurried away. As she sat waiting and watching the flames lick at the logs, Kelly's mind was suddenly filled with memories of the ranch. *We had such good times there, and I do miss everyone,* she thought. *Singing around the piano, playing games and having great conversation in front of the fire. We have to do that again, soon.*

Just then, from the corner of her eye, Kelly saw someone. Turning, she expected to see Samantha and Jared. "Merry Christmas, Kelly," she heard in a familiar Irish brogue. For a moment Kelly could only stare, unable to move. A second later she felt even more stunned when seeing Eric and Tom. Then Levi came down the stairs, carrying a baby.

Tears of joy rolled down Kelly's cheeks as she got up from her chair. "I don't believe it! I was *just* thinking about you!" she cried as Laura met her for an emotional hug. One by one, Levi and the boys each gave Kelly their heartfelt embrace. "Look at you two, you're young men and handsome ones at that," she told Eric and Tom. "How old are you now?"

"I'm fourteen, Eric's twelve," Tom replied somewhat proudly.

"You've sprouted up like weeds," Kelly said, shaking her head. Next come Samantha and Jared.

"We wanted to surprise you and it looks like we did," Samantha said, hugging Kelly.

"How . . . how *did* you pull this off without me knowing?" Kelly blurted.

"It wasn't easy," Samantha confessed. "The whole thing was Jock's idea, of course, he didn't have to twist anyone's arm," she jokingly added.

"What a *wonderful* surprise," Kelly said, choking back her tears. "Thank you, my dear, sweet husband, for thinking of this." Nearby, Jock only smiled and winked at his wife.

"And this is whom I've heard so much about," Kelly said, seeing Shelby Fay in Levi's arms. "May I?" Gently, Levi handed the baby to Kelly. "What a precious little gal you are! You're adorable, just like Kara said you were," Kelly whispered, seeing the doll-like face and big brown eyes looking at her.

With dimples, ivory complexion and dark curly hair, Shelby *was* beautiful. "Oh, what blessings you two have. Not only these great boys, but now this darling little girl," Kelly went on. "Jock, sweetheart, I guess this is as good a time as any to tell you and everyone my news. And Abby, please join us," she said, motioning for her and Jock to come stand beside her.

With a puzzled look on her face, Abby did as Kelly requested. By now, Emma, Charles, Gina, Pierre and even Sylvia had gathered in the great room to witness Kelly's look of surprise. Now they eagerly awaited her news.

"I'll see more of you later," Kelly told Shelby, kissing the baby's cheek and handing her back to Levi. Then, putting one arm around Abby's shoulder and one around Jock's waist, Kelly made her announcement. "In late June, we'll be welcoming a precious new life into our world as well," she said, again feeling tears of joy. "*We're* going to have a baby!"

Cheers erupted from everyone present, that is, except Abby. Jock hugged his wife and smothered her face with kisses, but from the corner of her eye, Kelly saw Abby walk to the far side of the room and slump in a chair.

"You've made this joyous season even more glorious," Jock whispered, taking Kelly in his arms.

At hearing all the well wishes and congratulations, Kelly knew everyone was happy for them. Jock was ecstatic. Although not wanting to leave her husband, Kelly knew someone else needed her attention at the moment. "I must talk to Abby," she told Jock.

"Everyone, please make yourselves at home. Sylvia and Charles have prepared us a lovely dinner, and it'll be ready by seven o'clock sharp. So get your appetites ready," Kelly heard Jock say as she headed Abby's direction.

"May I join you?" she asked softly. Making no reply, Abby slid to one side of her chair, making room for Kelly. "It seems something is bothering you, sweetie. Are you upset about us having a baby?"

"I wanted it to be just *us* . . . you, Father and me," Abby quickly replied, frowning and picking at her fingernail. "Why do we need a baby?"

"I thought you'd *love* being a big sister," Kelly replied, seeing the child's obvious jealousy. "I'm sure this baby will love *having* you as their big sister, because you're so smart and caring. That's what I think."

"I want you to love me, no one else. I was here first," Abby blurted.

"Abby, I've never seen you act this way, and I must say, I'm very surprised. Do you really think I'll love you less than I do now?" Kelly asked.

When Abby made no reply, Kelly went on. "Some mothers have *many* children, and no matter how many they have, they don't love the firstborn any more *or* less. We mothers have hearts too big to *ever* get depleted of love for our children," Kelly explained. "Do you think your Grand Mama loves your father differently than she does your Aunt Pamela or Uncle Ryan?"

For the first time, Abby looked at Kelly. Her eyes were intent as she seemed to ponder what she'd just heard. "Grand Mama is their *real* mother, you're *not* mine, but to this baby you *will* be," Abby spouted, bolting from her seat.

Pain ripped through Kelly's heart as she watched Abby run up the stairs. Never did she suspect this sweet, happy little girl would *ever* feel this way, or say such hurtful things to her. Certainly, if she hadn't had guests looking on, she'd have burst into tears from the devastation she now felt. Instead, Kelly left her chair and slipped down the hall to her bedroom.

Although trying hard to push Abby's harsh words and angry look from her thoughts, it remained, burned in her memory. *I can't believe this! What do I do? And how can I tell Jock all this? It'll break his heart.*

Not until she reached the bedroom and closed the door, did Kelly release her emotions. Throwing herself across the bed, she buried her face and let the sobs come. She cried not only because of Abby, but for other reasons, too. She missed her dad terribly, and knowing her mom would soon be moving away, just added to her heartache. *I can't let this ruin everyone's visit, I must not!*

"Darling, are you okay?" Jock asked, entering the room a moment later. "What is it? Please tell me what has upset you so," he coaxed, seeing her tear-stained face.

"Oh Jock, Abby doesn't want this baby. She's *very* upset with me. I never *dreamed* she'd feel this way."

"What do you mean, upset? What did she say?"

"Somehow she thinks I won't love her as much as this baby, because this will be my real child, and I'm not her real mother. Oh Jock, I didn't want to tell you all this, but I don't know what to do," Kelly cried. "We've *got* to make her understand."

"I'll take care of this, sweetheart, please don't worry," Jock said, taking Kelly in his arms. "It'll work out, and I won't let Abby or any-one ruin this time with your friends. I hate seeing you upset, for any reason."

For a moment Kelly closed her eyes, basking in the love and protection she felt in her husband's arms. Like so many times before, she found comfort knowing he would take care of things. But was it possible this time? She could only pray Jock could get through to his daughter . . . *their* daughter.

"Jock, I'd like Laura and Sam to join me back here, and Kara too, when she returns," Kelly requested a few minutes later. "Laura might have had these same problems with her boys, after all, Shelby is *their* half-sister. I'm sure we aren't the only family that's faced this."

"You're right," he replied, "and the more input we get, the better." After kissing his wife, Jock gently brushed aside a lone tear on her cheek. "No matter what Abby thinks, I'm *thrilled* about our new baby, and I'm sure in time she will be too," he said softly. "You're my life, Kelly. I can't imagine not having you with me. Please, don't ever forget how much I love you."

For a moment longer, Kelly looked into the dark sensual depths of her husband's eyes. "I'll go get your friends," Jock whispered, "please don't worry."

Getting off the bed, he left Kelly alone with her thoughts. *Dear God, there's got to be a way to help Abby get past this! Show us, give us the right words to say,* Kelly prayed, leaving the bed to pace the floor.

"Knock, knock," Samantha called out a moment later, "Kelly?"

"Come in, please," Kelly answered, trying to smile. "I'm sorry for leaving all of you like that, but it seems Jock and I have a problem and I need your advice. Please, have a seat," she offered, patting the bed as she, too, sat down.

"Kelly, what can we do ta help?" Laura asked. "For sure, if we put our heads together we can find a solution ta most anythin'."

"I'm hoping you're right," Kelly replied, looking at her friends. Once more, as Samantha and Laura listened, Kelly explained Abby's reaction to her announcement. "It crushed me! Abby and I've been so close. When the boating accident happened and we both nearly drowned, I felt sure we had a bond that *nothing* could sever. But, bringing a new baby into the equation seems to have changed all that," Kelly said, fighting a new round of emotion. "I had no idea she'd be this jealous."

"Nor did I," Samantha replied. "But, I suppose, when we think about it, Abby has never had to vie for anyone's attention. It's been only you three; before that, she was Jock's and Katherine's only child, too. No matter who she was with, Abby has always had center stage."

"The child needs a lesson," Laura interjected, nodding her head. "She needs ta see the other side of the coin. Like the kids that come ta the ranch. Poor kids, barely havin' enough ta eat at home or clothes ta put on their wee bodies. They have so little, yet, we see no selfishness among them," she said.

"Yeah, if it were summer, we could leave Abby there for a few days," Kelly said. "She might learn a thing or two about sharing, and realize the world doesn't evolve around her. You're right, Sam. She has *always* been the center of attention, so I guess it's easy to see why she's this way," Kelly remarked, leaving the bed. "Jock said he'd take care of it, but I'm afraid if he says too much, she'll feel that I'm making him take sides. I'd hate that!"

"Perhaps Abby's Grand Mama can talk to her. I hear she's a very wise woman, so maybe she can help Abby see the light," Samantha suggested.

"That's a good idea. Abby respects Cora, very much," Kelly replied. "All I know is: things will be very tense around this house until Abby accepts this baby," she told her friends. "Your boys weren't like this, were they?"

"Not for a minute," Laura replied, shaking her head. "Instead, they were countin' the days till my due date."

"I miss those boys," Kelly said, sitting on the edge of the bed. "I miss *all* of you, even the ranch hands," she admitted. Reaching for Laura's hand, Kelly gave it an affectionate squeeze. "I can't tell you how *glad* I am to see all of you again."

"Happy we are bein' here, for we've missed ya too," Laura replied. "And, how are ya doin' Kelly? I mean, since so much has happened?"

"Oh, since Kara is back in our lives, I've never been happier, at least until now," Kelly admitted. "Jock is *wonderful!* He's such a godly man and makes me feel so special everyday. It's not just the money or living in this lavish home, but rather it's *us*. Being together, walking in the park, laughing, talking. Of course, money makes it easier, but it doesn't promise happiness."

"That's something we *all* can attest to," Samantha stated. "We've all had it both ways. I *know* Jared and I could live on love," she teased, bringing a round of laughter from the other two. "He's the most affectionate man I've ever saw. And like Jock, he looks for ways to make me feel special."

"And how is Levi? Is *he* the romantic kind too?" Kelly had to know.

"Aye, that he is," Laura said, closing her eyes and smiling. "There's nothin' like those mountain men, ya know."

The room was instantly filled with riotous giggling when seeing and hearing Laura's comment. Like school girls, all three women lay across the king sized bed and laughed till tears ran down their faces.

Finally, a knock was heard. "May I join this party?" Kara asked, poking her head around the door.

"Kara, yes, come in," Kelly told her sister as the other two got up to greet her. While Samantha and Laura hugged Kara, Kelly watched while her heart filled with gratitude at having her sister back in her life.

"It's so good to see you," Kara said, "I'm sorry I wasn't here when you arrived."

"We're discussing Kelly's news and Abby's reaction to it," Samantha informed Kara.

"What news is that?" Kara asked, looking at her sister.

"The news that I'm having a baby in June," Kelly replied, watching for her reaction.

"A baby! You're *pregnant?*" Kara bellowed with eyes widened in shock.

"Isn't it grand?" Laura cheered. "There's nothin' like a wee child ta bring joy ta the heart."

"I had no idea," Kara replied, "what a *surprise!*"

"Jock is thrilled, but I'm afraid Abby is *not*," Kelly said, shaking her head. "Now I'm not sure what will happen."

"Abby will adjust, eventually. She's used to being in the spotlight, but now she won't be the only act in town," Kara said somewhat off handedly. "Don't worry, she'll come around."

"Before anyone could comment further, another knock was heard. "I hate to break this up, but dinner is served," Jock said outside the door. "I've come to beg your presence, if you lovely ladies would be so kind as to honor us," he said teasingly.

"I suppose we'd better go," Kelly teased back. "I can't expect to have you *all* to myself. But later, when everyone's in bed, let's put on our P. J's and sit in front of the fire and talk, like old times. Shall we?"

"Can't wait," Samantha remarked as the others agreed.

In no time, everyone was seated around the vast mahogany-wood table in the formal dining room. In the middle was a beautiful Christmas centerpiece with three red candles, greenery, and red canter berries.

Numerous trays and bowls of food sat ready. At each place setting, white Noritake china trimmed in gold, glistening silverware and Waterford Crystal stemware was perfectly arranged atop a red placemat. Overhead, a chandelier cast its shimmering glow on those seated.

"Before we start, I want to welcome each of you officially to our home," Jock said, getting to his feet. "Your presence here means so much to us, and I hope this gathering starts a tradition. Each year forward, whether here in Michigan, Montana, or New York, I hope we will all get together to celebrate."

"Here . . . here!" the others chimed in, nodding their heads.

"And now, please join me in asking God to bless this lovely dinner," Jock said, bowing his head. "Dear Lord, we thank you for all the blessings you shower upon us, and for each one who joins us around this table. Bless those we love that aren't with us, and we pray they, too, will experience the true meaning of this Joyous season. Bless this food and our time together. We praise and thank you, Jesus. In your Holy name we pray, Amen."

"Amen," the others said in unison.

From his place at the head of the table, Jock looked at Kelly at the opposite end. As their eyes met, he smiled and winked at her, bringing the usual feeling of joy to Kelly. And now, with a new life growing inside her, she felt certain she'd found her own real purpose. *And thank you Lord, for my wonderful husband! With Your help and his, there is nothing we can't do.*

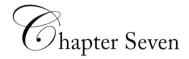

Chapter Seven

When dinner was over, everyone agreed they had eaten far too much to enjoy dessert now. It was then that Charles stood to his feet and took hold of Emma's hand, coaxing her up beside him.

"Mr. Beaumont, Mrs. Beaumont, friends," Charles began in his refined manner. "If you would permit me, on this auspicious occasion, I, too, would like to make an announcement. I'm most pleased to tell you that this lovely lady here, has honored me by becoming my bride in the very near future," Charles said beaming as he looked at Emma.

Cheers of congratulations once more erupted as everyone now stood to their feet. "To Charles and Emma," they shouted, lifting their water glasses in a toast to the happy couple. Seemingly dazed, Jock only shook his head as he looked at Kelly for confirmation.

With a grin, Kelly nodded and left her seat to give her mother and then Charles a hug. "I think you surprised your boss," she whispered to him.

"When's the big day? We need to know the particulars," Jared coaxed.

"In two weeks," Emma responded. "Just a simple wedding and then we'll be moving, to *Arizona!*"

Now, looking even more surprised, Jock left his place and joined them. "Well, I take it this is your two week notice?" he asked Charles.

"Yes, sir, it is," Charles replied. "I'm afraid working has no place in my new life. I've saved a substantial amount of money over the years, thanks to your generous salary, sir, and I've invested well. I bought a condo in Arizona and I plan to teach my bride how to play golf, that is, as soon as I sharpen my rather rusty game," he teased, smiling at Emma. "I admit it will be hard to leave you, sir, and the Pink Slipper, but we expect to visit often."

"And we expect *everyone* of you to visit us, too," Emma commented.

With his hand on Charles' shoulder, Jock looked at him. "You've been a fine chef, my man, and superb on every occasion. I only hope I can find another one *half* as talented as you," he said truthfully. "And Emma, we're going to miss you, too. I *see* why you declined our invitation to live with us. What about Aunt Gina? What are *her* plans?"

"Jock, I do appreciate you and Kelly's generous offer, but I fell in love with this wonderful man, and, well, I've always *wanted* to see Arizona," Emma said smiling at Charles. "As for Gina, she's returning to Alaska, but she just *might* become a snowbird and spend winters with us out there."

As they heard Charles and Emma talk and saw the happiness radiating from their faces, Jock and Kelly couldn't be more pleased. "You have your small wedding if you like, but we'll plan your reception; invite as many as you want," Jock offered, looking at his wife. "We insist on doing something quite spectacular, don't you agree, darling?"

"I certainly do," Kelly said, hugging her mom again. "And we'll miss you both terribly."

"As we will you, my dear," Emma replied, returning the embrace. After shaking hands with Charles and giving Emma a hug, Jock looked at Kelly.

"Did you know about this?" he asked his wife.

"Well, she *is* my mother," Kelly replied, smiling and winking at Emma. "Did we surprise you?"

"Shock is more like it, but I couldn't be more pleased. And now if you'll all excuse me, I think I'll go find Abby," Jock told the three. At his remark, Kelly looked at him.

"Oh Jock, be gentle. I don't want her to think you're siding with me against her," she said, feeling somewhat afraid.

"Don't you worry, sweetheart, I'll go easy," he assured her.

· · ·

Arriving at Abby's bedroom door, Jock knocked gently. "Abby? May I come in?" he asked as he waited. "Sweetheart, I need to talk to you, please open the door," he said when there came no response.

A moment later Abby slowly opened the door and looked up at her father. "You can come in if you'd like," she said, returning to her place on the floor by her music boxes. "What do you want to talk about?"

"Those things you said to Kelly," Jock told his daughter. "You hurt her very much and I want to know how you can say such things? Don't you know how much she loves you? After all she has done, even risking her life to save you?" he asked, studying Abby's face.

"But she won't love me when she has that baby," Abby blurted out. "I know how step-kids are treated. I'm not her *real* kid, so she won't love me as much as her *own* child."

"Abby, that's *simply* not true," Jock replied sternly. "Kelly loves you *very* much. We both do. You're nine years old and certainly not a baby anymore, and you having this attitude hurts Kelly and me a great deal," he scolded.

When Abby made no reply or showed no remorse for her actions, Jock went on. "I want you to stay in your room until you can apologize to your mom," he added, turning to leave. Just then his eyes fell on the numerous music boxes as an idea came to mind.

"Abby, you need to decide which music box you want to keep, because tomorrow I'm giving all the rest away," Jock told his daughter.

"But *why?*" she blurted out as her chin began quivering. "I can't decide *that* because I love them all!"

"Oh, I see. *You* can love all of your music boxes, but yet, you think Kelly isn't capable of loving more than one child, is that it? Aren't you being selfish, Abby, and unfair?" Jock asked sternly.

Although Abby kept her head lowered, he could see the tears rolling down her cheeks, yet she made no reply.

Turning, Jock headed for the door, but before leaving the room he looked back. Stubbornly, Abby gave no indication she would relent in her position toward the unborn child who'd arrive in six months, or toward Kelly who had generously given her all to make this house a home.

· · ·

After dinner, Jared and Levi found a quiet room to visit. "I thought we'd find a corner somewhere to talk," Levi told his long-time friend, patting Jared's shoulder. "It's been far too long, JB, so fill me in on the rat-race at the Medical Center."

"It's the same crazy politics, but amazing changes are happening in technology. Just like everything, neurosurgery has made great strides and it keeps us on our toes," Jared told Levi. "What about you? Ready to come back?"

"Not me," Levi quickly replied. "I get all the patients I want by doctoring the kids at summer camp, plus the staff and family. I'd *never* go back, not after finding Laura and being happier than I ever thought possible."

"I can see why," Jared said, nodding his head. "Laura is special all right, and those boys idolize you, and now that baby girl! I'd say you have it all, my friend. I felt sure Sam and I would have one on the way by now, but no such luck."

"Is there a problem?" Levi asked, sensing something in Jared's tone. "Infertility? Blocked fallopian tubes?"

"No, her gynecologist says nothing physical seems to be the problem. I was checked out, too, so now we're going the psychological route with a counselor to rule out that aspect."

"Is it the job she had? That was pretty high stress I'd think," Levi asked.

"Yeah, she had to do a lot of things she'd never do otherwise. Plus she feels guilty about her sister Shelly and how she died. Then her mom's mental breakdown afterwards," Jared admitted sadly. "Now, her dad returned to Ireland and she's wondering if she'll ever see *him* again." For a moment, the two men were silent as Levi pondered Jared's remarks.

"Not to change the subject, but any word on that kid sister of mine?" Levi inquired. "I think about her a lot, especially at Christmas," he admitted.

"Actually, I have," Jared replied. "Word is: Becky has gotten involved with the business world. I heard she left New York."

"Business? She *hated* paperwork and wasn't too organized. Did you hear where she went?" Levi asked, feeling shocked at such news.

"I'm not sure. Once I heard Chicago, then Los Angeles, but you know how rumors get started," Jared said. "I'll try to find out. She still has friends at the Medical Center. Have you tried to contact her?"

"Yeah, I wrote a few times. No response. Even tried to call, but her phone was unlisted. She hasn't forgiven me for giving up my practice and moving west," Levi replied, shaking his head. "I guess she still thinks I left because she broke up with you, my best friend."

"Well, she *did* break my heart, but later I realized we weren't suited for each other," Jared admitted. "It hurt, but I know our breakup had *nothing* to do with you quitting your practice and moving to Montana."

"No, I had had enough of hospital politics and hassle from the

HMO's," Levi replied. "And I've never looked back."

"Here you are!" Samantha announced from the doorway a moment later. "I have a mission: to drag you both to the piano for a sing-a-long. But, this place is so big, I *still* haven't found it," she admitted.

"Well, you don't have to twist *my* arm," Levi replied. "I'd *never* miss a chance to hear you sing or Laura play, so come along my friend," he told Jared, pulling him to his feet.

As they left the room, Levi and Jared followed Samantha toward the sound of jovial chatter down the hall. Sure enough, in another lovely and spacious room sat a shiny-black baby-grand-piano. Several comfortable looking chairs of soft blue fabric with a matching sofa were neatly arranged. Plush beige carpet was at their feet; overhead hung another glistening chandelier.

"Let's start with a classic," Kelly suggested. "How about 'Silent Night', since that's one of my favorites." Everyone agreed and waited for Laura to play the introduction to the favorite Christmas hymn.

In no time, the room was filled with music and song. It was during the second verse that everyone noticed Charles' clear tenor voice and Emma's lovely alto harmonizing. Soon the others quit singing just to listen. When the song ended applause rang out.

"What have we here? Mother, did you *know* this man could sing like this?" Kelly asked in amazement.

"Well, he *did* mention that he sang at Carnegie Hall once, but as a child, so I didn't question him further. Perhaps I *should* have," Emma teased. "And now, I would like to hear a solo." Applauding, the others cheered the request.

"With that voice, I'm sure he sang A cappella," Samantha remarked.

"At one time I did, but I'd prefer not to try it this evening," Charles told the others. "If you know 'Silver Bells', I'll give that a go," he told Laura.

Once more the room echoed with the melodious sound of Laura's playing and the man's remarkable voice. His eyes were most often on Emma who stood beside him. Again, there were cheers of jubilation when it ended.

"Now it's Sam's turn!" Eric blurted from his place on the floor. With everyone's urging, Samantha told Laura her selection. In no time, her lovely voice filled the room as she sang 'White Christmas'. On the last verse, she coaxed everyone to join in.

The room wasn't only filled with joyful singing, but it overflowed with love. Samantha and Jared stood arm in arm, gazing into each other's eyes; Kelly rested her head against Jock's chest as he held her close; Levi stood behind Laura as she played, his hands gently resting on his wife's shoulders. Charles and Emma stood side by side as their eyes met for an occasional tender glance. Only Kara stood alone, looking disheartened.

The hour passed quickly and when everyone seemed to have had their fill of singing, it was time for bed.

Although many seemed tired and ready for a good nights sleep, there were others who had different plans. As first cousins, Laura and Samantha had many things to catch up on. And, not having seen Kelly since before her wedding and Kara for several months, these four had much to talk about.

Finally it was time for their late-night gathering and session of girl-talk.

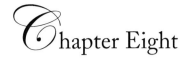

Chapter Eight

With the others now in bed, Samantha, Laura, Kara and Kelly were comfortably seated on a thick, soft blanket before the fire.

"Tis certain this brings wonderful memories of that first summer on the ranch," Laura told the others.

"Yes, we had some great times. Even those wild games of Dominos and Scrabble were a hoot," Kelly said, bringing a chuckle.

"I was only there a few weeks, but it certainly was life-changing! I had no idea I'd meet my future husband there," Samantha remarked. "How are things going with the camp? And, any word from Matte?"

"Aye, our dear sweet Matte is comin' back next summer. She's fit as a fiddle and has no lingerin' effects of the gunshot. Now with Shelby's arrival, she can't wait ta come and see her," Laura said smiling. "As for the ranch, tis goin' splendidly and applications are pourin' in for next season. There are so many hurtin' children, tis sad indeed."

"God Bless Matte, what a wonderful lady," Kelly remarked about the ranch's devoted housekeeper. "Are you getting enough donations to pay your expenses?" she then asked.

"For sure there are ups and downs, but Levi and I do our best so no child is turned away," Laura answered. "Tis hard at time, but ta see those smilin' faces makes it all worthwhile."

At that moment, Kelly knew what she'd be discussing with Jock before their friends left for home. As she thought about the ranch and her time there, Kelly suddenly thought about someone else.

"Have you any news about Ned?" she asked Laura, doubting she had.

"Aye, we hear he has started his own business," Laura revealed.

"What kind of business?" Kelly asked, grateful to know he was okay.

"He's selling and constructing log homes," Kara spoke up. "I talked to him some months ago. He's doing quite well."

"That's good, I'm glad to hear that," Kelly said truthfully. "He's a good man, and deserves a happy life."

"Since you brought this up," Samantha began, looking at Kelly. "Have you any regrets, for not marrying Ned?"

"Not one," Kelly quickly replied. "I wore his ring and *would* have married him. Ironically, my skiing accident stopped me from making that mistake," she told her friends, recalling the heartache back then. "Despite trying not to, I fell in love with Jock and it was then I realized what *real* love was. Marrying Ned would have ruined each of our lives, I know that, but he *is* a terrific guy."

"Is that the reason you got so upset, Kara, because you didn't know Kelly's true feelings?" Samantha asked in her investigative manner.

"I suppose, and I didn't give her a chance to explain," Kara admitted, somewhat sheepishly.

"She felt sorry for Ned and I can't fault her for that," Kelly said, clasping Kara's hand. "I heard how devastated he was after my accident and it *was* hard to understand, especially since I was engaged to Ned. After the coma and hearing I lost my leg, I had no intentions of marrying *anyone,* not ever."

"For sure, it would have been a shame if ya had not married Jock," Laura told Kelly, "'tis easy ta see the love ya have for each other."

"Yes, it would be," Kelly said, looking into the fire. "I'm happier than I ever thought possible."

"And I see it, too," Kara said nodding her head. "I was very wrong to accuse my sister like I did. The close call I had made me realize some things. And, Ned told me I should make things right with Kelly."

"He did? You never told me that," Kelly said, feeling surprised.

"We *all* can have secrets, dear sister," Kara remarked, bringing a laugh from the others.

"How about showing us your wedding pictures," Samantha suggested.

"I've never seen them either," Kara said, "so what better time."

"You're right," Kelly said, getting to her feet. "It was a glorious spring day and we planned it so fast, my head was in a fog," she remarked when she returned. Then, as everyone looked on, Kelly opened the thick white album.

Soon, comments were made over Kelly's dress, her hair, and how beautiful she looked. "What a lovely couple ya make," Laura said, studying the photos.

"Look at that necklace! Was that your wedding gift from Jock?" Kara blurted, scrutinizing the exquisitely cut gems.

"Actually, no," Kelly replied. "He gave me the heart-shaped-earrings I wore today. Surprisingly, this necklace came from Grandma Isabella."

"Grandma?" Kara blurted. "How's that *possible?* She and Grandpa were poor."

"Yes, they were, but Mother said Grandma was once engaged to a very wealthy man. He gave her this necklace as an engagement gift, but before they could get married, he was tragically killed," Kelly explained. "And, instead of selling it during the hard times, Grandma wanted to keep it for their first married daughter, which was Mother, and she was instructed to do the same."

"Tis a romantic story indeed," Laura exclaimed, shaking her head. "Who *was* this wealthy man?"

"Mother has no idea who he was or even his name, but I wish she did," Kelly replied. "I'd love knowing the full story."

"As would I," Kara blurted, studying the picture.

"It's a pity you don't have his name, if you did, we could track his family history," Samantha remarked. Each was silent as they finished looking a Kelly's wedding pictures.

"There's got to be *some* way to find the truth in all this," Kara said a moment later.

"Just give me a name, I'd *love* to solve a good mystery," Samantha replied, rubbing her hands in anticipation, bringing a chuckle from everyone.

When they closed the album, their discussion became more serious and for the next hour, the women shared their deepest feelings.

Laura talked about the many hurting kids that come into their lives every summer, and her own boys' futures, whether attending college or joining the military.

Surprisingly, Samantha admitted her fear of having a childless marriage, and her heartache of knowing Jared's immense disappointment.

"Have ya thought about adoptin'?" Laura asked.

"Yes, we've inquired, but there aren't as many babies these days. Girls are having abortions. It's become more popular to kill their babies than to adopt them to loving couples like us," Samantha told the others.

"We've even thought about going abroad to adopt a baby."

"Have you considered adopting an older child?" Kelly wanted to know.

"We've talked about it, and we're open to every avenue," Samantha replied.

When seeing her sadness, Kelly leaned close and hugged her. "I'll be praying God will send you a child," she whispered next to Samantha's ear. "You and Jared will be wonderful parents, so don't give up."

"Aye, ya can't give up," Laura chimed in, hugging her cousin. Lovingly, they shared Samantha's sorrow with a hug or gentle squeeze of her hand.

"Kara, Jock told us you'll be working for him," Samantha said, changing the subject. "Are you looking forward to the business world?"

"Somewhat, at least it's a job," Kara responded. "And it'll be nice to have some pull with my boss," she added teasingly.

The fire was a bed of hot embers before the conversation dwindled. While anticipating more fun tomorrow, the women finally decided it was time to turn in. After hugging each other goodnight, they all headed for bed.

. . .

By eight-thirty the next morning, nearly everyone was up and found Mrs. Beal preparing a buffet breakfast. "How can we help?" Kelly asked entering the kitchen, followed by Samantha and Laura. In no time breakfast was ready.

There were golden brown biscuits and white gravy, a variety of fresh fruit, scrambled eggs and sausage as well as Danish rolls. Orange juice, milk and coffee were also in good supply. By then, nearly everyone had arrived for breakfast. Still missing were: Abby, Eric, Tom, and Kara.

One by one everyone filled their plate from the hardy selection. Just as Jock was about to join the others at the table, the telephone rang. "It can't be the office, it's Christmas Eve," he said, glancing at his watch. "Please excuse me, I'll see who that is."

It was several minutes later when Jock rejoined the others. "Well that was a surprise," he announced. "Ryan is coming by later this morning, *and* he's bringing his girlfriend." To everyone, that was indeed good news.

"Finally, we'll meet this mysterious lady he's been keeping to himself," Kelly remarked. "I do hope they'll stay and not rush off."

"Me too," Samantha remarked, taking a sip of coffee. "Jared and I are so happy to know he's doing well."

During breakfast, summer plans were discussed as well as their next holiday gathering. "We'd love for you all to come to New York next Christmas," Jared offered looking at his wife.

"Yes, please do," Samantha agreed. "That'll be our excuse to have a house by then instead of an apartment," she teased, looking at her husband. "The kids can go ice skating, we'll go sightseeing, and of course, there is always plenty of shopping we can do."

"That *would* be fun!" Kelly raved as the others echoed their approval.

"New York, I haven't been back since I left there six years ago," Levi said thoughtfully. "But, I suppose I can handle it for a *few* days," he teased.

"Oh, it's snowing again," Kelly announced as she looked out the window. "And by the size of those flakes, it'll be piling up rather quickly."

"Ya don't suppose we'll be havin' a blizzard?" Laura asked. "One can expect drifts a-plenty in Montana with such snowfall, if the wind blows."

"No wind is expected, so we'll be fine," Jock assured their guests. "But, if we get snowed in, we have plenty to eat. Anyone need more coffee?"

Just then Tom appeared carrying Shelby Fay and all eyes were on the baby and her proud big brother. Quickly, Laura took her daughter so Tom could help himself to the newly replenished breakfast buffet.

"Are the others coming down?" Kelly asked, glancing toward the stairway, wondering if Abby was still pouting.

"I'm not sure. Eric's barely awake and I didn't see Abby," Tom replied. It was only a moment later when loud voices were heard upstairs.

One voice was obviously Abby's and the other had to be Eric. It was also quite clear they were having an argument.

. . .

59

"You can't tell me what to do!" Abby yelled, "I'm not a baby."

"Well you're acting like one!" Eric blared back.

Due to a headache, Kara was sleeping in and was suddenly jarred awake by loud voices in the hall. Feeling perturbed, she crawled out of bed and opened her door. "What's going on out here?"

Seeing Abby and her look of distain, Kara realized the child was being very inhospitable toward her young guest. With her hands on her slender hips, Abby was glaring at Eric. "He called me a baby!" she bellowed, pointing a finger. "And I'm not!"

"You're sure acting like one," Eric reiterated, shaking his head. "She said she didn't want Kelly to have a baby. So I told her she needs to grow up. She started whining so I called her a baby."

"Go on ahead, Eric, so I can talk to Abby, okay?" Kara coaxed. Due to her throbbing headache, she had to work hard at hiding her displeasure for being awakened in such a manner. Yet, she wanted to hear Abby's side.

Soon, the two were seated on Kara's bed, facing each other. "Let's talk about this, Abby. Why *are* you against Kelly having this baby?"

For the next few minutes, Abby told Kara what she already knew from the night before. But, while searching for words to rebuke the child, Kara had to admit she, too, had misjudged Kelly not so long ago.

"Abby, sometimes things aren't what they seem," she began, suddenly realizing someone had told *her* that once. "To you it looks as though Kelly couldn't love you as much as her own baby, but you're wrong. Not long ago *I* made a bad decision and mistakenly accused Kelly of something. It hurt her very much, *and* other people. Recently I learned how terribly wrong I was, just as you will. But meantime, everyone will be unhappy," Kara explained.

Although she seemed to listen intently, Abby had nothing to say. Kara could only wonder if she had gotten through to her. "I think we're missing breakfast, so why don't we go downstairs and see what's left, okay?" Kara finally asked.

Making no reply, Abby got up from Kara's bed and slowly headed for the door. Before leaving the room she turned. "Do you *promise* Kelly will still love me?"

"I *promise,*" Kara replied without hesitation.

. . .

After breakfast, Eric and Tom found a game to play and when Abby stood shyly nearby, they asked her to join them. "I'm sorry I called you a baby," Eric told her. "But you *were* acting like one. Ouch!" he yelled as Tom kicked his leg under the table.

After eating only a few bites of breakfast, Kara returned upstairs stating she was going back to bed until her headache subsided.

"We'll be in my office," Jock told Kelly as the men headed upstairs. "I have to prove I caught that record sailfish a couple years ago. They don't *believe* my fishing story," he teased, patting Jared and Levi on the back.

"I'll let you know when Ryan arrives," Kelly told her husband. The women soon busied themselves with getting ready for their day and the celebrating later that afternoon and evening. Everyone wore their festive attire of dressy pantsuits or slacks with shimmering tops.

"We're certainly having a white Christmas," Emma commented, looking outside to the still falling snow. "It's getting pretty deep out there."

Before long, the women had gathered in the great room where Gina soon had them spellbound with her tales of adventure. By now, Tom had tired of his game with Abby and Eric and was playing with his baby sister on the floor. It was just before noon when the doorbell rang.

"That must be Ryan," Kelly said, leaving her chair. Heading for the door, she felt pleased at seeing her brother-in-law again, and was especially excited to be meeting his new girlfriend.

· · ·

Seeing the numerous pictures of Jock's record fish had Jared and Levi fired up about deep sea fishing next summer. "I have to say, my good man, you *do* know how to have fun," Levi told their host. "And now you'll have to come to Montana and go fly fishing in one of our lakes," he offered. "It's quite different, but just as exciting I assure you."

Just then Eric knocked on Jock's open door. "I'm supposed to tell you Ryan and his friend are here," he informed the men.

"Thank you Eric, we'll be right down," Jock told him. "Okay Gentlemen, let's go see who this young lady might be that my brother has latched onto, shall we?"

While Jock hurried ahead, Levi and Jared followed behind making comments about the luxurious home and the still falling snow. "I just hope we don't get delayed at the airport," Jared commented.

"I had *that* displeasure before," Levi replied, shaking his head. As they reached the stairway, they could already hear the jovial greetings going on. "Sounds like a party," Levi teased as he and Jared descended toward the great room and the gathering of people.

As they neared the bottom, they stopped. Catching their breath, they watched as a young woman was being introduced to everyone.

"Am I *seeing* things?" Levi whispered as his heart began racing.

"If you are, so am I," Jared whispered back. As they stood watching, they saw a petite woman dressed in a long black skirt and red sweater. Her near-black hair was cut short in a flattering style. As the woman shook hands and spoke to those around her, there was no doubt, it was Rebecca North, Levi's estranged sister.

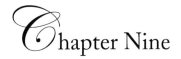

A hundred thoughts raced through Levi's mind when seeing his sister for the first time in over six years. *What will she do when she sees us? Get mad and run off like before?* Levi wondered, taking a deep breath. "She'll be mighty shocked," he whispered, glancing at Jared.

"Where *are* those two?" Jock was heard saying, looking toward the stairway. "Ahh, there they are," he added, seeing them. "Jared, Levi, come along. Ryan and Rebecca have arrived."

At hearing Jock's statement, Rebecca's gaze quickly followed his toward the stairs. Seemingly paralyzed, she only stared at her brother and Jared, her former fiancé.

In that brief moment, the pain of their last words came to mind as Levi slowly walked toward his sister. All else became oblivious as his eyes held hers, seeing astonishment, perhaps some anger. Then as he neared her, he saw tears welling up in her dark eyes; her chin quivered with emotion.

In the next instant she hurriedly took the few remaining steps and flew into his arms. "Levi, I can't believe this!" she wailed against his neck.

"Oh Becky, *Becky,* thank God! I never *dreamed . . ."* Levi's voice broke as he hugged his sister to him, hearing her sobs mingled with words of elation.

"You don't know how often I wanted to find you," she admitted a moment later, looking up at him. "You look wonderful, and I've missed you terribly."

"I've missed you, too," Levi confessed, brushing tears from her cheeks. Then, pulling her to his side, he held her close as his eyes scanned the faces of the others, seeing their questioning look. "Everyone, this is my sister," he could barely say. "We haven't seen each other in over six years."

Upon hearing Levi's statement, cheers filled the room. "I'm certainly glad to hear *that,"* Jock commented, shaking his head. "Otherwise, I wasn't sure what Laura might think."

"Aye, I'm glad ta know it too," Laura replied, joining Levi. "Hello again, Becky, I've heard about ya many times from this husband of mine."

"You've gotten *married?* The confirmed bachelor?" Rebecca blurted.

"Yes and there are other additions, too," Levi told her, motioning to Tom who was still playing with the baby on the floor. "This is our boy Tom, and our newest addition, Shelby Fay."

Saying nothing, Rebecca's eyes filled with new tears as she reached out and took the baby from Levi's arms. "What a beauty," she whispered as a lone tear ran down her cheek. "I've missed out on so much."

"I didn't know I was bringing such a valuable gift with me today, I'm Ryan," he told Levi, offering his hand.

"Ryan, a pleasure to meet you," Levi answered, returning the smile and shaking hands. "Indeed, you couldn't have brought anything more precious than this."

From the sidelines, Jared approached. "Hello Beck," he said motioning for his wife. "Good to see you again. You met her moments ago, but this is my wife, Samantha."

"What a *wonderful* surprise," Samantha said, giving Rebecca a hug.

"Thank you, my, I *do* have lots to catch up on," Rebecca commented, shaking her head. "This is so *overwhelming,* I feel I'm dreaming."

"As do I," Levi said, again putting his arm around his sister's shoulder.

. . .

For Ryan, the day had become one surprise after another. Not only was his friend Rebecca Levi's long-lost-sister, but an hour later, another surprise made her appearance.

Having decided to use Jock's office to call his mother, Ryan headed upstairs. Just as he neared the top, a beautiful blond in a long red dress stepped into view. Suddenly he realized this must be the elusive woman who was never around on his previous visits. He stopped. Their eyes met. Unable to tear his gaze from her face, he started toward her.

"Miss Kara Westin, I presume?" he said, approaching her.

"That I am," she answered smiling. "And you must be Ryan, the one I've heard so much about." Extending her hand, Kara took a step down. As she did, the heel of her shoe apparently caught on the carpet, causing her to fall forward, headlong into Ryan's arms. Catching her, he quickly put his arm around her slender waist, preventing her from falling down the stairs. Her cheek was next to his.

"I'm *so* sorry," Kara gasped, sounding embarrassed. "How clumsy!"

"Quite all right," Ryan replied, loosening his hold on her. "It isn't *everyday* I have a beautiful woman fall for me," he teased. "Are you okay?"

"Yes, thanks to you. I might have broken more ribs if you hadn't been here," Kara told him. "*Thank* you."

"I'm very happy to meet you, Kara," Ryan told her, looking in her eyes. For that moment, time stopped for him as blue eyes the color of which he had never seen before held his like a magnet.

"Me too," Kara whispered, slowly nodding her head. "Merry Christmas; I'm glad you're here," she added, sounding dazed.

"Merry Christmas," Ryan replied softly. "I'm glad I am too." During this exchange of words, Ryan held Kara's hand. Feeling transfixed in a state of awe, he became oblivious to their surroundings. No woman since Katherine, his first and only love, had touched him like this. Somehow he felt a sudden connection to Kara.

"I guess we should join the others," Kara said. "Thank you again for catching me."

"It was my extreme pleasure, I assure you," Ryan told her.

. . .

A cloud of euphoria hung over the Beaumont home for the rest of the afternoon. Not only were Levi and Rebecca celebrating their reunion, but Kelly especially noticed how enamored Kara and Ryan seemed to be.

I believe they've hit it off, so perhaps Ryan and Becky aren't really dating, Kelly thought, seeing no special attention paid toward each other. *Maybe we* will *see love blossom between these two.*

Being Christmas Eve, Jock and Kelly gave Sylvia the night off. In her greeting card was tucked a special bonus for her hard work. "Five thousand dollars!" she gasped wide-eyed. "This is far too generous!"

"Well, its Kelly's idea. *I* thought five dollars would have been enough," Jock teased, shaking his head.

"Oh Jock, what a thing to say," Kelly protested, lightly elbowing her husband. "You have a wonderful evening and Christmas day tomorrow, Sylvia," she said, giving the woman a hug. "We do love and appreciate you."

"You're very kind, thank you, Mrs. Beaumont," Sylvia replied, returning Kelly's embrace. "Thank you both." With that, the housekeeper put on her coat and exited through the door Jock held for her.

Wading through the snow, she headed toward a four-wheel drive vehicle where her husband sat waiting. As the couple drove away, Kelly and Jock waved from the doorway.

. . .

Although Abby joined them for dinner, she was noticeably quiet and refused to join in when Kelly tried to involve her in conversation. Her actions caused obvious hurt for Kelly and brought distinct displeasure to Jock. When she finished eating, Abby retreated to her room.

After dinner that evening, Jock asked everyone into the great room. When they had gathered, he stood by the Christmas tree and faced their guests.

"We thank you all for joining us on our first Christmas," he began. "I wanted to surprise my lovely wife, and I think we pulled that off *quite* nicely," Jock said, winking at Kelly who stood nearby. "But, there are other reasons too. We've had a remarkable year. Happiness has returned to this house and we've been blessed in so many ways. Because of that, we want to bless all of you," he said, bending to retrieve a stack of envelopes from under the tree.

No one spoke, but everyone looked puzzled as they glanced at each other. "Eric, would you like to help me?" Jock asked, noticing him sitting nearby.

"Sure," Eric blurted, jumping to his feet. Whispers soon filled the room as Eric started handing the envelopes to whosever name appeared. Some were addressed to couples, while others were named individually.

"If I missed anyone, I'll make sure you have yours before you leave this house," Jock announced as he put his arm around his wife's shoulder.

"You are so wonderful," Kelly whispered, looking at Jock. "I've never met a more generous man than you."

"It's one of my greatest pleasures, my darling," he replied softly. "I just wish everyone could be as happy as you've made me."

Suddenly the room filled with sounds of surprise. "I don't believe this!" Jared shouted. "Are you *sure* you want to do this?" he asked, looking at Jock.

"I'm sure," Jock replied, nodding his head and smiling. On the sofa, Levi and Laura looked at each other in disbelief, and then down at the check they held. Suddenly Laura was crying obvious tears of joy.

"An SUV? You're giving me *this*?" Kara wailed excitedly, hurrying to give Kelly and Jock each a hug. "Thank you both, *so* much!"

"I'm sorry it wasn't delivered today, but they promised first thing in the morning. That's why they sent a picture," Jock informed her.

"It's beautiful! I'd *never* be able to afford anything like this," Kara blurted, staring at the photo. "With all this snow, it'll be wonderful!"

"A simple thank you *just* isn't enough," Levi said, approaching Jock and Kelly. "You're helping make *a lot* of kids very happy. With this money, we can hire more help and not turn *any* child away next summer," he said, hugging Kelly.

"We're glad we could help," Jock told Levi as the two men then clasped hands in a heartfelt handshake. "You and Laura sacrifice so much of yourselves, this is nothing compared to all that."

"Wow! The note says this is college money," Eric said, "but what is it *exactly*?" he asked, handing it to his mother.

When Laura saw the government bond, her tears welled once more. Then, getting off the sofa, she headed for Jock and Kelly. "Ya just don't know what this means," she could barely say as she hugged Kelly first, then Jock. "Tis a mighty big heart ya both have, and I can't begin ta thank ya enough."

"Tom and Eric are wonderful boys and we want them to have a good education," Kelly told Laura.

"It's our pleasure to do this," Jock added, "Kelly adores those young men and I'm sure I'll feel the same after we spend time on your ranch next summer," he said, surprising both Kelly and Laura.

"Aye, ya must come ta see Morning Star," Laura quickly agreed. "We'd love ta have ya all season."

"We have a baby due," Kelly reminded them both, "but we'll come later."

"Yes, a baby indeed," Jock said smiling as he gently pulled Kelly in his arms. "We *will* be busy for awhile, but when everyone is ready to travel, we'll be there," he added.

Within the next few minutes, everyone had personally thanked Jock and Kelly for their lavish surprise. A honeymoon beyond their wildest dream was given to Emma and Charles. Aunt Gina was given a very generous check to help toward her next adventure in Alaska or perhaps a new destination.

To Samantha and Jared, Jock gave his beautiful vacation home in Hawaii. Not only for their help in saving Ryan's life in Austria, but because he didn't want Kelly living with Katherine's memories in yet another home. Instead, he would buy a lovely new place of her choosing, where they would make their own special memories.

When everyone had thanked them and made their gratitude known, it was Ryan's turn. Seeing his brother's face, Jock knew he, too, was surprised.

"I can't believe you did this," Ryan said, shaking his head as he drew near. Without hesitation, he threw his arms around Jock. "I never expected *anything* like this. Thank you, thank you for believing in me."

"You've proven yourself, little brother, many times over, so why not make you full partner in the Company? It's what Dad wanted all along," Jock told Ryan. "There's plenty for all of us and with the merger coming up *and* new contracts, we'll need to expand."

"Yes, and besides, you may need more money in the near future," Kelly teased. "If I'm seeing what I *think* I am."

Seemingly embarrassed, Ryan glanced at Kara who stood across the room. "I have to admit, she's one lovely lady," he told Kelly. "I'm just sorry we didn't meet before now."

"What's your connection to Rebecca?" Jock asked discretely, seeing the woman playing with Shelby who sat on her lap.

"We've dated, but nothing serious, not really," Ryan admitted. "She's a great person, good worker and fun to be with, but . . ." As his words trailed off, Ryan's gaze wandered toward Kara. Just then she looked his way and smiled. With noticeable elation, Kelly looked up at Jock and grinned.

From the corner of his eye, Jock suddenly noticed Abby on the stairs. Seemingly unsure of what to do, she sat down and peered at everyone through the railing. From where he stood, Jock could see her face and wondered if her stubbornness was ebbing.

"Excuse me for a minute," he told Ryan and Kelly. Soon he reached his daughter. "Abby, do you care to join us?"

"You said I have to apologize to Kelly, or stay in my room," Abby replied somewhat timidly, looking up at him. "So I guess I'm ready to apologize."

"That's wonderful, but are you doing it just so you can join us, or because you mean it?" Jock wanted to know.

"I'll mean it," Abby answered, continuing to look at her father.

"Do you mind telling me what changed your mind?" Jock then asked, wondering who or what had gotten through to her.

"Kara *promised* me Kelly would still love me, no matter what," Abby told Jock. "And will *you,* Father?"

Now, hearing his daughter's question, Jock felt a stab of pain in his heart. *It's obvious she's still unsure of me,* he thought, sitting down beside her on the stairs. Taking a deep breath, he began.

"Yes, sweetheart, I will *always* love you, no matter what. Just as Kelly will," he told her. "I know I did things in the past that hurt you very much, and I'm truly sorry for that. But I promise, nothing like that will *ever* happen again," he vowed, looking in Abby's big blue eyes.

For a moment Abby stared back, but said nothing. "You are very important to both of us, and the new baby will only add to our circle of love," Jock continued, fingering a curl over Abby's ear. "Shall I tell Kelly you want to talk to her?" he asked a moment later.

"Yes, in my room," Abby replied, getting to her feet. "I'll go wait." Breathing a sigh of relief, Jock got to his feet and headed back to Kelly's side. Quickly he informed her of what Abby said, seeing a smile brighten her face.

"Thank you, sweetheart," Kelly told him, "I'll go right up." With that, she headed for the stairs as Jock's eyes lingered after her.

A beautiful wife, my sweet Abby, and now a new baby. What more could I ask? Jock thought, feeling elated.

. . .

When Kelly arrived at Abby's bedroom, her door was open. "Abby? Are you here?" she asked, entering. Looking around, she noticed the child on the floor near her closet. In front of her were pictures scattered in disarray. Knowing Abby often looked at pictures of Katherine, her deceased mother, Kelly made no comment. Abby kept her eyes lowered.

"Hello sweetheart, your father said you wanted to talk to me,"

Kelly began, feeling unsure of Abby's mood. "May I join you?"

"I'm sorry," Abby told Kelly, picking up one of the pictures. "Father said I upset you and if I did, I'm sorry."

"Yes, I *was* upset, because I don't like seeing you unhappy, especially over something this important," Kelly explained, sitting in a nearby chair. "I can *never* replace your mother, Abby, but I do love you as my own daughter. And having this baby, or even a dozen more, will *never* change how I feel."

Suddenly, Abby looked up with eyes wide with surprise. "You're going to have a *dozen?*" she spouted. The look on Abby's face and hearing her remark brought instant laughter from Kelly.

"No, sweetheart, not even close," she replied after regaining her composure. "I'm afraid poor Sylvia would surely quit with *that* many children clambering for her oatmeal cookies!"

Although it was apparent she tried to remain stoic, Abby started laughing too. "Oh Abby, I miss hearing your laughter," Kelly said a moment later. "You are so dear to me, no one could *ever* take your place. Do you suppose we could forget about this misunderstanding and start over with a hug?" she added, holding out her arms.

For a moment, Abby only looked at her. Then, getting up from her place on the floor, she rushed into Kelly's arms. "I'm sorry, Mom, I *really* am!" she cried, as they hugged each other tight.

With a sense of relief, Kelly felt her life couldn't be more perfect, yet, unlike fairytales, she knew life was full of changes. But for now, she would savor what she had and bask in the love surrounding her.

Chapter Ten

Christmas Eve continued with more food, games and another singing session around the piano. Everyone was in high spirits and agreed it was turning out to be their most memorable Christmas ever.

Kelly's baby news along with Emma and Charles' wedding plans were exciting. But everyone agreed, Levi and Rebecca's reunion as well as Jock and Kelly's generous gifts were nothing short of astounding.

Although Rebecca was overjoyed at finding her brother, her heart felt renewed pain when seeing his baby daughter. Because of her new job and the move to Atlanta, she had managed to push her recent past from her mind. But after seeing Shelby, her guilt was back, fresh and hurting.

From her place near the piano, Rebecca could easily see Shelby Fay, her beautiful niece. *Why am I torturing myself? What's done is done,* she reasoned, fighting her tears. *Life goes on, and I'll have more children. Besides, the timing was all wrong, I wanted a career. Well, now I have one, so why am I so envious of Levi having Shelby?* Deep down, Rebecca had no answer.

For the finale around the piano, Charles and Emma sang a duet. When they had finished, everyone cheered and congratulated them both.

"A penny for your thoughts," Levi whispered next to his sister's ear, stepping up beside her. "I bet you haven't heard *that* one in a while."

"You're right, in fact, not since you said it," Rebecca had to admit.

"You seem a thousand miles away," Levi said, "*and* a bit sad."

"I'm still overwhelmed, I suppose. And feeling somewhat melancholy," Rebecca replied, quickly deciding on a distraction. "Do you ever think about our childhood? When Mom and Dad were still alive and well?"

"Sometimes, when I look at Tom and Eric," Levi told her. "I

think about how I was at their age. What I felt, what I wanted out of life. Things certainly took a different path than I ever imagined they would."

"Yes, I remember when you wanted to be a fireman, then a mountain climber, *then* a doctor," Rebecca teased, remembering how proud she always was of her handsome older brother. "Now look at you. From what you've told me already, you've been *all* of that since I saw you."

"Yeah, you're right. Since moving west and meeting Laura, I've had a full life, and I couldn't be happier," Levi confessed, gazing at his wife across the room. "Having her and the boys and now Shelby has given me more joy than I ever dreamed. I highly recommend having a family. How about you, sis? Are you ever going to get married and have babies?"

Levi's question caught her off guard, causing hot tears behind her eyes. "One day," Rebecca answered, trying to smile. "Right now I intend to be the best Sales Rep Beaumont Computers has ever had," she added, squaring her shoulders. "I find my job quite challenging."

"I must admit I was surprised to hear you had entered the business world," Levi told his sister. "But, life changes for all of us, as I can certainly attest. After meeting my family, I'm sure you can see why *I'm* so content," he added. "I hope one day soon you'll come and visit."

"I'd love to. Maybe next summer, but we *will* keep in touch," she assured Levi.

"Most definitely," he replied, bending to kiss her on the cheek. "Been meaning to ask, anything going on between you and Ryan?"

"Nothing serious," Rebecca responded, "it's a good thing too, since I see he suddenly has eyes for blonds."

"How do you feel about that?"

"It's okay. I sensed his reservation weeks ago. Ryan said he loved once in his life and there'd never be another one like that," Rebecca said, shrugging her shoulders. "There are plenty of men out there, so I'm not worried."

"Of course not, my beautiful sister," Levi replied smiling down at her. "I know one day you'll find just the right one."

"It's a blizzard outside!" Eric yelled, startling everyone. "Just look!" Upon hearing that announcement, everyone headed for the windows to peek through the draperies as Eric was doing.

Due to the thousands of Christmas lights adorning the yard, they could easily see the blowing snow and the drifts piling up outside.

"Wow, what a mess. I'm sure glad no one has to go out in that!" Kelly remarked.

"Our hotel isn't too far," Ryan commented, "so Rebecca and I should make that okay."

"Why risk it, Bro?" Jock quickly asked. "We can make room."

"Indeed, and we have *plenty* of food," Kelly assured their guests. "Please, don't *anyone* think of going out in that weather. Tomorrow is Christmas and we want you all here with us anyway."

"What about it, Rebecca? Mind spending the night?" Ryan asked as they turned from the windows.

"Well, I suppose under the circumstances," she replied, "if I can borrow something to sleep in."

"With all these women, they'll have *anything* you need," Levi told his sister. "This will give us more time to talk, cause I've barely gotten started."

As long as you talk, big brother, and don't ask me *too many questions,* Rebecca thought to herself.

. . .

By the time all gifts under the tree were opened and everyone had had their nightly snack, it was after ten-thirty. Soon, the younger ones were all in bed as were Emma and Aunt Gina. Charles was given the hide-a-bed in Jock's den. Tom and Eric would sleep downstairs, as would Ryan. Rebecca would take over the boys' bedroom on the second floor.

When sleeping arrangements were settled and everyone agreed it had been a full day, they headed for bed. Everyone that is, except Ryan.

After saying goodnight to the others, he poured another glass of Eggnog and sat down on the floor in front of the fireplace. Although his eyes were on the orange flames, Ryan's thoughts were on the past few hours. Not only did he think about his newly acquired partnership, but also Kara.

How did she get to me? I'm not a kid, and certainly not one to lose my head over a woman! I've had plenty of chances since Katherine. But no one has touched me like Kara has, Ryan thought, taking a sip of his drink.

Resting his head back against a nearby chair, he closed his eyes as she reappeared in his mind. Tall and elegant she stood smiling at him. Her blond hair piled atop her head, the dress accentuating her slender figure. *All that and she has the face of an angel,* Ryan thought, letting out a deep sigh. *Don't forget how she treated Kelly all those months. She does have another side to her,* he cautioned a moment later. *We all make mistakes,* he told himself.

For the next while, he pondered his feelings and possible scenarios. *I need to find a wife if I ever want a family. Is this a sign I'm putting the past behind me?* Ryan wondered as he gazed at the fire.

It was just a moment later when he heard a noise apparently coming from the kitchen. Surprised that anyone else would be up at this hour Ryan got to his feet and headed that direction. In the dim light he could only see someone's posterior as they bent down to look in the refrigerator.

"I thought I was the only night owl," he whispered, not wanting to startle this fellow insomniac. However, his plan failed when the person reacted to his words, bumping her head on the refrigerator.

"Ohhhh," she moaned, holding the top of her head. "You scared me!"

"Kara, I am *sorry,*" Ryan wailed when seeing who it was. Although he was elated to see her, he felt utterly foolish. "I didn't mean to startle you. Are you all right?" he asked, helping her to a nearby chair.

"I'll be fine, I just wasn't expecting anyone this time of night," Kara said, glancing at Ryan. "What *are* you doing up?"

"I've been enjoying the fire and another shot of Eggnog," he explained. "I'm a night person anyway, besides I wasn't sleepy. Why aren't you asleep?"

"I was in bed most of the day with a headache, and I'm a night person too," Kara replied, resting her head in her hands. "I just can't sleep."

"You've had a headache all day? Now I've made it worse," Ryan lamented, feeling even more guilty. "What can I get you, Kara? Obviously you came down for *something* from the refrigerator."

"I'll join you in some Eggnog, if you don't mind the company. But only half a glass," she requested.

"It's my pleasure," he assured her, retrieving the carton and pouring the creamy liquid. "There's a howling blizzard outside; I can't sleep and now I get a chance to talk to a lovely lady I've heard so much about. I'd say *someone's* on my side," Ryan teased, setting the glass in front of Kara.

"What did you hear . . . exactly?" Kara asked as Ryan sat down across from her.

"Oh, that I should meet you, that you're sweet and caring," Ryan told her. "Jock speaks highly of you, and of course your sister can't say enough about how great you are." For a moment, Kara's eyes rested on the glass in front of her, seeming to ponder his last remark.

"Even after the way I treated her," Kara stated somewhat sadly. "I was way off base with her, Ryan. I thought she married Jock for his money and I wouldn't give her time to explain. I was *quite* hateful to her."

"At least you admit it, and, I suppose it did seem questionable the way it happened," Ryan told her. "I know you hurt Kelly a lot, but she's not one to hold a grudge. That's why I admire her so much. We all do."

"Unlike me," Kara said as her eyes glistened with tears. "Since we're being honest, I have to admit I was jealous. Something Kelly has *never* been guilty of."

"Jealous? Why?" Ryan asked, feeling puzzled.

"Because she had two men who adored her, and one of them could give her anything she'd ever want," Kara confessed, surprising him.

I might be that one for you, Ryan wanted to say, yet he knew it was too soon. "We all find that special person in time," he told her instead. "You're a beautiful woman, Kara. Any man would be proud to have you on his arm."

"Like you, Ryan?" she asked bluntly.

Not wanting to divulge his feelings quite yet, Ryan could only return her gaze as her eyes bore into his. For a moment they were silent. Then, as if a light went on, Ryan looked past her beauty, into her soul. There he saw goodness, yet sensed her sadness and longing to be loved. He felt compelled to say more.

"I'm told, we *all* have that special person somewhere. That one we're meant to be with, that only God can put in our path," Ryan said, reaching for Kara's hand. "If your special person happens to be me, Kara, I'd be very happy indeed," he whispered.

A soft smile touched her lips before she lowered her eyes. Then, after drinking her Eggnog, she spoke. "I'm glad we had this talk, Ryan, but I suppose it's time we get some sleep," she told him.

"Perhaps so, but I'm not thinking about sleep right now," Ryan admitted. "I know you're leaving for Atlanta right after New Years. I'll be there too, and I'd like to show you around. I mean the sights of the city, not Beaumont Computers."

"I'd like that very much," Kara replied standing to her feet.

"I hope your headache is gone," Ryan said, still feeling bad for what happened. After leaving his chair, he took the glass from Kara's hand and placed it on the counter nearby. Again he looked at her. "I'm very sorry that happened. I'd never want to hurt you, Kara."

"Thank you, that's very sweet," she replied. Surprising him, Kara leaned forward and kissed him on the cheek.

Without forethought, Ryan placed his hands on her shoulders and looked in her eyes. Slowly he drew her close. Although he wanted to kiss her lips, he instead gently kissed her forehead and gave her a warm embrace.

. . .

By the time she reached her bedroom, Kara's head was reeling. *Wow! I've missed a lot by cutting myself off from family,* she thought. *He's a sweet guy just like they said, but he arrived with Rebecca. Mother says if we're patient things will work out the right way. Okay, we'll see,* she thought, climbing into bed.

Although her parents always said God cares about the smallest details, Kara doubted her marriage partner was a priority with the Almighty.

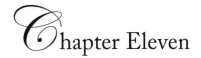

Chapter Eleven

Christmas morning dawned clear and calm. Although the blizzard was over, its resulting snowdrifts were easily seen glistening in the morning sun.

"Would you like to go sliding?" Abby asked Eric excitedly as they stood at the window. "We have a hill in the backyard."

"It can't be much of a hill," Eric replied, throwing a glance her way.

"It's a hill just the same! Forget I asked!" Abby snapped tossing her curls over her shoulder. Stomping away, she passed by Tom who sat in a chair reading but overhearing the conversation.

"I'll go sliding with you, Abby," Tom offered. "We don't need Eric."

"You'd *really* go?" she asked with eyes wide with excitement.

"Of course, why not?"

"Because you're big, I mean, you're not a kid like me," Abby told Tom.

"Well, I like kids, and I love the snow, so why not?" he admitted, laying aside the magazine. "Whenever you're ready, let me know." Upon hearing his remark, Abby smiled and hurried upstairs. "I doubt you'll be invited back here, at least by Abby," Tom told Eric when the girl was out of earshot. "Why do you keep insulting her like that?"

"I don't mean to, it just comes out," Eric said, shrugging his shoulders.

"If you ever want a girl to like you, you'd better cut it out," Tom advised.

"I'll *never* want a girlfriend, especially that one!" Eric spouted.

"Never is a very long time," Rebecca remarked, entering the room. "You'll change your mind in a few years."

"Mom said you're our Aunt Becky, is that right?" Eric asked, flopping down in a chair. "If so, how come you and Dad just found each other?"

As she seated herself on the sofa, Rebecca was quiet as she studied the cup she held. Then smiling, she looked at the boys. "That's a good question," she began, nodding her head. "We had a misunderstanding, many years ago. It was very foolish and I hope neither of you make that same mistake. It was my fault, Levi tried, but I didn't. So, we've spent all these years apart, lonely and heartbroken," Rebecca admitted. "Amazingly, we've found each other, and I've never seen him this happy. You're part of that reason."

"He's made us happy, too," Tom replied, "he's a great dad."

"Yeah, he saved Tom and me from a mountain lion! Did he tell you?" Eric asked excitedly.

"A mountain lion?" Rebecca shrieked. "No, please tell me." For the next while, Tom and Eric told their aunt about their camping trip up the mountain, and how Levi saved them from certain death.

"He risked his life for us, even before he *was* our dad," Tom told her.

Seemingly in shock, Rebecca slowly shook her head as she looked at them. "He loves you very much and I see why you love him too," she said as tears gathered. "I'm very glad he came to your rescue."

"Me too," Eric sighed heavily. "When you coming to Montana?" he then asked. "How about next summer?"

"We'll see, but it depends on my job," Rebecca told them. "I'd love to visit. Levi's been telling me all about the ranch."

"We can teach you to ride horses, and how to fish," Eric offered excitedly.

"My, I certainly wouldn't want to pass all *that* up," she teased, smiling.

"I'm ready to go sliding," Abby announced as she came downstairs. "Do you still want to go?" she asked Tom, zipping up her parka.

"Sure, let me get my things on," he told Abby. "It's been nice talking to you, Aunt Becky," Tom said politely. "If you'll excuse us, we're going sliding."

. . .

While the men were outside snow blowing the driveway and clearing off the front step and sidewalk, the women did breakfast dishes and cleared away gift wrappings from the night before.

"I can't believe you're all leaving tomorrow," Kelly remarked as they left the kitchen. "Three days just *isn't* enough." Everyone had to agree.

For the next hour, the women talked and laughed, sharing thoughts for the New Year just ahead. "I pray yer'll be havin' baby news of yer own, Sam," Laura told her cousin. "There's nothin' quite like hearin' the sound of a child around the house."

"We can see that," Kelly replied, "Levi just beams over Shelby Fay."

"Well, if Jared and I can't conceive we'll try to adopt, but like I said, there aren't a lot of babies available these days."

"Too many abortions going on," Gina spoke up. "I'll never understand a woman doing such a thing. Killing for convenience, that's what it is."

"And the poor girls don't realize the guilt they'll have later on," Emma remarked. "One day they'll see it was a baby, not a choice."

"Sadly it's become a big business," Gina explained. "The doctor doesn't only get paid for killing the baby, but is paid handsomely for the fetal tissue it produces. It all boils down to greed, pure and simple."

"How do you know so much about this, Aunt Gina?" Kara asked.

"I didn't *always* run a restaurant. For a few months I worked in a clinic," she explained, shaking her head. "I was so young and naïve back then. I was told we were there to *help* women with their problems. Not until a young girl bled to death was I told what *kind* of problems we treated," Gina remarked. "I left soon after, but since then the abortions have gotten even more heinous and they're killing full term babies!"

"Partial birth abortions," Kelly said shaking her head. "We must all do what we can to stop such horrific procedures."

As she listened, Rebecca could barely contain her emotions. Suddenly she remembered the life she once felt inside her. At first a tiny flutter, then as the weeks passed, a definite kick of tiny legs. "Please excuse me," she managed to say, bolting from her chair. As she raced upstairs, she feared her horrible secret had suddenly come to light.

Arriving at her bedroom, Rebecca flung herself across the bed as sobs racked her body. *I did that to my baby! How could I? What was I thinking? And why didn't anyone tell me how to cope with this guilt? How can I face everyone now that they know,* she sobbed.

"Becky, may I come in?" she heard Laura ask a few minutes later.

"Please?" Although wishing she could hide, Rebecca instead wiped her tears.

"Yes, come in," she answered. Slowly the door opened and Laura stepped inside, closing it behind her.

"Tis not our intension ta upset ya," she began, approaching the bed where Rebecca sat. "Tis a sensitive subject as we all know, for some more than others."

"Yes, it's hard for me," Rebecca admitted, wondering how much to say.

"We see it tis, and I don't mean ta pry, Becky, but talkin' it through might help," Laura offered kindly. "We aren't here as judge, but rather as friends hopin' ta heal the pain yer feelin'," she added, sitting down beside her.

Looking at Laura, her newly found sister-in-law, Rebecca did indeed see love, not condemnation. Truly her own guilt had condemned her most often in the past several months. Suddenly, she wanted to bare her soul, to rid herself of this guilt she'd carried. Despite what anyone thought of her, she must.

"Laura, the conversation wasn't all of it. Seeing your precious Shelby and playing with her, seeing her smile, hearing her giggles is hard," she confessed, fighting her tears. "All of it made me think about the baby I might have had, but chose not to. I killed *my* little girl," Rebecca wailed.

Instantly she felt Laura's arms around her, holding her like a child, cradling her. "Oh Becky, what sorrow ya must be feelin'," Laura whispered.

As she clung to Laura, Rebecca cried. Not only for what she did to her innocent baby, but for all the Christmas' void of *that* child's laughter. For missing those little arms around her neck, those tender bedtime kisses, all the joys she had witnessed Laura and Levi having with Shelby. She felt pitiful, knowing *she* had killed for convenience.

Finally, when her crying ceased, Rebecca pushed herself from Laura's arms and got to her feet. As she paced the spacious room, she knew she had to tell it all.

"I finally got this job, one I'd applied for months earlier. I didn't know what I'd do with a baby," she told Laura.

"Did ya tell the father? Couldn't he help ya somehow?" Laura asked.

"No, he didn't want the baby, or any part in raising it. Without a good job I couldn't afford a child," Rebecca said. "I was given no alternatives such as adoption, or counseling, *nothing.* They told me my 'crisis pregnancy' would be terminated and I could get on with my life after a few hours rest. Yeah, my pregnancy ended all right, but no one told me how to cope with this guilt or shame I feel."

"Tis only God that can take it from ya, Becky," Laura told her. "Surely, He alone knows the pain yer feelin' and wants ta comfort ya, if ya'll let Him."

Although she was far from religious, Rebecca knew somewhere there *had* to be a God, a divine entity. Knowing the vastness of the universe and seeing the intricate detail of a butterfly was surely proof of a supreme being. But, when thinking of a God who cared about our daily lives, who would comfort our pain and suffering, was far different. Yet, others felt certain of it and their lives reflected that peace in knowing such a Being.

"How do you *know* this?" Rebecca asked, sitting down beside Laura.

"By experience," Laura simply answered. "Aye, tis not an easy thing ta understand, but tis true nonetheless. God loves us and knows every detail of our lives, Becky. Despite all we've done wrong, He'll forgive us if we ask."

"I'll think about it," Rebecca replied a moment later. Once more on her feet, she went to the window and looked out. Facing the backyard, she saw the windswept landscape of snowdrifts and barren trees. Some distance from the house, she saw Abby and Tom romping in the snow.

"Those two remind me of how Levi and I were as kids," she told Laura. Leaving her place on the bed, Laura joined Rebecca at the window.

"Aye, Levi tells me about those years growin' up," she said. "He's missed ya, Becky. And now he's so grateful ta God for answerin' his prayers."

"Prayers? Levi prays?" she blurted. "I guess he *has* changed."

"For sure he has, and seein' ya again has certainly added ta our joy," Laura said smiling.

"Yes, for me too," Rebecca had to admit. "I only wish I would have done as well as Levi has. He's a hero, to many people. And I'm anything but."

"While we live and breathe, Becky, tis never too late," Laura said softly.

Making no reply, Rebecca could only think about her past mistakes, feeling certain nothing could make up for what she'd done to her baby. Nonetheless, talking to Laura had somehow lightened the load of guilt she was carrying. *Perhaps one day I'll find that comfort she's talking about,* she thought.

. . .

Despite the weather, Kara's SUV was delivered on Christmas Morning. After the man from the dealership demonstrated all the gadgetry to the new owner, he handed her keys to her tan-colored Denali. Due to the cold, a hurried look was given by everyone, all except Ryan.

"It's so beautiful!" Kara boasted, feeling the black leather seats. "I still can't believe Jock and Kelly gave me something this grand."

"They love you, and you needed a vehicle," Ryan told her. "By the way, is your headache better? I mean, after last night?"

"Yes, thank you. I feel very well, how about you?" Kara returned.

"Oh, I'm feeling *quite* superb," he said grinning. "I haven't had a chance to tell you, Kara, but I enjoyed our late night meeting, *very* much. Of course, it didn't help my insomnia. I'm afraid I didn't sleep much."

"Too much Eggnog?" Kara teased, glancing at Ryan. "Care to take a ride with me? I can't wait to drive this!" she said, changing the subject.

"I thought you'd never ask," Ryan teased back.

Not only was Kara delighted with her new vehicle, but she discovered Ryan to be quite interesting. *He's certainly a charmer. Nice looking too,* she thought as she headed her SUV down Lake Shore Drive. Already they saw snowplows out clearing and salting the streets after last night's storm.

"I know of a nice coffee shop up ahead," Ryan remarked as they drove. "I sure could use something hot about now."

"It does sound good, but are they open on Christmas?" Kara asked, secretly wishing for more time alone with Ryan.

"Maybe not, but I'm hoping they are," he admitted. Two minutes later, Ryan pointed to the 'Coffee Bean', a small quaint looking shop just off the road. "We're in luck," he cheered, seeing the lighted 'open' sign in the window. In no time they were seated in a small booth ordering flavored coffee.

For the next while, Kara and Ryan talked. No one subject monopolized their conversation, but rather, they touched on a variety of topics. Eventually the question of marriage and children came up.

"I suppose having a great new job would entice most women to forget about marriage and babies," Ryan remarked, studying Kara's face.

"Not *this* woman," Kara replied, shaking her head. "No job could take the place of being a mother, at least for me. I was hooked the first moment I saw Shelby Fay. From then on I knew motherhood was for me," she admitted. "This job is a necessity, nothing more."

Making no reply, Ryan lowered his eyes to the cup he held, but Kara clearly noted the grin on his face.

"What about you? Is having a family in your plans?" Kara then asked.

"Certainly, I've always wanted one. But, when things didn't work out with Katherine and she married Jock, I gave up. Since then I felt sure I'd never marry. No one could ever take her place, I was sure of it," Ryan confessed. "But now . . ."

"Yes?" Kara asked as her heart began racing.

"After meeting you, I *do* wonder if you might be that 'special someone' we talked about last night," he said softly, looking in her eyes. "There's no doubt you've stirred *something* inside of me, Kara. No matter how many women I've dated, they didn't," Ryan admitted, reaching for her hand.

She was speechless. Certainly other men had said sweet words to her, but this was different. She saw sincerity in his eyes, and she recalled Kelly's words. *Ryan dates a lot, but no matter how beautiful they are, he feels no special connection. Maybe I have touched his heart,* Kara thought. "That makes me feel very special," she replied, returning his gaze.

"Yes, you *are,*" Ryan answered.

Although wanting to hear more, Kara felt uncomfortable discussing such personal matters in this public place, especially when another couple seated themselves in the next booth.

"I suppose we'd better get going," she said, pulling her eyes from his. "Everyone will think we got lost."

"I guess you're right," Ryan agreed reluctantly.

After paying the check, they headed for the SUV. Upon hearing the appropriate sound for unlocking the vehicle, Kara looked at Ryan. "Care to drive me home?"

"I'd love to," Ryan answered as he opened the passenger side door for her. Once they were seated inside, Ryan hesitated. Then, after starting the motor, his attention was again on Kara. "I hope all this isn't scaring you off," he said, taking hold of her hand.

"Not at all," Kara replied, "I just regret all the months we've wasted, if you *are* my Mr. Right."

"I guess only time will tell, won't it," Ryan stated, gently caressing her slender fingers. "You have lovely hands, Kara. They match the rest of you," he said, lifting her hand to his lips.

Ryan's lips felt warm as they touched the back of her hand, and made chills when he kissed her palm. Then, looking in Kara's eyes, he began leaning toward her. *Is this for real? Or are we just playing games? I have to sort this out,* Kara thought, pulling her hand free.

"We better get going," she said, breaking the spell.

"You're right, forgive me, Kara, for being so eager," he said a moment later. In silence, Ryan headed the vehicle back toward the Beaumont estate.

We can't rush into this. How can we know our feelings this quickly? He's a fun kind of guy, but is *he the one for me?* Kara had to wonder.

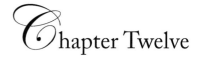

Chapter Twelve

The time had arrived to say goodbye. As the women hugged each other and vowed to stay in touch, the men finished loading the luggage inside Jock's SUV.

Standing away from the others, Rebecca tried to swallow the lump in her throat as she told Levi goodbye. "It's been great," she could barely say, choking back her tears. "I'm so *sorry* for what I've done to us."

With obvious emotion on his face, Levi pulled his sister into his arms and hugged her close. "All is forgiven, sweet Becky," he told her. "That's all behind us now, so from here on we'll make up for lost time, okay?" Unable to speak, Rebecca could only nod her head in agreement. "We can't let our mistakes in the past overshadow life today, now can we?"

"I'll try not to," Rebecca whispered through her tears. From Levi's remark, she could only wonder how much Laura had told him. If he knew what she had done, it was obvious he held nothing against her. "Take care of that precious family, okay? They're wonderful," she said, leaving Levi's arms.

"Yes, they are. I still can't believe God blessed me with so much," he said, smiling down at her. "Promise you'll come and see us?"

"I promise," she said, giving her brother a quick kiss goodbye. Within the next few minutes, Rebecca hugged Tom, Eric and Laura. Then, fighting that familiar hurt inside, she held Shelby one last time. "Goodbye you sweet baby," she whispered, seeing the wide dimpled smile that was quickly displayed for her. Then, Shelby reached out her tiny hand and touched Rebecca's face, causing renewed emotion to swell within her. Once more she felt the agony of remorse, knowing she'd never feel that tender touch from her own little girl.

With sobs building just beneath the surface, Rebecca quickly handed Shelby to Laura, giving a forced smile. With more goodbyes heard behind her, she ran upstairs to her room. No longer could she go on living with this guilt. Somehow, it must end. . . .

. . .

With the temperatures still below zero, the snow squeaked beneath the tires of Jock's SUV as it pulled from the driveway. Those inside the vehicle waved one last time, not seeing the tears spilling down Kelly's face.

Due to not having her luggage, Rebecca was eager to get back to her hotel room. And, because of business he needed to do, Charles offered to drop her off on his way, allowing Ryan to stay a while longer.

"Thank you for *everything,*" Rebecca told Kelly, giving her a hug. "It's been fun, and finding my brother again was a wonderful bonus. Thank you all for letting me share your Christmas," she said, looking at each one.

Then, after tying the belt of her coat around her, Rebecca pulled on her gloves and slipped past Charles who held the door for her. Soon, they were in the man's Jeep Cherokee and driving away.

"I *hate* seeing everyone go," Kelly said, dabbing a tear from her eye.

"The house *will* seem mighty empty," Kara remarked, nodding her head.

"I guess I'm next," Ryan remarked, glancing at his watch. "I have a meeting in Atlanta first thing tomorrow morning, so I have a flight this afternoon." When hearing that, Kara felt a tinge of disappointment.

"Oh Ryan, are you sure?" Kelly asked, "now that you're a partner can't you relax your hectic schedule?"

"Afraid not, being a partner brings *more* responsibility," he replied, "and of course a greater desire to see business grow."

"You're Jock's partner?" Kara blurted. "When did *that* happen?"

"This weekend," Ryan said grinning. "It was one of many pleasant surprises." At Ryan's comment, Kara knew what he meant and it brought a blush to her face. It was hard to miss the reaction of the others as they grinned at each other. "Now I have lots of reasons to get the job done," Ryan admitted, meeting Kara's gaze.

"I think it's wonderful," Emma boasted, looking at Ryan. "I know how much Jock depends on you and appreciates your hard work.

He's told me many times."

"Oh yes, Ryan, your brother is *very* proud of you for what you've accomplished," Kelly chimed in. "We all are." For a moment, Ryan said nothing yet seemed pleased to hear the accolades on his behalf.

"I must say, I never imagined I'd be working with my brother," Ryan confessed. "It was out of the question, but, a close brush with death will open our eyes to many things. Jock took very good care of me, so I owe him a lot. And now this partnership, well, I feel quite unworthy," he said, shaking his head.

"Nonsense," Gina quickly refuted. "Jock wouldn't have made you partner unless he felt you deserved it. And now, you'll *both* be Kara's boss."

"I promise I'll go easy on her," Ryan teased, winking at Kara. "If she works out, perhaps she'll be moved to a better position."

At Ryan's remark, Kara felt somewhat embarrassed, and excited. "Mother, we need to plan your wedding," she quickly stated, changing the subject. "I'd really like to help before I leave for Atlanta."

Just then the telephone rang. "Would you mind getting that, Ryan?" Kelly asked from her place on the sofa. While the women began discussing what Emma should wear for her wedding, Ryan left to answer the phone call.

It was several minutes later when he returned, looking astonished. Saying nothing, he only shook his head.

"Ryan, what is it?" Kelly asked. "What happened?"

"I can't believe it! I just *can't* believe it," he said, looking at the others. "It's Mother, she can *see!* She got her sight back, just today," Ryan blurted with obvious emotion.

"Praise God! It's a Christmas miracle!" Emma shouted with jubilation.

"That was my sister Pamela, calling from the hospital," Ryan told them. "Mother banged her head on the cupboard this morning and when she started feeling dizzy, Pamela drove her to the ER. As the doctor was examining the bump on her head, Mother started seeing. She told him she never knew he had such white hair!" he explained laughing.

"Oh Ryan, that is *glorious* news," Kara said, standing beside him. In the next instant Ryan's face grew solemn as he looked at her. Suddenly he threw his arms around Kara's waist, lifting her off the floor he began twirling her around.

"*Yes* its wonderful, *you're* wonderful, I *feel* wonderful," he told her as he lowered her back to the floor. All the while his eyes were on her face. "I think I'm in love with you," he then whispered so only she could hear.

In shock Kara only stared. "What, *what* did you say?" she stammered as her heart began racing.

"I'm in love with you. I know it's crazy, I can't explain it," Ryan said, looking in her eyes. "But I felt it from the moment I saw you."

"We must call Jock on his cellular and let him know about Cora," Kelly said from across the room. "He'll be ecstatic. After all these years, who'd ever guess she would get her sight back?"

Although Kara heard her sister rambling in the background, all she could think about was what she just heard from Ryan. "You don't have to say anything right now. You probably think I'm nuts," he told her. "It's a lot to digest, I know, especially since we just met." Then, adding to her surprise, Ryan turned and faced the others. "Do any of you believe in love at first sight?"

Seemingly dumbfounded, they all looked at each other, then back at Ryan. "Yes, I do," Gina announced nodding her head. "It happened to me. Of course, I didn't tell the guy until after we were engaged, but I knew he was the one for me from the moment I laid eyes on him."

"Great, that's good enough for me," Ryan blared. "I believe in it too." With that declaration, he looked at Kara and then leaned down and lightly kissed her cheek. "Ladies, I do believe I've been smitten by this lovely Kara, and if she'll have me, one day I hope to marry her." When hearing this, Kara felt embarrassed, but the others cheered.

"What's all the shouting about?" Abby asked from the stairway, sounding somewhat perturbed.

"Sweetheart, your Grand Mama has gotten her eyesight back," Kelly said excitedly. "She can finally see your beautiful face. Isn't that wonderful news?"

"I knew it, I just *knew* it would happen!" Abby squealed with delight as she raced to Kelly. "When can we go see her? Tomorrow? Please?" she begged.

"I'm sure we'll go as soon as your father can get away," Kelly told Abby. With that, Abby turned and looked at Emma and then threw her arms around the woman's waist.

"Thank you, Grandma Em! Thank you!" she cried, closing her eyes as she hugged her. "You were right, now I can't *wait* to see Grand

Mama." Just as quickly, Abby turned and ran back upstairs, leaving everyone staring.

"What did she mean, Mother?" Kelly asked. "What did you tell her?"

"About miracles," Emma replied. "I told her if we earnestly pray for something, and have faith to believe, God will answer. So, we've been praying her Grand Mama would see again," she explained to everyone. "When it didn't happen right away, I also told Abby that God has a different timetable then we do. But, He *will* answer."

"She's never mentioned this," Kelly told her mother, sounding surprised. "No *wonder* she's so excited now that it's happened. And I have to say thank you, too, Mother," she added, giving Emma a hug.

"Thank God, not me," Emma quickly replied. "We've had many miracles in our family, and now we've had one more. God saw the faith of that little girl and heard her heartfelt prayers."

By now, everyone was shedding tears of joy and were seemingly lost for words. Ryan had his arm around Kara's shoulder; Kelly and Gina brushed aside their tears; Emma stood with her face and hands lifted skyward. "We Praise you Lord and thank you for this miracle."

For the next hour gaiety filled the house. Not only was Cora Beaumont's restored eyesight reason to celebrate, but Ryan's declaration of love for Kara had everyone excited.

"How do *you* feel about Ryan's announcement?" Kelly asked when Ryan left the room.

"I'm shocked," Kara replied feeling overwhelmed. "I knew he liked me, but saying it like this is—"

"*Exciting,*" Gina chimed in, putting her arm around Kara's waist. "You need a good man, dear, and from what I can see, he's all of that and more."

"Yes, he *is,* but I have to wonder if his excitement over his mother got the best of him," Kara told the others. "You know how people are sometimes."

"Don't concern your pretty head about *that,*" Ryan said, surprising them upon his return. "I meant every word." With his eyes on Kara, he slowly approached. "I hate to leave, but I really have to get going," he told everyone. "My only consolation is that I'll see you in a week or so, in Atlanta," he said looking at Kara. "As for the rest of you, have a wonderful New Year," he added, giving them each a hug. "It's been a most *thrilling* Christmas gathering."

After the others returned his well wishes, Ryan took Kara's hand and led her away to the kitchen. There, facing her, he put his hands on her shoulders. "Kara, I meant every word I said," he told her tenderly, looking in her eyes. "I *am* in love with you. I can't believe it either, but I *know* it. This will take some getting used to, so I'm not going to rush you into anything. We'll move at your pace, my lovely Kara," Ryan said, brushing her cheek with his hand. "All I ask is: let me prove my love," he whispered.

With Ryan's tender look and words of love aimed at her, Kara felt sure she was in a dream. "I don't understand any of this, but yes, I'll give you that chance," she could barely say.

Gently, Ryan wrapped his arms around her and silently they clung to each other. "I guess I'll see you in Atlanta," Kara told him a moment later.

"That you will, my dear," Ryan replied, kissing her forehead. Then, as he gazed into her eyes, he slowly lowered his lips to hers.

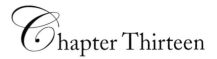

During the next two weeks, everyone was busy making wedding plans for Emma and Charles. The sun felt especially warm on January sixth when the family gathered in a quaint little church near Romeo, Michigan.

"Mother, I do believe God is shining His face down upon you today," Kelly said while helping Emma get ready.

"I feel blessed in so many ways, I can hardly believe it," Emma replied tearfully, looking at those around her. "My two precious daughters, my wonderful sister, and now another darling man as my husband. I'm truly *overwhelmed* with thanksgiving."

"No one deserves it more, Mother," Kara said, leaning down and touching her cheek next to Emma's.

"Amen to that," Gina added, taking her sister's hand. Then, while sharing tears of joy, each gave the bride one last hug before leaving the room.

For her wedding attire, Emma wore a lavender ankle-length-chiffon with matching wide-brimmed hat and low-heel-shoes. Her blond hair hung in soft curls just above her shoulders. At her neck she wore a gift from her groom, a strand of perfectly matched pearls.

With emotions high, Kelly and Kara watched their mother exchange vows with the man they, too, had grown to love and respect. The church ceremony included only the family, but a lavish reception with hundreds of guests was held at an elegant hotel.

"I never thought I'd be this happy again," she told her girls and Gina, giving them each a hug following the ceremony.

"We know he'll take good care of you, Mother," Kelly said, choking back her tears. "He's a wonderful man."

"And he's lucky to have *you,* Mom," Kara added, sniffling. As she dabbed her own eyes, Emma looked at her girls.

"I want you both to know how proud I am of you," she began. "You've been so supportive of my marriage to Charles. Some children *aren't* when their parent remarries."

"We want you to be happy, Mother. We know Dad would too, so how *could* we deny you that chance? Besides, you're too young and beautiful not to marry again," Kelly said. "But, we'll miss you terribly."

With a new round of emotion, Kelly and Kara said goodbye. "Have a *wonderful* honeymoon," Kara whispered, wondering if one could be in her near future.

With cheers and well wishes shouted after them, Charles and Emma climbed into a black stretch limousine that would take them to the airport. From there, Pierre would fly them on Jock's company plane to the Caribbean for their two week honeymoon.

A private island resort awaited their arrival. Supplied with anything they could want or need, their secluded bungalow not only assured them privacy, but tour guides and servants were at their beckon call. It promised to be memorable in every way.

. . .

Following her mother's wedding, Kara returned to Atlanta. Upon her first day back in the office, she was surprised to see a box of expensive chocolates sitting on her desk. Thinking they came from Ryan, she was surprised when the card read: *Congratulations on your new job. Welcome aboard!* Signed, L. C.

"They came from Mr. Carlyle," a co-worker told Kara. "He does that for all new employees, even though he isn't even our boss."

"He must be very kind," Kara replied, laying the candy and card aside.

Despite Ryan's promise to show her the sights, Kara saw him only briefly each morning. However, since she found the training more challenging than expected, she was grateful to have a good night's sleep, instead of a date.

Nearly a week after her return from Michigan, Kara received an early morning call at her office. "Hello Miss Westin, welcome to Beaumont," a male voice greeted. "Are you enjoying your new job?"

For a moment, Kara sorted through her memory. *This guy sounds familiar, have I met him since I arrived?* "It's coming along, thank you."

"I *am* sorry to cut this short, but an urgent call is coming in. I look forward to seeing you this afternoon at the staff meeting," he added in haste.

For the next while, Kara tried to match a face to the man's voice. Finally, she conceded to wait until the meeting.

. . .

It was two o'clock that afternoon when Ryan poked his head around the corner. "Hi beautiful," he greeted, winking at Kara. "You ready for a break?"

"I could use one," she replied, returning his smile as a warm feeling swept over her. *It's pretty nice having a boss who cares so much, it certainly has its advantages,* she decided, closing the computer program she was using. "Are you here for the meeting?"

"Among other reasons," he said, taking her by the hand. "Come with me, my dear. I have something to show you upstairs."

Soon they were on the elevator heading for the twentieth floor of the huge office building. Here the executive offices were located. However, it wasn't where a young trainee would have occasion to go *or* be invited, unless of course her boss and half owner of the company would take her.

When the elevator doors opened, Kara felt as though she'd stepped into a different world. No longer was she among desks, computers and ringing telephones. Instead, she felt plush wine colored carpet beneath her feet; chairs upholstered in rich looking material sat sporadically along the wide hallway. She saw shiny wooden doors of intricate design with gold name plates.

The world of the upper echelon, Kara thought as they passed each office.

"It's just ahead," Ryan said, pointing and giving her a smile. "I can't wait to show you."

Upon hearing his remark, Kara was reminded of a little boy wanting to show off his new toy. Certainly the man beside her was no child. Tall, with light brown hair and hazel eyes, Ryan was quite good looking, admittedly however, not the gorgeous hunk his brother Jock was.

Finally, they stopped in front of another shiny door with a gold name plate. "This is it, my office," Ryan told Kara, "at least for the time being."

As she looked closer, Kara did in fact see Ryan's name on the sign. "Ryan Beaumont . . . Vice President," she read aloud. "This is wonderful, Ryan. Congratulations," she added, giving him a quick kiss on the cheek.

"For *that* you get the twenty-five cent tour," he teased, opening the door. For the next several minutes, Ryan showed Kara his spacious new office with its beautiful oak wood desk and burgundy leather chairs. In an adjoining room was a massive oak conference table with eighteen brown leather chairs. A wall of windows looked out over the city.

"What a view!" Kara remarked as her eyes scanned the surroundings. Downtown Atlanta was in the distance. In the foreground, the now barren trees and dead winter grass would surely be beautiful when spring arrived. "It's all so grand, Ryan. *Thank you* for sharing it with me," she told him, turning from the window.

"Will you have dinner with me tomorrow night?" Ryan asked, looking at her. "I'm sorry we haven't made it before now, but this new plant opening is taking more time than I expected."

"And my head is full of charts and graphs and trying to remember which is for what," Kara said jokingly. "It's early to bed for me these days. By the way, isn't there a meeting this afternoon?" she asked.

"Yes, so we better get going," Ryan said, glancing at his watch. "I've missed you, Kara," he added, taking hold of her hand. "I can't quit thinking about you, I want you to know that."

Not waiting for a reply, Ryan opened the door to his office and the two headed down the hall for the elevator. *How do I feel about this man?* Kara wondered. Whether it was due to her tired, stressed out feeling over her new job, or for other reasons, right now she wasn't sure what she felt.

. . .

The sounds of chatter greeted Ryan and Kara when they arrived at the meeting room. "I'll join you later," he whispered as he escorted Kara to a chair.

Nodding her head, she sat down and watched as Ryan headed toward the podium. Nonchalantly she looked around, returning a smile or nod from those nearby. As she gazed toward the front table, Kara saw Ryan and other well-dressed men talking.

What she saw next made her gasp. *It's him! That's who called me this morning, it's Lorenzo!* She could only stare at the man, the one who had saved her life months before.

"It's time we get started," Ryan said, facing the employees. "Due to other obligations, Jock can't be here today, so I'll try to update you on things."

As Ryan talked, his words soon became lost to Kara as her mind wandered back in time, to her accident *and* Lorenzo. *Who is he? Does he work for Beaumont Computers too?* Kara pondered, looking at him. *He looks different; distinguished; more handsome. His beard is gone, and he doesn't look so tired or sad,* Kara decided, staring at the man.

While Ryan rambled on about reports and updates on new government contracts, Lorenzo took notes. From where she sat, Kara watched his every move. *He wears no wedding ring; he's left handed; he looks comfortable in a suit,* she decided, thinking of questions to ask Ryan.

"Now that I've covered all that, I'll let Mr. Carlyle fill you in on the rest," Ryan said, motioning toward the man.

Carlyle . . . so that's his name. He's the one who sends chocolates, Kara thought, feeling stunned at such revelation.

"Thank you, Ryan. It's good to see everyone again," Lorenzo began, his eyes finding Kara. "Very good, indeed," he added before looking away. It was obvious that his lingering attention directed at her didn't go unnoticed by those sitting nearby. Several turned in their seats and looked at her, bringing a blush to Kara's face.

"As you know, my company has worked hand in hand with Beaumont Computers for the past few months," Lorenzo continued. "We do the technical research on the computer chips before you make them. Our goal to keep those planes and missiles flying is a joint effort," he remarked. "Each of you is important to the success we achieve-or the failure. No company is greater than its employees and that's one reason why I'm here today, to tell everyone we'll be looking for those who are dedicated, ethical, and deserve promotion," he said, bringing a round of applause.

"Another reason for this meeting is: to announce the merger of Beaumont Computers and the Carlyle Research Corporation."

With that, the room erupted in cheers and applause as everyone stood to their feet. During the standing ovation, Ryan and Lorenzo shook hands and patted each other on the back. Finally, the room quieted.

"In closing, I commend you all for your hard work and

encourage you to keep it up. We at CRC are eager to start this new venture with Beaumont and with each of you, thank you all."

With Lorenzo's conclusion, more cheers reverberated throughout the room. It was obvious how everyone felt about him. While she watched, Kara felt entranced by Lorenzo's easy appeal and the kind, easy manner she was privy to once before, but didn't appreciate. She again saw his gentle side and his genuine concern for others.

After Ryan thanked everyone and dismissed the meeting, he stood talking to Lorenzo. In a daze, Kara joined the others as they headed back to their perspective jobs, all the while her mind flooded with questions about this man who had suddenly reappeared. *What is it about him? And why does he have such an affect on people, and on me?* Kara wondered, finding it hard to breathe. *I don't even know him. . . .*

. . .

As they finished their business, Ryan and Lorenzo left the meeting room. "By the way, how is Miss Westin working out?" Lorenzo asked as they walked, surprising Ryan. "She's certainly a lovely young lady."

"Yes indeed, beautiful in fact," Ryan replied, nodding his head. "And she's doing a good job I'm told. Have you met her before?"

"Yes, some time back," Lorenzo admitted. "I was pleasantly surprised to see her name on the roster of new employees. I always read your newsletter and happened to see it."

"We met over Christmas. She's Jock's sister-in-law," Ryan revealed. "I'm just sorry we didn't meet earlier. She's *quite* fascinating."

"Is she happy here?" Lorenzo asked, again surprising Ryan.

"She seems to be, but after training she'll be moving to our satellite office in Detroit," Ryan informed him. "And, if I have my way, she'll soon be promoted, to being my wife," he boasted, feeling confident.

"Is congratulations in order?" Lorenzo asked solemnly.

"No, not quite yet," Ryan admitted. "It's nothing official, but when this new plant is open I'll have more time to pursue that goal."

Making no comment, Lorenzo kept his eyes forward. Feeling inquisitive about the man's earlier remark, Ryan had to ask. "Where *did* you meet Kara?"

"In Michigan, after her accident our paths crossed," Lorenzo explained.

Quickly, Ryan remembered the explosion that made news headlines for days. *That was during Kelly's and Kara's estrangement,* he thought. "Those days were hard for everyone," he commented, deciding not to reveal any more.

As the two men arrived at Ryan's office, the subject of Kara was dropped. Instead, they decided on their next meeting when Jock could be present. "It's going to be a good year," Ryan said then, shaking hands with Lorenzo.

"Somehow I believe you're right," Lorenzo agreed smiling.

. . .

When Ryan asked a second time for Kara to join him for dinner, she accepted. With another stressful week behind her, she decided a night out might be what she needed to unwind.

After pondering her attire for the evening, Kara decided on a long navy-blue skirt and a light blue turtleneck with gold accessories. Her long hair was in a soft twist atop her head with wisps of shiny curls hanging at the ear and nape of her neck.

"You look beautiful as always," Ryan said, giving her a quick kiss on the cheek when he arrived at her door.

"Thank you, sir," she replied smiling. "And I'd say you, *too,* look mighty handsome this evening." Tonight, Ryan's dark slacks, light gray shirt and dark gray sports jacket did indeed enhance his slender physique.

"We've waited far too long for this evening," Ryan told Kara. "Now, since all those negotiations are over, life should again return to normal."

For a moment, Kara wanted to ask about Lorenzo, but thought better of it. Tonight she'd forget about business and the hubbub she'd been hearing in the office, no matter how intriguing it was. *Royalty? Surely not, but we all know rumors run rampant in the work place,* Kara decided.

"I'm ready if you are," she said instead. In no time, she was seated in Ryan's shiny black Lexus sedan. "This is wonderful, it smells new."

"It is," Ryan replied, pulling from the curb. "I decided a Vice President needed a decent car, so I found enough time one afternoon to buy one."

As soft music played on the stereo, the two were silent as they entered the freeway. The lights of Atlanta glistened in the distance against the black Georgia night. Overhead, the new moon reminded Kara of a piece of silver fingernail hanging in space.

"It's a lovely night," she remarked as they drove.

"Yes, it is," Ryan said, finding Kara's hand in the dark. "It's always lovely when I'm with you," he added glancing at her. "I want *all* of our evenings to be special, no matter where we are."

"Thank you, Ryan. You're very sweet," Kara told him truthfully. "Why wasn't Jock at the meeting yesterday?" she decided to ask.

"They flew to Dallas to see Mother," Ryan told her. "None of them could wait another minute. Just think of it, Mother has never seen her children, or her only grandchild. I told Jock I'd hold down the fort until they got back. They'll be home this weekend."

"How exciting," Kara replied. "When will your mother get to see you?"

"Hopefully soon," Ryan answered. "It's Mother's birthday next month and we're planning a real celebration this year. Can you imagine how she must be feeling?" he remarked. "Regaining her eyesight after *all* this time?"

"No, I *can't* imagine," Kara said, shaking her head. Admittedly, she hadn't thought about Cora Beaumont's miracle since arriving in Atlanta, nor anyone else for that matter. "I really should call Kelly, perhaps this week my training will get easier," Kara said. "Mother and Charles should be arriving in Arizona soon. Aunt Gina must feel lost without Mother around," she rambled on. Suddenly, Kara felt terribly homesick to see those she loved.

It was twenty minutes later when Ryan exited the freeway. Soon they were among bright neon lights and elaborate looking establishments. As they stopped in front of one, Kara saw people in evening attire exiting luxury cars and scurrying out of the cold night air. Next it was their turn.

After giving his vehicle over to the parking attendant, Ryan took Kara's hand as they headed for the entrance. A friendly doorman greeted them, and upon entering the popular night spot, Kara heard music.

In no time she felt energized and eager to enjoy the evening. *I'm going to have fun, and forget about Beaumont Computers,* she vowed taking Ryan's arm.

Chapter Fourteen

From the small corner table where she and Ryan were seated, Kara looked around the spacious room. At the far end was an orchestra. Its musicians, dressed in bright red shirts, white jackets with black bow-ties, were playing lively renditions of all-time favorites. Soon Kara was tapping her feet and swaying to the rhythm.

As her eyes adjusted to the dim light, Kara noticed people of various ages. At some nearby tables people laughed and talked, while at another a lone couple gazed at each other, seemingly oblivious to those around them.

"May I have this dance?" Ryan asked, taking Kara's hand.

"I'd love to," she replied, getting to her feet. With her hand in his, Kara followed Ryan as they threaded their way through the crowd to the dance floor.

When hearing a familiar love song, Ryan drew her into his arms for the slow-dance. The music, the romantic atmosphere soon held Kara in its grip. *I could get use to this,* she thought, closing her eyes.

As they danced to the slow steady rhythm, Kara thought about her feelings for Ryan. *Could I love this man? Would I even be here if he wasn't a Beaumont? I can't say, but for now I'll enjoy the perks of having the attention of a rich boss,* she decided.

"This is wonderful, we must do it more often," Ryan whispered next to her ear. Then, looking up at him, Kara replied.

"It *is* nice, I haven't danced in years."

"I don't just mean dancing, my dear, but being together, you and me. We *could* make it permanent, in the near future," Ryan said softly. When hearing this, Kara didn't know what to say. Just then the song ended.

"Let's get something cool to drink, shall we?" she suggested, discounting his remark. Hand in hand they headed back to their table.

After ordering their drinks, Kara tried to reason with herself. *This is your first serious boyfriend, he's rich, attentive, what you've always wanted, so what's the problem? He loves you and would give you anything you want, just like Jock does Kelly,* she debated. *Yes, but Kelly loves Jock. If I married Ryan without loving him, I'd be the gold-digger!* Kara thought disgustedly.

When their drinks arrived, Ryan broke the silence. "I'd like to make a toast," he said, lifting his glass.

"Of course," Kara replied, following his lead.

"To you, Kara," he began, looking in her eyes. "May your life be filled with love and laughter, may our friendship ever bloom," he said, touching his glass to hers.

"How very sweet, thank you," Kara told him. When looking at Ryan, she saw sincerity in his eyes. *I believe he* does *love me. He's a wonderful guy, so where are my feelings for him?* she wondered, sipping her pina-colada.

"I'm sorry," Ryan said, reaching for her hand. "I said I wouldn't rush you, but it appears I am," he told her.

"No, I wouldn't say that," Kara quickly replied. "I just wish I was as certain of *my* feelings," she added, deciding to be honest. "You're a great guy, and I really like you, but that's not enough to consider marriage, agreed?"

"Yes, marriage is hard enough when two people love each other," Ryan said, nodding his head. "Thanks for being honest, Kara." As Ryan stared at the glass he held, Kara saw his look of disappointment. Once more she was reminded of a little boy, this time looking sad and rejected. "Do I at *least* have reason to hope?" he then asked, surprising her.

"Mother says there is *always* reason to hope, about anything. I guess that's true of us, too," Kara replied. Although he made no comment, Ryan softly smiled at her.

"Hey, Ryan!" a man greeted loudly, "I haven't seen you in eons." The sudden appearance of this rather boisterous person brought the tender moment to an abrupt end. "What a surprise," he continued, slapping Ryan on the back.

"Hello Mike," Ryan said, getting to his feet and offering his hand. "Yeah, it's been awhile," he added, sounding somewhat perturbed for the interruption.

"Aren't you going to introduce me?" Mike asked as he studied Kara. It was obvious Ryan was not thrilled to acquaint Kara to this rather pushy individual.

After polite words were exchange, Kara once more turned her

attention to those around her. Since her childhood, she was intrigued with watching people. Tonight was no different.

From where she sat, Kara had full view of several tables and the entrance. Couples were still arriving. Some mingled with friends and occasionally a lone man or woman entered the room.

As her eyes drifted across the sea of faces, Kara suddenly caught sight of a familiar one. *I know that guy, but from where?* When the rather lanky fellow maneuvered his way through the crowd, she noted the swagger in his step.

He's from Montana. No city dude can walk like that, she decided. *It really is a small world,* she thought, taking a sip of her drink.

While searching her memory for who he was or where she'd met him, she saw him stop at a table where several others were seated. However, in the dim light it was impossible to see their faces. *It'll come to me, if not, I won't sleep tonight,* Kara thought, sorting through those she'd met out west.

"Kara, I *am* sorry," Ryan apologized several minutes later. "He used to work for Jock. Would you care for another dance before we order dinner?"

"That sounds good," Kara replied, still thinking about the familiar looking man. Once more, she and Ryan headed for the dance floor. Although she hoped to see the man close up, the crowd made it impossible.

Again, having finished a spirited fox-trot, the orchestra began playing another slow song. "My kind of music," Ryan said, taking Kara in his arms.

As Ryan gently guided her across the dance floor, Kara closed her eyes as she enjoyed the moment. Yet, she had to wonder. *Will this spark of interest I feel for Ryan ever burst into flame? I won't settle for mediocre love. I want the kind Kelly and Jock share. The kind Mom and Dad had. Nothing less will do,* she vowed. *Mom says if I'm patient, the right one will come along. The trouble is, everyone thinks its Ryan. . . .*

"Don't look, Kara, but I think you have an admirer," Ryan whispered, surprising her. "He's been watching you, and can't say I blame him."

When hearing Ryan's comment, Kara opened her eyes and looked at him. "So many are dancing, are you *certain* he's looking at us?" she asked.

"It's you, not me he's looking at," Ryan answered. "He's at the table behind you, against the wall. You'll see him."

In the next moment, Ryan guided their dance steps so Kara was now facing the table over his shoulder. At first, she saw a man's face hidden behind the glass he drank from, then . . .

"I don't believe it!" Kara uttered in shock. "It can't be!" Excitement swept over her as she stared back at the man. "Excuse me, I have to go," she said, slightly aware of Ryan's reluctance to release her.

Is it really Ned? So far from Montana? Kara thought, seeing the familiar smile aimed at her. Already he was on his feet. Suddenly she felt tears burning her eyes. Then she was standing in front of him.

"I can't believe this," Ned whispered, shaking his head. "I told these guys it couldn't possibly be you, not this far from Michigan. But it is. It's *really* you. And you're beautiful as ever," he said softly, scanning her face and hair.

With everyone looking on, Ned suddenly threw his arms around Kara and hugged her. "You're like a breath of mountain air," he whispered in her ear.

Trying to contain her tears, Kara felt overjoyed to see Ned. "I've missed you, but until this moment, I didn't know how much," she whispered back.

. . .

It was nearly midnight when Ryan and Ned shook hands and said their polite remarks. Then, turning his attention to Kara, Ned looked at her. "This was a *wonderful* surprise," he said, hugging her goodnight. "You've made my trip to the big city tolerable," he added.

"I've missed having you around," Kara told Ned, clinging to him. "We do need time to catch up on things." It was obvious to Ryan, Kara hated to leave Ned, and as they drove off the two waved one last time.

Now, heading his car toward the freeway, Ryan wondered at Kara's silence. "It certainly was an eventful evening," he finally commented, glancing at her. "I'm sure you agree."

"Amazingly so," Kara sighed, laying her head back against the seat.

"Ned seems like a nice fellow, they all do. Atlanta is always popular for conventions, but I must say, 'Log Home Builders' is a new one to me," Ryan said, trying to make small talk.

"Log homes are intriguing. Ned thinks a convention is good publicity. They're not only sturdy, but beautiful, too, in the right setting of course."

"Of course," Ryan agreed, sensing it wasn't only Ned's log structures Kara found intriguing. *Don't give up without a fight, this is only your first date. Ned leaves in two day, then you'll have her all to yourself,* he thought happily.

As he merged in with the freeway traffic, Ryan thought about the evening. Admittedly, his hope of having Kara in his life permanently did look bleak. *I can't dismiss her history with Ned. He loved Kelly, and Kara is her twin. She's just as beautiful* and *available,* Ryan reasoned. *Obviously I have some obstacles to overcome if I want to win Kara's heart. I'll just have to make more time to spend with her,* he decided, knowing she still had weeks of training.

"I enjoyed tonight, did you?" he asked, reaching for Kara's hand.

"Very much, thank you," she replied, "it was a *most* enjoyable evening."

"How about having breakfast in the morning? Then I can show you the city, as I promised weeks ago," Ryan suggested.

"I'm sorry, but I promised to meet Ned for an early lunch," Kara replied. "He wants to show me pictures of the houses they've built. He brought them along to display at the convention. I can't *wait* to see them," she said excitedly. "Since he's leaving so soon, we decided to spend the day together."

"Understandably," Ryan responded, trying to curb his disappointment. "How do you *really* feel about Ned, Kara?" he blurted out in his next breath. "I mean, he's a young handsome guy, single, obviously hard working. He sounds dependable. I'd think *any* woman would fall for him. Am I right?" he asked.

"He's a very dear friend," Kara admitted. "We go way back, to the first summer Kelly and I arrived at Morning Star Ranch. Ned was deputy sheriff and always took his job serious. The best thing he did was rid this world of Frank Webster, the lowest scum on earth," she told him. "After that, we were *all* indebted to him. He fell in love with Kelly, and well, the rest you know."

"It appears he likes *you* a lot too," Ryan said, keeping his eyes on the road.

"Like I said, we're friends," Kara answered, "we'll always be,

I'm sure."

With that, Ryan made no further comment, yet, he couldn't forget the way Kara and Ned looked at each other, not only when they talked but while they were on the dance floor. *No matter what, I'm not giving up on you, Kara,* Ryan vowed silently as he slowed for the exit.

In no time, they arrived at Kara's apartment in an upscale neighborhood. "Are you finding things comfortable here? Is there anything you need?" Ryan asked, pulling into the parking lot.

"No. It's lovely, and I'm very comfortable, *thank* you," Kara told him. "I'd *never* afford such luxury if you and Jock weren't paying for it."

"We do it for all our trainees, but I wanted something a little nicer for you, Kara," Ryan confessed, parking his car.

"I appreciate that, but I assure you it wasn't necessary," Kara replied. "I had a good time tonight, Ryan. Thank you, and I do hope you understand about tomorrow with Ned," she added, looking at him.

"Certainly, it's what old friends do," he replied, trying to sound up-beat. Realizing the late hour and knowing he was past any further discussion about Ned, Ryan got out and went around to Kara's car door. "Will you have dinner with me on Sunday?" he asked as they headed toward her apartment.

"Possibly, give me a call Sunday morning, okay?" she replied. When she had found her key and unlocked the door, Kara turned to face him. "You are a sweet man, Ryan. I'm sorry I can't say what you want to hear, but right now I'm not in love with *anyone,*" she admitted. "As for the future, no one knows. Good Night, Ryan," she added, looking at him.

"Good Night, Kara," he said softly, taking her hand. Fighting his desire to kiss her, he looked in her eyes. "Have a nice time with Ned," he told her.

With that, Ryan turned and headed down the walkway to his car. *How ironic. Jock battled Ned for Kelly's love, and now, will I have to do the same to win Kara? What strange twists of circumstances will bring about my success? It might be Ned who wins* this *time,* Ryan heard from that small inner voice.

. . .

After Ryan left, Kara closed and locked the door, feeling relieved to be alone.   Absentmindedly she tossed her purse and wrap on the sofa as she sat down. "I can't believe he's really *here,*" she muttered, smiling to herself. *Ned looks so good, and he's fun, now that he's not pining over Kelly. I've really missed him, a lot,* Kara admitted feeling surprised at how much.

For a long while, Kara thought about the evening. She remembered the smooth way Ned danced, how he held her, how he looked at her. Suddenly she realized her thoughts were filled with Ned, not Ryan, the man proclaiming his love for her. *This is crazy, Ned and I are just friends. . . .*

Finally, as she got up and headed for bed, Kara knew she'd be getting little sleep tonight. Instead, she must try and sort out these new emotions, regarding Ned.

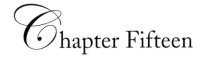

Chapter Fifteen

It was early when Kara opened the blinds and looked out. The pink tinge of the approaching sunrise filled the sky with cotton candy clouds and brought a gasp of delight. "How *beautiful!* It's going to be a glorious day!" she sang out, gazing toward the heavens.

Although she had had little sleep, Kara felt eager to start her day. Admittedly, it was due to seeing Ned again and having time to talk without the scrutiny of others.

She had just wrapped her newly shampooed hair in a towel when her telephone rang. "Who'd be calling this early?" she muttered, glancing at the clock. "Good Morning," she greeted, pulling her robe around her.

"Hello Kara. It's Ryan, I'm sorry to call so early," he said apologetically.

"Oh, Ryan, that's okay, what's up?" Kara responded, sensing urgency in his voice. "Has something happened?"

"I'm afraid so," he told her. "Jock just called. Kelly's in the hospital, in Texas. He said there's a possibility she might lose the baby."

"No! What *happened?*" Kara wailed in shock.

"She started labor, but, they aren't sure why, so they're running some tests," Ryan informed her. "They planned to fly home today, but of course that won't happen now."

As Ryan talked, Kara thought about her sister and how much this baby meant to her. "Does Mother know about this? Is there anything *I* can do for Kelly?" she hurriedly asked.

"Jock is calling Emma now. For the moment there's nothing we can do, except pray Kelly and the baby will be all right," Ryan replied. "Jock said he'd call me as soon as they get the tests results."

"Ryan, *please,* let me know too, the minute you hear," Kara told him.

"You'll be with Ned today, how will I reach you?" he asked. For the first time, Kara regretted not having a cellular phone. Mentally she vowed she'd have one, by tomorrow if possible.

"I'll call *you*, I have your cell number," she reminded him, wondering if she should call off her day with Ned. "Ryan, if Kelly needs me, I'm going," Kara blurted, fighting a lump in throat. "Understood?"

"No question, my dear. We'll *both* be going," Ryan replied tenderly.

When the call had ended, Kara no longer restrained her tears. Freely they ran down her face as she thought about Kelly and Jock, and the crushing heartache if they lost their baby they already loved so much.

. . .

Although she had planned earlier to dress meticulously for her day with Ned, Kara instead paid no special attention as she put on a pair of jeans and black turtleneck sweater. Her shiny blond hair simply hung loose around her shoulders, and a pair of small gold earrings was her only accessory.

Just before it was time to leave to meet Ned, Kara called Ryan. "Any word?" she asked, when he answered.

"Nothing yet," he replied. "I know it isn't easy, but try not to worry, Kara. Kelly has the best doctors around, so I'm sure they'll take very good care of her," he assured her. "Just enjoy your day with Ned and call me whenever you like."

"Thank you, Ryan. I will," Kara said, ending the call. Minutes later, she was on her way to meet Ned. The promise of a glorious day was suddenly gone. The sky was now overcast, matching the gloom that encircled Kara's heart.

. . .

The restaurant where Ned sat waiting for Kara was across the street from the convention center. As hoped, Ned and his two employees had gleaned helpful information regarding the business of building log homes, not only in construction, but in advertising ideas. For that, Ned felt their trip to Atlanta had proved worthwhile.

Admittedly, since he arrived, Ned couldn't wait to leave the big city. That is, until he saw Kara last night.

As time drew near for their meeting, he felt nervous. *She's a familiar face, a friend. Of course I'm excited to see her. And she reminds you of Kelly,* Ned finally admitted to himself.

From his table he stared through the window, yet, seeing nothing but memories as they paraded through this mind. For the past eight months, Ned had done everything he could to forget Kelly. But now, after seeing her twin sister, memories broke down the barrier he had built around his heart.

He thought about Kelly's skiing accident and how she'd lingered near death for weeks. Once more he was at her bedside, seeing her wrapped in bandages and attached to IV lines and monitors. He prayed, yes, for hours he begged God to let her live. Finally, they knew she would. Then, after months of rehabilitation, Kelly announced she'd never marry *anyone,* for fear of being a burden after losing her leg.

Oh Kel, you would never be a burden, not to me. I guess Jock convinced you too. I hear you two are happy, for that I'm glad, Ned thought, remembering their final meeting.

"I'm sorry I'm late," Kara said, jarring Ned from his thoughts.

"Oh, you're not late, I'm early," he replied, getting to his feet and giving Kara a quick hug. "How are you?"

"I've been better," she said, taking the chair across from him. "Kelly's in the hospital." For an instant, Ned felt he'd been punched in the stomach.

"What's wrong? Is she okay?" he asked, feeling dazed.

"Jock called Ryan, Kelly's in labor and the baby isn't due until June. They're running some tests," Kara said in haste.

"Kelly's going to have a *baby?* I had no idea," Ned uttered in shock. Hearing this brought renewed pain and memories of how he and Kelly had once planned to have their own family one day. Sadness enveloped him. "I hope she'll be okay," he managed to say.

"Me too," Kara answered with obvious emotion. "This baby means so much to them, it'll be heart-wrenching if she loses it."

When the food server came to get their order, they both decided on coffee. For Ned, his appetite had vanished.

"I'm sorry to unload my bad news on you, Ned," Kara said after steaming cups of coffee were placed in front of them. "I'm sure you don't care to hear it."

"It *is* hard to hear, but not for the reason you think," Ned stated, shaking his head. "You think I'm bitter for what Kelly did to me, but I'm not. It's hard because I hate hearing that she's hurting, in *any* way."

"You're still in love with her?" Kara asked, studying his face.

"I didn't think so, until now," Ned replied, feeling quite disheartened.

"How and *why?* After all she put you through?" Kara asked abruptly. In that moment, Ned had to wonder the same thing, but had no answer.

Certainly, in the months following their break up, he was driven to forget about Kelly. Rather than dwell on his heartache, he concentrated on his new business, working sixteen-hour-days until exhausted sleep kept him from dreaming about Kelly or the life they once planned.

"I guess Mother was right again," Kara sighed a moment later.

"And that is?"

"We never forget our first love. *Was* Kelly your first love, Ned?" Kara asked, adding cream in her coffee.

"Yes, she certainly was," Ned answered, remembering the first time he saw her. "When she opened the door and I saw her that day, I thought she was an angel. I knew my life would *never* be the same, and I was right."

"Kelly is one lucky girl," Kara remarked, fingering the handle on her cup. "But I, on the other hand, have *yet* to find true love."

"From what I witnessed last night, that Ryan fellow seems quite smitten with you," Ned argued. "You probably have hordes of men scrambling after you, but you just aren't noticing."

"Hardly, oh yeah, Ryan says he loves me, but he's only one," Kara refuted.

"And there's that guy behind you who seems pretty intrigued," Ned told her, nodding.

Just then, the well-dressed man in question headed their direction. As he drew near, Ned guessed him to be in his early thirties. Then, the man stopped at their table.

"Good Morning, I do hope you'll forgive my intrusion, but Kara, I need a word with you," he said, looking solemn.

"Lorenzo, certainly," Kara replied, looking surprised. "How did you find me? Is anything wrong?"

"This is the nicest restaurant near the convention center, and I was told you might be here. I'm Lorenzo Carlyle, again I apologize, but may I join you?" he asked Ned, offering his hand.

"Ned Whitmore, yes, of course," he replied, returning Lorenzo's handshake. Soon the man was seated next to Kara.

"I just got a call from Ryan." When hearing that, Kara's hand flew to her mouth in noticeable surprise.

"I was supposed to call Ryan! It's Kelly isn't it?" she gasped in alarm.

"Yes, I'm afraid the news isn't good," Lorenzo replied. "Kelly's lost the baby." Again, for the second time, Ned felt an invisible hand punch him in the stomach. He felt weak, thinking of what Kelly must be going through.

When Kara began crying, Lorenzo put his arm around her shoulder and drew her close, comforting her. "I'm so sorry," he whispered. "Is there anything I can do?"

"I need to call Jock. I need to know how Kelly's doing," Kara said, wiping tears from her cheeks. "I have to find a telephone."

"My car is right outside, it has a phone you can use," Lorenzo offered.

"Please come with us, Ned," Kara requested. Although wishing to be alone, Ned accepted the offer. Certainly, he too, needed to know how Kelly was.

In no time they were seated in Lorenzo's Mercedes sedan. From the backseat, Ned listened to Kara's conversation with Jock. It was hard to hear about Kelly's sorrow, and harder still knowing he could never comfort her, even as a friend.

Dear God, help Kelly get through this, both she and Jock, he hurriedly prayed. *Ease the heartache they must be feeling.*

"No! Are you serious?" Kara suddenly blurted, shaking her head. "But how can this be? She's too young, too healthy!" At hearing Kara's comments, Ned tried to brace himself for more bad news. Just then, Lorenzo reached out his hand and placed it on Kara's shoulder, casting her a tender look.

"Okay, I'll call Ryan, right away. Thank you Jock, and please, give Kelly my love," Kara said, ending the call. For a moment, she buried her face in her hands and cried. "It's just *awful!* Poor Kelly," she wailed.

"What is it, Kara?" Ned prompted, feeling the blood drain from his face.

"The doctors are saying Kelly has *kidney failure,* that's why she lost the baby. I don't *believe* this is happening!" Kara cried out shaking her head.

Overwhelmed at such news, Ned felt too weak to move, yet, he had to get away. He had to be alone with this ache that was crushing his heart.

"You have my number. Call me, *please.* I need to know how she is," he could barely say as he opened the car door and got out.

Just then it started raining, mingling with tears that now ran down Ned's face.

. . .

"I'm truly sorry," Lorenzo said, taking hold of Kara's hand. "I wish I could ease your sadness in some way," he added tenderly.

"Oh Lorenzo, you seem to always be here when I need someone," Kara said, wiping her tears. "How do you manage that?" Making no comment, the man only shook his head and smiled. "I just can't believe my sister is so *sick,*" Kara again cried, recalling Jock's words.

In the next moment, she was gently coaxed into Lorenzo's arms. Strong yet comforting, they enveloped her.

"Let it go, Kara, get it all out," he whispered. As Kara rested her head against Lorenzo's chest, she cried openly for her sister. She wept for the time she wasted in her jealousy and for uncertainties that now lie ahead. And for Ned, whose heart was surely breaking, too, at this very moment.

Tenderly Lorenzo held her, saying nothing. Finally, when she couldn't cry anymore, Kara pushed herself free of his embrace. "Thank you, Lorenzo. I'm glad you're here," she whispered, looking in his eyes.

"I'm glad too," he replied, brushing a tear from her cheek. "I live ten minutes from here, let me take you home. I'll call Ryan and have him meet us there. Then I'll have my company plane readied," Lorenzo offered.

"Thank you, but I have my rental car. I'll follow you," Kara replied.

"Not to worry, I'll have someone pick it up later," he told her. "Don't be concerned about anything, except your sister. At a time like this, *nothing* else matters," Lorenzo added softly, smoothing Kara's hair

After buckling their seatbelts, Lorenzo pulled from the parking space. In no time they were on the freeway. Resting her head against the seat, Kara looked out her window.

Absentmindedly she gazed at beautiful homes in the distance, but her mind was filled with questions regarding the hours and days just ahead.

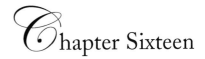

Chapter Sixteen

During the past few years as a business man, Lorenzo learned if he showed his appreciation to his employees, they in turn would show greater devotion to him and their assigned jobs. Although he took great pleasure in entertaining people, it was never in his home. Instead, he rented beautiful hotels or resorts for those special occasions. For reasons of his own, his private life was off limits to the outside world. Today however, as he drove with Kara beside him, Lorenzo was breaking that staunch rule.

One day you will know who I am, but for now, I'll take care of you and make sure you have everything you need, Lorenzo thought, glancing at Kara. *Beautiful, strong spirited, yet loving. All the qualities befitting the Carlyle name.*

As he drove, Lorenzo wondered when things had changed. *Once I needed you to help me achieve a goal, but now I need you for myself. How quickly you've taken hold of my heart, Kara.*

"If Kelly needs a kidney, I'm giving her one of mine," Kara suddenly blurted out. "I've been thinking about it, and that's what I've decided."

Lorenzo was stunned. "That's a pretty hasty decision don't you think? Perhaps you should consider it more fully," he cautioned.

"There's nothing to consider. We're twins so I'm a perfect match," Kara replied, sternly.

"Let's hope it doesn't come to that," Lorenzo responded, turning into his driveway. *I have my own reasons to keep you safe and well.*

· · ·

When Kara entered Lorenzo home, she caught her breath. From outside, the house looked similar to other elite homes they'd driven by, but seeing the interior reminded her of a cold European castle she'd seen in books. Cathedral ceilings and walls were painted olive green and the furniture was big and cumbersome.

Antiques, certainly not my style, she quickly decided, scanning the room.

"Please have a seat, Kara. I'll fix us some tea, or would you rather have coffee?" Lorenzo asked kindly.

"I'd prefer orange juice, if you have it," she replied. "Thank you."

"I'm sure that'll be no problem," he said, turning to leave.

After taking a seat on the high-back sofa, Kara turned her attention to the huge portraits hanging on the walls. One by one she studied the faces. With silent scrutiny their eyes stared back at her. *Distinguished, some are quite handsome, but they all look so stern,* Kara decided.

"Those are a few of my ancestors, if you're wondering," Lorenzo said, entering the room and setting a silver tray on a nearby table.

"I've been looking for some resemblance and I don't see much," Kara told him. "And they're all men. Weren't there any women in your ancestry?"

"A few, but the Carlyle family had mostly sons for the past several generations. And most never married, and those that did, I'm afraid didn't live long enough to have many children."

"How dreadful," Kara replied, thinking of Kelly at that moment. "It's sad when couples are childless, or lose the ones they do have."

"Undoubtedly," Lorenzo said, handing Kara a glass of orange juice. "I found some pastries, please have one. I know you haven't eaten."

"Thank you, but I'm really not hungry," Kara replied, sipping her juice. "How soon will Ryan be arriving?"

"I haven't reached him, but I'll try again in a few minutes," Lorenzo said, sitting down beside her. "How do you feel about Ryan, if I may ask?"

"I like him, he's very nice," Kara replied, feeling surprised at the question.

"Are you in love with him, or with Ned?"

"No, I'm not in love with *anyone?* Why do you ask?"

"I'm just wondering who might have that special place in your heart. That's all," he said softly, his eyes lingering on her face.

"What about you, Lorenzo? Why aren't *you* married?" Kara then asked.

"I won't marry just any woman. There are guidelines. The Carlyle name needs quality, and certain attributes are required."

"My, that sounds like those staunch blue-blood families that demand their *code of standards*," Kara teased, squaring her shoulders. Saying nothing, it was obvious Lorenzo didn't find her remark humorous. "I'm sorry, I didn't mean to compare you to *that* kind of family," she added in haste.

"Would *that* kind of family be so terrible?" Lorenzo asked, studying the glass he held. "I mean, would royal ancestry be *unthinkable*, to you?"

Suddenly Kara remembered the recent rumors she'd heard. *Perhaps it is true. But wouldn't Ryan or Jock mention this? Surely they would know if Lorenzo comes from royalty,* Kara reasoned, searching for an answer.

"No, I didn't, I mean, well, *is* it true?" Kara stammered, deciding she had to know. "*Are* you from royalty?" Saying nothing, Lorenzo left his seat and walked to a cabinet and opened a drawer. After retrieving a large book, he returned to the sofa where Kara sat.

"I've heard that pictures can speak volumes, so these should help answer your questions, Kara," he said, opening the album. "This is my family. Unfortunately, most of them are dead."

As he turned each page, Lorenzo told Kara who they were. Unmistakably, each one looked as stately as their titles of Earl, Duke, Prince, Nobleman. "My great-great grandfather was King of a tiny country I can't even pronounce," he admitted. "Part of my family came to America from Scotland before I was born."

Slowly, as she studied each picture, Kara was surprised to see such high ranking ancestry, but felt more shocked that she would be privy to such details.

"Do you have a picture of your mother, or grandmother?" Kara asked, after seeing mostly men in the photos.

"Yes, of course," Lorenzo replied, skipping to the back pages. "This is my paternal grandmother, Sabrina De Marco Carlyle, and my mother, Gabriella."

In a portrait setting, an older woman was seated while a younger one stood behind her. *They're quite lovely, but their eyes look so empty and cold,* Kara thought as the women stared from the page. Then, Kara caught her breath at what she saw.

"It can't be, but it is, I'm sure of it!" she gasped, taking a closer look. "This diamond necklace looks *exactly* like Kelly's, the one handed down from my grandmother," Kara exclaimed. "*What* a coincidence!"

"It may be similar, but it's not the same, I assure you," Lorenzo replied emphatically, shaking his head. "My Great-grandfather paid a handsome sum to guarantee only two such necklaces be made to his exact specifications. Their value is substantially more than just a piece of jewelry," he told Kara, closing the album. "Whoever possesses the necklaces is deemed to be in charge of running the Carlyle estates, both in Scotland and in America. Its owner relinquishes that responsibility only when they became incapacitated or die."

"Why were there *two* necklaces?" Kara asked, suddenly enthralled with such information. "And, how is its owner chosen?"

"Great-grandfather was the ruling head of our family. Prince Ferdinand B. Carlyle III. I'm told he saved the family fortune from Scottish mongrels, much like the Mafia we hear of in this country," Lorenzo explained. "So, he was made the connoisseur, as it were, of the Carlyle wealth. His word was law. Although he was a bit eccentric, no one questioned his decisions," he continued, getting to his feet. "But, commissioning two necklaces did *indeed* prove to be a mistake. One of them was *misplaced* by my uncle, my father's brother. Unfortunately, he was killed in a boating accident soon after," Lorenzo said, replacing the album in the drawer. "We surmise the necklace is at the bottom of the Atlantic."

"What if the necklace fell into the wrong hands?" Kara asked, finding the whole idea quite intriguing. "*Could* that person claim the estate?"

When hearing Kara's question, Lorenzo was silent as he walked to the table. There he refilled his glass with orange juice. "*If* they knew Great-grandfather's instructions regarding the necklace," he said hesitantly.

"And if there *are* two necklaces *and* different owners, then wouldn't they *share* the estate?" Kara asked, still pondering Kelly's necklace. As she waited for Lorenzo's answer, she couldn't help noticing the frown on his face.

"It's *quite* impossible," Lorenzo said assuredly. "As I said, one is at the bottom of the ocean and the other necklace is in Scotland with my mother. May I refresh your drink?" he asked, changing the subject.

"No, thank you. I'm fine, but I'm wondering about Ryan. Please call him again, we do need to be on our way," Kara said, getting to her feet.

"Certainly, and Kara, since my family history isn't for public knowledge, may I ask that you be discrete and keep this between us?" Lorenzo said, taking hold of her hand.

"Rumors are flying around the office. Are you aware of that?" Kara asked in return. "*Someone* got wind of your royalty."

"Rumors come and go, but *no* one knows for certain, not until now," Lorenzo replied.

"Not even Jock and Ryan?"

"Nothing has prompted such discussion," Lorenzo answered. "We're business partners. Business tactics *and* problems take precedence over boring family history, I assure you," he said stoically.

"Why did you tell me? You barely *know* me?" Kara questioned. Making no comment, Lorenzo looked at her hand he held, then in her eyes.

"Many reasons," he said softly. "Trust, friendship, a kin ward spirit. I find all of those in you, Kara."

The look in his eyes spoke volumes and caused a strange weakness to wash over Kara. "I *will* keep your secret," she barely managed to say. For a moment longer his magnetic dark eyes held hers. Then she looked away.

"Thank you, Kara, and now I'll go call Ryan," he said, sounding relieved.

When Lorenzo had gone, Kara quickly sought the stability of a nearby chair. *His house is eerie and cold, but the man is not. His presence wraps love and protection around me. And I find no reason to doubt him,* Kara thought, wishing for more time.

Now, trusting her legs to hold her, Kara left her seat and meandered around the room. Scores of questions bombarded her mind, not only about Kelly, but also Lorenzo and his surprising trust in her. *This is too bizarre. Why would he tell me and not Jock, his business partner? Could Kelly's necklace be the lost Carlyle heirloom? I promised I wouldn't say anything, besides, Grandmother couldn't possibly have known royalty,* Kara decided, shaking her head. Yet, deep down, there lingered thoughts of uncertainty.

· · ·

Within an hour, Ryan had arrived and Lorenzo's company plane was said to be ready. "We have one slight hitch I'm afraid," Lorenzo told the two. "My pilot is in bed with pneumonia so unless you can fly the Lear, Ryan, I'll have to go with you."

"No, I'm sorry to say, I never got my license," Ryan admitted. "I could get Pierre to come after us I suppose."

"That's not necessary, I assure you," Lorenzo protested, "it's the weekend and I have nothing pressing."

"Thank you, Lorenzo," Kara spoke up. "The sooner we leave the better. Ryan, I do need to get a few things, will you take me?" Kara asked.

"Let's go. Lorenzo, we'll meet you at the airport in an hour," Ryan said.

"By then I'll have the flight plan and be ready to go," Lorenzo answered.

In no time, Ryan and Kara were on the freeway heading for her apartment. "This day has certainly turned out differently than expected," Kara remarked, shaking her head. "Have you spoken to Jock since this morning?"

"Yes, about two hours ago. He's worried sick about Kelly, and rightly so. She'll be having dialysis tomorrow morning," Ryan said, reaching for Kara's hand. "I'm so sorry about all this. I wish there was something I could do."

"You are, Ryan. Going with me and being there for moral support means a lot," Kara answered, wondering if Lorenzo would be staying for a few days. "If Kelly needs a kidney transplant, I'm giving her one of mine," she quickly added.

"Are you sure?" Ryan blurted, glancing at her.

"I'm sure, after all I *am* the best candidate to be her donor," she replied. As they drove in silence, Kara thought about the future. *I won't let Kelly be dependant on dialysis for the rest of her life, not when I can help. But, how will having only one kidney effect each of us? Can we still have children? Or would it be too risky? It won't be long and I'll have all those answers,* Kara decided.

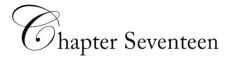

Chapter Seventeen

As she gazed through the porthole window of Lorenzo's plane, Kara was in awe of the scene outside. *Cotton-ball clouds, towering over fields and towns,* she thought, feeling more relaxed than she thought possible.

Despite the reason they were flying to Texas, Kara felt unusually calm and reassured that things would be fine with Kelly. *Is it Lorenzo's soft words? Or the tenderness in Ryan's eyes that brings such comfort?* Kara wondered, laying her head back against the seat. With the two men in the cockpit, Kara had the cabin to herself. Snuggled under a warm cover, she closed her eyes hearing the soft drone of the engines. In no time it had lulled her to sleep.

. . .

Sorrow gripped Kelly's heart. Questions and waves of guilt washed over her as she and Jock awaited test results. Finally, the time had come. They would know what caused her kidney failure.

With a frown creasing his forehead, the young nephrologists, Dr. Reed, pulled a chair up beside Kelly's hospital bed and sat down. After flipping through the chart in his hands, he looked up.

"After learning about your skiing accident, Mrs. Beaumont, it explains the trauma we see on your kidneys," he began. "Without your pregnancy, this might never have happened, but the normal stress of carrying a baby was too much, I'm afraid," the doctor said solemnly. "When your kidneys quit working, it wasn't long until the toxic build-up caused your miscarriage."

"Can they ever return to normal?" Jock asked, holding Kelly's hand. "I mean, since she's no longer pregnant, will they start working again?"

"That's hard to say, perhaps with medication and a few sessions of dialysis they'll rejuvenate somewhat," Dr. Reed replied. "You are basically a very healthy young woman, so there is always reason to hope."

"We've seen our share of miracles," Jock said, looking at Kelly. "And we certainly aren't giving up on seeing another one."

"One question, Dr. Reed," Kelly said. "If just one kidney starts working, will I be able to carry a baby to term?"

"If it proves viable, yes, one healthy kidney should handle pregnancy just fine," he replied, nodding his head.

As the doctor explained dialysis, he held little of Kelly's attention. Instead, her thoughts were on the future. *Dear God, I need Your strength to get through this, don't let bitterness or disappointment fill my heart. Help me to accept whatever lies ahead,* she prayed.

"Try not to worry. That miracle might be just around the corner," Dr. Reed remarked with a lopsided grin before leaving the room.

"He's right, my darling," Jock told Kelly, kissing her hand. "God is still in charge, and although we lost our precious baby girl, she's being cradled in the arms of Jesus," he whispered, caressing Kelly's cheek with the back of his hand.

Although she mourned for her baby, Kelly drew comfort from those words. With certainty she knew he was right and that one day she'd see that precious child she had carried for such a short time.

. . .

When Lorenzo landed his plane in Dallas, they were met by Pamela Beaumont, the youngest sibling of Ryan and Jock. After cordial greetings and introductions were made and Lorenzo had given instructions regarding his plane, they loaded into the shiny red Cadillac Pamela was driving.

"How far is the hospital?" Kara asked, buckling her seatbelt.

"Not far, but it's *too* late to see Kelly now," Pamela replied sharply. "She has dialysis in the morning so she needs her rest."

When hearing that, Kara looked at Ryan sitting beside her in the backseat, hoping for a rebuttal to Pamela's statement, but none was forthcoming.

"Certainly it wouldn't hurt to stop by for a *brief* visit," Lorenzo said from the passenger seat. "Kara's very concerned about her sister. I'm sure you understand," he added. Although Pamela made no comment, her ire was obvious as she pulled from the curb, squealing the tires.

"I see you still have a lead-foot," Ryan said jokingly, again bringing no reply from Pamela. "Okay, Pammie, cool your jets. We've *all* had a long day."

An air of tension suddenly filled the car as its driver swerved in and out of traffic. Despite trying to be tolerant, Kara found herself envisioning her hands around Pamela's neck. But, instead of carrying out that urge, she gritted her teeth and watched the blur of city lights out the car window.

· · ·

What Pamela showed in rudeness, Cora Beaumont revealed in genuine hospitality when they arrived. As they pulled in the driveway, they saw Cora and Abby standing in the doorway.

"Welcome, all of you," the woman cheered waving her hand. First to exit was Ryan.

"Mom, it's so *good* to see you," he called out as he raced toward her. With her arms outstretched, Cora welcomed her son. For a moment, Kara stood watching as Ryan and his mother shared their heartfelt greeting. Abby, she noticed, stood nearby saying nothing.

"Oh, Ryan, my boy, you're more handsome than I imagined," Cora said, choking back her tears as she studied her son's face for the first time.

"Mom, I still can't believe it!" Ryan said shaking his head. "You can really see!"

Emotion filled Ryan's voice as he again wrapped his arms around his mother.

"Mom, this is Kara," he said a moment later, motioning for her to join them.

"Oh, I'm so happy to finally meet you," Cora said, giving Kara a hug.

"What a pleasure to meet *you,* Mrs. Beaumont," Kara replied. "I've heard so much about you." Then, with a smile, the woman looked at Kara.

"You're a lovely young lady, just like your sister," Cora said, gently touching Kara's cheek. "My, I'm so blessed to see you, to see *all* of you."

By this time, Lorenzo had unloaded the few pieces of luggage from the car and stood quietly nearby. Pamela had disappeared through a side door.

"Abby, aren't you going to greet your Uncle Ryan and Aunt Kara?" Cora asked the child. Meekly, Abby did as her Grand Mama instructed.

"And this is Lorenzo, in the flesh," Ryan announced, introducing the man.

"I've heard about you many times, Lorenzo," Cora said, extending her hand. "Welcome, and thank you for flying Ryan and Kara here," she added.

"It's my pleasure, Mrs. Beaumont. Mothers are special people, and from what I hear from your sons, you're Mother of the Year, *every* year," he said kissing Cora's hand.

"That's right," Ryan said, putting his arm around Cora's shoulder.

"Oh, you're too kind, Lorenzo. And, *please* call me Cora," she said, looking up at him. "And you too, my dear," she told Kara. "Come in, please. We need to get you settled, I know you must all be very tired."

As Cora showed everyone to their rooms, Kara couldn't help noticing Abby and her quiet demeanor. *Something is bothering her. I'm sure she's just worried about Kelly, especially since she lost her mother to illness. I'll see if I can cheer her up,* Kara decided.

When she had gotten settled in the lovely room she would be using, Kara left it to join the others in the kitchen. There, Ryan and Lorenzo were enjoying the refreshments Cora had made.

"There she is," Ryan remarked when seeing Kara. "Come along my lovely, I know you *must* be famished." After getting to his feet, Ryan took hold of Kara's hand and helped her up on the bar stool beside him. As she was seated, Kara glanced at Lorenzo in time to see the scowl he aimed at Ryan.

Is he mad? Or is that jealousy? Kara wondered. "Thank you, Cora, this looks yummy," she told the woman, seeing the variety of food and a chocolate cake. "Has Abby gone to bed already?"

"No, I think she's just in her room," Cora replied. "She's having a hard time with all this," she added softly.

"I'm sure she's very worried . . . considering the past," Kara responded.

"Abby's having a hard time about the baby. You must know how she rejected it at first, and now she feels guilty, that it was her fault somehow."

At hearing the explanation, Kara remembered the heartache Abby caused Kelly and the bitterness toward the new baby. Certainly, it was easy to see the child's reasoning. "Maybe I can help her see it isn't her fault. Any new word on Kelly," Kara asked, spooning potato salad on her plate.

"No, but Jock should be calling any minute," Cora replied, glancing at the kitchen clock. "He said he would talk to you then."

"I was hoping to see Kelly this evening, but I guess we arrived too late," Kara remarked, trying to forget the lingering resentment she felt toward Pamela.

"Where *is* Pamela?" Ryan asked, somehow reading her thoughts.

"She had a date. She's been seeing a nice young man," Cora explained. "I *do* hope this one works out."

Upon hearing Cora's statement, Kara had to wonder why any man in his right mind would get serious about Pamela Beaumont. *If he sees that quick temper of hers, I've no doubt he'll hit the road!* Kara decided.

"I've heard about your business talents, Lorenzo, but nothing personal. So, may I ask about your family?" Cora said kindly. "Are you married?"

For a moment, as everyone waited for his answer, Lorenzo seemed to ponder how much to say. "No, I've never married, but there's always a possibility, if the right woman comes along," he replied, glancing at Kara. "So far, my work and other interests have kept me quite occupied."

"Life is fleeting," Cora stated, looking at Lorenzo. "Profit margins and bank accounts make for poor company on those cold nights," she advised, patting his hand in a motherly sort of way. "Don't wait too long. As I've told Ryan, the years slip by awfully fast."

"I for one am taking your words to heart, Mother," Ryan spoke up. "If I have my way, by year's end *I'll* have a wife," he said, leaning his shoulder against Kara's as he looked at her.

Before anyone could comment, the ringing telephone was heard. "That'll be Jock," Cora said, leaving to answer. As they waited everyone was silent. However, the look on Lorenzo's face reminded Kara of those of his ancestors.

Grim, harsh, unyielding, is that what royalty is like? Are they so used to being in control that they flaunt their displeasure for all to see? Kara had to wonder, feeling a chill. *What is Lorenzo* really *like? And what does he want? Why* did *he confide in me about his family, and the necklace?*

Suddenly, Kara had a strong suspicion Kelly's necklace was the Carlyle heirloom. *Like a glove it all fits, but I promised not to say anything about his family. Now I'll just have to play along with him until I know for sure,* Kara decided hastily.

"Yes, it's Jock," Cora said a moment later. "He wants to speak to you."

Leaving her seat, Kara hurried to the phone. Although she had great concern for her sister's condition, Kara had to admit other questions hounded the back of her mind. Sadly, she realized these she must handle on her own.

. . .

It was late when Kara finally went to bed. As she lay in the dark, her mind replayed the conversation with Jock regarding Kelly's condition. The news provided hope that her kidney function would resume.

"We're praying for a miracle," Jock had told her confidently. When hearing that, Kara vowed to remain optimistic.

If Kelly is released tomorrow after her dialysis, at least that's a start, Kara thought, hoping for some quality time with her sister. Then, once more her mind was on Lorenzo. *How long will he stay? He doesn't need to be here, since Jock can fly us back to Atlanta,* she reasoned. *If I'm going to discover the truth, I need to be nice to Lorenzo. Play up to him.*

Suddenly a light went on in Kara's head. *Sam! She said all she needs is a name and she can get information on Grandmother's wealthy fiancé. That's it! I'll call her first chance I get,* she thought excitedly.

Snuggling under the covers, Kara closed her eyes feeling confident she would learn the truth about Mr. Carlyle, *and* the mysterious diamond necklace.

Chapter Eighteen

Despite feeling sad about Kelly's miscarriage, everyone was elated to hear she would be released from the hospital Sunday afternoon following dialysis. With the news of her improved kidney functions there was an air of celebration among those at the Beaumont home.

It was Sunday morning. Cora and Abby had gone to church; Pamela was still in bed; Kara, Ryan and Lorenzo sat in the kitchen drinking coffee.

"Kara and I'll be flying back to Atlanta with Jock," Ryan told Lorenzo, getting up to make more coffee. "We really appreciate you getting us here, but there's no reason for you to stay now," he added.

Upon hearing Ryan's announcement, Kara saw Lorenzo's jaw clench and his eyes narrow as he looked out the nearby window. Seated across from him, Kara could easily see the anger on his face. "Then I'll take my leave tomorrow morning," he said finally with a forced smile.

"We do appreciate all your help, Lorenzo," Kara said, reaching for his hand. "I can't thank you enough for flying us here so I can see my sister."

For a moment, when their eyes met, Kara saw his look change from its rigid stare to that of tenderness. "Anything for you, Kara," he whispered, covering her hand with his own. "I *am* happy for the good news about Kelly."

"Thank you, me too," Kara said, feeling somewhat guilty for the flirty and deceptive role she was playing. "Hopefully, things will soon return to normal."

"And we can get on with *our* plans," Ryan interjected, returning to his seat beside Kara. "And, I'm *not* talking about computer chips or mergers, but *fun* things, *exciting* things," he went on, putting his arm around Kara's waist as he smiled at her.

To Kara, it seemed that Ryan was prodding Lorenzo's already heightened jealousy, or at the least, his anger. Certainly, without Ryan knowing Lorenzo's background, he wasn't aware of the man's controlling nature, or his lineage of authority.

I've got to defuse all this somehow! Two headstrong men, each stroking his ego, and *wanting his territory,* Kara surmised, searching for a way out.

"Good Morning," Pamela greeted as she entered the kitchen. "Oh good, fresh coffee," she muttered, retrieving a cup from the shelf. Still wearing her bathrobe, Pamela looked disheveled yet, still attractive despite having no make-up on and her short brown hair in disarray.

"Good Morning," they all replied. For Kara, the appearance of Ryan's spoiled sister couldn't have come at a better time.

"Late night, huh," Ryan commented, removing his arm from Kara's waist. "Who's the guy? Do I know him?"

"I doubt it, he's from Canada," Pamela replied, filling her cup with coffee. "It's nothing serious, despite Mother's hopes and dreams."

With that announcement, Pamela took the seat next to Lorenzo. After finger-fluffing her curls, she gave an enticing look from the corner of her eye. "So *you're* the new partner I've heard about," she said with a flirtatious tone. "I *am* sorry if I was rude last night," she added, smiling at Lorenzo. "I was a bit rushed, that's all. Nothing personal," Pamela rambled on, resting her elbows on the counter and aiming a sultry look at him.

"It's not me who needs an apology, Miss Beaumont, its Kara," Lorenzo told the woman rather sharply. "It is *she* you offended, not I." With that remark, Lorenzo got up from his seat and headed for the door. "If you'll excuse me, I need some fresh air," he said, taking his jacket from the nearby closet.

At Lorenzo's words and his immediate exit, Pamela was noticeable embarrassed. "Wow! That was worth a fortune!" Ryan blurted with a belly-laugh. "The mighty Pamela gets a taste of her own medicine."

"Oh shut up!" she fired back, grabbing her cup from the counter. In a huff Pamela hurried from the room. Like Ryan, Kara had to cheer Lorenzo's quick response to the woman's obnoxious behavior.

"Is she always so—"

"Disgusting? Yes, I'm afraid so," Ryan admitted, shaking his head. "She needs a good *spanking*. I *do* pity the man who marries that one!"

· · ·

Were it not for his anger toward the Beaumont siblings and his concern for the future, Lorenzo would have enjoyed his walk, seeing the rolling hills and the lovely homes sparsely dotting the countryside.

Instead, his mind was in turmoil. With his collar up and his hands buried in the pockets of his leather jacket against the brisk morning air, Lorenzo stepped from the porch of Cora's prestigious home and headed for the road, going nowhere in particular.

Ryan, you have no idea who you're dealing with, or what I'm capable of, Lorenzo thought, seething with anger. *And that sister of yours! What a disgrace to poor Cora, thinking she could entice me with her harlot ways! Not a chance! All this nonsense when I'd rather be courting Kara for the woman she is,* not *for what she can help me do. Oh Kara, I wish things were different. You're smart, courageous, beautiful, and the first woman I've ever desired for my wife. If only that necklace* was *at the bottom of the Atlantic and I wasn't a Carlyle.*

As he walked, Lorenzo wanted to forget the coming days, the events that would change his life. *Kara will never understand what I must do, and she'll hate me.*

"Don't forget you're a Carlyle. We have honor to uphold and a duty to keep what is ours!" Again his mother's words echoed through his mind.

If only I were an ordinary man, with an ordinary family background. I could win Kara's heart without deception. What if I forgot this whole thing? I could tell Mother Kara's on to me, that she's too smart to fall for such a scam. And, what if she is? Then my mission fails and *I lose the woman I love,* Lorenzo sighed, wanting only to tell Kara the truth.

· · ·

As expected, Kelly arrived home that afternoon following dialysis. For Kara it was a tearful reunion, knowing her sister no longer carried the baby she wanted so badly. And now, the added concern for Kelly's health. Not until everyone else had made their greeting did Kara approach her sister.

"Hello Kel," Kara said, hugging her. "It's so good to see you. How are you?"

"I'm so glad you're here," Kelly whispered with emotion as she returned the embrace. "I'm tired, but hopeful. Dr. Reed said my kidneys could 'kick in' and start working again."

"That *is* good news, but if they don't, you can have one of mine," Kara offered, holding Kelly's hand.

For a moment, Kelly only looked at her sister, seemingly in

127

shock. "Are you serious?" she could barely ask.

"Yes, I've thought about it a lot. It's what I want to do," Kara replied. With the sofa nearby, Kelly held her sister's hand and tugged her along as she sat down. With Jock, Ryan and Lorenzo having a conversation in the kitchen, and Cora, Abby and Pamela elsewhere, the twins were free to talk.

"I don't know what to say, Kara. It's such a big sacrifice," Kelly said, her eyes filling with tears. "I never dreamed—"

"I'd be so selfless? Well, I must admit it isn't like the old Kara, but I've changed. I don't think like I used to. I love you, and I can't *imagine* my life without you," Kara admitted. "And I know you'd do it for me. By the way, are Mom and Charles coming to see you?"

"Yes, next week," Kelly replied, her shock still evident. "We talk every day and since they're getting settled in Arizona, I told her to wait. Oh Kara, my dear, sweet sister, *thank you* for that wonderful offer, but Jock and I are praying for a miracle," Kelly said. "My next dialysis is Wednesday, by then perhaps we'll have more good news."

Just then, Ryan entered the room, carrying an album. "Lovely ladies, may I interrupt for a moment?" he asked, approaching. "I've been looking at these pictures of your wedding, Kelly. I was there, but I'd forgotten how beautiful it all was," he added, flipping through the pages.

By now Jock and Lorenzo had followed Ryan into the living room. "And that necklace you're wearing, Kelly, is *very* fine," Ryan said with a whistle.

"Yes, I'm sure you remember it came from our maternal grandmother," Kelly replied. "It certainly surprised me."

When hearing comments regarding the necklace, Kara looked at Lorenzo. Again his jaw was set, but instead of showing anger he seemed nervous.

"Did you see the necklace, Lorenzo?" Kara had to ask. "Isn't it beautiful?"

"It's exquisite, and *indeed* an interesting story," he replied, taking a seat across the room.

"Sweetheart, my orders are to make sure you rest this afternoon, so how about it?" Jock asked Kelly, bending down to kiss her cheek.

"Yes, I *am* a little tired," she replied, taking Jock's hand. As the others looked on, Jock helped Kelly off the sofa. "Please excuse me everyone, I'll see you after my nap."

"We'll be here," Kara said, "have a good sleep." As Ryan sat down beside her, Kara looked at Lorenzo, noticing his somewhat fidgety behavior. *He's got something in his craw. I wonder if it is that necklace? Or perhaps Ryan is the problem? Tomorrow I'll call Sam and tell her I have a name, she said that's all she needs to start investigating. What if it did come from Lorenzo's family? Then what?* Kara wondered, somehow feeling certain that it had.

. . .

After Sunday supper, Ryan began complaining of nausea and a headache. As evening approached he grew worse, so with apologies to Kara and the others, he went to bed. Likewise, Jock and Kelly were in bed by ten-thirty; Pamela left to meet a friend and Abby had coaxed the others into playing Monopoly.

Surprisingly, the friendly competition had everyone laughing and Abby's earlier sadness soon disappeared. However, after two hours, Cora declared she had had enough of 'going broke', and announced it was well past her bedtime. "And young lady, I think that goes for you too," she told Abby.

After saying good night to Abby and Cora, Kara and Lorenzo were alone for the first time since arriving in Dallas. Much to Lorenzo's pleasure.

"I'm sure you need *your* sleep, since you're flying out in the morning," Kara told him as they sat alone at the table. "Don't let me keep you up, I'm a night owl so I get my second wind about now," she chuckled, putting all the game pieces back in the box.

"Actually, I am too," Lorenzo replied, feeling elated to have Kara to himself.

"I do think it's a full moon, would you care to take a walk?" he asked, expecting her to decline.

"Sure, why not?" Kara replied, surprising him. "I'll grab my coat." As Kara left the room, Lorenzo wondered at his good fortune.

First Ryan gets sick and now Kara agrees to take a moonlight walk with me? How do I play this? he wondered. *Quit playing games, be honest and let it happen naturally. Deception only brings regret,* his thoughts suddenly cautioned as he retrieved his jacket from the closet.

"I'm ready," Kara said from the doorway a moment later. "Let's go." Quietly the two opened the door and slipped outside. "Oh, look at that sky," Kara cheered softly. "*This* is why I'm a night person."

Sure enough, the giant orb and a million stars slowly paraded their splendor across a stage of black. Even the winter landscape, bathed in a silvery glow, was a magical sight as the two started walking. "I *love* the country, don't you?" Kara asked excitedly, keeping her eyes skyward.

"Yes, I always did," Lorenzo replied, looking at Kara. "I like the solitude, the fresh air, and certainly nights like this."

"Where *did* you grow up, Lorenzo?" Kara then asked.

"I lived mostly in Scotland until I went to University in London. After that I traveled between New York, Scotland, and now Georgia," he replied. "So my roots aren't very deep."

"That's sad, at least to me," Kara remarked. "I think a permanent home with a mom and dad, friends, and close relatives is important. That kind of life gave Kelly and me stability. And it's what I want for my kids. Don't you agree?"

"If life was only that simple, it *would* be wonderful," he replied, wishing he could explain why his never would be. For him, a Carlyle, life was anything *but* simple. At that moment, he wanted nothing more than to tell Kara the truth, about everything. The necklace, the family honor he was expected to uphold, and the anguish he felt for deceiving her.

Seeming to sense his sadness, Kara stopped suddenly and looked at him. "Lorenzo, *please* tell me the truth. I *must* know," she begged, "is Kelly's necklace one of those you told me about?"

At that moment, Lorenzo wanted the earth to open up beneath him. If only it would. *Anything* to prevent him from having to lie to Kara. In that instant, his mind filled with a million questions as he searched for an answer.

"What are you saying?" he asked, stalling for more time. "Why would you *think* that?"

"Because I *saw* both necklaces, yet I can't understand why you'd deny it," Kara fired back. "And I noticed how you acted when we talked about it. You were nervous, edgy, and could barely sit there and listen. That's why. I promised to keep quiet about your family history, but I *will* find the truth, Lorenzo. If not from you, then a different way."

Never before had he been confronted by such courage, at least from a woman *and* a commoner. Certainly, if he wasn't in love with

Kara, he would have walked away, giving no answer. Or, his sharp tongue would have her in tears. But not this time. Instead, his heart was in shambles and his plan to use Kara to get the necklace back had suddenly lost its power.

As he searched for the right answer, Lorenzo looked at Kara as she waited. With the moonlight on her face and hair she looked even more beautiful. "Please, Lorenzo, where's the trust, the kin ward spirit you said we shared?"

"Oh Kara, don't you know by now that I love you?" Lorenzo blurted, taking hold of her hand. "Because of that, I *can't* lie to you, not anymore. Yes, *yes,* you're right, it *is* the missing necklace. Nonetheless, with the family's blessing I'm expected to retrieve it, by *any* means necessary. Whether by deception, blackmail, even kidnapping," Lorenzo confessed as he looked at her. "It's my duty *and* honor as a Carlyle to get it back. It's not my wish, Kara, it's my *obligation.* That's just how it is."

In the moonlight, Lorenzo saw Kara's eyes well with tears as she ripped her hand free of his. Her face held a look of shock, perhaps even hate.

"You were *willing* to do those things in order to steal my grandmother's necklace?" Kara shouted. "It was a gift from the man who loved her, and she loved him! This is rotten, so if this is royalty, then give me poverty! At least we poor folk don't have a mind ta steal dreams from the dead!" she scorned, feigning a mountain accent. With that, Kara stormed off toward the house.

"Kara, please, *please* forgive me," Lorenzo begged, racing after her. "I have to explain, please listen."

"Explain? Explain what?" Kara seethed in rage, stopping to look back. "That you wanted to use me, to use *all* of us? I wondered how you happen to be there at the fire. Now I know. You were following me, wanting me to lead you to Kelly and the necklace. Isn't that right?"

"No Kara, I already knew where the necklace was. I knew Kelly had it. Yes, I admit I wanted your help, and I did follow you. I was at the Blue Lagoon, every few days, watching you, hearing you laugh. Lately, I've come to realize it was during those times that I began falling in love with your," Lorenzo admitted as Kara stared back at him. "I just happened to be nearby the day of the fire, picking up dry cleaning. I'm so glad I was. I heard the explosion, and when I ran out and saw it was the restaurant, I was terrified that you might be there," he explained. "I dropped everything and ran toward it. For a split second I saw you, then the wall caved in on you. I knew I *had* to get you out."

Now, remembering the horror of that day, Lorenzo felt sick to his stomach. "Kara, I'm so sorry, I never wanted to hurt you or Kelly, or take back that special gift your grandmother left behind," Lorenzo said truthfully.

"Just leave us, Lorenzo. Your secret is safe with me, as long as I never see you again," she said with an icy stare. "You can tell your family you failed. Because as long as I have breath, you'll *never* get that necklace," Kara warned. "And if you're worried about us trying to take half of the Carlyle estate, you can forget it. Greed doesn't run in *my* family!"

Then, with tears streaming, she turned and walked away as Lorenzo stood watching. Nothing in his life had prepared him for such rejection. Not only did he fail at his duty, but most of all he failed at winning the heart of the only woman he had ever loved, and now he had no more chances to even try.

As you wish, my darling Kara. As you wish. . . .

Chapter Nineteen

Hot tears poured from Kara's eyes as she lay in the dark, remembering Lorenzo's words and his plans. *Blackmail? Kidnapping? Thievery at any cost? They belong in prison not a castle. I see no honor! Yes, perhaps he* did *rescue me from certain death, but I wish I'd never met the man!* Kara fumed, punching her pillow. *I can't even tell my family about him. I have to pretend, and act like there's nothing wrong. How do I do that now?*

The sun was coming up before Kara finally fell asleep.

. . .

Long before sunup, Lorenzo had taken his shower and was dressed, waiting now for someone to drive him to the airport. Having planned to call a taxi, he decided it would appear rude to leave Cora and the others without saying goodbye. Although he dreaded the long flight back to Atlanta without having had any sleep, he knew that challenge was far easier than facing Kara one more time. Seeing the bitterness she obviously felt would be intolerable.

"Good Morning, Lorenzo," Cora greeted cheerfully entering the kitchen.

"Good Morning, Cora," he replied, trying to sound normal. "It's another beautiful day."

"Yes indeed, *every* morning is beautiful, especially now that I can see," Cora said looking out the window. "While I was blind, I tried to remember what things looked like. I lost my sight as a child, so I did have a few memories. But my, when seeing a sunset, or the morning sun spilling through my window or the gentle rain falling on the earth, I must say they're far more breathtaking than I remembered."

As he sat listening to the soft Texas drawl of this woman, Lorenzo felt a soothing to his turbulent spirit. "I'm happy for you, Cora," he told her. "I can't even imagine what you went through."

"It *was* hard, but somehow I always knew the good Lord would let me see again, at least for awhile before I die," Cora said as she made coffee. "Having my babies and not seeing their tiny faces, or their beautiful eyes looking back at me, was by far the most painful," she admitted. "I had conjured up an image in my mind what they would look like, but I must say, each one is more lovely than I had imagined. And, my dear, sweet husband was such a handsome man. But, not until a month ago did I see his face in our wedding pictures," Cora told Lorenzo.

"If you were blinded as a child, you have the whole world to explore," Lorenzo commented, thinking what adventures awaited this lovely woman.

"Yes I do," Cora laughed, "and one day, when things are back to normal for Jock and lovely Kelly, I'm gonna do some traveling."

As he sat listening, Lorenzo couldn't help comparing Cora to his own mother. *What a difference. This woman I'm hearing has more charm than any Carlyle I've ever been around. Sweet, caring, grateful for the simplest things. My mother could certainly take some lessons from this lady,* Lorenzo thought, suddenly feeling quite envious of Jock and Ryan.

"Good Morning you two," Jock said, entering the kitchen. "I never can beat you up, now can I?" he teased, giving Cora a kiss on the cheek.

"Not when I have this beautiful sunshine waiting for me," Cora teased back. "And, I've been enjoying the company of this fine young man. I do hope I haven't bored him to death while he's been waiting for his morning coffee."

"Not at all, Cora, it's been delightful I assure you," Lorenzo said, regretting to see it end. "I'm leaving this morning, Jock. Could you drive me to the airport?"

"I hope not before you've had your breakfast," Cora interjected as she began mixing pancakes. "I'll have these ready in two shakes of a lamb's tail," she drawled smiling.

"Well, how can I refuse such speedy service as that?" Lorenzo teased, making a mental note to send Cora some flowers when he got home.

While Jock found the butter and syrup, Lorenzo began setting the table. As promised, Cora soon had a stack of golden brown pancakes and a plate full of sausage ready to eat. "Seeing all this, I'm certainly glad I stayed," Lorenzo admitted.

Despite his inner turmoil and fear of seeing Kara before he left, Lorenzo enjoyed breakfast with Jock and Cora. As he watched the jovial bantering and genuine love between the two, Lorenzo was reminded of what he never had.

Indeed, the relationship he had with his mother was staunch and even cold at times. Certainly, he'd had the best education money could buy, yet, all the degrees he had acquired failed to bring true happiness or the kind of love he witnessed on this Texas morning.

. . .

For Kara, the departure of Lorenzo was a relief. Whenever his name came up she remained silent, refusing to express any feelings about the man.

When Ryan's bout with the flu had run its course, he spent hours with his mother, discussing things Kara felt were family matters.

It was during these times that she and Kelly had their talks and Abby and Jock enjoyed their daily horseback ride. It was Tuesday morning during Kara and Kelly's time alone that Ned's name came up.

"I saw him, did I tell you?" Kara asked, sipping her coffee.

"You saw Ned? Where, when?" Kelly asked, seemingly interested.

"In Atlanta, at a dinner club. He was in town for a Log Builders convention and we happened on each other. It was great seeing him."

"How is he, Kara? Is he doing okay?"

"He was until he heard about you, and the baby," Kara replied, deciding to be truthful. "He still loves you, Kelly. Despite his best efforts, you're still under his skin, *and* in his heart. I'm supposed to call him and let him know how you are. I must do that today," she said, regretting she hadn't done it before now. "Ned looks good, and his business is growing."

"I'm glad," Kelly said. "Oh Kara, he's such a great guy, I was hoping he had found someone by now."

"Perhaps he will one day," Kara remarked. "He's glad you and Jock are doing so well. And he's genuinely concerned about your health."

"Tell Ned hello for me, and let him know I'm getting better," Kelly told her sister. "This is just a setback, nothing more."

"Yes, we all have setbacks now and then," Kara remarked leaving her seat. "Some are greater than others, but we manage to get through them."

"It sounds as though you're going through one of your own," Kelly stated. "Anything you care to talk about?"

"No, it's nothing really, just an observation," Kara replied, looking out the bedroom window. "I'm so sorry you're going through this, Kel. And I'm sorry for all those months I wasted being jealous and ignoring everyone."

Turning from the window, Kara knelt down in front of her sister and looked up at her. "We only have each other, and I vow *nothing* will ever come between us again, not ever!"

"Me too," Kelly said, bending down to give Kara a hug. "And Kara, thanks for telling me about Ned. I want us to *always* be honest with each other. No matter how much it may hurt us, okay?"

"Okay, that's a deal. No matter what it is, we must stick together," Kara agreed. Suddenly she thought about Lorenzo and was grateful that Kelly knew nothing about the significance of her necklace, or that if it weren't for a boating accident, Lorenzo's uncle would have been their grandfather.

"Excuse me, but there's a phone call for either of you," Cora said, knocking on Kelly's door. "I believe she said Aunt Gina."

"Oh, yes, thank you, Cora," they both chimed excitedly. "We'll be right there." Hurriedly, Kara and Kelly went to take the call.

"Aunt Gina, how nice to hear your voice," Kelly greeted. "How are you?" From where Kara sat, she watched and listened as Kelly explained their fervent hope and trust that God would heal her. Then the conversation changed.

"Well no, I wasn't aware of any such diaries. Where did you find them?" Kelly asked as a frown creased her forehead. "I'm sure Mother knew nothing about them, or she would have told us," she remarked. "Let me ask Kara." Covering the mouthpiece, Kelly looked at her sister. "Were you aware that Grandma Isabella kept a diary for years and they're stored in Mother's attic?" she asked Kara.

"No, I had no idea," Kara replied, feeling stunned. "Did Gina find them?"

"Yes, she's getting rid of things so Mother can sell the house and she found a box in the attic filled with Grandma's things, including her journals."

Upon hearing this shocking news, Kara felt sick. Surely now the truth would surface regarding their grandmother's fiancé, his name and ultimately the necklace and its claim to the Carlyle wealth.

In a daze Kara paced the living room floor as Kelly resumed her conversation with Aunt Gina. *How will I explain that I knew this all along?*

Kelly and I vowed we'd have no secrets, but how can I expect her to believe this happened before I made that promise? Kara wondered. Suddenly, she realized she may not have seen the last of Lorenzo Carlyle after all.

When Kelly finished her talk with Aunt Gina, it was Kara's turn. "Hello Aunt Gina, it sounds like you're busy," Kara said, trying to sound upbeat.

"In shock would be a better definition," Gina replied. "Kara, it'll take me a month just to sort through things. Would you have time to come and help me?"

When hearing that, Kara's mind filled with a plan. "Yes, of course. I know Mother is getting settled in Arizona, and Kelly's in no shape to help out, so yes, I'll tell Jock and Ryan I need to do this. I'm sure they'll understand."

"Thank you dear, I hate to take you away from your job, but I had no idea I'd find all this in Emma's attic!"

"When did you discover this, Aunt Gina?" Kara asked, wondering if she'd had time to read any of the diaries.

"This afternoon, just hours ago," she replied. "I was so shocked, I just *had* to call someone. Emma and Charles are out enjoying all that sunshine I suppose so I haven't gotten hold of her as yet."

"Aunt Gina, don't worry Mother with this right now. I'll come and help you. You and I can surely get through all of Grandma's things in short order. Is the house sold already?" Kara asked, feeling eager to get started.

"No, but we've had some serious inquiries, so we need to clear these things out as soon as we can," Gina told her. "But, we can't just throw it all away. It would be a crime not to go through everything."

"Yes, of course, we must do that," Kara answered, "it's hard telling what we might find in those boxes." With a promise to be there as soon as she could, Kara ended her call with Aunt Gina. Not only did she need to confiscate those journals and the truth they were sure to reveal about the necklace, but Kara had to avoid any further contact with Lorenzo and his royal greed, at all costs.

. . .

After talking to Ryan and Jock about helping Aunt Gina, Kara was grateful for their understanding. "I will miss you, my lovely," Ryan said, giving her a hug. "But, I for one don't want Aunt Gina on my case, about anything. She's not one I'd care to tangle with," he teased.

"Nor do I, thank you," Kara teased back. "I'll leave tomorrow. The sooner I leave the sooner I can get back to what I need to do."

"*And* to me," Ryan said, taking Kara's hand. "Let's go horseback riding, okay? It's such a lovely day, it's a shame to waste it."

Just then the doorbell rang. With the others not available, Ryan went to answer. "Wow, someone must rate pretty well around here," Kara heard him say. A moment later, Ryan stepped from the foyer with a huge bouquet of pink roses. After setting the vase on the nearby table, Ryan looked for a card.

"Let's see who has a secret admirer," he said, pulling the tiny white envelope from its place. "These are for *Mother?* My, she must be doing something *very* fine," he teased, raising his eyebrows. "Shall we go find her?" he added, motioning for Kara.

Feeling curious, Kara went along with Ryan to the family room to find Cora who was knitting while Abby sat reading a book. "Oh Mother, I have a little surprise for you," Ryan began teasing, handing her the card. "There's a big bouquet of flowers sitting in the living room for you. Is there anything you want to tell us?"

"Flowers? For me?" Cora asked, looking surprised as she opened the card. A smile appeared on her face as she read it. Then, without saying a word, she carefully replaced it inside the envelope. "My, how very thoughtful," she remarked softly. "Thank you, dear. I'll go see my flowers as soon as I finish this row."

Dumbfounded, Ryan and Kara looked at each other. It seemed as though Cora had no intentions of telling them who had sent her such an elaborate bouquet. "Well, Mother, we're waiting," Ryan prodded, tapping his foot in jest. "Do you have a Southern gentleman who we should know about?"

"No," Cora simply replied, keeping her eyes on her knitting.

"*Are* you going to tell us who sent you those flowers?" Ryan again asked.

"No," Cora said as a smile touched her lips. "Only that he's a very nice man and obviously very thoughtful."

"Okay, Kara and I are going horseback riding," Ryan said, seemingly surprised at his mother's stubbornness. Indeed, Kara was somewhat curious too, but any woman could have an admirer, and she *certainly* didn't have to share him with the world.

. . .

The afternoon was glorious for Kara as she and Ryan rode horses across the rolling hillside. White fences gleamed in the sun against the backdrop of green pastures from the mild winter they were having. Lovely ranch style homes sat amid well landscaped yards with evergreen trees as well as shrubs native to Texas. It was truly a peaceful setting and somehow the stillness brought tranquility to Kara's trouble heart.

"I'm in love with you, Kara," Ryan suddenly remarked as he rode beside her. "And, I love everything about you, I hope you believe that."

"Thank you, Ryan. Yes, I do believe you love me," Kara replied, wishing she could reciprocate that feeling. "I care for you, Ryan. Very much, but I can't say I'm in love with you, at least not yet."

"Well, caring *is* a start," he said lightheartedly. "I can wait. But, you do seem troubled about something. Can you tell me about it?"

"Oh, it's just a lot of different things," Kara replied, knowing she couldn't delve into the real issue hounding her. "It's Kelly, my new job, helping Aunt Gina, and my future."

"Your future I can take care of, if you'll let me," Ryan offered. "I'd love nothing better than to give you all the things you have ever wanted, my lovely. I want to show you the world, to buy you your dream home, to spend quiet evenings in front of the fire," he said, looking at her. "I want to take you to all the romantic places on earth, to dance under the stars," he expounded happily, lifting his eyes and hands skyward.

Certainly, when hearing Ryan's plans for their future, Kara felt life with him would be filled with all those things she'd always dreamed about. *Am I crazy? How can I* not *love this man? He's fun-loving, sweet, caring, generous and quite handsome. What more could I ask?*

As she gazed across the meadow they rode through, Kara knew until certain issues were behind her, she could never sort out her true feelings for Ryan. *I have to find those diaries and make sure no one else learns about Kelly's necklace, and make sure Lorenzo doesn't find a way to get it.* Somehow, she wasn't sure the man had given up on his bag of devious tricks.

"I'm sorry, Ryan. But right now my mind seems so jumbled up with things, I can't think straight," Kara told him. "This isn't fair to you and I wouldn't blame you if you looked elsewhere."

"It won't happen. I'm here till the end, Kara," he said solemnly.

"I'm a patient man, so whenever you're ready, I'm here. Shall we gallop?"

With that, Kara nudged her horse's side with her boots, bringing instant response. Soon, her long hair was flying behind her as she and Ryan galloped side by side. *If only life could be so carefree,* she thought, knowing tomorrow would surely start another venture of uncertainty.

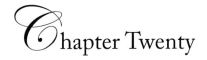

Chapter Twenty

With a last word of encouragement for her sister, Kara hugged and kissed Kelly goodbye. Today, would be another session of dialysis and with more tests they would see if Kelly's kidneys were in fact improving. Although she hated to leave before the news, Kara wanted to reach Romeo and her grandmother's diaries before Gina read them. For Kara, life had become one huge rollercoaster.

"I'll call you tonight," she told Kelly, waving from the car. In no time she and Ryan were on their way to the airport to catch her morning flight.

"How long are you staying in Dallas?" Kara asked, sensing his sadness.

"Just until tomorrow," Ryan said as he drove. "I need to get back to Atlanta. If Kelly improves, Jock will fly her home as soon as the doctors give their okay."

"Is the merger with Carlyle Research completed?" Kara asked. "Since I work there now, I was wondering how that works. Do you and Jock own more of the company then Lorenzo?"

"Look at you," Ryan teased. "Aren't you Miss Business-woman."

"I'm just curious, since I *am* in the family," Kara replied, not wanting to sound nosey. "Mergers aren't my forte, but they *are* interesting."

"It's pretty technical, with a lot of business jargon, like stock options, percentages, liquid assets and such, but as we speak, Beaumont Computers holds more than CRC does," Ryan informed her. "Our attorneys take care of such matters, and our accountants handle other details. Jock and I drum up business by getting government contracts. I'm very proud of you, my dear, for being so interested," Ryan concluded, reaching for Kara's hand. "It's unusual for women to care about such matters."

"I guess I'm a multifaceted female," Kara teased, not daring to express her real motive. *I just hope Lorenzo doesn't try some dirty trick, right now, nothing would surprise me,* Kara thought, remembering his confession sixty-two hours earlier.

. . .

Since leaving Dallas, Lorenzo thought of little else except Kara. Over and over he relived their moonlight walk and analyzed every word. He wondered what he might have said differently, yet, any other answer would have been a lie. He wanted, no, he *needed* to tell Kara the truth. But now, having done so, he lost any chance of winning her heart. The reality of that left him depressed and feeling lifeless.

Everything he tried had failed. And now he had to tell his mother, the family Matriarch.

"Might as well get this over with," Lorenzo muttered, wishing to avoid the confrontation that was sure to ensue. As he dialed the long overseas number to Scotland, he wanted only to sleep, to close out the world he had created by his mistakes.

Finally, there was an answer. "Hello, this is Lorenzo, calling for Gabriella," he told the servant, trying to prepare himself for her onslaught.

"Hello Lorenzo, I do hope you have good news for me," the woman said shortly.

At that moment, Lorenzo thought about Jock and Cora and the love they showed for each other. Their mother/son greetings were cordial and kind, certainly not like the one he just heard in his ear.

"No Mother, I'm afraid I failed," he told her. "I did not get the necklace, so we might as well accept—"

"I will accept no such thing!" Gabriella blared at him. "Failure is not a word we use, Lorenzo. We try until we get it right, do you *understand?*"

"Why does it matter?" he fired back. "They have no idea of its value, other than it's a keepsake from their grandmother. They won't pursue *anything* even if by some miracle they learned of Great-grandfather's ruling."

"Of that you can *not* be certain! And, if other issues come to light they're bound to want a share of our wealth," she argued.

"What issues, Mother? There are none, other than Uncle Henry gave his intended bride a lovely gift. Of which they have no *bloody* idea

142

of its worth!" he yelled, wishing only for this ordeal to end.

"I will *not* be spoken to in this manner!" Gabriella blurted back. "When you can be civil to me, then you may call me. Until then, you are expected to succeed at *your* obligation *without* fail! That is all I will say on the matter," she concluded, hanging up in Lorenzo's ear.

When the call had ended, Lorenzo felt numb with despair. Suddenly, he realized nothing Gabriella did could compare to what he was feeling now, after hurting Kara.

Remembering the hurt in her eyes, hearing the hatred in her voice tore through him like a knife. *I won't put you through anymore, my darling. You don't have to worry about me. Kelly's necklace will remain hers,* he vowed silently. *Gabriella is certain to pay other people to do what I can't, but I will protect my sweet Kara, no matter what,* Lorenzo promised in his heart.

· · ·

It was late Wednesday afternoon by the time Kara arrived at her mother's house in Romeo. Since Aunt Gina hated to drive in freeway traffic, Kara took a taxi from the airport. With her thoughts on the newly discovered diaries, Kara was eager to get started.

"Oh my dear, I'm so glad to see you," Gina cheered, giving Kara a hug. "Just look at me! Dust from head to toe. This is *quite* an unexpected job, I assure you. Why Mother didn't burn all these I'll never know. I for one don't want people knowing my deepest thoughts and feelings," she said, shaking her head. "Let's have some coffee and I'll fill you in."

"Have you started reading any of them yet?" Kara asked. "I mean, are you *going* to read them?"

"Well why not? Mother won't care, and she had no great secrets, at least none that I'm aware of," Gina commented, filling two cups with coffee. "I'm sure it's just a bunch of daily drudgery. Of course, there *is* that one major event in her life, you know, the guy she was engaged to? The filthy rich fellow who died before they could say 'I do'? I *would* like to know more about that."

When hearing Aunt Gina's comment, Kara knew she had her work cut out for her. Trying to find *that* journal and keep it from the prying eyes of her aunt wouldn't be easy. "Since I'm here now, Aunt Gina, I want you to take it easy. You look as though you could use a day of rest. Why not let *me* take the dusty attic for a few days and you work on something down here," Kara said in her most persuasive manner.

"Nonsense, my dear," Gina answered shaking her head. "It'll be *much* more fun if we do things together. Besides, while we work you can fill me in on Kelly and your job in Atlanta, and that sweet young Ryan," she rambled on, smiling. "Any news I should know about? You know, here comes the bride kind of news?" she added teasingly.

"Nothing yet," Kara said, suddenly wishing she had a special bottle she could close Aunt Gina up in. At least until she finished things in the attic.

"Well, he's certainly a fine young man," Gina went on. "I do hope things work out between you two."

When the telephone rang a moment later Gina went to answer. As she waited, Kara decided there was no use wasting time. After gulping down the last of her coffee, she carried her one small suitcase upstairs to her old room.

Quickly she changed into a pair of old jeans and a baggy top and pulled her hair up, covering it with a kerchief.

Since Gina still hadn't joined her, Kara made her way up the creaky narrow steps to the attic. *I see why we never came up here much! This is spooky,* she thought, opening the door to the dark cubby-hole-room.

As she stepped inside, Kara noticed a dank musty odor mingled with the smell of dust. The light from one small window revealed boxes in disarray and their contents scattered across the floor. One lone light bulb hung from the rafters and when Kara reached up and turned it on, it cast a dim yellowish glow, certainly not enough to read by.

In haste Kara looked through the boxes, searching for the diaries. She found tattered black and white photos of people she didn't know; tiny dolls with yellowed and torn dresses and small boxes filled with hair ribbons, but no books of any kind. *Where are they? Did she really see them?* Kara wondered, looking around the dingy area.

"That was the realtor," Gina called out from the bottom of the attic steps. "He's bringing someone by to look at the property, so I need to be downstairs when they arrive. You can wait until they've gone so we can work together, dear," she suggested.

"Oh no, Aunt Gina, you take care of business and I'll get started up here," Kara called back. "By the way, where *are* the journals?"

"Oh, I brought them downstairs, we can't read them up there in that dingy light," she said, turning to leave. "I'll be up to help as soon as I can."

At Gina's announcement regarding the journals, Kara's heart sank. *Well, so much for that idea! I'll have to take my chances while we read them together.*

Deciding to start on the box of old pictures, Kara took them down to her room to sort through them. *I might find a picture of Grandpa and Grandma when they were young, and I wouldn't want to throw them away,* she thought.

When she had reached her bedroom, Kara covered her bed with an old sheet and dumped the contents of the box on top. Slowly she began looking for someone familiar. Carefully she searched, tossing those she didn't recognize back in the box for her mother and Aunt Gina to go through later.

Suddenly, something caught her eye. There, amid dozens of photos of ordinary people who were farming, picking apples or doing mundane jobs, was a picture of a man and woman wearing formal attire.

Grabbing the picture, Kara studied the faces. *He looks familiar, but who is he?* she wondered. Then she knew. *He looks like Lorenzo! Is this his uncle who loved my grandmother? It has to be! They resemble more than any of those I saw in Lorenzo's album!* Kara decided, feeling stunned. "I'm *sure* that's Grandma Isabella," she muttered seeing the beautiful fair-haired woman smiling back at her.

Not knowing why she did, Kara glanced at the back of the picture. To her surprise there was something written. Although passing years had faded the words, Kara could still make them out. *Our wedding day, Mr. and Mrs. Henry Carlyle.* In disbelief Kara could only stare at the words as she slumped to her bed. "They were married?" she gasped, shaking her head. *But why were we told otherwise? Does Lorenzo know about this?*

In that moment, Kara realized she had many more questions for the man. *Surely Grandma wrote about this in her journals,* Kara decided, feeling certain that neither her mother or Aunt Gina knew anything about this.

After regaining her composure, Kara put the photo in her dresser drawer for safe keeping. Only then did she resume her task of sorting through the remaining old pictures.

After learning her grandmother was married to a wealthy Carlyle, Kara wondered even more about the necklace in Kelly's possession.

Grandma was a rightful owner, then why didn't she demand her share? Instead, she and Grandpa Kline were paupers. Did she think by passing it down it may one day bring the wealth her family was entitled to? Oh, Aunt Gina, I do believe we have a mystery to solve and there's no way I can keep this to myself. . . .

. . .

By the time Gina joined her, Kara had looked through most of the photos and had set aside several she wanted to keep. "I do believe Emma just sold her property," Gina boasted as she entered Kara's bedroom. "They seen like such a nice couple and they *love* the orchard."

"That's good, Mother will be pleased," Kara replied, only half listening to the woman. While Gina rambled on, Kara wondered how to break the shocking news she had just learned. *Aunt Gina never minces words so why should I?* she decided, taking a deep breath.

"Aunt Gina, do you remember saying earlier today that Grandma didn't have any secrets?" Kara began, "well, it seems that she did."

"Are you certain? What secret is that?" Gina asked, looking puzzled.

"Let me show you something," Kara said, retrieving the picture from her dresser drawer. "Who is this?" she asked, handing it to Gina.

For better light, Gina went to the window and studied the photo. "It looks like my mother when she was a young woman, but, oh my, could *this* be the mystery man?" she asked, glancing at Kara.

"Read the back," Kara told her aunt. Seemingly puzzled, Gina did as she was told. A moment later, her eyes widened in shock and her mouth gaped open as she stared at Kara. Then, plopping on the edge of Kara's bed, she appeared dumbfounded as she shook her head.

"Oh, this, this is *shocking!*" Gina gasped. "We had no idea. Mother told us a far different story, but why?"

"We have to read her diaries to find the answer to *that,*" Kara replied. "And perhaps we'll learn more surprising details."

"I guess *anything* is possible now," Gina remarked, fanning her face with the photo. "Oh dear, I *am* afraid we've opened a can of worms. No, I believe it's more like a box of dynamite!"

"I have to agree," Kara said, realizing there was much more to all this than just the necklace. "Shall we get started?"

"Let's go," Gina said. "I do believe we'll be having one of those late nights, my dear," she added, letting out a deep sigh.

As they descended the stairs to the living room, Kara's mind was buzzing with questions. *I'm afraid I haven't seen the last of Lorenzo after all. . . .*

· · ·

After stopping to eat a quick bite of supper, Kara and Gina then spent well over an hour arranging the journals in order, from the earliest to the latest.

"Mother was certainly diligent at keeping records," Gina said, shaking her head. "And she started so young."

"Well, now we begin," Kara remarked, eyeing the pile of small books.

"Yes, and lets mark every page that pertains to that secret husband of hers," Gina said, handing Kara a pack of post-it-notes.

With their beverages nearby, Kara and Gina took their place on the floor within easy reach of the dusty volumes. The moment had come to begin their adventure through countless joys and heartaches of decades past.

For Kara, these diaries were sure to answer questions she already had, but after today, she could only wonder what other secrets would come to light.

Chapter Twenty-one

As she lovingly opened the tattered and yellowed pages, Kara thought of that young girl whose world was contained inside. Although it was long ago, that world had surprisingly entangled with her own. With calm reverence Kara began her invasion into those private thoughts.

Early on, she smiled as she read the childish notations regarding a beloved cat and the boys who teased the young Isabella mercilessly during school. On most pages she wrote about friends, teachers and a cute boy at school and another one at summer camp. One by one Kara and Gina skimmed through the early life of a girl who eagerly yearned to be a woman.

As the hours passed, they occasionally read aloud one of Isabella's entries that was especially funny, or sad. As Kara read, she wondered when the young Isabella had jotted down her thoughts. *Was she in her nightgown before bed? Or perhaps when she first arrived home from school?*

The winters are long and filled with drudgery. How I long to feel the warm sand between my toes as I stroll along the beach. No longer will I complain about the added work of summer Mother has me do.

The howling winds bring such mournful sounds outside my window. If only I could sleep until spring arrives as other creatures do. Father told Mother and I of the violent storm he was in. Sometimes I fear his fishing boat will surely be crushed beneath such towering waves.

In many ways, Kara soon realized she and her grandmother were very much alike. At times, she felt certain she might have written these same words, revealing her inner most thoughts, her fears and dreams.

Ah, spring has arrived at last and soon the wind's chill will change to its warm ocean breeze. Again the sand and surf will be mine to enjoy.

As she read, Kara saw her grandmother blossom from a girl into a young woman. Her handwriting changed from short childish sentences to delicately penned thoughts. And so they continued. *January 1952,* she read silently as she carefully opened the faded-pink cover of the next journal.

Inside, Kara was surprised to find a flower pressed between its pages. Gently she touched it only to have it disintegrate into powdery chafe, causing a distinct musty odor. *Is this what age smells like?* Kara wondered. *Grandmother was seventeen when she wrote this. Obviously she already had romantic feelings.*

I can not know tomorrow, but with certainty I shall find my one true love. He's out there somewhere and he, too, dreams of me, and awaits that day when our paths shall meet.

Today I walked along the seashore and I couldn't help but envy the gulls as they fly so untamed, so free. How lovely it would be to always breathe the salty air and hear the roar of the waves. One day I shall live by the sea.

Oh what a glorious day, for I have met the man I hope to marry! How could such a handsome man look at me with such adoring eyes? Dare I hope his smile was meant to cause my heart to soar? For surely he achieved that and much more. It matters not that he is older, for surely love knows no bounds.

Each entry was a peek inside the heart of a young girl. Now, all these years later, Kara was transported back in time, feeling the same anticipation.

I saw him again today, he waved at me from the hill's crest and I waved back. Mary said he's just being friendly, but I think she's jealous since he never looks at her, not like he does me. One day I will find the nerve to talk to him. . . .

Last night I dreamed about him. He kissed me and it was wonderful. I will carry thoughts of how it felt until the day he takes me in his arms and tells me of his love. My dream is surely a sign, so now I will wait. . . .

It happened and it was glorious! I saw him at the store and he said hello. I thought my heart would burst with joy at the sound of his voice. His eyes are dark and they seemed to look inside me. If that is true, then he knows of my love for him. I watched him walk away and he looked back at me and smiled.

I am excited for today I learned his name from Miss Miller at the store. Henry Carlyle. He lives in the big house overlooking the cove and it appears I am not alone in my wishes to make his acquaintance.

I heard others say he is rich and owns a castle in a foreign land. Does he think me a child? Tomorrow I will beg Mother for some coloring for my lips.

"I found it, Aunt Gina," Kara announced, sticking a bright pink post-it-note on the appropriate page. "Grandmother was seventeen when she met Henry Carlyle."

"Oh my goodness," Gina replied, looking surprised.

"What is it? What's wrong?"

"Mother was barely twenty-two when Emma was born. It appears her courtship *and* marriage to Mr. Carlyle was a short one doesn't it," she stated, shaking her head.

"It appears so," Kara said as more questions came to mind. Eagerly she resumed reading.

Today my heart leaps with joy. I met Mr. Carlyle on the path and although he was dressed quite handsomely and I was barefooted, he stopped to say hello. My embarrassment soon dissolved due to his gentle manner and kind words to me. My heart races with delight as I recall the way his eyes lingered on my face.

As she read, Kara felt transfixed in time. Suddenly, these worn and weathered pages, filled with the stirrings of young love, revealed a heart not so unlike her own. *Oh Grandma, if only we could have known all this before you died,* Kara thought sadly. Stopping only long enough to take a drink of water, Kara resumed reading.

Although making Mr. Carlyle's acquaintance this summer caused my spirit to soar with delight, I now feel endless sadness knowing he is gone. Only his promised return next summer will keep me from dying from pure loneliness.

Each day I mark the calendar, waiting for summer. My friendship with Mary is strained with her refusal to understand or believe this devotion I feel for Henry. Soon I'll be eighteen and will no longer need my parents approval and if he should ask, I would leave everything behind to marry him. Without Henry here, even the seashore has lost its beauty.

"Aunt Gina, did you know *your* grandparents? I read no mention of siblings and rarely does she mention her parents. Do you know about them?"

"My grandmother was a twin, but her sister died at birth," Gina explained, laying aside the journal she was reading. "They lived in Maine and my grandfather had his own fishing boat. From what I understand, he and his crew were lost at sea during a bad storm," she told Kara. "It was said that my grandmother never recovered from her loss and died of a broken heart."

"How *sad*," Kara replied, wondering why she'd never heard that story before. *I'll be asking Mother about that,* Kara thought as she resumed reading.

For the next while, Kara and Gina continued to read in silence. "Listen to this!" Gina shouted, surprising Kara with her outburst.

'Tonight, Henry entrusted me with surprising news. His recent demeanor was of great concern to me, fearing he had found another to share his love. Instead, a bitter family quarrel is certain to leave him penniless. He tells me he must relinquish all assets of the Carlyle estate, including the castle in Scotland.'

"Did you hear that, Kara? He owned a castle, so he must be royalty!"

"It appears so," Kara replied, knowing now why no pictures of Henry appeared in Lorenzo's album. "Do you suppose he and Grandmother were engaged by that time?"

"I can't tell or I missed that particular journal," Gina told Kara. "This is *amazing!* Wow, just think, we were *that* close to being rich and having our own castle."

"Let's keep reading, or do you want to quit for the night?" Kara asked.

"Are you *kidding?* Who can sleep with all *this* going on!" Gina spouted.

After stretching their legs and hurriedly eating a snack of cheese and crackers, Kara and Gina resumed reading. Clearly it was a mystery why her grandmother left behind evidence of a marriage she'd never told anyone about.

At eighteen Kara's grandmother wrote: *My heart soars each time I see Henry. Truly he is a man of his word and a gentleman the kind I've never known. My greatest pleasure is just being with him, walking along the beach or sailing in his sloop off the coast.*

I am mindful of his growing adoration, but he seems troubled over our age difference. I assure him no man could ensnare my heart as he has done so completely. Surely, I would marry him tomorrow if he would ask.

Henry spoke today of Sabrina, the woman his brother recently married. He seemed troubled and when he could no longer contain his anger toward her, he told of a necklace that would assure this woman her place of importance. He vowed she would never rule over him.

Closing her eyes to rest them, Kara nodded her head. *You were right, Mother, the truth is buried just so long and then it comes to light. Certainly, Lorenzo has no truth in him, but its all here to see. Oh Grandma, if only I could have known you better,* she thought, blinking back her tears. "When I finish this, Aunt Gina, I'm going to bed," Kara said yawning.

"Yes, I know dear, we'll soon hear the neighbor's rooster crowing," Gina replied. Once more they resumed reading, finishing what they had started.

Several pages later, Kara eyes flew open at what she read:

It happened, tonight Henry asked me for my hand in marriage. He warns me of his family's rebuke due to my common place, but he is willing to relinquish his place of honor if need be. Truly I have no doubt of his love. . . .

Mother and Father accepted my news with a surprisingly gentle manner. As much as I want their blessing, their denial of it would not change my mind. Only God Himself will stop me from marrying Henry.

We have it planned, next week I will be Mrs. Henry Carlyle. Henry has it arranged and gave me money for my wedding dress. Tonight he brings my engagement gift and assures me he will tell me of its importance.

"Aunt Gina, I found it," Kara said, turning the page. "This is about Kelly's necklace, the one Grandmother left. "Listen to this."

"I fear my eyesight is harmed from its dazzling brightness. My tongue can not explain such splendor nor my throat give it fair display. Henry says it is far more valuable than its glittering gold and diamonds, for whoever wears this has control of the Carlyle wealth. He tells me Sabrina now wears one too."

"Who is Sabrina?" Gina asked, looking puzzled.

"She is Henry's sister-in-law, and a controlling power it seems," Kara said, deciding she would have to reveal all she knew sooner or later. "My mind is too boggled to understand all of this, let's wait until morning, okay?"

"Good idea," Gina answered, marking her last page. "This is all so unbelievable I'll have to mull this over for awhile. Goodnight dear."

After giving her aunt a hug, Kara headed upstairs. "How can we ever sort this out, or understand such things?" she muttered arriving in her room. *One thing's for sure, Lorenzo does come from an honor bound family, just like he said. . . .*

. . .

Despite her weariness Kara had a restless night. She tossed and turned amid dreams of scowling faces and of her grandmother crying. *Surely the impact of her marriage and Henry's death is within those pages. What kind of rebuke* did *she get from the Carlyle clan?* Kara wondered. *And how much of this does Lorenzo know?* For the first time, she began to understand what Lorenzo's life must have been like. *Certainly, I don't want to see him again, but it is sad,* Kara decided, remembering the moonlight walk and how pathetic he sounded.

. . .

When Kara awoke just three hours later, she remembered. *I forgot to call Kelly, and Ned! Where's my brain? Inside those journals,* she quickly decided.

Despite her few hours of sleep, Kara crawled out of bed, took her shower and got dressed for the day. She had just finished combing her hair when Aunt Gina yelled from the bottom of the stairs.

"Kara, you have a phone call, dear. It's Ryan," she called out in a melodious tone. "Shall I have him wait or will you call him back?"

"I'll be right down," Kara yelled out. *Was I supposed to call him too?* she thought, recalling their last words at the airport. Hurriedly she ran downstairs to take the call. "Hello Ryan, was I suppose to call you?" she asked.

"No, but Kelly waited up," Ryan told her. "She decided you were probably too tired or involved in your job. How's it coming?"

"It's coming, and I am sorry I didn't call Kelly. Are you still in Dallas?"

"No, I just left, but she has good news," Ryan said happily.

"Oh Ryan, are her kidney's working?" Kara asked excitedly.

"I should let her tell you, but yes, they've improved a lot, so we're all very hopeful. I'll let her tell you the other good news," Ryan added.

For the next few minutes their talk involved Atlanta and how much he missed her. When Ryan asked about her grandmother's things,

154

Kara downplayed the subject, knowing Lorenzo's name was sure to come up.

When her call had ended with Ryan, Kara called Kelly to get the good news Ryan spoke of. "Hi, Kel, I'm sorry about last night. Aunt Gina and I got involved and the time got away from me," she said. "How are you?"

"We're praising God because our prayers are being answered," Kelly said excitedly. "My kidneys are starting to function on their own. If my blood tests are good tomorrow, we can fly home on Saturday."

"That *is* good news," Kara cheered. "I can't wait to see you. Things here are progressing. Aunt Gina thinks Mother has a buyer for her place and we're busy cleaning out things."

"I wish I was there to help," Kelly told her.

"I know, Kel, but I'll fill you in. You just keep getting better, okay?"

"Thanks, I will, I'm sure of it. We'll see you when we get home," Kelly concluded as they said goodbye.

With Kelly's good news, Kara called Ned next, making her apologies for not calling sooner. He made no comment while she told him about Kelly. Finally, he spoke.

"I've been worried sick, Kara. I'm glad she's better, and losing the baby? How's she taking that?" he asked.

"She's sad, of course, but they haven't given up," Kara told him. "Ned, how are you?"

"Better now," he sighed. "I'll always worry about Kelly, I guess."

"Ned, Kelly says hello and she's glad about your business. She's hoping you'll find someone special to share your life," Kara told him.

"Yeah, well, maybe someday," Ned replied. "Right now I'm not looking." After a few comments about their meeting in Atlanta, the call ended, leaving Kara wondering how he could still love Kelly after all that had happened.

Now that's true love. Some women are just lucky I guess, Kara decided.

$\mathcal{C}$hapter Twenty-two

It was late morning when Kara and Gina resumed their probing of Isabella's journals. Again, Kara read her grandmother's innermost thoughts penned in delicate and perfectly spaced words across the page.

This time tomorrow I will be Mrs. Henry Carlyle and look forward with wondrous anticipation at such an honor. Although Henry is quite displeased with regard to his family's behavior toward me, I have no thought for it. I'm sure, as time passes, they will know me for the devoted wife I truly will be. . . .

After our splendorous honeymoon aboard the Queen Mary, I find no words to describe how I feel. If I should die tomorrow, I have no regrets for I have surely reached the height of happiness because of my wonderful husband. However, I do sense his concern regarding repercussions from his family due to our marriage.

Tonight my heart weeps at hearing Henry's life has been threatened. Could his family hate me although we've never met? I wish to give back the necklace, but Henry refuses to bow to their threats. He promises to be careful. . . .

As she read, Kara had to wonder. *Was Henry's boating accident really an accident? Could his own parents and brother have murdered him?* Suddenly, she recalled Lorenzo's words. *Kidnapping, blackmail, if they're capable of that, why* not *murder?* A chill swept over Kara when thinking about who now had the necklace. *Is Kelly in danger? They obviously know she has it.*

"Aunt Gina, anything yet about Henry's death?" Kara asked, hoping to find these last missing pieces. Looking up, Kara noticed Gina wasn't reading, but rather gazing out the window. "Aunt Gina, are you okay?"

Slowly Gina turned her head and looked at Kara. "We never knew. Why didn't our mother ever tell us?" Gina said flatly, shaking her head.

"What Aunt Gina, told you what?"

"Emma is my *half* sister. She is Henry Carlyle's daughter." A wave of disbelief washed over Kara when hearing those words. Her mind went numb.

Then, while trying to grasp such news, Kara suddenly realized what this meant. "Then *Mother* is a Carlyle heir, *she* is entitled to half of their wealth," she blared, jumping to her feet. "Aunt Gina, this is *unbelievable!* Did you hear me?"

"*Why* didn't we know, why all these years later?" Gina asked again.

"I don't know, Aunt Gina. But I do have a few words to ask a certain person," Kara announced, going to the phone.

After dialing, she listened for an answer. "Hello Ryan, are you busy?" Kara asked, feeling her heart racing.

"Hi Kara, yeah, I'm here slaving away," he said in his usual joking manner. "Did you miss me already?"

"Ryan, I'm sorry to cut this short, but is Lorenzo around anywhere? If he is may I please speak to him?" she asked, realizing she was reneging on her own promise.

"No, he left for the day. He said he wasn't feeling well," Ryan replied. "Anything wrong? Something maybe *I* can help you with?"

"No, I'm afraid it's not about business, at least not Beaumont kind of business," she answered, knowing Ryan would be more than a little curious. "It's about something he and I talked about while we were Dallas, I'll fill you in later," she said. "Thanks Ryan, I'll catch up with him tomorrow. And you too."

In haste she hung up the telephone before Ryan could ask any further questions. With her mind in a whirl, Kara thought about this shocking news. "*This* is why Grandma didn't throw these journals away, she *wanted* us to find the truth," she told Gina. "It was all she knew to do."

After reading about Emma being her half sister, Gina excused herself. "I have to get some fresh air, this has bowled me over," she told Kara as she headed for the door.

Obviously being kept in the dark all these years is harder for Gina to grasp than learning who Mother's real father is. She's a Carlyle!

Just then, another truth popped into Kara's mind. *That means Lorenzo and I are related!*

. . .

When Lorenzo arrived at home, he downed three Excedrin with a glass of water and laid down on his bed. Since early this morning his head pounded. *Mother and migraines, it's a combination that never fails,* he decided, thinking about her surprising phone call that morning, before sunup.

'I won't stand for it, do you hear me? I'm giving you fair warning, so whatever happens, it's on your hands,' Gabriella had threatened. When he asked why the family couldn't let the necklace go, he got an even stronger retort. *'You don't need to know the reason, just obey my wishes! I'm the head of this family and the sooner you understand that, the better!'*

When his headache eased a bit, Lorenzo dozed off. A short time later the ringing telephone woke him. As he waited for the answering machine to pick up, he was surprised to hear Ryan's voice. "Hey partner, I hate to bother you. Just letting you know Kara tried to reach you. She said it's about your conversation in Dallas. I guess she'll—"

"Hi Ryan, I'm here. When did Kara call?" Lorenzo ask, feeling his heart leap.

"Oh, bout an hour ago."

"Do you have her number? I don't mind calling, my headache is finally better," Lorenzo stated, trying to mask his excitement. As Ryan gave him Kara's telephone number, Lorenzo couldn't believe this streak of good fortune. Especially after what happened just days before. "Thanks Ryan, I'll see you tomorrow."

Taking a deep breath, Lorenzo dialed the Michigan number. "Hello," he heard Kara say on the third ring.

"Hello Kara, this is Lorenzo. I heard you wanted to speak to me?"

"Yes, Lorenzo, I do, but not on the phone. All I will say is this: it has to do with Kelly's necklace, *and* the Carlyle family. I've learned some *very* interesting facts, and I need to know if you are privy to such details. When can I see you?" Kara asked, surprising him.

"I can fly up there, if you'd like," he told her. "I could leave in an hour, be there by late afternoon and rent a car. I'll call from the airport to get directions. Would that be okay?"

"Fine, I'll be waiting," Kara said abruptly, hanging up in his ear.

Interesting facts? Whatever they are must *be important for her to call me,* Lorenzo thought, remembering their moonlight walk. Hurriedly, he changed his clothes, grabbed his coat and left the house. Despite hearing Kara's cool tone, Lorenzo, nonetheless, was elated about seeing her again.

From his car phone he requested his plane be readied right away. *I've got to call Ryan,* he thought, wondering how much to say.

Reluctantly he dialed the office. "Hey Ryan, I wanted to let you know I may not be in tomorrow after all. I have some business to take care of," he informed Ryan. "I'm leaving right away so I'll catch you later."

Before Ryan could inquire about his urgent matter, Lorenzo hung up. *He isn't stupid, he'll connect this to Kara's phone call eventually,* he decided.

Again he thought about Kara's call. *Could these facts she mentioned be connected to what Gabriella won't tell me?*

· · ·

That afternoon, Kara found it hard to think of anything but the shocking secrets they'd uncovered. And knowing Lorenzo would be arriving later today only added to her restlessness.

"I *can't* read anymore, Kara. It's too shocking, you finish if you'd like, but for me, I've learned enough," Gina said shaking her head. "I'll be in the attic cleaning, if you need me."

"Aunt Gina, I'm sorry you found out like this," Kara said, giving her aunt a hug. "When should we tell Mother? Do we call? Do we wait until we see her, what do you think?"

"She and Charles will be arriving in a few days to get some of her things," Gina told Kara. "I'm sure we can wait until then."

"Yes, it's better if we have the proof in front of us, I'm sure Mother will be just as shocked as we've been," Kara replied, nodding her head. "I may skim through the remaining journals, at least until Lorenzo arrives."

"Is this the same Lorenzo fellow that saved your life?" Gina then asked.

"Yes, he is. I haven't said much about him, but he ties into all of this. Do you want to know how?" Kara asked realizing the time had come.

"Yes, but this calls for a fresh pot of coffee," Gina stated, heading for the kitchen. In no time, coffee was brewing and the two women sat at the kitchen table. In depth, Kara began telling her aunt about Lorenzo, even their moonlight walk in Dallas.

"That man really *does* love you," Gina remarked when Kara had finished the details. "He was devious, yes, but it's obvious *you* are now more important than the necklace. If you weren't, he would *never* have told you the truth."

"But how can I believe him? He might be saying that just to trick me," Kara argued, trying hard to forget the tenderness in Lorenzo's eyes that night.

"That wouldn't be to his advantage, he risks you telling *everyone,* even the authorities about this," Gina argued back. "And if the necklace *did* come up missing, or someone *was* kidnapped, they'd know who did it."

When hearing Gina's explanation, Kara had to admit she was right. "I suppose, after reading Grandma's journals, I *can* see what Lorenzo's up against. Even Henry had threats, perhaps they've threatened Lorenzo as well. What a ruthless bunch, hiding behind their *royalty.* And now, I find *I'm* related to those people!" Kara blurted, leaving her seat at the table.

"You and Lorenzo are second cousins," Gina remarked. "Kissing cousins some have called it," she added grinning.

. . .

It was four-thirty when the ringing telephone jarred Kara from her nap. After her sleepless night and trying to finish the journals, she'd fallen asleep on the sofa. As she hurried to answer, Kara remembered Lorenzo's imminent arrival. "Hello, this Kara," she greeted still half asleep.

"Hello Kara, this is Lorenzo, I'm at the airport. Where would you like to meet me? Or should I come to your house?" he asked.

"Yes, come here," Kara told him. "I'll fix some sandwiches, I'm sure you're hungry."

"I can stop and get something," Lorenzo offered. "Or we can go out. I'm sure we can find a quiet place where we can talk."

At hearing Lorenzo's offer, Kara looked around the disheveled kitchen. *Certainly this isn't the best place to invite anyone,* she thought, seeing piles of dishes sitting on the cupboard and open boxes half filled.

"We *are* in the middle of packing, so I guess eating somewhere else might be the best idea," Kara told him. "Here's how to find me." For the next few minutes she gave Lorenzo directions to her mother's house in Romeo.

When finished with the call, Kara hurried upstairs, mentally calculating how soon he'd be arriving. "Aunt Gina, Lorenzo's at the airport. He asked to take me out for dinner. Do you mind?" she yelled up the steps to the attic.

"Of course not, dear," Gina said from the doorway. "Have a good time, but I expect a full report," she teased, seemingly in a better mood.

In haste Kara washed her face, applied a dab of color to her lips and combed her hair, leaving it loose around her shoulders. *What to wear? Certainly there isn't much here,* she decided, thumbing through the few items she hadn't moved to Kelly's or to Atlanta. *Nothing fancy, this is* not *a date,* Kara reminded herself.

Finally, she retrieved a pair of black jeans, boots and a turquoise colored sweater from her closet. While she got ready, her mind darted all direction.

Certainly Grandmother revealed secrets no one knew about, and now it raises even more questions, Kara thought. *Was Henry murdered by his family? Why didn't they go after Grandma, after all* she *had the necklace? And Grandpa Kline? What about him? I must finish reading, surely I'll find a few more answers,* she decided, wondering what reaction Lorenzo would have to all this.

While Kara waited for the man to arrive, she gathered the appropriate journals together, making sure the pages were well marked to backup her news. With only five left unread, she promised to get to those later. *It won't take long with Lorenzo, besides, he has to fly back tonight,* she decided.

Nearly an hour later, a knock sounded on the front door. Surprisingly, Kara felt a tinge of excitement. *Nerves, it's just nerves at having to see him again,* she assured herself.

"Hello Lorenzo, please come in," she said after opening the door.

"Hello Kara," he said softly as their eyes met. "How are you?"

"I'm fine, thank you," she said politely, tearing her eyes from his. "I'll just grab my coat and we can go," Kara added, turning from the doorway.

When she'd gotten her coat, Lorenzo stepped inside. "Please allow me," he said. While he held Kara's coat and she slipped her arms into the sleeves, their close proximity caused her awareness of Lorenzo's tantalizing cologne.

"Thank you," she said, tying the belt and avoiding his eyes. "I guess I'm ready." With that, Lorenzo held the door for her and closed it behind them.

He is a gentleman, but when he learns we're related, I'm sure he won't be so cordial, Kara thought as they headed for his rental car.

"I noticed a nice dinner club some miles back, would that be okay?" he asked after they were buckled in their seats.

"Anywhere is fine, just so we can talk without everyone overhearing our conversation," Kara replied, expecting him to deny what he was about to hear.

"Kara, just so you know, I'm happy that you called," Lorenzo told her as he pulled from the driveway. "I know this is just business, nothing more, but it's still very nice to see you again. And just so you know, my feelings haven't changed," he added as he glanced at her.

"Lorenzo, I'm afraid things *aren't* what they appear," Kara replied, suddenly remembering *he* had told her those very words some months back. She could only wonder why.

"What *is* your news, Kara?" Lorenzo asked, looking at her. "Please tell me." As she looked straight ahead, pondering where to begin, Kara felt his eyes on her. She decided to dive right in.

"For starters, we're related," she blurted out as she looked his direction. "Your Uncle Henry is my biological grandfather."

Now it was Lorenzo who looked straight ahead, saying nothing. "It's green," Kara prodded as he sat staring. Slowly, Lorenzo started through the intersection and then headed toward a parking lot.

"Lorenzo? Are you okay?" Kara had to ask, seeing his stalled expression.

"That's *got* to be it. She's afraid of what this would mean," he whispered, bringing the car to a stop. "This is dangerous, for all of you, Kara."

"What do you mean, Lorenzo? Have you heard something?" she asked.

"I know my mother. She will stop at *nothing* to keep what she has, and she must know who Uncle Henry married. Don't you see, Kara, it all fits," he said excitedly. "With this necklace, Kelly, your mother or even *you* can claim what is rightfully your half of the Carlyle wealth. And it scares her to death!"

"Did you ever suspect Kelly or me as being rightful heirs of the Carlyle wealth?" Kara then asked. "Is *that* why you followed me in the first place?"

"Honestly no, but I know why mother didn't tell me. She knew I'd *never* go along with her scheme," Lorenzo told her. "It's no more fair for her to have the wealth then anyone else, with the necklace. It was Great-grandfather's ruling and she does well with it until it threatens her position."

"Lorenzo, I found another bit of disturbing news in Grand-mother's journals," Kara told him. "She said that Henry was threatened because he married her, and he had to relinquish his inheritance. Did you know that?"

Again, Lorenzo stared out the window in silence, seemingly disturbed by this added revelation. "When I was very young, I overheard a family dispute between my grandmother Sabrina and my father," he began. "She was saying Uncle Henry was a disgrace and would not see *any* Carlyle wealth. I remember my father being very distressed, but no matter what he said, Sabrina wouldn't back down," Lorenzo concluded.

"What about your father? Did he agree with Gabriella on family matters?" Kara asked, wondering if *anyone* stood up to the Carlyle women.

"I believe they only tolerated each other, certainly *I* saw no love between them," Lorenzo confessed sadly. "Father died when I was nineteen. For many years he seemed depressed and I always felt it was due to Henry's death. Honestly, Kara, I admit it's quite likely Henry's death was *no* accident."

When hearing Lorenzo admit such possibilities, Kara felt a wave of fear wash over her. "If they killed Henry, they're not afraid to kill again," she said, thinking about Kelly and her mother.

"As long as I'm alive, my dear Kara, *no* one will harm you or those you love," Lorenzo said, reaching for her hand. "I *promise* you. I'd give my life for you, *please* believe that." As their eyes met, Kara once more saw the look of tenderness, and love.

It's hard to believe this man, the one I thought was evil and heartless, is vowing his protection over me. He's my relative, I must stop this from going any further. "How *did* Henry get the necklace to give my grandmother?" Kara asked, pulling her hand free of his and changing the subject. "Surely it wasn't just lying around somewhere."

With noticeable disappointment Lorenzo looked at her, then pulled his eyes from Kara's face. "No, from what I was told, Henry took it from the castle's vault. Once he knew they were going to disinherited him, for marrying a commoner, he got angry and took it, the most valuable asset anyone *could* have," Lorenzo explained.

"Certainly, after Henry died, my grandmother would be the most likely target wouldn't she? Do you know *why* they didn't go after her?" Kara asked.

"I'm not sure, perhaps she out-smarted the family's detectives, *or* the hit-men couldn't find her," Lorenzo replied. "It does seem unlikely however."

"Maybe I'll find those answers when I finish reading Grandma's journals," Kara remarked. "Shall we have dinner, or have you lost your appetite?"

"I must admit, Kara, I *never* suspected anything this bizarre, but it all fits," he told her. "Unfortunately, *nothing* my mother does surprises me when it comes to controlling things. Yes, I *am* still hungry," he said, forcing a smile.

As they again headed for the restaurant, neither of them spoke. Kara's mind was in turmoil, as was her heart. *What is wrong with me? He's my cousin, but why do I wish now we weren't related? Things really* aren't *what they seem, or what I first thought,* Kara decided, looking out her car window.

. . .

During dinner, there was no mention of the necklace or the Carlyle family. Instead, Lorenzo asked about Kara's childhood and her life's dreams. Suddenly he hungered to know everything he could about her. While she talked, he watched how her eyes sparkled and how her hair cascaded around her shoulders, even how her nose wrinkled when she laughed.

As he listened, Lorenzo wished he could take Kara away from all the turmoil that was sure to come. To love and protect her was his only desire.

"Lorenzo, when I was in the hospital you made some comments I wondered about. Can you explain what you meant?" Kara asked, studying his face.

"Such as: things aren't really what they seem, and I can sense things about people, are those the ones you're referring to?" he asked.

As Kara nodded her head, he began. "In case you had noticed me lingering around the Blue Lagoon and thought I was stalking you, I wanted you to know I wasn't, thus the remark things aren't what they seem. And the other is also true," Lorenzo explained. "I *do* sense things about people, their sadness, fear, loneliness. I watched you at work, and when you thought no one was looking, your face changed from a lovely smile to sadness. I felt you were carrying a heavy burden," he said. "Was I right?"

For a moment, Kara seemed to ponder his question, then she answered. "Yes, I *was* unhappy. I had cut myself off from my family due to my own stubbornness. It took the explosion to wake me up, Lorenzo. How foolish we humans are sometimes."

"Yes aren't we?" he laughed. "I'm very glad you've made up with your family," he added reaching out to pat her hand. "I wish I could say the same."

Both were silent as they finished their meal. For Lorenzo, he thought about his mother and what she might be up to. Certainly their last conversation gave him reason to suspect she planned something.

"Kara, I'm quite concerned about what Gabriella might do," he said, finishing the last of his prime rib. "She's quite determined to get the necklace."

"Why do you call your mother by her first name?" Kara asked frowning. "It seems so odd to me."

"I suppose due to our strained relationship," he answered truthfully. "She's never acted like a mother, nor do I feel she loves me. Somehow I got the feeling she had me around out of duty, nothing more."

"How sad," Kara replied, looking at him. "I'm sorry for that, Lorenzo. My mother is just the opposite of yours, I've *never* doubted her love and devotion. She loves me unconditionally, no matter what I do wrong she is always there ready to forgive me. That's the kind of mother I hope to be one day," she added.

"I have no doubt you will be," Lorenzo said softly, looking at Kara. "Well, I'm ready if you are," he then said, regretting to see the evening end.

When they stepped outside the restaurant, they were surprised to see it was snowing. *This will be interesting to fly home in,* Lorenzo thought, remembering the forecast for clear skies through tomorrow. In no time they were in the car and headed back to Romeo.

"What *do* you think Gabriella might try?" Kara then asked as they drove.

"I'm not sure, but when she called this morning, it was obvious she isn't giving up," he told Kara. "Will you come with me, Kara? Away from here where she can't find you?" Lorenzo asked. "She knows where you are, and she knows you work in Atlanta."

"What about Kelly? Or my mother?" Kara asked in haste. "We can't *all* hide like scared rabbits. And I refuse to be intimidated by someone I don't even know." Somehow Lorenzo wasn't surprised at her response.

"Obviously we have to tell Kelly and Jock about this. And your mother," Lorenzo told her. "We *must* be cautious."

"We?" Kara asked, "surely you aren't in danger."

"You don't know Gabriella. Since I've refused to help, I'm now her enemy," Lorenzo said sighing, wishing he could convince Kara to leave with him.

"But you're her son! Would she *really* chose wealth and power over you?"

"Unmistakably, you see Kara, evil knows no bounds and I've seen an evil side to Gabriella since I was a child," Lorenzo admitted sadly.

"Then who *did* show you love? Who nurtured you as a child? Surely someone did," Kara replied. "Otherwise you'd be evil too."

"There *was* someone who loved me, her name was Carlota. She would spend hours with me," Lorenzo said as memories flooded his mind. "When I was eight she died and I missed her terribly. No one ever explained who she was other than a maid who worked in the kitchen."

It had been years since Lorenzo thought about his childhood and Carlota. Tonight, when hearing Kara talk about her mother brought renewed envy, just as he felt when seeing Jock and his mother Cora together."

"I must say, Lorenzo, I was wrong about you," Kara admitted, surprising him. "I see a caring man, one who is hurting far more than I ever imagined. I'm sorry for misjudging you, can you forgive me?"

As Kara spoke, she reached over and laid her hand on his arm.

The feel of her touch and hearing her gentle remark would make leaving her tonight even more difficult. "Of course, but there's nothing to forgive. You had every right to think what you did," Lorenzo replied.

It was after ten o'clock when Lorenzo got Kara home. By now the snow was swirling, making it hard to see the roadway.

"You can't *possibly* fly out in this," Kara said as they pulled in the driveway. "If you don't mind a regular sized bed, we have a spare room you can have for the night," Kara offered. "Then tomorrow we can discuss our next move in this necklace dilemma."

When hearing Kara's offer, Lorenzo was delighted at the possibility of spending more time with her. And certainly, a plan of action was needed against Gabriella's fury. "Thank you, Kara, I am afraid I wouldn't get far in this," Lorenzo replied, seeing the accumulation of snow.

"Then it's settled, lets go see if Aunt Gina is still awake," Kara suggested.

"Please wait," Lorenzo said as he exited the car. Quickly, he went around to Kara's side and opened her door. After taking her hand, the two headed up the steps to the front door of the house. Before Kara could turn the knob, Lorenzo stopped her. "Kara," he said, taking hold of her arm. "I have to say something. I'm *sorry* for everything you've been through, because of me and my family. I'd *never* hurt you, no matter what," he whispered as he looked in her eyes. "I love you Kara."

Without hesitation, Lorenzo then lowered his lips to hers, kissing Kara with all the tenderness he felt toward her. At first he felt her stiffen in shock, then relax under his embrace as he wrapped his arms around her. Finally, she responded to the velvety touch of his lips against her own as she kissed him back.

When their kiss ended, neither one spoke, but their embrace lingered under the glow of the porch light. Suddenly, nothing else matter. Not the swirling snow or the recent revelations that brought uncertainty into their lives.

"What are we doing?" Kara finally whispered. "We're related, Lorenzo."

"Not enough to matter," he replied softly, resting his cheek against her hair. "Let me take care of you, my darling Kara. I can't imagine life without you, not now. You're the only thing that makes life worth living for me," he confessed tenderly.

Pushing herself from Lorenzo's arms, Kara looked up at him.

"There are so many obstacles, so much we still don't know," she told him.

"All I know is: I love you and I want you as my wife," Lorenzo said, brushing a snowflake from her cheek. "I know there are still some unanswered questions, but nothing will change my love for you."

At that moment, Lorenzo knew his life was changed forever. No longer did the Carlyle name bring honor or hold any obligation for him. Finally, at age thirty-four, Lorenzo Carlyle was free of the chains that held him. No longer would Gabriella dictate his life or make him feel guilty. Many people had helped to open his eyes, but Kara most of all.

On a moonlit night in Texas, she managed to pull down the walls he hid behind, revealing what he really was. Greedy, corrupt, deceitful. All the things she wasn't or never could be. Suddenly the blinders fell from his eyes showing the evil beneath the veneer of wealth and royalty. He would be forever grateful.

Chapter Twenty-three

When Kara crawled in bed that night, she knew sleep would be in short supply. Although she tried pushing Lorenzo's words to the back of her mind, she found it impossible to forget his declaration of love, or his kiss.

Then she thought about Ryan and his plans for their future. *Well, you wanted what Kelly had, two rich, handsome man, willing to give you the world on a platter. Now you have that too, so why aren't you happy?* Kara scolded herself.

Suddenly she realized it wasn't easy, trying to decipher one's own feelings. For the first time Kara understood what Kelly went through. *She loved Ned, but was* in *love with Jock.* "Who am *I* in love with?" she uttered in the dark.

As she tossed and turned, Kara's mind filled with memories of both men. The times they spent together, the way they each made her feel. As the night wore on, she knew it was impossible to analyze her own feelings. *Too much is going on. Our lives could be in danger; we've just uncovered Mother's true identity. How can I possibly think straight about this?* Kara lamented as she rolled over yet again. Daybreak was touching the horizon before she fell asleep.

. . .

"Hey sleepy head, time to get up. There's a mighty handsome man sitting in our kitchen waiting just for you," a voice coaxed as Kara became aware of bright sunlight on her face. "Coffee's ready, the snow is melting and it's a glorious morning, my dear."

Finally, the words registered in Kara's mind. "Oh, what time *is* it, Aunt Gina?" she blurted, sitting up in bed. "It must be very late," she added, briskly rubbing her face with her hands.

"The sun is well up," Gina replied, sitting on the edge of Kara's bed. "I'd love to hear about last night, but I *assume* it went well," she said softly, giving Kara a kiss on the cheek.

"Tell Lorenzo I'll be down in a few minutes," Kara only replied, still trying to clear the grogginess from her mind.

"That I'll do," the woman told her niece, leaving the room. "I'll keep him entertained until you arrive."

As she hurriedly showered, Kara's mind was again on Lorenzo and his confessions of last night. *I can't think about this now, we have to alert Kelly, Mother and Aunt Gina of the danger we're in,* she thought as she toweled herself off.

Moments later, after dressing in blue-jeans and a red turtleneck sweater, Kara gave her hair a few quick swipes with a brush. Then, pulling it back, she secured it with a gold clasp, allowing her long mane to hang down her back. Small gold earrings finished her attire as she glanced in the mirror one last time.

Then, taking a deep breath, Kara opened her bedroom door and headed downstairs.

. . .

Although he was enjoying Gina's company and his third cup of morning coffee, Lorenzo found his mind wandering back to the kiss he and Kara shared last night. While trying to concentrate on his conversation with Gina, he couldn't help noticing her sweet smile and perky personality. A moment later he heard Kara on the stairs, bringing him to his feet.

"Good Morning, Lorenzo. I'm sorry to keep you waiting, it seems my sleepless night caught up to me," Kara said apologetically as she approached him. "Did you sleep well?" Stopping in front of him, she reached out her hand.

"Good Morning, Kara," Lorenzo replied softly, taking her hand and leaning down to kiss her cheek. "I must admit my sleep was inadequate as well," he added smiling. "But, you look radiant as always."

Although hearing no comment, he saw a slight blush appear on Kara's face as she returned his smile. "I need coffee, Aunt Gina," she said then, tugging her hand free of his. "We have a full day ahead of us."

"Yes, dear, I'm eager to hear what you two have to say," Gina replied, filling a cup with coffee. "After yesterday, it's obvious we don't know everything."

"Lorenzo, would you please tell Aunt Gina *who* is after the necklace and why?" Kara asked, stirring cream in her coffee.

From the look on Gina's face, it was obvious the woman was bracing herself for more bad news. With his coffee cup refilled, Lorenzo began revealing his family's plot to retrieve the diamond necklace from Kelly. Quietly the two women listened. Only now and then did a gasp of disbelief escape Gina's lips.

For the next while Lorenzo confessed his part in the devious plan. Not only did he admit how he found them through private investigators, but how he set the stage to meet Jock and become his partner.

"It was all for our ultimate goal of getting what we felt belonged to the Carlyle family," he said, suddenly realizing how dirty and cruel it all sounded. "Because of Kara, I finally see how heinous and corrupt my family is. She opened my eyes to the truth," he added softly, reaching for Kara's hand. "Please, can you ever forgive me for my part in all of this?" Lorenzo pleaded as he looked in Kara's eyes.

"Of course," Kara whispered as her eyes welled with tears. "We *all* have skeletons in our closet," she added, grasping his hand with both of hers. "I'm just glad you're on *our* side now."

"Amen," Gina was heard saying, dabbing the corner of her eye.

When he finished revealing the ugly contempt of Gabriella and the way she manipulated him *and* others, Lorenzo somehow felt better. Telling the truth of his own actions helped to relieve some of the guilt weighing him down. "For the rest of my life, I'll do *whatever* it takes to protect each of you from that woman," he vowed.

· · ·

It was late afternoon by the time Lorenzo prepared to leave for the airport. After telling their guest goodbye, Aunt Gina excused herself, feigning an urgent need to drive to the store for a few things.

"If you hear or see *anything* unusual, please call the police right away, okay?" Lorenzo pleaded, studying Kara's face. "You can't be too careful, I know Gabriella and she'll stop at *nothing* to get what she wants," he reiterated, wrapping his arms around Kara. "I couldn't live if anything happened to you."

"I promise we'll be careful, but you're in danger too," Kara told Lorenzo, realizing for the first time how bad she'd feel if he was hurt, or worse. "Please be careful, Lorenzo, you're more vulnerable than we are.

Surely they know where your plane is, and where you live," she advised with concern.

"I'll be back as soon as I can, it should only be a few days," Lorenzo told her, still holding her close. "I'll be talking to Ryan and Jock, they need to know everything and if they decide against the merger, well, I can't blame them."

Then, releasing Kara from his embrace, Lorenzo looked in her eyes. "I meant everything I said last night, Kara. I love you very much. Yet, I know Ryan does too. The question is: where is *your* heart in all of this?" he asked, gently brushing a strand of hair from her face.

For a moment, Kara pondered his question. "At this moment, I'm not sure, Lorenzo. Truly you've both proven your kindness and at times have brought me great joy and excitement. Yet, I can't say its love, for *either* of you," Kara admitted. "Perhaps there's been too much going on in my life. First the explosion and my friends dying, then my new job; Kelly's health scare and now all this. I haven't had much time to analyze my feeling, I guess," Kara told him.

"I understand," Lorenzo whispered. "Just as long as I have a chance, that's all I ask. Goodbye Kara," he said, slowly lowering his lips to hers. This time, Kara had no hesitation in her response.

· · ·

With Lorenzo gone, Kara suddenly felt terribly alone. For a time she wandered from room to room, seeing the faded green sofa and the now marred furniture her father had painstakingly built many years before. *You had only the barest of tools, yet you cut and sanded each piece with such love and care.*

Oh Dad, so much of you is in this house. I can still hear your laughter and words of advise, Kara thought, fighting her tears. "What would you think of all this, I wonder?" she uttered, plopping down in the overstuffed green chair. *How do I decide, Dad? You always said I'd know when the right man comes along. Does this mean neither Ryan or Lorenzo is the right one?*

Due to her lack of sleep, Kara was about to lie down for a nap when the doorbell rang. Deciding it would be Aunt Gina with her arms full of groceries, Kara hurried to answer.

Instead of her aunt, two men in suits towered over her. "Good afternoon," one of them greeted. "We're looking for the owner of the

174

property. Would that be you?"

"No, actually, the owner is my mother," Kara replied, deciding they were connected to the sale of the place. "She's not here at the moment. Perhaps I can help you."

"And you would be?" the other man asked, peering inside the house.

"Kara, Kara Westin. My Aunt Gina will be home soon. She's been handling the business while—" Before Kara could finish, the two men reached out and grabbed her by the arms. In that split second, Kara knew who they were. "Help please, help!" she screamed as loud as she could.

Instantly a cloth was placed over her mouth and nose. A strong, sharp odor filled her sense and within seconds she slumped helplessly into the waiting arms of her captures.

. . .

When Gina arrive home, she was surprised to find the front door ajar and Kara was nowhere in sight. "Kara, are you upstairs?" she yelled after setting her bag of groceries on the table. "She must be in that dusty old attic," she uttered, smiling at her niece's tenacity.

For the next few minutes, as she busied herself with putting the groceries away, Gina couldn't help thinking about Lorenzo and his eerie revelations regarding his family. *They're a power hungry bunch, certainly no one I'd want to meet in a dark alley,* she thought, shaking her head. *We'll certainly have to be on guard, especially poor Kelly, she's the one with the necklace,* Gina decided as she folded the grocery bag and put it away.

Just as she started upstairs to find Kara, the telephone rang. "Hello," she greeted, glancing at the wall clock.

"Hello Aunt Gina," the voice responded, sounding upbeat.

"*Kelly,* how wonderful to hear your voice," Gina gushed. "How are you dear? Are you still in Texas?"

"No, we just arrived home and I couldn't wait to let you and Kara know my good news. My kidneys are *working* again, Aunt Gina!" Kelly blurted. "The doctors believe they've seen a miracle and we do too!"

"Oh Kelly, how wonderful, let me call Kara to the phone. She'll be *so* happy," Gina told her niece. Seconds later she was hurrying upstairs.

"Kara, it's Kelly on the phone. She's home and has some news to tell you," Gina called out. When reaching her niece's bedroom and seeing no sign of her, she then opened the door to the attic. "Kara? Are you up there?"

Only silence greeted her; not even the dingy glow of the yellow light was seen. Sudden fear washed over her as she remembered finding the door ajar earlier. "Oh Dear God, don't let this be true, *please,*" she begged, racing back downstairs. *I can't tell Kelly about this, not over the phone,* Gina quickly decided.

"Kelly, I'm sorry, Kara must have stepped out for a minute. But, please come over right away," Gina requested. "I know you must be exhausted, but it's very important that I see you. There's been some alarming discoveries in your grandmother's diaries and I must talk to you," she told Kelly, trying to stay calm.

"You sound upset, Aunt Gina," Kelly replied. "Are you okay?"

"Oh Kelly, I'm afraid it's not good news. How soon could you and Jock be here?"

"Right away, but is it necessary that Jock come too?"

"Yes dear, it is," Gina hurriedly replied. "Please hurry." When the call ended, Gina crumpled in a heap on the floor next to her mother's journals. Tears poured down her cheeks as she wailed in despair. Suddenly, deep in her gut, she knew beyond any doubt Kara was missing because of Gabriella's order.

Quickly Gina dried her tears. *Enough of this! We have to use our heads if we're going to help Kara,* she chided herself, drying her face. "I have to tell Lorenzo," she uttered, remembering the business card he gave her that morning. Getting to her feet, she raced to the kitchen to find it.

Frantically she searched the kitchen counter. At last she found the card and again headed for the telephone. *He won't be home yet, oh please, let him have his cellular on,* Gina prayed as she dialed the number.

"Oh thank God you answered," Gina blurted when hearing his voice.

"Gina, what is it?" Lorenzo asked with noticeable concern.

"It's Kara, she's missing! When I arrived home from the store, the door was open and she was nowhere around," Gina quickly replied. "I've searched the house and she's *gone,* Lorenzo," she wailed in anguish.

"I'm turning around, Gina. I've barely reached altitude so it won't take me long," he told her. "I know who has her. They didn't waste any time, did they," he said with anger in his voice.

As she hung up the phone, Gina thought about Emma. *How can I tell my sister her daughter's been kidnapped? And on top of everything, she has to be told she's a Carlyle, the rightful heir to a fortune,* Gina agonized as new tears burned her eyes. *A fortune that people are ready to kill for. . . .*

$\mathcal{C}$hapter Twenty-four

A new kind of anger welled up inside of Lorenzo; the kind he'd never felt before. Years of scorn and hate filled words had killed any love Lorenzo might have had for his mother, Gabriella. But this time she'd reached a new low, even for her. "You won't get away with this! Not this time!" Lorenzo screamed inside the cockpit of his Lear Jet. His body shook with rage when thinking of anyone having their hands on Kara.

He knew the scenario. Too many times Gabriella's goons had paid a visit to those she wanted to intimidate. Oh, they did their home-work all right. They knew what to say to put their unsuspecting prey at ease, then they pounced.

Oh Kara, my beautiful Kara, I'll find you, I promise. I said I'd protect you, but I failed! I should have insisted you leave with me, he grieved. *I knew Gabriella was up to something. She warned me. I should have* known *it would be you, since you're the most vulnerable. Where will they take you? Perhaps somewhere different? Out of my reach? But Gabriella will call, gloating at her success, I know her,* Lorenzo thought as he clenched his teeth in rage.

It was twenty minutes later when he was cleared for landing at Detroit's Metro Airport. Already a plan was forming in Lorenzo's head. Yet, he knew there was nothing he could do until he heard Gabriella's demands. *She'll want the necklace, pure and simple. But, she'll make me squirm first. She always turns the knife,* he thought, shaking his head. *Why didn't I see your rottenness before now? Because you are just like her,* a small voice taunted. "No, I'm *not* like her, not anymore!" he yelled with disgust.

Just as Lorenzo taxied his plane to the private hangers, his cel-lular phone rang yet again. He looked at the number, it was Gabriella's. Quickly he turned on the tape recorder attached to his phone. "You didn't waste anytime," he greeted, trying to contain his anger.

"You were warned, my dear boy. Now *weren't* you?" the woman taunted.

"This time you've gone *too* far, Gabriella," Lorenzo warned in return. "I know the truth, about *everything*. You lied to me all these years, but father was right. He said your schemes would one day lose their power and now they have."

"How *dare* you talk to me of such nonsense!" she blared back. "I hold the trump card in my hand. If I don't get the necklace, your fair-haired maiden will no longer have her lovely locks, nor will she be a maiden. I'm sure you know what I mean, Lorenzo," she said laughing the hideous cackle he heard so often.

"If you so much as touch a hair on Kara's head, you will rue the day you was born, Gabriella!" Lorenzo shouted as he ended the call.

In order to ease the rage that shook his body, Lorenzo closed his eyes and pictured Kara's face. He remembered the smell of her hair as he held her just hours before. He could feel her lips, soft and delicate as they met his.

Then, the vision was gone as he thought about Gabriella's threat. The thought of those hoodlums touching Kara made him shake with renewed furor.

. . .

While she waited for Kelly and Jock to arrived, Gina rehearsed how she'd break the news of Kara's disappearance. *No matter what I say, it'll be devastating,* she thought shaking her head. *And poor Emma, how can we tell her?*

When the telephone rang a short time later, Gina hurried to answer, hoping by some miracle it might be Kara. "Hello," she answered, holding her breath.

"Hello Aunt Gina," Ryan greeted happily. "How's it going?"

"Not too well, I'm afraid," she replied. "Oh Ryan, Kara is *missing*."

"How's she missing?" Ryan asked, his tone now solemn. "Tell me what happened, Gina."

Tearfully, Gina began telling Ryan everything she'd learned earlier regarding the necklace and Gabriella. "Lorenzo was right. That woman is vile and it's hard telling *what* she'll put poor Kara through," she said, choking back her emotion. "Lorenzo rescued Kara once before, so I pray he can this time, too."

"Rescued Kara? What do you mean?" Ryan asked, sounding

180

shocked.

Quickly, Gina told Ryan how Lorenzo pulled Kara from the rubble after the explosion months earlier. "He saved her life, Ryan, and then stayed at her bedside in the hospital for days."

"I wasn't aware of this," Ryan barely replied. "Thank you for telling me."

"I'm sorry Ryan," Gina said, hearing defeat in his voice. "I know you love Kara, so I'm sure this is quite a shock."

"Yes, yes it is," Ryan admitted, "but the main thing now is to get Kara back, safe and sound. I pray Lorenzo can pull that off."

Moments after her call with Ryan ended, Gina heard the door open. "Aunt Gina? We're here," Kelly called out as she and Jock stepped inside.

"Oh Kelly, Jock, thank God you've arrived. This is just *awful.* I'm so sorry to have to tell you this," Gina blurted, rushing to give them each a hug.

"Aunt Gina, what is it?" Kelly urged, taking hold of the woman's hand.

"It's Kara, dear, she's missing!" Gina sobbed, giving way to tears.

"Missing?" Kelly gasped, glancing at Jock. "What do you mean?"

"Come in and I'll tell you everything," Gina said after regaining her composure. "We know who has her, *and* why," she said, leading Jock and Kelly into the living room.

Again, Gina retold Lorenzo's shocking news to Kelly and Jock. Next, she told of the stunning discovery in the diaries regarding Emma being a Carlyle.

"This is *unbelievable,*" Kelly could barely say, shaking her head. "All this over Grandmother's necklace?"

"It's what the necklace stands for, *and* the fortune it controls," Gina said.

"Lorenzo was in on this?" Jock asked solemnly, speaking up for the first time. "Are we sure we can trust him now?"

"Yes, he admitted his part in all this, but I truly believe he *has* had a change of heart. Love has a way of doing that," Gina replied. "He loves Kara."

"Are you *sure,* Aunt Gina?" Kelly asked in surprise. "How does Kara feel about him?"

"I don't think the poor girl has had enough time to decide *how* she feels," Gina replied. "Everything happened so fast." Just then the doorbell rang. "Perhaps that's Lorenzo returning now," she said hurrying to answer.

. . .

Upon Lorenzo's arrival, he reiterated his shame for his earlier actions. "I can't blame you if you hate me and never want to see me again," he told Jock and the two women. "But, in any case, I promise I *will* rescue Kara from Gabriella, no matter what it takes," he vowed, looking at each one. "You see, it's Kara who finally opened my eyes to what I was. And, I didn't like what I saw. Gabriella is evil and I was becoming just like her, I'm afraid," he confessed sadly.

"Do you have *any* idea where they've taken Kara?" Kelly asked, fighting her emotion. "How do we even start looking for her?"

"I have one person I can trust, and he might know *something* that will be of help," Lorenzo replied. "He oversees things around the castle where Gabriella lives. Although he pretends to be a loyal servant, I learned last year he despises Gabriella for the beating she gave one of his staff."

"Are you saying you think they took Kara to *Scotland?*" Gina gasped.

"That's my guess," Lorenzo told them. "Gabriella wants her victims nearby," he added.

"You must call this woman and tell her she can *have* the necklace back," Kelly blurted out. "Nothing is worth my sister's life! We don't *want* her castle or anything she has."

"Yes, I understand," Lorenzo replied, "but I know Gabriella. She isn't about to let it be an even exchange, not now. She'll want something more, 'for her trouble' as she puts it," he added, suddenly feeling sick with disgust.

"But what? What could she possibly *want* besides the necklace?" Gina asked, studying Lorenzo's face.

"I'm sure she'll let me know in a few hours," he answered, knowing in his heart it could be of far greater worth than the necklace. "In the meantime, if you don't mind, I think it's best if we stay together, that way when I hear from Gabriella, we can decide our next move."

"Yes, yes of course," Jock replied, taking Kelly's hand. "Emma and Charles are arriving tomorrow, they'll have questions, so it's better if you're here with us."

"This will be a long night," Gina remarked, dabbing her eyes. "I'll fix coffee and something to eat." Leaving her husband's side, Kelly followed her aunt into the kitchen. As he watched the gloom settle over the two women, Lorenzo felt renewed guilt for what he had caused.

. . .

Desperately, Kara fought to escape the black hole that enveloped her. She knew she must. She felt horrible pain. It seemed an invisible hand was squeezing her head and she feared it would soon burst like an over-ripe melon. Beyond that she heard the distant drone of engines.

When trying to move she couldn't. Something held her. She worked to clear the fog from her mind, to remember bits and pieces.

Two men . . . grabbed me . . . why? Somehow, despite her violent headache, Kara fought for memories that lingered just below the surface. *A man's face, a conversation. She remembered screaming. . . .*

Although trying hard to retrieve more, Kara was too weak. Once more her mind and body gave in to the darkness coaxing her to its quiet relief.

. . .

Hours later Kara opened her eyes. She felt weak and nauseated, but her headache had lost its crushing grip. In the dim light she looked around the small compartment to see she was on the floor. *Am I in an airplane, or a boat?* She could only wonder from the steady hum of an engine and the occasional sensation of turning a new direction. Later came the familiar sound of skis against water.

"The Golden Goose has landed," a man said, surprising her. "She's tied and ready for the plucking," she heard amid a round of laughter.

That's me they're talking about! I have to get away, but how? Kara thought frantically as she tried to free her hands. *It's useless, I have no power over these guys!* she decided helplessly.

'Never give up, as long as we're breathing, there's always hope! God will never leave us if we trust Him.' Suddenly, her parents' words came to mind.

I'm sure God has forgotten about me long ago, she thought, realizing her carnal attitude the past many months. Yet, right now, Kara had to admit she had nowhere else to turn.

"Okay little girl, tis time ta meet the Queen herself," a new voice said just then. The engines had stopped. Except for the shuffling of feet Kara heard no other sounds. "On yor pins, lass," a man said in a thick Scottish brogue.

Suddenly Kara felt a firm grip on her arms as she was pulled to her feet. A bright light then hit her in the face, bringing pain to her still aching head.

"Ahh, such a pretty one ta be facin' Gabriella," he told her. "God be with ya, lass, cause she'll show ya no mercy."

Gabriella? Sudden memories came to mind. "Am I in *Scotland?*" Kara asked.

"I'm not at liberty ta tell ya, but ya'll know soon enough," the man said as he cut the tape binding Kara's ankles and wrists. "I'll get some ointment for the welts, lass, but it won't be right away," he whispered, glancing over his shoulder.

"Thank you," Kara replied softly, grateful to be freed. "What's your name?" she asked.

"Mitchell," he replied. "I'll try ta help ya all I can, lass."

"Hurry up in there!" a man yelled from outside. "We don't have all night!"

Just then, Kara's nausea suddenly returned. "I'm going to be sick."

"Here we come, but ya might want ta stand back. It seems the ride has made her a bit unsettled," Mitchell warned, helping Kara out of the seaplane and up the three wooden steps.

Just as she stepped onto the pier, Kara could no longer hold it. Instantly, vomit spewed like a fountain hitting one of the men with full force, covering his suit jacket and trousers in the smelly substance.

"Ahh!" he yelled in disgust, stepping back. Unaware of his close proximity to the edge, the man lost his footing and fell backwards, plummeting into the water. With twilight fading, the water looked black and foreboding.

In shock, they stood watching as he began thrashing his arms and legs amid the icy depths. "I can't swim!" he screamed. "Help me, please!" he yelled as he began choking. "*Please,* don't let me die!"

"I'll get help!" his cohort yelled, racing toward the marina.

"Throw him a rope," he ordered over his shoulder.

"Tis a pity, Gabriella is losin' her best flogger," Mitchell commented, his tone void of any compassion. Kara could only watch, hearing the man's plea for help.

Should I save him? Although he kidnapped me and brought me here against my will? If he drowns it's one less evil person on this earth, she reasoned. *Still, he is a human being and I am responsible,* her conscience blared. Just as she decided to dive into the shadowy depths, she heard voices behind her.

"Move out of the way!" someone ordered, pushing her aside.

Then, a younger man threw a life preserver out on the water. "Grab hold of it!" he yelled. A moment later he retrieved it by its rope and tossed it again. "He's a goner I'm afraid," he said solemnly. "No one can live long in ice water."

In shock, Kara realized she was responsible for someone's death. The thought made her sick. *I should have helped. I'm a strong swimmer. How could I just stand by and do nothing?*

"You caused this!" her kidnapper yelled in her face as he raised his hand. Before Kara could duck she felt a blow to the side of her head which sent her sprawling across the pier. "Just wait till Gabriella hears of *this!*"

Stunned, Kara could only hold her head as it again ached with intensity. *God, get me out of this mess! Please, don't let me die over here,* she pleaded, feeling helpless against such vile people.

"Twas an accident, pure and simple," Mitchell argued in Kara's defense. With a glare, the other man walked to the end of the pier and looked across the water. Then, unlike anything Kara had ever heard, the man let out a scream. An icy chill ran up her spine when hearing his tortured wail of despair.

"They were cousin's," Mitchell whispered, kneeling down beside her. Having dipped his handkerchief in the frigid lake, he now carefully placed it on the side of Kara's head. "This'll help till I can get ya some ice."

"Thank you again," Kara said, feeling grateful for the man's kindness.

Within minutes there was a hubbub of activity. Three men in wetsuits walked past her and headed for the end of the dock. Several vehicles arrived carrying men in uniforms. While everyone's attention was on the task of recovering the body, Kara glanced at her surroundings.

If I could just hide somewhere, surely I could find help in the morning, she reasoned as her heart began racing. Several buildings sat along the shoreline, none had lighted windows. From where she huddled near the seaplane, Kara counted six men now some distance away.

Although she felt dizzy from the earlier blow to her head, she slowly got to her feet. Now feeling confident she could make a get-away, Kara strained her eyes to catch a glimpse of her assailant. Mitchell, too, had joined the others.

Lord, don't let them see me and please help me find a place to hide, she prayed. Some distance away a sign read: Marina. Dozens of boats, covered in heavy white plastic, sat on trailers side by side. *Could I possibly get inside one of those? I can't wait forever, so here goes,* Kara thought, making sure no one was looking.

In the next moment she began hurrying toward the marina, running on her tip-toes, trying to avoid the clomping of her boot heels against the wooden pier.

Arriving at the front entrance, Kara glanced inside. She saw no one. Quietly she opened the door and went in. It was then she heard loud voices and pounding feet as the men ran after her. Fear rose up inside her as she frantically looked for somewhere to hide.

Just then she caught sight of a cellular phone lying on the counter. Hoping to later call for help, she grabbed it as she raced toward the backdoor.

The voices grew louder. Her heart hammered inside her chest as she feared the worst. She spied a row of scuba tanks as a thought flashed through her mind.

When the men came through the front door, Kara opened and slammed the backdoor, then darted behind the tanks leaning against the wall. "Get after her!" a man ordered. Quickly, her pursuers ran past her hiding place and out the backdoor.

For the next several minutes, Kara stayed quiet, straining her ears to hear. Then the men returned. "She can't be far so get yer lanterns and check every inch of this place! We'll find her and when we do, she'll be floatin' in her icy grave, just like poor Kenny," the familiar voice growled in contempt.

· · ·

As she waited, Kara was too afraid to move. Her body was numb from sitting in such a cramped position.

It was much later when two men returned. "Out-fooled by a young lass; Morgan won't be livin' this one down," one remarked as they both laughed.

"Tis sure we won't be gettin' paid fer our time," another replied in a thick brogue. "I have ta admit, I hope she gets clean away, serves um right. From what I hear, Gabriella will boil her own kin in oil if it pleases her."

When hearing that remark, Kara cringed in horror. *Poor Lorenzo! What price will he pay for rebelling against that hateful woman? Can't anyone stop her?*

"Have ya seen my phone?" Kara heard one ask. "It was right here earlier."

"Just give it a jingle, if it's around yer'll hear it," the other suggested. In fright, Kara hurriedly placed the phone on the floor and slid it as far away from her as she could. Seconds later a piercing ring filled the room.

"How'd it get in there? Maybe our *criminal* had it," he teased, entering the backroom.

Like a frightened animal, Kara held her breath. The man bent down to retrieve his phone as his eyes moved along the row of tanks. He leaned in, peering between them.

In the dim light Kara could see his boyish face and collar-length hair. The mingled odors of sweat and grime permeated her senses as he came closer.

Just when Kara felt sure he saw her, he stood to his feet. "We can go home now, Jake," he said, "tomorrow's another day and I'm tired."

Within minutes the marina was dark and quiet. *He saw me, I know he did. I can't stay here. He'll be back with more men to catch me,* Kara thought.

Cautiously, she crawled out from her hiding place, trying to relieve the cramps and numbness in her body. The only light was from the sign over the front counter. *I can't stay here, but what now?* she thought frantically.

For a moment Kara stood as her eyes searched the room. Then she noticed a beige telephone hanging on the wall. *Could I call Lorenzo? Not without his number, but I can call Aunt Gina,* she decided, remembering the business card he gave her.

She dialed the operator. "I need to make a collect call to the United

States, please," Kara said, glancing around. When the woman asked for her name and the number, she gave it and then waited. It seemed like hours before Kara heard a ringing on the other end.

"Hello, this is Jock," she heard a second later.

"I have a collect call from Kara, do you accept the charges?"

"Kara? Oh yes, yes," Jock said excitedly.

"Jock! Thank God I got through," Kara gasped as tears stung her eyes.

"Kara! Where *are* you?"

"I'm not sure, but I escaped those men, at least for the time being," she hurriedly said. "I need to reach Lorenzo."

"He's right here, Kara," Jock informed her.

"Kara, where have they taken you? Describe it," Lorenzo quickly coaxed over the line.

"We landed in a seaplane. One of the men fell off the pier and drowned. I managed to get away," Kara explained, glancing around. "There was a man named Mitchell, he was helping me. Do you know who *he* might be?" Kara suddenly asked.

"Oh, Mitchell, yes, if he was there, then you're near the castle, in Loch Lomond," Lorenzo told her. "What else do you see?"

"Boats, covered in white plastic sitting on trailers," Kara quickly told him. "I'm hiding in a Marina, but I can't stay here," she said, nervously looking around. "I'm sure one of the men saw me earlier."

"Perfect, Kara I know exactly where you are. Down the road is the Highland Inn. The proprietor is a man named Rowan, he's a friend of mine—"

"Someone's coming!" Kara gasped before Lorenzo could finish. "I'll try to find Rowan," she blurted before hanging up the phone.

Quickly, Kara stepped through the doorway to the backroom. Outside she heard voices; her legs grew weak from fear. *This is impossible! Dear God, what am I going to do?*

Just then a beam of light came through the window and swept the backroom where Kara was. In haste to hide behind a cabinet, she tripped over a box. In the light she could see what it contained. *Wetsuits? It is! Of course, they go with scuba tanks,* she reasoned, pulling one from the box.

Quickly, while keeping her eyes on the ones outside, Kara removed her boots and pulled the rubbery pant legs over her jeans. Next, she donned the top over her sweater. *This'll have to do,* Kara decided realizing the suit was somewhat too large.

Then the doorknob rattled. "It's locked, so no one's here," some-one said softly. "Now's our chance, we grab the money and run. I know there's no alarm," a male voice remarked.

They're burglars! Kara realized as she hurriedly stuffed her long hair inside the cap of the rubber-suit. A second later she heard breaking glass. A hand reached through to unlock the door just as Kara pulled on her boots.

Now dressed in the near-black wetsuit, Kara was easily overlooked in the shadowy room. She crouched behind the cabinet as the intruders passed by.

Seconds later, the two thieves were heard rifling the cash register. Just then, several bright lights suddenly appeared through the front win-dows.

"Come out with your hands up!" someone ordered with a bull-horn. "You're surrounded so you might as well give up."

A string of profanities and words of blame were exchanged between the two robbers before they did as they were ordered.

Just then two men came through the backdoor and immediately went to the scuba tanks and began moving them away from the wall. "I think the lad was dreamin'," Kara heard one say. "There's no sign of her."

Fearing the men would hear her heart pounding, Kara crouched in a fetal position on the floor, holding her breath. *Dear Jesus, don't let them see me,* she prayed, knowing they were barely two feet away.

"Well, which one of ya is a faired-hair lass?" someone out front asked as others began laughing. "It seems we have squelched yer plan fer the night, lads, but can ya tell us if yer eyes have crossed a fair maiden this evenin'?"

"No, but better if we had," one of the would-be robbers remarked. When hearing that, the two men near Kara walked away laughing.

"We'll be takin' a closer look, since she can't be far," someone commented.

I have to get out of this place before daylight, Kara thought, still unsure of what to do.

Chapter Twenty-five

After his brief conversation with Kara ended so abruptly, Lorenzo quickly told the others what was said. "She got away, for now. Kara's a brave young woman and knows how to use her head, but she's outnumbered. So I have to say, those of you who believe in miracles, keep praying. Perhaps it'll even up the score a bit," Lorenzo told them.

"We've no doubt about that," Kelly replied. "Is she hurt? How did she sound?"

"She's scared, of course, but seems to be unhurt," Lorenzo answered. "I'm flying to Scotland as soon as I can get there."

"Take my Citation X," Jock offered. "They just did maintenance so it's ready to go. It's faster and better for the long haul," he added.

"Thanks Jock, you're right. And I *do* need to get there as soon as I can," Lorenzo replied, nodding his head. "From what Kara described, I'm sure I know where they took her."

"God speed, my man," Jock told Lorenzo, offering his hand. "If we can do anything from this end, just let us know."

"Thank you Jock, thank you *all* for being so forgiving of my past mistakes," Lorenzo said, returning Jock's handshake. "You've shown true kindness and love in everything you've done."

"Please bring my sister home soon, *and* unharmed," Kelly told Lorenzo.

"I'd give my life for Kara," he said solemnly. "I love her very much." As he turned to leave, Lorenzo knew in his heart he spoke the truth. Without Kara his life had no meaning.

. . .

Fearing she'd be discovered if anyone came inside the marina, Kara inched her way to the backdoor, staying in the shadows. *Don't leave me now, Lord. Help me find that Inn Lorenzo talked about, please,* she begged.

As she got to the door, the broken glass from the break-in crunched beneath her boots. She froze with fear as she listened. Someone entered the front door.

"Come out with your hands up!" a man yelled as beams of light filled the room.

Without forethought, Kara opened the backdoor and started running. With surprising speed she raced down the graveled path behind the marina, past numerous boats veiled in their winter garb. Shouts of warnings were heard behind her. "Stop or I'll shoot!"

I'll not stop, you'll have to shoot me in the back! Kara thought in defiance. Just then a bullet whizzed by her. To her right was the lake, looking eerily dark under the half moon. *They'll think they hit me, or I've drowned,* she reasoned just as another shot rang out.

Taking a deep breath, Kara leaped from the path into the water.

. . .

"Looks like ya got her, if not, that icy Loch will make short work of it," the deputy said shaking his head. "Tis a pity fer such a young lass ta meet her end this way."

"Aye, yet no doubt better than in Gabriella's dungeons," the Captain said, holstering his weapon. "We'll find her body at daylight," he added.

"With ole Kenny drownin' like he did, and the girl givin' us the slip, I'm sure Gabriella would be floggin' us all if she had the chance," the deputy commented as they headed back.

"No doubt," the Captain sighed, realizing he would again be hearing Gabriella's words of wrath aimed at him.

"No meaner woman have I ever laid eyes on! I hear tell, even poor Lorenzo has a price on his head," the deputy remarked, letting out a deep sigh.

. . .

Within seconds of her plunge in the lake, Kara realized why Kenny had drowned so quickly. The water was frigid. *Without this wetsuit, I'd be dead too,* she thought, swimming underwater.

Finally, when feeling her lungs would burst, Kara surfaced. She could see the shoreline some fifty yards or so away. Two men were talking and their voices carried across the water. *Just as I hoped, they think I'm dead. Now I've got to find that man Rowan, somehow,* Kara thought, scanning the shore for lighted windows.

When she felt sure the men had left, Kara slowly started back toward shore. Suddenly she felt weak, her arms and legs drained of all energy.

Rolling onto her back, Kara began floating as she gazed skyward. Millions of stars danced against the night's black tapestry. Instead of thinking about the past many hours or the danger she was facing, Kara was suddenly reminded of another star-studded night not so long before. *Oh Lorenzo, will I ever see you again? And what will become of all this? Everyone must be so worried about me,* Kara thought, as she again starting swimming toward shore.

. . .

Flickering candles sat half way up the stone wall, casting eerie shadows across the three persons below. With her dark-green-caftan billowing out behind her, Gabriella paced the floor as her tirade continued. "What utter fools! Spineless incompetents!" she raged at the two men. "How *dare* you let her get away! Without her I'll *never* regain what is rightfully mine!"

"But poor Kenny was in the Loch, dyin'," Morgan argued. "How can ya expect us ta forget about him?"

"I expect you to do your job!" the woman ranted, stopping to point her bony finger in the man's face. "You find her! And *if* you fail, you *both* will feel the whip on your backs!" she blared, glaring at the men. With that, Gabriella stomped off through the darkened doorway.

As the two stared after her, they heard her footsteps echoing throughout the stone tower.

"Demon filled, that's all I can say," Mitchell declared shaking his head.

"Aye, I'm afraid I have ta agree," Morgan replied sighing.

. . .

After Lorenzo refueled in New York, he headed for Scotland. He was grateful for Jock's Citation X. *Intercontinental, it'll save time, and time is a precious commodity right now,* he thought, estimating his arrival.

"Hang on, my sweet innocent Kara. Just stay out of sight," he uttered softly. He had barely cleared the coastline when his phone rang. Since he was expecting another call from Gabriella, Lorenzo flipped on the recorder.

"Well, Gabriella, what a surprise," he greeted sarcastically. "How's every little thing going for you these days?"

"Don't be so smug, Lorenzo. I have an offer to make," she began. "Since I have your fair-maiden, I thought perhaps you might be in the bargaining mood."

"Gabriella, you don't *have* Kara, and I doubt you ever will," he replied. "Why can't you admit she outsmarted those goons of yours and you're left with *no* trump card. And if I have my way, the *rightful* heir of the Carlyle fortune will be in charge any day now," he taunted the woman.

"How, *how* did you hear such rubbish?" Gabriella fired back. "*Your* Kara will be in *my* shackles before nightfall, and I will see you dead before I'm ever replaced!"

"Well, Gabriella, I always thought you hated me, and now I know," Lorenzo replied. "I must say, you could take some lessons in motherhood."

"I'm *not* your mother!" she yelled back. The line went dead before Lorenzo could reply. Although he sensed it many times, he felt stunned.

"Then who *is?*" Lorenzo uttered as his mind filled with new unanswered questions.

· · ·

Less than a mile from the Marina sat the Highland Inn. Because of the dance the night before, its few overnight guests were still in bed. Due to the winter season the rooms were sparsely occupied, yet, a small band was made available by the generous proprietor named Rowan.

This morning, the forty-year-old American had awaken before daybreak. Despite his late night, Rowan felt a sudden need for a morning jog. After donning his sweat-suit and running shoes, he left his private quarters and hurried down the backstairs of his Inn. *This reminds me of my competition days,* he thought, recalling his stringent routine as a weight-lifter.

The air felt brisk as he drew in his first deep breaths. While doing his usual stretching exercises, Rowan debated where to run. *Up the road or along the beach?* he wondered. Finally, because of the fog moving in, he chose the latter. *I don't need a motorist hitting me,* he decided, heading for the water.

. . .

A warm hand against her cheek and a soft voice began pulling Kara from her deep sleep. "Wake up Miss, open your eyes," he told her. "What a lucky thing I happened along, you're freezing. Can you tell me your name?"

"Who, who are *you?*" Kara shivered, trying to clear her grogginess. Then, she remembered her circumstances. In haste, she wondered what she'd do if he meant her harm.

Amid the grayish morning, Kara looked up at the man. A dark colored stocking cap was pulled down over his ears. His face was broad and wore a neatly trimmed beard; his eyes were deep set. Quickly she assessed this one looking back at her. She felt she could trust him. "Please, I'm looking for an Inn. Will you help me?" she asked, trying to sit up.

"An Inn? Well, the only Inn in these parts is 'The Highland Inn', up the beach a short way. I'm sure they can accommodate your needs," he told her, taking hold of her arm.

"Yes, that's it," Kara said with her teeth chattering. "The proprietor, Rowan, do you know him?"

"May I ask what your business might be with this Rowan fellow?"

"He's a friend, of a friend; I was told he'd help me," Kara told the man, glancing up and down the beach. "Please, would you help me find it?"

"Of course, Miss. And who might this friend of yours be?"

"Lorenzo Carlyle," Kara said, trying to remove her water-soaked boots.

"Let me help you, Miss," the man told her, pulling them off. "We need to get you inside. I'll go get my car. It's too far to walk without shoes."

"No, no *please,* I can make it," Kara pleaded, glancing around her. "Don't leave me here alone. I'm in danger."

"What kind of danger, Miss?"

"I was kidnapped, and brought here, but I escaped in the water. I'm afraid they'll find me," Kara explained as she shivered from the cold. "Please, don't leave me."

"As you wish," the man said, helping her to her feet. "Lean on me and I'll try to keep you from any pit falls."

"Thank you, thank you so much, Mr.—"

"Just call me Rowan, Miss," he grinned, glancing at Kara. "I must say, you're the most remarkable surprise *I've* ever found on the beach."

"Thank God," Kara uttered as she hobbled along, using the man's arm for support.

Neither one spoke as they headed toward the Inn. Patches of fog shrouded them; only their unhurried footsteps over the rocky terrain broke the stillness. An occasional squawk from a water foul was heard in the distance.

When barely half way to the Inn, Kara's little bit of strength faded. "I have to rest a minute," she whispered, letting go of Rowan's arm.

"Have you eaten anything lately?" he asked, helping her to a large rock.

"No, not since they kidnapped me," Kara replied, finally pushing the rubber cap from her head. When doing so, her mane of hair fell around her shoulders. *That feels better,* she thought, resting her head on her knees.

"If you'll allow me, Miss, we need to get you inside," Rowan remarked. With that, the man easily picked her up in his arms and began carrying her. "I can assure you, Miss, it won't be long until you'll have your fill of a scrumptious breakfast, with plenty of hot coffee."

As she was being carried, Kara could barely keep her eyes open. Right now, she wasn't sure what she needed most. A hot meal or a nice warm bed.

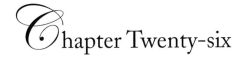

Chapter Twenty-six

With her sister missing and her mother and Charles due to arrive from Arizona this morning, Kelly had little sleep. *How do I tell Mother all this? And what can we possibly do to help Kara?* Kelly wondered, running a comb through her short-curly hair.

"Breakfast is ready my darling," Jock said, poking his head around the corner. "Did you get any sleep at all?" he asked, studying his wife's face.

"Not much, but I'm sure poor Kara got even less," Kelly replied, fighting her tears. As hard as she tried, she couldn't forget Lorenzo's description of Gabriella. "Jock, I feel so helpless, isn't there something *more* we can do?"

"I'm sure our prayers are working, sweetheart," he told Kelly, brushing his hand against her cheek. "God won't forsake her. Somehow I feel Kara is safe," Jock said, wrapping his arms around her. "I know it's hard right now, but we *must* keep the faith," he whispered, "for Emma."

"Mother has more faith than ten people," Kelly remarked, looking up at Jock.

"Yes, I know," he replied, "but this time she has a pretty big shock to digest. Not only Kara's kidnapping, but also discovering her true identity."

For the first time, Kelly wondered how her mother *would* take the shocking news found in those old diaries. "You're right as always, Mother does have a lot to swallow," Kelly replied.

. . .

For the third time in five minutes, Gina nervously glanced outside. "Oh Kelly, how will Emma take all this?" she asked, turning from the window. "She is so happy with Charles, but now this bomb is about to hit her."

"Emma's faith gets her through, and the love of her family," Jock reminded Gina.

Making no reply, Gina had to agree. Emma did accept things in stride, no matter what happened. *But this is different. We were lied to all these years, about so many things! And by our own mother,* Gina thought, seeing her mother's diaries neatly piled on the living room floor.

. . .

"Hello everyone!" Emma shouted a short time later as she and Charles came through the front-door. "What a lovely surprise, having you all here to greet us," she added, hurrying to give Kelly a hug.

"Hello Mother," Kelly replied, returning Emma's embrace and glancing at Jock for moral support. "It's so good to see you again."

For the next few minutes, hugs and words of welcome were exchanged amid tears of thanksgiving over Kelly's recent recovery. Certainly, Emma's arrival brought a surge of gaiety to the old house, although short lived.

"Where's Kara?" Emma asked, looking around. "Is that girl still in bed?"

"No Mother, Kara isn't here," Kelly said as her heart began racing. "Come and sit, we have things to tell you," she added, taking hold of Emma's hand.

"What is it dear, you sound so serious," Emma said, following Kelly to the wore-out sofa. Just then she eyed the journals on the floor. "What are all those books?" she then asked.

"Those are Mother's diaries," Gina spoke up. "They were in the attic."

"My goodness, I had no idea," Emma replied, shaking her head. "Go ahead, my dear, tell me your news."

Taking a deep breath, Kelly fought the lump growing in her throat. *Dear God, give me the right words,* she quickly prayed. Lifting her eyes to her mother's face, she began.

"Mother, we didn't have the heart to tell you and Charles this over the phone, but Kara is missing. We have reason to believe she's alive, but she's been kidnapped," Kelly informed them.

All color drained from Emma's face. She glanced at Charles across the room who was instantly at his wife's side, holding her hand.

"Kidnapped? But why? How?" Emma asked, glancing from one

to the other. "Tell me, tell me everything. I *have* to know."

"It's about the necklace, Mother. Grandmother's necklace," Kelly began.

"It wasn't just a gift from her fiancé, I'm afraid it holds much more importance than that," Gina spoke up. "Not only is this confirmed in Mother's diaries, but Lorenzo tells the same story."

"Lorenzo? The man who saved Kara's life?" Emma asked, looking stunned. "Is *he* the one who kidnapped her?"

"No Mother, but he knows who has her and he's on his way to Scotland to rescue Kara," Kelly informed her mother.

"*Scotland?*" Emma gasped, getting to her feet. "Oh dear God, why would that necklace cause *anyone* to kidnap Kara? Who would *do* such a thing?"

"Her name is Gabriella Carlyle," Gina interjected.

For the next while, Kelly and Gina revealed who Gabriella was and what part the necklace played in controlling the Carlyle fortune, including a castle in Scotland. As she listened, Emma nervously paced the living room floor.

"We'll give it back! *Nothing* is worth my daughter's life!" Emma blared, choking back her emotion. "Why didn't Mother's fiancé tell her about this? Surely *he* knew its importance when he gave her the necklace."

"There's more you don't know," Gina told her sister. "We found photo's, upstairs, proving that Mother and her fiancé, Henry Carlyle were *married.*"

"*Married!* Are you sure? But why would she tell us otherwise?"

"That we don't know," Gina said, glancing at Kelly. "And, we've learned other secrets too," the woman said, dabbing the corner of her eye.

"What sister, what *is* it?" Emma prodded.

"Oh Emma, Henry Carlyle was *your* father! Not the man who raised us," Gina explained through her tears.

Looking dazed, Emma only stared at Gina, saying nothing. Then she walked to the living room window and looked out. "I can't believe this. All those years Mother lived with this secret?" she whispered. "Not *once* did she hint at anything, but why? Sister, you read her diaries, did she say *why?*" Emma asked as her voice quivered with emotion.

"Oh Mother, I'm so sorry! What a horrible thing to come home to," Kelly sobbed, bolting from her seat and throwing her arms around the woman. Across the room, Gina covered her face in anguish. The men sat as silent observers.

Never before had Kelly seen her mother so distraught. Although she was always the calm, coolheaded one, Emma seemingly had lost her resolve. *Who can blame you, Mother? These shocking secrets hidden away in your own attic, and now Kara is kidnapped because of them!* All Kelly could do was cry as she hugged her mother.

For a time no one spoke. This house, that minutes before heard the sound of a happy reunion, was now shrouded in sorrow, *and* unanswered questions.

A moment later Emma began softly praying. For the first time Kelly heard the desperation of her mother's prayers. She sensed her faith and trust in a God who promises to see us through anything, no matter what.

"Lord, we love and praise You for who You are. We thank You for what You've done already and for what You're going to do. Please protect and deliver Kara from harm," Emma prayed in earnest.

It was barely a minute later when the ringing telephone broke the sorrowful silence in the room. From his seat, Jock hurried to answer. As the others waited, they watched as a smile slowly appeared on his face. "This *is* good news, Lorenzo," they heard him say. "Thank you, we'll be waiting, *and* praying," he concluded before hanging up the phone.

"Does he have Kara?" Kelly quickly asked.

"No, not yet. But he knows where she is," Jock relayed. "Thank God she's safe, with a friend of his. It seems the man found Kara on the beach, wet and cold, but alive and uninjured."

Words of thanksgiving and tears of relief were in abundance after hearing the good news.

"Oh that poor child," Gina cried, shaking her head. "She must have been scared to death."

"What is Lorenzo doing now? Is he bringing her home?" Emma asked from her seat beside her husband.

"When he arrives there he'll get a few hours rest, then he and Kara will head for home," Jock replied. "He said everything should work out fine, unless Gabriella learns of her whereabouts."

"Oh Jock, does Lorenzo think that could happen?" Kelly asked as a new wave of fear washed over her.

"He knows Gabriella won't give up easily, so Lorenzo is quite sure she'll have men out looking for Kara, and for him too, once he arrives," Jock said.

Just then Jock's cellular phone rang. "Hello Ryan," Jock greeted after seeing the caller ID. "Yes, Lorenzo called with good news."

For the next few minutes, Jock relayed Lorenzo's news about Kara. "I know, Ryan, but *someone* has to be at the office. I *promise* I'll let you know the minute I hear anything," Jock vowed. "And, when Kara gets back, I'll come to Atlanta so you can come see her."

After the call, Jock expressed Ryan's concern and frustration for having to mind the business. "He feels left out," Kelly remarked. "Any man would under the circumstances."

"Yes, especially knowing Lorenzo shares his feelings for Kara," Gina remarked.

"What do you mean?" Emma asked, looking puzzled. "Is there *more* I should know?"

"Yes, Mother. It seems Lorenzo *also* loves Kara. He made that quite clear, so I'm afraid Ryan isn't the only man smitten by my sister," Kelly informed her.

"Oh my, it seems to be raining pitchforks and hammer handles," Emma sighed, shaking her head. Closing her eyes, she leaned against her husband as he wrapped his arms around her.

. . .

When his call to Jock ended, Ryan leaned back in his chair and closed his eyes. First, he felt relief for Kara's apparent rescue, then another thought came to mind. *Lorenzo will be the hero, and what woman could resist a man who saves her life, twice?* he thought, recalling Gina's shocking revelation yesterday.

Why didn't *Kara tell me? Or Lorenzo? They both had ample time,* Ryan thought, remembering their many conversations. *He even stayed at Kara's bedside after saving her life, and now he's gone off to save her again. I see the way he looks at her, on every occasion.* "Who can compete with all that?" he muttered, feeling quite hopeless.

. . .

Due to Kelly's recent illness, Jock decided it was best if they went home for the night and returned the next day. It was well past ten o'clock by the time they left for home.

"I don't know about you two, but I'm going to bed," Gina told Emma and Charles a short time later.

"Good night, sister," Emma said, hugging Gina. "We'll talk tomorrow." Although making no reply, Gina's lingering embrace tightened around her. Then, with tears welling, she looked at Emma one last time before hurrying from the room.

"Are you all right, my dumpling?" Charles asked, taking Emma's hand.

"I will be," Emma could barely whisper, trying to smile.

"It's been a long day, shall we turn in?" With a nod, Emma leaned against her husband as they slowly headed for the bedroom.

Soon, husband and wife were snuggled in each others arms. As he often did, Charles began humming softly. With the tender melodious sound lulling her, Emma was soon asleep. However, an hour later she awoke with the shocking news from the diaries echoing through her mind.

Leaving her husbands arms, Emma rolled over on her side as she stared at the dim light coming through the window. *Why Mother? Why would you keep such secrets from us?* As she sorted through memories, Emma searched for a hint, a remark they might have said to reveal such secrets. She found none. *Dad treated me no differently than he did Gina, his own flesh and blood. And there was no hint of a previous marriage, even when you talked about the necklace, why Mother? Surely you knew we'd learn the truth one day. Is that why you left your diaries in the attic?* Emma wondered.

Suddenly, an overwhelming need to know the truth came over her. *You must have kept those aged journals so we* would *learn the reasons behind all this,* Emma decided.

Now, wide awake, she quietly slipped out of bed and donned her robe. Trying hard not to disturb her husband, Emma opened the door and stepped from the room. She heard the familiar creak in the floor as she slowly headed down the hall. Thoughts and questions tumbled through her mind. *Is Kara safe? Will Lorenzo reach her in time? Dear God, this is too much to grasp, give me peace about this,* she prayed.

As she reached the living room, Emma stopped at the doorway. The moon's glow filtered in through the living room window, casting an almost magical aura across the spacious, yet sparsely furnished area. Tears burned her eyes as she thought about life years earlier. *So much happened in this place,* she thought, filled with sudden nostalgia.

With the stillness of night wrapped around her, Emma sat down in her favorite chair. Although she planned to read her mother's diaries, she was suddenly amid a storehouse of memories. As though standing on the edge of time, she looked back to those days when this old house was filled with gaiety, *and* sadness.

What fun we had singing, laughing, celebrating so much in this place. Once more she heard the giggles and happy squeals of Kara and Kelly as their chubby little legs propelled them full speed down the sidewalk to meet their father when he arrived home from work. Like hundreds of times before, Emma saw Carl bend down and kiss his daughter's cheeks, then playfully chase them toward the front door amid more squeals of delight.

Vivid memories of Kelly and Kara paraded through her mind. Again she saw them grow from pudgy-faced little girls into the age of awkwardness with gangly legs and a newly acquired shyness. Then, seemingly overnight, they blossomed into statuesque young women with happy, outgoing personalities.

She thought about their family camping trips to the Upper Peninsula; picking apples and peaches in their orchard; the girls' adventurous high school years.

There was sadness too. Dad's Pancreatic cancer; Mother's stroke that left her paralyzed and unable to talk during her two remaining years. That was hard on all of us, Emma thought as a lump appeared in her throat. *Then, losing Carl to a sudden heart attack. Kelly's skiing accident that nearly killed her, and now Kara's kidnapping!* Emma shuddered. *Could this have been avoided if we'd known about the necklace?* she wondered shaking her head.

As she turned on the nearby lamp, Emma looked at the journals piled on the floor. Carefully she sorted through them, seeing the bright colored post-it-notes Kara and Gina placed in those they had read days earlier. *Just five remain, will I find my answers in these?* Emma wondered as she open the first faded cover.

With respectful awe, Emma's eyes were first drawn to the lovely penmanship. The precisely formed letters penned by this young woman who, years later, would be unable to hold even a pencil. Finally, blinking back her tears, Emma began reading the fragile and yellowed pages.

A finer man I could never hope to find. Although Henry's love and devotion has taken my life beyond my wildest dreams, I feel a cloud of uncertainties overshadowing us.

Threats from Henry's family has brought growing restlessness to my beloved husband. Although he tries to hide it, I see the frown of worry on his handsome face. If only they would leave us alone!

Not only has Henry lost his inheritance, but I sense more trouble brewing. I fear they won't be happy until we are dead. If only I could meet them, I would beg for their understanding and give back the neck-lace. Henry is adamantly opposed.

Only when I lie in Henry's arms do I feel safe and wish the night would never end. Henry tells me not to worry, but each day I see his growing concern.

As she read, Emma felt the torment being expressed. With each entry of those by-gone-days, a young bride's frustration was apparent. *Oh, Mother, if only you and Henry could have lived your life in peace,* Emma thought, dabbing a tear from the corner of her eye.

For several pages, the daily entry was missing. *Those days must have been extremely difficult,* Emma thought, pondering what had taken place. Two pages later it resumed.

We feel such torment I find no words to describe it. Henry's brother brings vicious threats from his wife, Sabrina Carlyle, the owner of the first necklace. As I lie in Henry's arms, I sense his deep concern for our future. Do I dare tell him my news? Will it add to his worries, or perhaps bring a smile back to his face?

I did it, I told Henry my wonderful news. His face beamed as he twirled me in his arms and smothered me with kisses. He is overjoyed about the baby. He tells me we are leaving Maine for a safer place. Henry says it's a surprise.

When reading this, Emma's eyes filled with tears. *How sad. These are my parents and they lived in fear. Is this Carlyle family a bunch of monsters? Are they demon possessed?* Emma reasoned with disgust as she resumed reading.

Such sickness I've never known, yet, in a few months we'll have our precious baby. Due to my nauseated weakness, Henry stays at my side most of the day. He is packing our belongings. He says we will drive until we find that special place just for us.

With each page, Emma felt more drained as she read the shocking details of this tormented past so long ago. "I must finish this," she muttered softly, seeing only a few more entries.

Today we cried for our baby. Henry and I fear he or she shall never have a normal life. How can we protect our child from such evil? Henry says we must move far away and change our names.

Now, closing the first journal, Emma gazed through the window to the moon that had inched its way across the heavens. *Henry Carlyle was my father, and he loved me,* Emma thought, suddenly longing to know him better. Silent tears streamed down her face as she thought about the parent she had never known.

Would you have told me the truth, Mother, if you'd been able during those last years? You couldn't talk, or write, so perhaps you wanted to, Emma decided.

Chapter Twenty-seven

At the Highland Inn, a half dozen guests still lingered in front of the warm fire. With breakfast over they now enjoyed their morning coffee. Some talked about the latest terrorist attack while others discussed the gloomy winter weather.

In the kitchen, the staff whispered about the pretty young American upstairs. "Ya heard the orders, if anyone comes askin' bout her, ya know nothin'!" Edwina, the head cook ordered in her usual gruff manner. "Rowan will have yer head if ya spill the beans," she warned, glaring at those around her. "As far as yer concerned, she doesn't exist, do ya *hear* me?"

With a nod and a quick glance at each other, the four female workers resumed their chores. No doubt the women found it all rather romantic. Not only had Rowan discovered the fair-haired woman on the beach, but had carried her upstairs to a room and gently laid her on the bed.

Then, after drawing a warm bath, he ordered Edwina to help the young woman undress and into the tub. It was hard for the maid to miss the strange looking rubber suit when she entered some minutes later to turn down the bed for their new guest.

In haste, Rowan had called the staff to the kitchen and instructed them to keep the woman's whereabouts a secret. "In her condition, she needs time to rest and gather her strength," he told them. "Her presence here is of *no* ones concern. Is that understood?"

Never before had they known their gentle natured boss to sound so stern. When a hardy breakfast tray was readied, Rowan himself delivered it to the guest room. From the hallway, two of the maids listened as he knocked lightly on the bathroom door, announcing its arrival.

Due to their curiosity and lingering near the door a moment too long, the maids were highly embarrassed when Rowan caught them eavesdropping.

Although she barely remembered getting there, Kara felt the warm water driving the chill from her body. Lovingly, the soft scent of lavender caressed her jangled nerves and coaxed her to that place between sleep and awareness.

Am I really here? Or am I dreaming? she wondered, remembering the icy lake and how she struggled to reach shore. *Am I safe now?* Then Kara remembered the man, the kind one who carried her. Just then a rap was heard on the door.

"Miss, your breakfast is ready. It's on the bedside table," Rowan told her. "And your bed has been turned down. You have a good rest and don't worry about anything, you're safe now," he added softly through the door.

"I can't thank you enough," Kara told him. Then a thought occurred to her. "Sir, I hate to impose any further, but would you please call Lorenzo? Tell him I'm here with you."

"I've already taken care of that," Rowan assured her. "He's on his way here to get you."

"That's wonderful, thank you, Rowan," Kara replied feeling relieved.

Although a bath had never felt more enjoyable, Kara couldn't wait to eat. Eagerly she dried off and wrapped the fluffy pink towel around her. The smell of food only heightened her ravenous condition. Like a refugee, she gobbled down the hefty serving of steak and eggs, slices of fruit and hot biscuits with butter. Food had never tasted so good.

It was barely ten minutes later when Kara finished her last bite and drank the last drop of milk and hot coffee. Then, after donning the flannel gown laid out for her, she crawled into bed. *Blessed sleep, thank God for blessed sleep,* she thought, closing her eyes.

. . .

It was nearly noon by the time the three men arrived on the beach. Although the fog had lifted, dark-gray clouds hung low over the lake, giving it an ominous appearance. Rain fell in a steady drizzle.

Now, with new information concerning their fugitive and her

possible gunshot wound, they expected to find evidence of her demise. However, to avoid another round of Gabriella's wrath, the men hoped to find the young woman alive, regardless of her condition.

"Take it slow so ya won't miss anythin'," Morgan told Mitchell and the rookie officer, pulling the cap of his rain-slick over his head. "Spread out and cover every inch," he added as they started walking.

As they began the search, Morgan had to wonder who he hated more, the young woman who caused Kenny's death or the woman who brought misery to so many lives, including his.

He was desperate to be free of Gabriella; he wanted to tell the truth about what he knew. But who'd believe him? She was La Gabriella, the Matriarch of not only the Carlyle fortune, but of the region. Everyone feared her for what she might do if they crossed her. Even the local authorities cowered at her demands.

"I found somethin'!" Mitchell called out a short time later. "Over here."

"Did ya find her?" Morgan anxiously called back.

"No, but it seems the lass is barefoot," he answered, picking up a water soaked boot. "It appears she took a dip in the Loch."

"She can't be far, not without shoes," Morgan said, looking up and down the beach. "The Highland is just up the road, she might have managed that."

"It seems a bit unlikely, without help," the young cop argued.

"Ya don't know *this* one!" Morgan fired back. "We'll be payin' the Inn a visit, and if nothin' more, we'll have a cup of coffee fer this chill I'm feelin'."

. . .

Although Arden, Loch Lomond had barely twelve thousand residents, Rowan had yet to meet Gabriella. And, after hearing of the woman's less than congenial personality, he hoped his luck continued. However, after making Lorenzo's acquaintance three years earlier, a strong bond had quickly formed.

Despite his happy-go-lucky demeanor, Rowan's six-foot-four, two hundred seventy-five pound physique of solid muscle had always been enough to squelch anyone from challenging his word. Today he had no reason to think otherwise.

Because of Lorenzo's friendship, Rowan felt honored to help in any way he could. *The man's in love, that's for sure,* Rowan decided, recalling Lorenzo's words of relief and gratitude. *Now, if my staff will just follow orders we'll have nothing to worry about and by tomorrow he and his lovely lady can be on their way,* he thought, entering his office.

With his desk facing the Inn's entrance, Rowan could easily see anyone coming or going. Knowing it would still be hours until Lorenzo's arrival, he decided to catch up on some paperwork.

It was just after one o'clock when three men came through the door. From his desk, Rowan watched as they removed their rain gear and placed them on a hook near the entrance. Then, quietly they stood looking around before whispering among themselves.

They look a little suspicious, no doubt they're the ones Lorenzo warned me about, Rowan decided, leaving the seat behind his desk.

"Good afternoon, Gentlemen," he greeted happily as he approached. "Come in and warm yourselves. What brings you out on a day like this?" he asked, watching their reaction.

"Tis business I'm afraid," one of them replied.

"What kind of business?" Rowan asked, noticing their eyes scanning the spacious lobby.

"Police business," the younger one answered, flashing his badge. "We have a fugitive on the loose. A young woman, fair-haired, slender built. We think she might have come here either last night or this morning," he told Rowan. "Did ya see anyone like that come through yer doors?"

"No, can't say that I have," Rowan replied. "Fugitive you say. What kind of crime did the woman commit?" he asked then.

"We're not at liberty ta say," the third man quickly answered. "Can we talk ta yer staff? They might have seen her."

"If I haven't seen your fugitive, then my staff hasn't either," Rowan told the men. "No one comes through these door without me knowing it. But, to satisfy your questions I'll round up the few that haven't left for the day," he offered, hoping his cooperation would hurry these men on their way. "If you'll have a seat, I'll bring them down," Rowan added, pointing to a sitting area.

It took only a few minutes to locate those who were finishing up their chores before leaving. Once more Rowan reiterated his earlier warning to keep their American guest a secret. Then, nodding their assurance to follow his instructions, the four young maids followed him downstairs to be questioned.

"We're lookin' fer a young woman, she might have a gunshot wound, but fer sure she's wet and cold," the older man told the young women. "Have ya seen anyone like that hobblin' through yer door?"

Standing nearby, Rowan watched and wondered how his staff might take such questioning. Quickly they glanced at each other. "No sir, we've seen no such person hobblin' through our door," one replied while the other three agreed by shaking their head.

For a moment two of the men glared at the maids with obvious intimidation. "Well, I guess that answers your questions, Gentleman," Rowan commented, ending the interrogation.

"The woman is a fugitive so yer'll be in serious trouble if yer hidin' her," the young officer warned. "That goes for all of ya."

"We'll keep that in mind," Rowan replied, "and if we see anyone suspicious we'll be sure to let you know right away. In the meantime, try to stay dry out there," he added jokingly while motioning for the maids to leave.

As they put on their rain gear, the same two men now looked daggers at Rowan, showing their obvious displeasure. A moment later, after the men had left the Inn, Rowan somehow felt he'd be seeing more of their prying eyes.

. . .

By the time Lorenzo landed Jock's Citation at the Glasgow airport it was nearly midnight. For the past hour he fought to stay awake. His neck and back felt stiff and achy. After calculating his sleep, he realized he had had very little the past two days and now it was catching up to him.

As he taxied to the usual hanger, Lorenzo felt uneasy. *Just my luck,* he thought, seeing Garrett, the mechanic he'd had an earlier run-in with.

"I heard ya left these parts," the man said when Lorenzo exited the plane.

"People come and go," Lorenzo replied, trying not to say too much.

"New plane?" Garrett asked, scanning the Citation X. "Tis a beauty."

"Yes, it cuts the air like a bullet," Lorenzo commented. "It's a fine plane."

"Are ya stayin' long?" Garrett asked, wiping his hands on a

grease rag.

"Plans can change, but I'd like it fueled and ready by noon tomorrow," Lorenzo told him. "That's all it'll need."

"I'll take care of it," Garrett said with a half smirk.

"Thanks," Lorenzo said, nodding as he turned to leave. A sudden knot grabbed at his gut. *I don't trust that man as far as I can throw a bull by the tail. He'll do anything for a quick buck and if he's a mind to, he'll call Gabriella and tell her I'm here,* he thought disgustedly.

Although he had spent many winters in Scotland, Lorenzo had never gotten used to the damp icy cold that cut to the bone. Tonight, the chill felt worse than usual as the wind whipped around him.

Twenty-one miles, that's all I am from my lovely Kara, Lorenzo thought, squeezing his six-foot frame inside the compact rental car. The insistent rain made the road hard to see as Lorenzo left the airport for his destination.

. . .

For a moment, when Kara first opened her eyes, she felt disoriented. Then, in the dim light, she saw the flowery top and ruffle of the canopy bed she slept in. *I'm safe now, Rowan rescued me. Lorenzo will be here soon and we'll be going home,* she thought confidently.

When she stretched her arms and legs, they felt stiff and sore. Closing her eyes, Kara remembered being so horribly cold, and hungry. *Thank you, God, for sending help my way,* she thought, pulling the covers up around her neck.

For a moment more, Kara thought about her ordeal and the men who would surely be after her. *Lorenzo will keep me safe, I know it,* she decided as she once more drifted off to sleep.

. . .

The longer Lorenzo drove the sicker he felt. His headache had worsened as did the stiffness in his back and neck, he felt chilled, despite having the heater on full blast. *I'm just tired, after some sleep I'll be fine,* he told himself. But as he drove, passing over Erskine toll bridge and then on to Dumbarton, Lorenzo had to admit these few miles never felt so long.

Although the drizzling rain had stopped, strong wind gusts pushed and pulled at the tiny European car, making the drive even worse.

I can't get sick now, Kara needs me. Everyone is depending on me to get her home safely. "I *won't* get sick," Lorenzo said out loud, willing it so.

Finally, he saw the last road sign taking him to Highland Inn; past the Marina, past Duck Bay. At last he saw it. With lighted windows and a sign out front, the two story Inn stood like a beacon of safety.

After parking and turning off the motor, Lorenzo leaned his head against the steering wheel, trying to gather some strength. If it weren't for the chilling cold, he'd have fallen into an exhausted sleep.

I have to get out of this car. Rest and warmth are just inside that door. Kara needs me. I can't let her down. I've come too far, Lorenzo reminded himself.

With chills racking his body, Lorenzo opened the car door and slowly climbed out. His head pounded, his legs threatened to give way as he headed for the entrance. Never before had he felt so cold, so weak. Then, just feet from reaching the door, Lorenzo's legs could no longer hold him. Helplessly he crumpled in a heap on the cold, wet concrete as everything went black.

. . .

Although he hired a front desk attendant during tourist season, Rowan managed the job in the winter. Rarely did a late night traveler appear at his door, but if they did, Rowan could easily hear the bell from the cot in his office.

Tonight, due to Lorenzo's intended arrival, Rowan waited up. "Where are you, my friend," he muttered, glancing at his watch for the hundredth time.

As he opened the glass doors on the fireplace to add another log, Rowan thought he heard something outside. He stopped to listen. *Just that blasted wind,* he decided.

A moment later, Rowan absentmindedly walked to the main entrance and looked out. "What the—" he gasped, seeing someone lying outside. Within seconds Rowan was beside the man, peering into his face.

"*Lorenzo,* can you hear me?" Rowan wailed, putting his hand against his friend's cheek. "You're burning up," he muttered in shock. When getting no response, Rowan quickly placed his arms under Lorenzo's knees and around his back, lifting him off the ground. Carefully he maneuvered through the door and then up the stairs to a room.

I'm sorry Edwina, it appears I'll need your help after all, Rowan thought, feeling grateful that his cook offered to stay overnight and help with Kara. For now, Rowan realized his Inn had suddenly become a place of refuge. No matter what, he was ready to do all he could to help.

$\mathscr{C}$hapter Twenty-eight

It was barely light when Kara was awakened by voices out in the hall. A moment later she heard a knock on her bedroom door. "Yes, come in," she called, quickly sitting up in bed.

"Sorry ta wake ya, Miss, but we have a bit of an emergency," a young maid told Kara, hurrying to a nearby closet. "Mr. Rowan is requestin' your presence down the hall." As she spoke, the petite young woman removed a long robe from a hanger and retrieved a pair of slippers from a dresser drawer. "Ya can wear these, Miss."

"Thank you, is anything wrong?" Kara asked as she threw off her covers and quickly put on the items handed her.

"You'll know soon enough, Miss. Please come with me," she told Kara.

As she followed the maid from the room, Kara felt stunned at such abruptness. *Is it Lorenzo? Or those men who are hunting for me?* she wondered.

They had gone only a short way when the maid stopped at a door and motioned for Kara to step inside. Although feeling puzzled, Kara did as she was instructed. When she entered the room, she noticed Rowan and a stout looking woman standing at someone's bedside.

"Please come in, Kara," Rowan whispered as he approached. "It's Lorenzo. I'm afraid he's *very* ill."

Feeling too stunned to speak, Kara's eyes darted to the one lying in bed. A hundred questions flashed through her mind as she slowly walked toward him. For a moment she didn't recognize him. *It is Lorenzo!* she then realized.

From the bedside lamp, a dim light rested on Lorenzo's ashen-colored face. *Oh Dear God, this can't be happening!* Kara thought, feeling her legs go weak.

"Have a seat, Kara," Rowan told her, taking hold of her arm.

"What, what is *wrong* with him?" Kara could only whisper.

"He collapsed outside last night," Rowan quickly informed her.

"We're not sure, but he came to long enough to say he had a crushing headache and his neck hurts. That plus his high fever, the doctor says it might be meningitis."

"*Meningitis?* Shouldn't he be in the hospital?" Kara wailed, feeling numb with worry.

"Yes, the doctor says he *should,* but someone has to be responsible for him," Rowan explained. "I know his mother lives nearby, but under the circumstances—"

"No! Not Gabriella," Kara blurted. "She hates Lorenzo and we don't *dare* let her near him. We just can't!"

"Is there anyone else?" Rowan asked quietly.

"What about his business partner? Would that work?" Kara asked, thinking of Jock.

"Do you think he'd assume responsibility? I would, but my cash is tied up in this place," Rowan explained.

"I'm *sure* Jock would, I just need to call him," Kara replied, getting to her feet. In no time Rowan led her into his office downstairs.

Despite the danger she could still be in, Kara's only concern was Lorenzo. Although it was the middle of the night in Michigan, Kara dialed Jock's number. "Hello," he answered sleepily.

"Jock, this is Kara, I'm sorry for calling so early, but—"

"Kara, that's okay, are you all right? Did Lorenzo arrive?" Jock hurriedly asked.

"Yes, yes he did, but he's *terribly* sick," Kara said in haste. "Jock, he needs to be hospitalized, but since he's unable to sign papers, they'll need someone who'll be responsible for him. Would *you* be that person."

"Yes, yes, of course, but Kara, what happened?" He wanted to know.

"I'm not sure, they said he collapsed and was unconscious; he might have meningitis," Kara informed him, trying hard not to cry. "Thank you, Jock."

"Kara, where are you? Are you safe from those men?" He questioned.

"I'm safe for now," Kara told him. "I'm at an Inn, the one Lorenzo told me about. His friend Rowan has been wonderful, but I need to go now," she told him. "I'll have the hospital call for your okay. And Jock, please tell Kelly and Mom to pray for Lorenzo, he's *very* ill," Kara said, choking back her tears.

"We will, you're *both* in our prayers. Kara, how can we reach you?"

"You can call here to Highland Inn, Rowan will know where we are," Kara said as Rowan handed her a business card. "Here's the number," she said, reading it from the card. "I'll call you as soon as I know what's going on with Lorenzo, I promise. Goodbye and thank you so much!"

As she hung up the telephone, Kara let out a sigh of relief as she looked at Rowan standing nearby. "Jock will take care of it," she told him.

"Now I'll call the ambulance," Rowan replied, putting the phone to his ear. After he had dialed the number, he looked at Kara. "Try not to worry. Lorenzo's a pretty tough guy, and I'm sure he'll be better in no time."

While fighting her tears, Kara said nothing. In her heart she felt unsure of Lorenzo's recovery. Then she thought about her own situation and the men who were looking for her.

Dear God, what am I going to do? I'm so afraid, for me and *Lorenzo,* Kara thought, heading back upstairs.

When she had reached Lorenzo's room, Kara found the same hefty looking woman at his bedside, placing a cool cloth over his forehead. "How is he?" Kara asked softly as she approached the bed. "Any change?"

"Not that I can see, Miss," the woman replied. "'Tis the fever that worries me most. How are *you* doin', Miss?" she then asked.

"Much better, thank you," Kara told her. "Please, call me Kara."

"And I'm Edwina," she said, "I'm the cook around here."

"Thank you, Edwina, for taking care of Lorenzo like you are," Kara said. "Have you known him long?"

"Aye, since he was a wee lad," she told Kara, glancing at her. "'Tis a pity ta see him this way, so sick, so helpless."

"Do you know his mother?" Kara then asked, wondering if she might tell Gabriella of their whereabouts. For a moment the woman hesitated as she seemed to ponder the question.

"Aye, indeed, I knew his mum," she whispered, nodding her head.

"Knew?" Kara asked when hearing the past tense.

"A pure gem she was, kind and caring, and she loved her little boy, that she did," Edwina remarked softly, brushing her hand against Lorenzo's cheek.

"Are you, do you mean, Gabriella *isn't* Lorenzo's mother?" Kara stammered, feeling stunned at such news.

"No, Miss, she is *not,* and tis time he knew," Edwina said. "No mum would put a price on her own child's head as that woman has done."

"A price? You mean there's a *reward* for Lorenzo's capture?" Kara gasped, feeling renewed shock.

"Aye, as of yesterday," Edwina said sadly. "Not only is he sick, but that woman has her bums lookin' fer him."

When hearing this latest news, Kara felt sick. *Dear God, what more must we deal with?* she wondered as she found a nearby chair. *We're both in grave danger, and now Lorenzo can't defend himself, let alone take care of me!*

For the first time, Kara realized, *she* now had to be the protector. "Thank you for telling me this, Edwina," she said. "I'm going to get dressed; I'll be going to the hospital too."

As she headed for her room, Kara felt dazed. When thinking of the reward for Lorenzo's capture, she felt an invisible hand twisting her insides. *With Lorenzo so sick we can't run, and what chance do* I *have against those horrible men?* Kara reasoned in fear.

When she reached her bedroom, Kara fell on her knees beside her bed. "Dear Father in heaven, I don't know what's going to happen, but we need You to take care of us. Forgive me for doubting Your Power, Dear God, for surely I have seen it many times. Please, keep us safe, Dear Jesus," Kara tearfully prayed.

Getting to her feet, Kara noticed her bed was made. Lying across the foot of the bed were her newly laundered blue jeans and red turtleneck sweater. "Oh, bless those wonderful maids," she muttered as she pulled off her night clothes. "I have no shoes!" she gasped, remembering her ruined boots. "Now what?"

By the time Kara had dressed, washed her face and hurriedly braided her hair, she heard noises in the hallway. Just then a knock sounded at her door. Rushing to open it, Kara was surprised to see Rowan standing there holding a box. "You might need these," he said, handing Kara the rather large parcel.

If only they were shoes, Kara thought as she untied the string. As she lifted the lid from the box, she caught her breath. "Boots, you bought me boots!" she cheered, throwing her arms around Rowan's neck. "Thank you, thank you so much," she said as she hurriedly tried them on.

Not only did they fit, but they were much like the ones she had ruined in the lake. "They're perfect," Kara said walking the length of the room and back. "How did you know my size, and amid this dilemma how did you even *think* about getting them?" she asked Rowan.

"Honestly, I'm not sure, the thought came to mind you'd need shoes and I just guessed at the size," he told Kara. "I'm glad they fit so well."

"I have someone watching out for me, there's no *doubt* about that!" Kara replied, looking and pointing heavenward. "And thank *you* for helping out with those plans," she added, patting Rowan's muscular arm.

"It does appear divine intervention has been at work since you've arrived in our fair land, my dear," Rowan agreed. "Let's just hope it continues. By the way, the ambulance just arrived for Lorenzo."

"Edwina said Gabriella has placed a reward for Lorenzo's capture, will the hospital be safe for him?" Kara asked with renewed concern.

"I guess it depends on who knows about it *and* how greedy they are," Rowan replied as they left Kara's room. "Gabriella isn't well-liked, but I doubt her money is rarely turned down."

When hearing Rowan's remark, Kara felt a wave of fear. *Isn't there anyone who can stop that woman from her evil deeds?* she thought with growing frustration. *Does Lorenzo have any idea Gabriella isn't his mother? And if she isn't, then who is?*

By the time Kara and Rowan reached Lorenzo's room, the paramedics were readying their patient and trying to get some respond from him. "Sir, my name is Ben and we're here to help you, we're taking you to the hospital. Can you open your eyes and look at me?"

"There's been no response since two this morning, only his writhin' in pain," Edwina informed them. "Nothing more."

Following a hurried glance at each other, Ben and his helper worked with precise movements to load Lorenzo onto the stretcher. "Who'll be meeting us at the hospital?" Ben asked, looking at Kara and Rowan.

"I'll be coming with you," Kara quickly replied, "if I may."

"We don't usually allow anyone to ride with us," Ben replied, giving Kara a quick once over. "Are you his wife?"

"No, just a good friend," Kara answered, feeling surprised at the question. "Please, I *must* go with him. He has no one else," she quickly added.

"Come along then," he told Kara. Just as they all started to leave the room, Lorenzo moaned and barely opened his eyes. Quickly, Kara moved close.

"Lorenzo, it's me, Kara. We're taking you to the hospital and I'll be right here with you," she said, taking hold of his hand. "You're very ill, but you're going to be fine. I won't leave you alone, I *promise,*" she told him, feeling a slight squeeze from his hand.

With great effort Lorenzo tried to speak. Finally, as Kara and the others waited, he choked out three words. "I love you," he barely whispered.

Then, with tears burning her eyes, Kara reached out and touched Lorenzo's fiery-hot cheek. "I love you too," she said softly, swallowing her emotion. Feeling surprised at her own words, Kara followed behind the stretcher as they took Lorenzo from the room.

Why did I say that? Was it only a response, or is it truly how I feel? Kara wondered. *I can't think about it right now, there'll be time later to sort out my feelings,* she decided as she watched the men load Lorenzo in the ambulance.

It was mid-morning, but the cold, gray day gave no indication that above the thick blanket of clouds the sun was shining. As she climbed inside the ambulance and sat on a small bench beside the stretcher, Kara took hold of Lorenzo's hand. It, too, felt hot and despite her slim medical knowledge, Kara became aware of his rapid but shallow breathing.

"It's okay, Lorenzo," she whispered. "I'm here with you, no matter what, we're in this together," she said, gently touching his cheek with her hand.

For the first time, Kara felt this was where she belonged, at Lorenzo's side. As she watched his face grimace with pain and heard his jagged breathing, something touched her heart. *Is this love, or just pity for his miserable condition?* Kara asked herself. For now, she had no time to sort it out. Instead she thought about the easy target she had become. *Will someone find us and turn us over to Gabriella and her henchmen, or can we escape her grasp again?*

After Ben radioed ahead regarding their patent and their esti-mated time of arrival at the hospital, the driver pulled from the Highland's entrance and onto the road. Ben was in the back with Lorenzo and Kara.

"You aren't from around here, are you?" he asked Kara, surprising her.

"No, I'm an American," she replied. "I've never been to Scotland before, until recently."

"You're the woman everyone is looking for, the one who outsmarted Morgan and his puppet cops," he told Kara smiling. Feeling stunned, Kara could only look back at him, wondering how he knew so much.

"*Please,* you won't tell, will you?" Kara begged. "They kidnapped me and brought me here for ransom. I barely escaped, but they're looking for me and if they find me it's hard telling what Gabriella will do to me *and* poor Lorenzo," she explained. "If you'll help us, I can assure you a most generous reward."

"How generous? From what I hear, that Gabriella woman is offering a pretty hefty sum herself," he told Kara after taking Lorenzo's blood pressure.

"We'll double it, *whatever* it is," Kara quickly promised. For a moment, while he started an IV in Lorenzo's arm, Ben was silent.

Finally he spoke. "There's not much I can do for you, Miss. If I could I'd help you, without *any* reward, but Morgan has his cronies everywhere."

"Do you mean the people working in the hospital will tell Morgan about Lorenzo being a patient?" Kara wailed. "If they do, we'll be helpless! I can't run and leave Lorenzo and he's too sick to go *anywhere.*"

"I'm afraid you're right," Ben replied, nodding his head. "But perhaps if you disguise yourself some way you won't fit the description so well."

"Disguise? But how, with what?" Kara asked, looking around the vehicle. "Can you help me find something?"

For a moment, Ben studied Kara. Then, reaching inside a small cabinet he retrieved a cap. "Here, put this on," he told her.

Doing as instructed, Kara twisted her braid atop her head and covered it with the dark blue cap, pulling it low over her forehead. "Thank you so much. This will certainly help," Kara told him, realizing she wore the same clothes as when they kidnapped her. "Do you have a spare shirt around here somewhere?"

"I'm afraid not, Miss. I wish I could do more, but I *will* keep my ears open," Ben assured Kara. "Morgan is a bully and he works for the meanest woman on earth, so I'll try to warn you if I hear anything," he told her.

As they drove, Kara's mind filled with possible scenarios. *We're both so vulnerable, what are we walking in to?*

"Okay, Miss, here's the hospital and it's a good thing. I'm afraid your friend has reached the critical stage."

When hearing that, Kara filled with despair. *Lorenzo is deathly ill, I have no money, no car, no friends to call, and I could be recognized in five minutes and carried off to Gabriella's fortress. Dear Lord, if You get us out of this mess, I'll never complain again,* Kara vowed as she watched the men hurriedly unloaded Lorenzo from the ambulance.

With a tug, Kara pulled the cap lower over her forehead as she followed behind Lorenzo's stretcher. Taking a deep breath, she squared her shoulders as they stepped through the doors of the small hospital. At that moment, Kara felt certain danger lurked just around the corner, yet, there was nothing she could do but wait and see. . . .

$\mathcal{C}$hapter Twenty-nine

Upon their arrival, Kara was told she needed to see the front office girl to admit Lorenzo. Soon she was being questioned by a young woman regarding her own name, the patient and the one responsible for expenses. Because Ben assessed Lorenzo's condition as critical, the patient was hurriedly taken away down the hall and through double doors.

After giving Jock's name and telephone number to the admitting girl, Kara was told to step to the next window. There she was greeted by a stern-looking middle-aged woman. When seated, Kara sensed the woman's immediate dislike of her as she roughly flipped through the pages of information. When she got to the one containing Lorenzo's name, the woman's rather beady eyes looked over the top of her glasses at Kara with a scrutinizing glare.

"What relation are *you* to this man?" she asked sharply.

"We're friends," Kara replied, feeling sure this woman could pass for a Nazi interrogator.

"You are obviously American, where are you staying?" she then asked in the same angry tone all the while staring at Kara.

A sudden alarm went off in Kara's head when hearing such an irrelevant question. "No place in particular," she answered. "I'll be going home to the United States very soon," she quickly added.

"So, you are a vagrant," the woman snapped as her lips puckered in a pious expression. "There are *laws* against such wanderings."

"I'm not loitering, nor is my *wandering* anything for you to be concerned about," Kara fired back. "I can assure you, my friend *and* I will be out of here the minute he can travel."

As though she had been slapped, the woman stiffened her back and pulled her chin against her chest. "We'll see about that!" she huffed, bolting from her chair. Feeling disgust at such rudeness, Kara watched the woman stomp off down the hall and disappear inside a room.

While staring after her, Kara already regretted her quick temper.

Why can't I keep my big mouth shut! she lamented. *I bet she's going to call Gabriella right now and tell her we're here. Now what?* Kara wondered, slumping back in her chair. Glancing around, she saw two women nearby who had obviously overheard the heated exchange. When Kara looked their way, they quickly lowered their eyes and mumbled something to each other.

I need a restroom, maybe I'll hide in there for awhile, Kara thought leaving her seat. With the nurses station at the far end of the hall from where she was, Kara looked for the familiar sign: Restroom . . . Women. Gratefully, she found one a few doors down the corridor.

For such a small hospital, Kara was quite surprised to see the large, almost elegant, restroom and lounge. A small pink sofa and several matching chairs were in the powder room as well as a mirrored wall. For the first time she got a glimpse of herself wearing the cap. *Wow, I do look different!* Under most circumstances, Kara would have laughed at the vision looking back at her, but not this time. Instead, she felt desperation weighing her down.

As she entered one of the stalls to use the toilet, Kara could no longer contain her emotion. Silently, in the confines of that tiny cubicle, she let the tears roll freely down her face. She cried for Lorenzo whose illness had taken him beyond knowing or caring what danger lurked nearby. Gallantly, his body struggled with an unknown invader, yet, if Gabriella found him, Kara feared Lorenzo would have an equally dangerous enemy to overcome.

Now I've made things worse by losing my temper with that woman! If they come here looking for us, it'll be my fault, I'm to blame! Kara sobbed. *What can I do? I'm helpless against such vile people. David was just a boy against a giant, Daniel had to face hungry lions, yet they weren't defeated.* Suddenly, Kara was reminded of the Bible stories she'd heard so often in Sunday School and from stories her parents read to her and Kelly at bedtime.

"With Your help, Lord, we'll get through this too," Kara whispered, drying her tears on her sleeve. *When God is for us . . . who can be against us? No enemy shall prevail against me!* Over and over in her head, Kara repeated the Bible verses she'd learned so many years before.

Moments earlier Kara had felt defeated and desperately alone, but now a renewed confidence welled up inside her. *I won't be afraid! I will not fear!* she vowed. *The Lord is on our side and besides, Mother, Kelly and everyone is praying. So Gabriella doesn't have a chance of winning.*

· · ·

Three hours had passed since their arrival at the hospital and still Kara had not seen Lorenzo. Although feeling frustrated, she vowed *nothing* would cause her to lose her temper. Having asked to see Lorenzo, she was told he was having tests and the doctor would talk to her when he could. So she waited. Although pretending to read a magazine, Kara was keeping a constant vigil of those arriving through the front door.

Adding to her uncertainties was her gnawing hunger. With no money, the vending machines were of no use to her. As she sat waiting, Kara saw people coming and going, but rarely did anyone give her more than a passing glance.

Slowly the minutes ticked by, then another hour passed. When her frustrations had reached a breaking point, Kara finally saw the doctor heading her way. His white lab coat was in stark contrast to his Scottish red hair.

"I'm Dr. Lennox and you are—"

"Kara Westin," she replied, reaching for his extended hand. "How is Lorenzo?"

"Very sick, I'm afraid," he told Kara, sitting down beside her. "The tests confirm our suspicions of Viral Meningitis."

"What can you do? From what I've heard antibiotics won't work, so then what?" Kara asked, feeling panic growing inside her.

"Rest, lots of rest," the doctor told her. "We're building up his immune system so it can fight it off. And we're keeping him sedated."

"May I please see him?"

"He's sleeping, but I'll take you," the doctor replied in a kindly manner.

Saying nothing, the two walked down the hall to the Intensive Care Unit and in no time, Kara was standing at Lorenzo's bedside. After checking the chart, doctor Lennox left Kara alone with his patient.

In silence Kara looked at Lorenzo. She felt relieved to hear a more steady rhythm in his breathing. A peaceful look was on his face. Gently she reached out her hand and laid it over his, wondering at the tears filling her eyes.

For the first time, Kara had to believe what her heart was telling her. Suddenly she realized how desperately she'd miss him if he were to die. "I love you, Lorenzo," she whispered. "You *must* get well, we have so much living ahead of us, *please,* don't leave me."

With her other hand, Kara carefully brushed a lock of Lorenzo's hair from his forehead. Now, as she touched his feverish brow, Kara knew she could no longer deny her feelings. *I haven't given poor Ryan a thought. Did it take all this to wake me up to real love?*

"Miss, you have a telephone call," a young nurse informed Kara. "There's a telephone just through that door," she said, pointing.

"Thank you," Kara replied, deciding it must be Jock calling. Although hating to leave Lorenzo, she was eager to hear a friendly voice.

"Hello, this is Kara," she greeted.

"Well, welcome to Scotland, Miss Westin," a voice cackled on the other end. "I hear you are baby-sitting my son while he's ill."

Gabriella! Panic gripped Kara's throat. Frantically she searched for something to say back at this woman who was bringing so much pain to her family. "I hear Lorenzo *isn't* your son," Kara blared. "So why can't you leave him *and* my family alone?"

"Oh, I see Lorenzo has found himself a feisty one," Gabriella smirked. "Well, I have ways of taming the likes of you, so I'm looking forward to having some more, fun, shall we say? I'll be seeing you soon, my dear, so there's no use running away," she laughed as she hung up in Kara's ear.

Desperately, Kara wondered what to do. *I can't leave Lorenzo, but here Gabriella's men are sure to find me. So what now?* Just then she saw Dr. Lennox step through a doorway. Her heart raced as she headed toward him.

"Dr. Lennox, please, may I have a word with you?" Kara asked, scanning her surroundings. "It's very urgent."

"Of course, come this way," he told Kara.

Once inside a small office, Kara hurriedly told him about Gabriella and her connection to Lorenzo. She explained how the two men would be trying to catch her and would harm her and Lorenzo. "I got away once, but with Lorenzo so sick I hate to leave him," Kara said. "If I *have* to run is there a security guard to keep watch over Lorenzo? He *must* be protected."

"I've heard of this woman, but certainly she'd never be so brazen as to harm a patient undergoing treatment," he said, shaking his head. "That could get her arrested."

"Not when the cops are on her payroll," Kara quickly replied.

"At least the ones around here don't mind if she breaks the law, even when trying to kill me."

"Unfortunately, I've been to London on sabbatical, so I'm not aware of who or *what* she controls," he told Kara. "I'll do all I can to make sure Lorenzo is not harmed. And now, you must try to avoid these people," he added, opening the door to the office. "I'm sorry you've had to endure such treatment at the hands of my countrymen."

"Yes, thank you," Kara told the doctor before stepping into the hall. Quickly, she looked up and down the corridor scanning for suspicious looking men. *I have to call Jock and let him know what's going on,* she thought, heading for the telephone she'd used earlier.

It was only a few minutes until the operator had Jock on the line, asking if he'd accept charges. Then they were connected.

"Kara how are things going?" Jock quickly asked.

"Not so good, I'm afraid. Gabriella knows where we are. Obviously someone here told her about Lorenzo and she called *me!* She as much as told me her hit-men are coming after me and there's nothing I can do about it," Kara quickly informed Jock. "I *hate* to leave Lorenzo, but if I don't run, they'll have me. Hard telling what Gabriella will do if she gets her hands on me."

"Do you have *anywhere* to hide? Can Rowan help you?" Jock asked.

"Rowan isn't here and we're miles from the Inn. I'm not sure where we are exactly," Kara told him "We're near Loch Lomond, that's all I know for sure."

"How is Lorenzo? Will he be better soon?" Jock wanted to know.

"He's got Viral Meningitis and he's very ill, Jock. The doctor says he needs lots of rest so they're keeping him sedated. He isn't aware of *anything* and I'm so worried about him," Kara said as her voice broke. The line was silent as Kara regained her composure. "I have to go, but if you don't hear from me by tomorrow morning, you'll know Gabriella has me," Kara told him.

"Be safe, Kara. I've got the hospital's number so I'll call and check on Lorenzo. When you call, I'll let you know how he is," Jock hurriedly said. "Go Kara, find somewhere to hide. God be with you."

In haste, Kara ended the call and headed for the women's restroom. *Surely they won't come in there looking for me,* she thought, glancing up and down the hall one last time. Just before she ducked inside, Kara saw two men coming through the front door. Her heart nearly stopped when she recognized the one called Morgan. *I'm sure they didn't see me, so I'll stay in here all night,* she decided. *But that woman, she's the squealer so* she'll *come looking for me,* Kara reasoned, feeling renewed panic.

A young woman and a little girl were just leaving when Kara entered. Now with the restroom empty of people, Kara hurried to the stall at the far end. *Well, this in home for tonight,* she thought, locking the door.

It had been more than twenty-four hours since Kara had eaten. Hunger gnawed at her stomach and her head felt achy. *Oh, what I wouldn't do for a nice juicy hamburger, or even a dried-out sandwich,* she thought, wondering when her next meal might be.

When she heard anyone come in, Kara held her breath as she waited. Not until she heard conversation or someone using the toilet did she let out a sigh of relief. The minutes ticked slowly by as she sat listening, waiting.

As she sat in her tiny metal cage, Kara suddenly realized how hilariously funny this all was. *I can just hear Mother and Aunt Gina laughing about this, me sitting on a toilet all night, hiding,* Kara thought, wondering if she would ever get the chance to tell them about it.

Now, with time on her hands, Kara let her mind wander, trying to forget the danger she was in. She thought about her mother and Aunt Gina and how worried they must be. Thoughts of home were comforting as she lulled herself with memories. While she was thinking about Kelly and the closeness they shared, Kara suddenly became aware of someone in the room.

She froze. Then she knew. *She's here! That woman is looking for me,* Kara thought as her heart began pounding. One by one the stall doors were pushed open as footsteps came closer.

Frantically, Kara climbed atop the toilet seat, readying herself to leap if the woman managed to undo the latch. Then it was Kara's cubicle being pushed. *Dear God, help me!* she pleaded, knowing she'd been discovered.

Just then a woman yelled. "This is the women's restroom. Get out of here you pervert! Get out before I call security!" she ordered loudly.

With a string of obscenities the man left. *It wasn't the woman at all, it was Morgan,* Kara thought, climbing off the toilet seat. Knowing she must leave, Kara unlocked the door and slowly opened it. *He's gone, but he's waiting outside. When this woman leaves he'll be back,* she reasoned, leaving the stall.

A moment later, an attractive silver-haired woman exited the cubicle and looked at Kara. "Did you see that man?" she asked as she headed for a sink. "Of all places for a weirdo, in a hospital!" she ranted while washing her hands.

"Thank you Ma'am, for what you did," Kara began, glancing at the door. "You just saved my life. That man is after *me.* He kidnapped me and I escaped, but he and his partner are determined to catch me. He found my hiding place just before you came in and now he's waiting outside. Would you please help me?" Kara begged, not knowing what the woman could do.

"Are you serious? That man *kidnapped* you?" the woman wailed with eyes wide in shock. "Honey, I don't have a thimble full of respect for a man who harms a woman so you *bet* I'll help!"

"Thank you, thank you *so* much!" Kara said. "I'm not sure what you can do, but I need to get away from here. I came with a friend who's very ill. I hate to leave him, but I can't stay here, not now."

"Well, I have a big burly husband waiting right outside and if I tell him that man is trying to hurt a pretty young gal like you, he'll make mincemeat out of him," the woman told Kara. "So, we're going to walk right out of here and out to our car. Then, we'll take you anywhere you need to go," she added, taking hold of Kara's arm.

"Thank you, Lord!" Kara uttered softly as they headed for the door.

Sure enough, when they stepped from the restroom, Kara saw the biggest man she had seen in a very long time leaning against the wall, waiting. Not fat by any means, the man was tall and broad-shouldered. His powerful chest and arms bulged beneath the beige colored sweater he wore. When seeing them, he smiled and headed their way.

"Bran, sweetheart, we're going to help this young lady," she said softly, glancing around. "She's in danger and we must get her *out* of here."

For a moment he studied Kara's face saying nothing. "If you say so," he answered, smiling at his wife. "You just walk between us, Miss, and we'll head for that door," he told Kara.

With a sense of relief, Kara nodded and smiled as the three of them started down the hall toward the entrance. As they approached the front desk, Kara saw Morgan and his cohort standing only a few feet away, staring at them.

As they passed by the two men, Kara heard a muffled warning aimed at her. "We'll get you," Morgan said under his breath. With that, Bran stopped abruptly and stepped back so he was directly in front of the man.

"*That* sounded like a threat, and where I come from, no gentleman threatens a lady," Bran said quietly as he leaned closer. Due to his massive size, Bran dwarfed Morgan and his ally as he glared down on them.

"Now, if you're smart, you won't do *anything* to upset me," Bran said in a kindly manner. "These two ladies and I are walking out this door, and if you *were* to do something stupid, I'll have to hurt you," he warned, running his hand over Morgan's shoulder. "And I'd *hate* to ruin this very nice coat you're wearing."

If I only had a camera! Kara thought when seeing the color drain from their faces. *They're cowards when they're dealing with a man!*

"Now, are we clear on this?" Bran asked as he kept his voice lowered. Although there were a handful of people sitting a short distance away, no one seemed to notice what was taking place. "Do I hear a yes?" Bran prompted as he smiled at both men.

Without saying a word, both Morgan and his partner only nodded their heads sheepishly, glancing at each other. "Good, now if you'll go have a seat over by that desk, we'll be leaving," Bran told them, nodding toward a couple of empty chairs. "I'll be watching, so don't leave your seats for at *least* five minutes. Understood?"

Having the look of two rowdy boys being sent to the principal's office, Morgan and his friend headed for the empty chairs. When they were seated, Bran nodded curtly and with his arms around the waists of his wife and Kara, he guided them through the doors and down the sidewalk.

"I can't thank you enough for what you did," Kara said, sighing with relief. "They would surely have me in their clutches by now if it weren't for *both* of you."

"Bran deals with that kind of ilk on a regular basis," the woman said.

"Why, are you a cop?" Kara asked, feeling amazed at her good fortune.

"Something like that, but not exactly," Bran admitted. "Here we are."

Now in the parking lot, they stopped beside a shiny black SUV. As he glanced toward the hospital's entrance, Bran opened the passenger's door for his wife and the backdoor for Kara and helped them both inside.

"Now young lady, where can we take you?" Bran asked after climbing in behind the steering wheel.

"To the Highland Inn, the owner saved my life just recently," Kara confessed. "And now you've saved my life today."

"By the way, my name is Iona, what's yours?" the woman said, turning in her seat.

"Kara Westin, I'm from Michigan in the United States," she told them.

"Wow, and we're from La Cross Wisconsin," Iona blurted. "Small world. We're here checking out a job for Bran."

"Wisconsin? I thought you might be from England," Kara remarked, thinking she heard a slight British accent.

"We lived there for ten years, before Wisconsin," Iona replied. "We move a lot."

"Tell me about those men," Bran said as he pulled from the parking space.

"You'll find this hard to believe, but it's all true," Kara began. As Bran headed his vehicle south down the only road within miles, Kara told the couple about the necklace and how it led to her kidnapping. Also its connection to Lorenzo and the woman once thought to be his mother. She explained the past few days and how she escaped her kidnappers by hiding and how desperate she was when Rowan found her.

"Lorenzo was coming to take me home when he got deathly ill and now I'm afraid they'll do something to him as he lies on his sick bed. Gabriella seems to run everything."

"I wish we could do more to help you," Bran told Kara. "But we're due to fly out of here tomorrow morning."

"Oh, you've done so much already, *both* of you," Kara replied. "You don't know how hard I was praying and I *know* you were my answer," she added, feeling grateful.

"Perhaps so, Kara. *Something* urged us to come this way," Iona said, nodding her head.

"Yes, she was quite emphatic about coming to see the hospital this trip," Bran remarked.

"Just why *were* you at the hospital?" Kara asked for the first time.

"This is where my father practiced medicine, many years ago," Iona told Kara. "Because of his hard work, that hospital was built, but I'd never seen it."

"Yes, we've talked about coming here since we got married, but we never made it," Bran said, smiling at his wife. "It seems it was our destiny to be here now, Miss Westin," he added.

"God *does* works in mysterious ways," Kara replied nodding her head. "I'm learning that more every day."

Silently they rode. As for Kara, she was beginning to understand the faith her mother often spoke of. '*Trust God, Kara. You'll never go wrong when you do.*'

"It appears we've found the Highland Inn," Bran said, breaking the silence. "It looks like a refreshing hide-away," he added, turning in the driveway.

"I'm sure it is, under normal conditions," Kara replied from the backseat. "Rowan and his staff are wonderful. Please come in so you can meet them."

"I guess we have time," Bran said, looking at his wife. When he had parked his vehicle, Bran hurriedly exited and went around to open the door for his wife and then Kara.

"I'm sorry we have to leave tomorrow, I'd love to stay a few days," Bran said, gazing at the well-kept structure. "One day we'll do that."

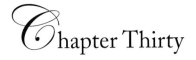

Chapter Thirty

Having left that morning on business Rowan wasn't at the Inn, but Edwina showed genuine hospitality by serving them delicious sandwiches, spice cake and coffee. Kara had seconds.

After lunch, Bran and Iona prepared to leave despite Kara's urging them to stay longer. "Thanks again for saving my neck," she told them, giving one last hug.

"You take care of yourself *and* that friend of yours," Iona said, giving Kara a card. "Here's our Wisconsin number, be sure to call when you get home."

"I certainly will," Kara replied smiling. As she watched the couple drive off, Kara felt sad to see them go. *Thank you, Lord, for sending those people to help me. I'm sure by now I'd be in Gabriella's grip if they hadn't shown up in the nick of time,* she thought, heading back inside.

Weariness weighed on her shoulders as she thought about the days ahead. "What now?" Kara muttered, thinking about her family. *Will I ever see them again?* she wondered in despair. *Don't think such things, you can't give up!*

As she reached the large open room near the entrance, Kara stopped and looked around. *I'll sit here and wait for Rowan,* she decided seeing a comfortable looking seat. Soon she was curled up in the over-stuffed chair and feeling the warmth from the fire.

Although she peered at the flames, Kara's mind was on Lorenzo. Suddenly a chill ran through her. *He has people caring for his illness, but who'll care for his safety? Surely, not even Gabriella would take him from the hospital when he's so sick,* Kara decided, recalling the doctor's words about sedation. *I have to trust he'll be okay. We'll both be okay, somehow, we will be,* she told herself over and over.

Lying her head back, Kara closed her eyes. *Why am I worried? God has His hands on every circumstance, I know that now.* With a deep sigh, Kara closed her eyes, feeling at ease about the future. No matter what happened, she somehow knew everything was going to turn out okay. With that in mind, she fell into a restful sleep.

. . .

Despite his explanation of what happened, Morgan was again on the receiving end of Gabriella's wrath. "*Cowards,* spineless cowards!" she yelled. "You're not worth your salt let alone the money I pay you! Two men outsmarted by one snip of a girl. How utterly stupid!"

"No, it wasn't *just* the girl!" Morgan yelled. "Anyone that size must be a body guard."

"Well, since you can't seen to catch *her,* we'll make her come to *us,*" Gabriella announced as she paced the floor of her study. With its stone walls and floor, the room's icy coldness was matched only by its occupant.

"How? She'll never agree ta come here?" Morgan disputed, glaring at the woman. *If you only knew how much we all loath you!* he thought in silence.

"She will, if she *ever* wants to see Lorenzo again," Gabriella sneered.

"But, you can't mean, you'll actually *try* and bring Lorenzo here!"

"Not me you idiot! *You'll* bring Lorenzo here!" she screeched. "That is *if* you can handle a man who is sleeping!"

"How can we pull that off? He's being watched," Morgan protested.

"I have connections in that hospital, so all you need to do is go get him and bring him here. Or is *that* too hard for you?" Gabriella taunted sarcastically.

"But, the man is sick. From what I hear he's critically ill," Morgan replied. "How can we *possibly* bring him here and take care of him?"

"That's up to Miss Westin. Perhaps *she'll* come and see to his needs, knowing his condition," Gabriella smirked, nodding her head. "If not, well, poor Lorenzo might not make it. So, I expect *you* to have him here by midnight. Is that understood?"

In shock, Morgan could only stare at the woman. *You've done some rotten things in your life, Gabriella, but taking a dying man from his hospital bed?* "He's your son. Can you *really* do this?" he had to ask.

Gabriella's only reply was her loud hideous laughter as she stomped from the room.

. . .

Distant voices and the jostling of his bed was slowly arousing Lorenzo from his deep sleep. Although unable to open his eyes, he sensed people were arguing around him. "You'll answer to Gabriella if you try to stop us," a somewhat familiar voice warned.

"And I'll call the Constable. I'm sure *he* isn't on that woman's payroll," someone else threatened.

"Let's be off with him before anyone else shows up," a third person said.

When hearing Gabriella's name, Lorenzo fought desperately to clear his mind of the drugged stupor he was in. But no matter how hard he tried, it was useless. His mind drifted in and out of recent memories. He sensed Kara's presence. He remembered her voice, and her hand against his face. As his mind teetered on the edge of awareness, Lorenzo felt something special had happened. But what?

A sudden movement jarred his body, and he felt something hard and cold as renewed pain gripped his neck and head. For a moment he wondered what was happening, but it didn't matter. He was too tired to care. Lorenzo wanted only to slip back to that place where he felt nothing.

. . .

From the door of the hospital, Ben could only watch as the ambulance drove away carrying Lorenzo, the critically ill patient he'd helped just hours before. *What chance does that poor guy have now? That witch sure won't help him,* Ben thought angrily shaking his head. Adding to his disgust, was the realization of how many people were being paid by Gabriella to do her dirty work.

Ten-fifty-five, my shift is over. Now I must go to Highland Inn and tell that sweet young Kara what happened here tonight, he thought sadly, remembering his offer to help if he could.

Just as he was about to leave, Dr. Lennox came hurrying through the front door. "What happened here?" he asked Ben, sounding out of breath.

"Well Doc, I'm afraid you're missing a patient. With help from two of our own ambulance drivers, Gabriella's thugs snatched Lorenzo from his bed," Ben quickly relayed.

"Oh, Miss Westin warned me, but I'm afraid I didn't put much stock in her words," Dr. Lennox said, shaking his head. "If that young man dies, I'll be partly responsible."

"I was just about to leave for the Highland to let Kara know what happened," Ben remarked. "Is there anything you want me to tell her?"

"No, I feel I must apologize in person," Dr. Lennox replied, glancing at his watch. "Do you mind if I follow you, unless you'd care to ride with me?"

"I live that direction so we'll both drive," Ben answered.

With obvious remorse showing on his face, Dr. Lennox accompanied Ben to the parking lot. In no time the two men had their vehicles headed toward Highland Inn. For Ben, no matter how hard he tried, he found no easy words to tell Kara about her friend. Nor could he find any way to ease his own guilt for not having done more.

. . .

With a scream, Kara woke up from the nightmare she'd been having. *Gabriella had me and Kelly. She was torturing us!* she thought, covering her face with her hands. "It was only a dream; she'll never have Kelly, *or* me," Kara whispered in the dark. Yet, she knew the possibility of her own capture was real. *I'll stay here at the Inn. Rowan said I could until Lorenzo gets well. Then we can leave this place, for good,* Kara thought, climbing out of bed.

Going to the bathroom she splashed water on her face. Then leaning close, she studied her face in the mirror. *You look terrible! Gaunt, unkempt,* Kara thought, seeing the pale image looking back at her. *No doubt. I haven't had makeup or even face cream since I was kidnapped,* Kara reasoned noticing the now visible lines. With a sigh, she returned to her bedroom.

Eleven o'clock, oh, I wish it were morning so I could call about Lorenzo, she thought, glancing at the bedside clock. From a small table, Kara retrieved a magazine. Climbing back into bed, she fluffed the pillows and leaned back to read, hoping this would take her mind off of her dream and Lorenzo's illness.

Sometime later, Kara was surprised when a knock sounded at her door. "Yes, come in," she called, expecting Edwina who was staying overnight.

"Kara, I'm sorry to disturb you, but you have two visitors downstairs," Rowan said from the doorway. "They need to speak to you; it's quite urgent."

"Is it about Lorenzo?" Kara asked as her heart began racing. In haste, she threw back the covers and grabbed her robe. "Rowan, is it *Lorenzo?*" she asked again, reaching the doorway.

"Yes, it's concerning Lorenzo," Rowan said solemnly. When hearing the man's noticeable sadness, Kara's fear escalated as they hurriedly descended the stairs. As they neared the fireplace, she saw two men get up from the sofa and look at her.

"Dr. Lennox? Ben?" Kara greeted as her legs grew weak. In her heart, she felt sure her greatest fear had become a reality. "No, don't tell me he died. He *couldn't* have," she wailed.

"No, Miss Westin," doctor Lennox began as he walked toward Kara, "he didn't expire, but I'm afraid your concerns for his safety have nonetheless come true," he said, reaching for her hand.

When hearing that, Kara's other hand flew to her mouth. "Dear God, not Gabriella!" she gasped as he legs gave out. Quickly, Dr. Lennox and Rowan grabbed Kara, keeping her from crumpling to the floor.

"Sit here, Kara?" Rowan said, helping her to the sofa.

"I'm so sorry I didn't heed your warning, Miss Westin," the doctor told her. "I doubted *anyone* could be so heartless as to nab a patient from their hospital bed, but apparently you were right about this woman."

"I'm sorry too, Kara," Ben spoke up, sitting down beside her. "I've learned my own co-workers will do *anything* for money, but I'm here to help however I can. Here's my number."

In stunned silence Kara took the card. *This is my fault. I know Gabriella took Lorenzo because of me. How will he survive now, without care? What can we possibly do? Something, I must do something!* Kara decided.

"Dr. Lennox, what does Lorenzo need besides rest? In case I find him, what can I do to keep him alive?" Kara asked, forming a plan.

"Find him? What do you mean?" Rowan asked.

"Gabriella wants *me,* and if I let them find me, I'm sure they'll take me to where Lorenzo is. If that's the case, I can help him if I have the supplies with me," Kara told the others.

"He needs nutrients to build up his strength," Dr. Lennox began. "Rest if vital. He'll need something for pain *and* his fever. If we're lucky, what he's gotten the past few hours has helped."

"Where can I get these things?" Kara asked. "I need them right away."

"I'll get them for you. Can you come with me now?" the doctor asked.

"That's not necessary. I'll bring them back to her," Ben offered. "It's late and Kara's been through enough already. It's the least I can do," he concluded.

"Thank you, thank you all," Kara said, glancing at the three men. "I'd be lost without your help, and your kindness. I'll never forget what you've done for me. One day, I hope Lorenzo and I can repay you."

When thinking about the danger ahead *and* Lorenzo's condition, Kara felt sure her heart would break under its sorrow.

"We'll be going now, and I'll send those items we spoke of," Dr. Lennox told Kara. "Good luck, Miss Westin." With that the kindly doctor grasped Kara's hand. "If you need my assistance for *anything* else, please call me." With a nod, Kara watched as Rowan escorted Ben and Dr. Lennox to the door.

She felt weak with despair; hopelessly outnumbered, yet, grateful for these strangers who were willing to help. *I must call Jock, they need to know about Lorenzo,* Kara thought, lying her head back and closing her eyes.

Dear God, please help Lorenzo. Don't let him die, Kara pleaded. Strangely her tears had dried. In their place was stoic determination. Visions of Lorenzo drifted through her mind. This time, instead of seeing his face grimacing in pain, she saw the tenderness in his eyes whenever he had looked at her. She remembered their moonlight walk. Here, amid her anguish, Kara's eyes were opened. *No more doubts, no more questions, my sweet Lorenzo. It's you I love. Why has it taken me so long to see it?* she wondered.

. . .

The annoying sound of high-pitched laughter was inching Lorenzo toward awareness. With great effort he opened his eyes only to be blinded by a bright light just above his face.

"Well, well, who *have* we here?" a female voice taunted. "Oh, I *do* believe it's Lorenzo, the headstrong, defiant, and disobedient one."

Gabriella! No! Lorenzo thought in despair, trying to clear his grogginess. *How did I get here?* When trying to move his arms, he couldn't. Was it weakness or restraints, he wasn't sure. *Kara? Is Kara here too?*

"Gabriella," Lorenzo barely whispered. "What, do you want?"

"Oh, I want many things, Lorenzo. Much more now that you *defied* me," the woman sneered. "But, since you're in no shape to help, I'll have to depend on your girlfriend."

When hearing that, Lorenzo tried all the harder to regain his senses. Mentally he sorted through what he felt, assessing his strength. Pain gripped his head and neck, his back hurt, and weakness engulfed his body. *Not Kara, please,* he wanted to say, yet, it would do no good. He knew Gabriella.

In the next moment an eerie sound resonated around him. From the far recesses of his mind, a memory surfaced. Not since he was young had he heard the desolate sound of cold iron clanging together. *Dungeon, I'm in the dungeon!* Lorenzo realized as he gave way to the heavy weight of hopelessness . . .

. . .

After her call to Jock, Kara sat waiting for Ben's return. Having brought a warm blanket, Rowan wrapped it around Kara's shoulders and then seated himself nearby. "You should get some rest, Kara," he urged, leaning back in his chair. "I'll wait up for Ben."

"I couldn't sleep, not with Lorenzo in such danger," Kara protested, staring at the flames. "It's hard to comprehend such greed, such evilness as that woman has."

"Yes, but she, too, will have her end," Rowan replied nodding. "We all must face our Maker one day."

"That's a certainty, and my only consolation," Kara replied.

"Tell me about your family," Rowan then said, hoping to take Kara's mind off of this latest dilemma.

Without hesitation, Kara began talking about her sister Kelly, and their mother, Emma, the most important people in her life. With emotion she spoke of their strength, their strong faith and unconditional love.

"They sound exceptional. I hope I can meet them one day," Rowan told Kara. "There's nothing like strong family ties."

"You're right, but sometimes we don't realize that soon enough," Kara said.

When hearing Kara express the relationship she and her family enjoyed, Rowan felt a tinge of envy. After all, wasn't that what everyone wanted?

Chapter Thirty-one

After Ben arrived with the supplies from Dr. Lennox, Kara went to bed. Although exhaustion had drained her body as well as her mind, she tossed and turned as sleep evaded her. *Poor Lorenzo, what must he be going through? And what will Gabriella do to us both when I get there?* she wondered.

Dear God, this is in Your Hands. Give me strength to do what I must, Kara prayed as she snuggled beneath the covers. Finally, she could asleep.

· · ·

As he shuffled along the corridor carrying a tray of food, Mitchell's ire grew. "She's the devil himself, pure and simple," he muttered shaking his head.

Panting from the long walk, the old man sat the tray on the floor when he arrived at the dungeon. Leaning against the wall to catch his breath, Mitchell peered though the bars. "Lorenzo, are ya alive in there?" he called out.

When hearing no sound, he opened the heavy iron door, retrieved the tray from the floor and stepped inside. *Tis certain Gabriella lost all decency long ago,* Mitchell thought fuming, setting the tray on the rickety stool.

Now at Lorenzo's side, Mitchell studied his face in the dim light. *Ya look like a dead man! How could she do this ta ya?* "Lorenzo? Can ya hear me?"

When barely a moan was heard, Mitchell touched Lorenzo's face. "Yer as hot as a fryin' skillet," he uttered out loud. "I brought ya some soup, and hot tea, but don't worry, I'll go get ya some help."

Leaving Lorenzo, Mitchell headed back to the kitchen. *Have ya no shame, man? Will ya be a coward till yer dyin' day and not save Lorenzo after he's stood up fer ya?* the man scolded himself, thinking of the dirty work he'd done for Gabriella.

When he arrived at the kitchen, Mitchell was silent, making sure none of Gabriella's snitches were in sight. "Lorenzo needs ta be fed, he's burnin' up and right now he's not worth a sway back mule," he said solemnly.

When hearing the man's remark, one of the kitchen girls quickly gathered a few items and placed them in a basket. "I'll see ta him right away," she said, glancing around the room. With a nod, Mitchell sighed with relief.

. . .

In another part of the castle, Gabriella was giving a new round of orders. "I want you to spread the word, if this little snit wants to see her beloved Lorenzo alive she must come to *me,* here! She has twenty-four hours and if she refuses, then his demise will be *her* fault," Gabriella announced as her face twisted in a hateful sneer.

"Why would she *agree* ta such a thing?" Morgan asked.

"Love, *that's* why!" Gabriella fired back. "Some lose their hearts for love, *and* their heads!" she snapped viciously.

"You don't intend ta *kill* them, do ya?" Morgan asked, knowing the extent of her hatred. *I won't be party ta murder, not again,* he vowed silently.

"I *won't* lose what is mine, no matter what!" she yelled glaring at him. "Is that clear?"

"Yes, I understand," Morgan replied as he glared back at her.

"Very well then, go find that girl and bring her to me!" Gabriella ordered.

As he turned to leave, Morgan knew he had reached the end. *I have to be free of that woman! I can't, and I* won't *live like this anymore. After I bring that girl here, I'm through! But she'll hunt you down. You know too much,* his thoughts quickly warned. "Then I'll make sure she won't!" he muttered under his breath.

. . .

As Kara dressed that morning, she thought about things she might need. *I'm sure Gabriella will search my bag, so I'll hide it on me,* she decided, wondering how it might be done.

242

When she had finished, Kara went downstairs to find Rowan. "I have a favor to ask, if you don't mind," she told him. For the next few minutes, Kara gave Rowan a list of small items she wanted to take with her, just in case.

"That's a very good idea," Rowan replied, "and I think I have everything." When the two had finished gathering the items requested, Kara asked Edwina to come to her room to help.

For the next hour, Kara and Edwina devised a plan to hide things in unsuspecting places. Taking the length of rope, they intertwined it in Kara's hair as an apparent accessory for her one long braid. Then, after winding the plait atop her head, Edwina hid a small screwdriver beneath it next to Kara's head.

Under her bulky red sweater was taped a zip lock bag holding book matches and a tiny flashlight. Inside the top of one boot was a long slender knife in a sheaf.

"That's everything," Kara said, looking in the mirror. Then turning, she faced Edwina. "Thank you, for *everything*. You've been so kind since I arrived and you've helped immensely," Kara said, giving the woman a quick hug.

"I am pleased ta help, Miss," Edwina replied kindly. "Are ya sure ya have ta go? For sure Gabriella is nothin' like ya have ever seen before. I know *first* hand," she added, looking at Kara.

"How do you know?" Kara asked, feeling puzzled. "I worked there, but her cruelty drove me away," Edwina said. "That's how I knew Lorenzo's mum." Now, with the door open, Kara had to ask.

"Who was she, Edwina? What was her name?"

"Carlotta," Edwina said sadly. "A precious girl she was, but doomed from the start."

"Doomed? What do you mean? And who is Lorenzo's father?" Kara asked, feeling sure he wasn't her blood relative after all.

"Doomed because of Gabriella's wrath. Carlotta was found dead at the bottom of the stairs; an accident we were told, but we knew better," Edwina said in anger. "The poor girl was hauled off like yesterday's rubbish. No funeral, nary a prayer was said fer the lass."

"How horrible!" Kara gasped, suddenly feeling sick to her stomach. "Not even Lorenzo's father could give Carlotta a decent burial?"

For the first time, Kara saw the woman's stoic veneer give way to emotion. With her head down, Edwina picked at a thread on her sleeve, seemingly searching for the right words.

"He didn't know, until too late," Edwina said sadly. "He was in London, and by the time he returned home, Carlotta was buried like a dog. He, too, died an untimely death."

"Who *was* he, Edwina? Did *he* work for Gabriella?" Kara asked.

"Lorenzo's father was Gabriella's husband, John Carlyle," Edwina replied looking at Kara. "His marriage to Gabriella was a sham, arranged by their parents when the two were barely out of nappies. Tis for sure they had no love, only bitterness. When Carlotta was hired ta work at the castle, her sweet manner soon won John's heart."

"Couldn't John get out of his loveless marriage?" Kara asked then.

"He tried, but by then, Gabriella controlled everything, even John. When he learned a baby was on the way, he was thrilled and when Carlotta died, I'm sure John lived only for his son," Edwina replied.

When hearing this, Kara felt weak with sorrow and sought the edge of her bed.

"How horribly sad," she uttered. "Poor Lorenzo, he knows *nothing* of this. And now *he's* on the receiving end of Gabriella's wrath. But why would she raise Lorenzo as her own son?" Kara asked Edwina.

"Tis a puzzle indeed, but it seems Gabriella wanted Lorenzo for her own purposes. Ta use and control for her own sick pleasure. Now it seems ta be the case," Edwina concluded.

In shock Kara could say nothing. *Lorenzo's in grave danger! Hard telling what that woman is doing to him,* she thought, feeling eager to be on her way. "Thank you, Edwina, for telling me all this," she could finally say. "It seems there are *many* skeletons in the Carlyle closet."

"I must be gettin' back ta the kitchen," Edwina told Kara. "Be careful, Miss, Gabriella will stop at nothin' ta get what she wants."

"Yes, I see that," Kara replied, walking Edwina to the door. When the woman had left, Kara again seated herself. Now, as the time drew near for her to meet Gabriella face to face, Kara prayed. "Dear God, You know every evil thought and plan Gabriella has devised. I need wisdom and Your protection," she prayed in earnest.

For a moment longer, Kara sat trying to visualize the days ahead. *No matter what she plans, we're going to get through this!* Kara thought confidently.

Then, grabbing the backpack containing the medical items and some bottled water, Kara gave one more glance around the bedroom. *I'm sure the next place I sleep won't be nearly this cozy,* she thought. With a deep sigh, she headed for the door.

. . .

After eating lunch, Kara made one last call to Jock and Kelly, informing them of her plans. Despite their begging her not to go, Kara remained firm in her decision. Quickly she relayed what she'd learned from Edwina. "Gabriella must resent him and wouldn't think twice about killing him," Kara said. "I must have faith that it *will* work out, somehow. I'll try to get word to Rowan so he can call you," she concluded.

After an emotional goodbye, Kara squared her shoulders and told Rowan she was ready to leave. Just then she saw a kitchen maid heading her way.

"Tis a cold and drafty place, Miss, ya must take this," she told Kara, handing her a dark colored winter coat.

"Thank you, very much," Kara said, feeling overwhelmed at her kindness. "I promise to do my best to bring it back." Making no reply, the petite maid only smiled and nodded her head.

Within minutes, Kara and Rowan were in his vehicle heading toward the castle. "No matter what time it is, call whenever you have the chance," Rowan told Kara. "I wish I could do more to help you, Kara. I feel I'm delivering you to the lions."

"You've done so much already, and I so appreciate your every kindness. From you *and* your staff," Kara replied. "One day, when this is over, I hope Lorenzo and I can come back for a *real* vacation. It's beautiful here."

"I hope so too," Rowan answered, reaching for Kara's hand. "You'll *always* have a place here, with or without Lorenzo."

When hearing Rowan's statement, Kara shuddered as a chill ran through her. "Do you think Lorenzo will survive all this?" she asked.

"I don't know, Kara. I certainly hope you both do. That's the place," he said, pointing.

Sure enough, in the distance Kara saw a grayish white structure sitting on a hill. Looking at it, she was reminded of books she'd read about the medieval times, when gallant warriors rode horses into battle. *It looks eerie and cold. Why would* anyone *fight over such a place as this?* Kara had to wonder. "Is all this land included with the castle?" she asked, seeing the surrounding fields and rolling hillside.

"I hear that it is," Rowan answered, slowing his vehicle. "There are also herds of cattle and sheep. "If I owned it, I'd knock down that dreary old castle and build a spacious new Inn. I'm sure the view is grand indeed."

When they entered the drive leading to the entrance, Kara felt her heart racing. "Well, this is it," she said softly as her eyes sweep the foreboding structure now in front of her. "Thank you, Rowan, I do hope we'll be celebrating in your lovely Inn very soon," she told him, trying to smile.

"Godspeed, Kara," Rowan said, again reaching for her hand. "I'll keep the fires burning." When he started to get out, Kara stopped him.

"I can do this," she said nodding, feeling renewed confidence. Straightening her back, Kara opened her door and climbed out. Before Rowan could back his vehicle to leave, the massive wooden door opened and for the first time, Kara saw that one who had caused so much pain.

Shivers ran up Kara's spine when seeing her. Wearing a long black dress, the woman looked much older than she would have guessed. Gabriella's rather long face was framed by straight black shoulder length hair. Cold grey eyes bore into Kara's as she approached. "Miss Westin, how very pleased I am to see you," Gabriella greeted in a sarcastic tone. "Do come in."

With only a nod, Kara stepped through the door and into a dark dreary room. She searched for the right words, but nothing came to mind. *I can't make her mad, it will only add to her fury,* Kara cautioned herself.

"What have we here?" Gabriella blared, grabbing the backpack from Kara's arm. Without hesitating, the woman dumped its contents on a huge wooden table. "Do you expect me to allow this?" she yelled.

"It's for Lorenzo, *please* let me help him," Kara pleaded. "He's very sick and he needs these. What good is he to you if he dies?"

"He means *nothing* to me, but obviously he does to you," Gabriella smirked. "Why would *I* care if he dies? Or you, for that matter? You've caused me nothing but trouble, the whole lot of you!" she yelled, pounding her fist on the table.

Suddenly, Kara realized there was no compromising with insanity. *This woman is crazy! She's filled with pride and arrogance. Nothing*

I say will change her mind. Dear God, just let me find Lorenzo. . . .

Just then Morgan entered from another room. When seeing the man, Kara was surprised. Instead of his icy stare aimed at her, he glared at Gabriella behind her back. "I beg you, Gabriella, allow me to give these few things to Lorenzo, certainly your kindness would be most appreciated," Kara said, hoping to find some hint of decency in the woman.

"Kindness? Or weakness?" she smirked. "That's what you're hoping for, Miss Westin, that I will weaken in my stance. Long ago, I learned only the strong prevail, and those who cower to no one!" she blared defiantly. With that, Gabriella spun around to see Morgan standing behind her. "Take this woman to Lorenzo," she ordered. "When you've finished, come to my study. I have another job for you to do." With that, Gabriella shot a daggered look at Kara before stomping out of the room.

Much to Kara's surprise, Morgan quickly gathered the items strewn across the table and threw them inside the pack. "Follow me," he told Kara as he slung the strap over his arm.

In haste, Morgan led Kara from the room and down a long dimly lit hallway with walls and ceiling made of rough hewn stones. Only the light from sporadically placed candles lit their way. The echo from their hurried footsteps is all that was heard. *What a horrible place to live!* Kara thought, feeling the penetrating cold.

The farther they went, the narrower the walkway became until soon it seemed no more than a tunnel. Finally they reached an intersection where stairways converged. From a wall hook, Morgan retrieved an oil lantern. "Watch your head," he advised Kara as he chose the stairs leading downward.

Here, in the bowels of this Gothic structure, Kara suddenly felt far from the world she knew. Its dank, musty smell not only brought a wave of nausea, but oppression weighed heavily on her young shoulders.

Step by step they slowly descended the crooked, narrow opening. *It's the dungeon! It must be!* Kara decided, feeling more hopeless as they proceeded downward.

With barely enough light to see her way, Kara had no warning until they finally stepped into an open area. "Here we are," Morgan announced. In the dim light, Kara saw black iron bars from floor to ceiling. Then Morgan opened the heavy iron door and stepped back. "For what it's worth, I hope these *do* help Lorenzo," he added, handing her the pack as he motioned her inside.

"Yes, thank you," Kara replied as she stepped through the door. "Is Lorenzo here?" she asked when seeing no one.

"Right over there," Morgan said pointing to a dark corner. "Welcome to Gabriella's dungeon, Miss Westin." A wave of depression swept over Kara when Morgan confirmed her fears. Then, when the man closed and locked the door, her legs threatened to give way.

"Please, we need that light," she yelled after Morgan as darkness closed in around her. A moment later, the man returned with a small candle and placed it in a wall sconce.

"That's the best I can do," Morgan told her.

Just then Kara heard a moan. "Lorenzo?" Inching her way cautiously toward the sound, Kara saw him. "Oh Lorenzo, what has she *done* to you?"

Leaning close, Kara could hear his short rapid breathing and could barely see his features in the dim light. Gently she touched his cheek. "It's Kara. Can you hear me?" she asked, feeling his fiery hot skin.

"Kara, Kara," Lorenzo barely whispered a moment later.

"Yes, Lorenzo, I'm here. Whatever happens, we're together," she said softly, choking back her tears. "I love you and I want to spend the rest of my life with you, my sweet man." Suddenly, the truth of those words hit Kara. *God, please don't let us die in this horrible place! Let us live so we* can *have a life together,* she quickly prayed.

"I won't make it," Lorenzo then uttered.

"Yes, Lorenzo, you will! Don't give up, please, you *can't* give up," Kara pleaded. "I brought medicine to help. I have it right here."

Quickly, Kara threw off her coat and removed the zip lock bag taped to her belly. After removing the matches and small flashlight, she looked through the pack to find the liquid medication and Dr Lennox's instructions.

Moments later she was helping Lorenzo take a dose of each item she had brought. When finished, Kara stood quietly at his side while she gently caressed his face and forehead. "You must rest, Lorenzo. I'm here now, and you'll be better soon," she said through her tears.

As she waited for Lorenzo's breathing to slow, Kara's mind flooded with memories. Suddenly, every kind word and deed he had shown her came to mind. His comforting arms, his eyes filled with love and the way he stood up for her when others wouldn't. *You saved my life, Lorenzo, and I promise, with God's help, I'll save yours too,* she vowed silently.

Finally, when Lorenzo fell asleep, Kara used the flashlight to look around the dingy space. *This is barbaric! She's truly insane!* she thought, seeing only gray stone walls and floor. A wobbly looking stool sat in the corner and the cot where Lorenzo lay was filled with musty smelling straw. A raggedy brown blanket was his covering.

Dear God, we need a miracle! Please *get us out of this horrible place!* Kara pleaded, trying not to cry.

In despair, Kara leaned her back against the iron bars and slowly slid to the floor. Then, burying her face in her hands, she sobbed with unrelenting sorrow. Amid her wails of anguish, a small voice spoke to her. *Don't give up. You told Lorenzo to hang on, so why can't you? Yes, I must fight. I must, no matter what it takes!* Kara thought, reaching inside for that stubborn determination she was use to having.

· · ·

By the time Gabriella had finished giving him a list of 'chores' for the next several days, Morgan had made a decision. Although he stared at the woman, Morgan saw other faces, those he had killed or kidnapped at her request. *I sold my soul fer blood money, but now tis time ta end it,* Morgan thought, feeling relieved at the decision.

"What are ya plannin' ta do with those two in the hole?" he asked, having no doubt of their sorrowful fate before he asked.

"How do I *usually* treat defiance?" Gabriella smirked, giving him a sideward glance. "They'll feed the rats like the others."

For the first time, Morgan felt repulsed when thinking of their agonizing fate. *Starving ta death, then eaten by rats!* The thought made him shudder. *Tis true, I had my run-ins with Lorenzo and that girl caused Kenny's drownin'. Well, at least they won't live long enough ta starve,* Morgan reasoned.

When Gabriella dismissed him with the usual wave of her hand, Morgan smiled to himself when thinking of his plan. *Ya killed for this place, Gabriella, now tis only fittin' that ya die here,* Morgan thought grinning to himself. *Dynamite should do nicely. . . .*

. . .

It was late that afternoon when Morgan told Mitchell of his plan. "Are ya sure of this? Tis true she deserves it more than anyone I know, but we're sure ta be found out," Mitchell protested, rubbing his wrinkled forehead.

"Tis a known fact we have dynamite fer clearin' stumps from the field, so anyone could be blowin' the place up," Morgan argued. "Regardless of what they may think, tis harder ta prove."

"Aye, for sure Gabriella won't be missed by anyone I know," Mitchell replied, nodding his head. In agreement, they made plans for the next day. One by one, they advised the staff to leave the castle no later than three o'clock, that is, except for Gabriella's snitches.

Chapter Thirty-two

Even with the winter coat, Kara was freezing. Back and forth she paced the dark prison, concentrating on the sound of her boots clomping against the stone floor. Soon she began humming. It wasn't a song, but rather, a soft soothing tone. Somehow, it brought a sense of calm.

When Lorenzo called out in his delirium, Kara hurried to his side. "Yes, my love, I'm here," she told him softly, brushing her hand against his cheek. When feeling her touch, Lorenzo quieted. "Just rest, Lorenzo, I'm right here."

As she stood beside him, Kara thought about the life they might have had. *Dad said I would know when I met the right man, but why did it take me so long?* Kara wondered, wishing things had been different. *Someday, people may write a song about our tragic end! A modern day Romeo and Juliet,* she thought sadly.

Time inched by. *It's impossible to tell night from day in this place,* she thought, shining the light on her wristwatch. *Nine o'clock. Time for Lorenzo's medicine.* Once more, with her arm under his head, she lifted it slightly while holding the light in her hand. In her other hand, Kara held the small cup with the medication while Lorenzo slowly swallowed a few drops at a time.

"Dear God, take this horrible sickness from Lorenzo's body, make him well," she prayed. *We* will *get out of here; someone will rescue us. I have to believe that!* Kara thought with confidence. "Go to sleep, sweetheart," she told Lorenzo, caressing his face. "You must rest and not worry, everything will work out. And very soon you *will* be better."

Not until Lorenzo slept peacefully did Kara leave his side. With cold and hunger nagging at her, she felt exhausted. When she could no longer stand on her feet, she found the corner closest to Lorenzo.

Sitting on the floor, Kara drew her knees us and pulled the coat over them. *Thank God for that generous young woman,* she thought, closing her eyes.

Sometime later Kara was aroused from her sleep. *Was I dreaming?* she wondered, feeling as though someone had touched her. When trying to move she couldn't. Every joint felt stiff, locked in place from the cold dampness. In her same cramped position, Kara listened for Lorenzo. *He's alive and sleeping sound,* she thought when hearing his slow, steady breathing.

Suddenly another sound caught her attention. Straining to hear, Kara tried hard to decipher the strange noise in the dark. *It's nearby, but what is it?*

With great effort, she straightened her legs and reached in her coat pocket for the light. *Two o'clock. I did sleep some,* Kara thought, glancing at her watch.

Then for no apparent reason, she swept the small beam of light around her. She screamed. She froze in fear when she saw yellow beady eyes looking back at her. *Dear God! Not rats!*

One was on the bag of medicine. "No you don't!" she yelled, scrambling to her feet. Amid her quick movement, Kara heard the high pitch squeaks as the rodents scurried off. With her heart racing, she lifted the pack off the floor and placed it on the stool.

I hate rats! I should have known they'd be in this place! Kara thought as tears burned her eyes. Once more, all she could do was bury her face in her hands and cry with frustration.

. . .

As was Gabriella's routine, she ate breakfast alone. To her surprise, no one had mentioned Lorenzo and the girl. *Those spineless ones usually beg for my leniency. Why not now? They sided with Lorenzo against me so why aren't they begging for mercy on his behalf?* Gabriella wondered, drumming her knobby fingers on the table.

Perhaps I'd better make sure no one has helped them escape. Besides, they need to realize they put themselves there for defying me! she grinned, feeling pleased she had again outsmarted a much younger woman.

After drinking the last of her coffee, Gabriella left her seat and headed for the dungeon. With her chin raised and shoulders back she walked briskly down the long corridor. *This is mine, all mine and no one will ever take it from me! When will people learn they can not defy me and live!* she thought smugly.

At the usual place she retrieved the oil lantern from its hook and lighted the wick, using the nearby candle. Then she started down the narrow stairway. Soon she arrived at her destination. Without a word she pulled on the door, making sure it was still locked. Although she lifted the lantern to see behind the bars, she saw only dark shadows.

"My, I *do* hope you're enjoying the accommodations," she taunted, hoping to arouse some response. Instead, only silence. "I suppose it *is* still early, so I assume you had a good nights sleep?" Gabriella continued. Finally, with no remark forthcoming, she felt curious. "Perhaps you both died of shear fright."

Cautiously, Gabriella unlocked the door and stepped inside the darkened area, holding the lantern. With the light so near her face, it was impossible to see past a few feet. When she saw the cot, she headed toward it. "Wake up Lorenzo, your *mother* is here," she sang out sarcastically, expecting the girl to be huddled in fear.

Suddenly, a hand pushed Gabriella from behind, propelling her headlong into the wall. The lantern flew from her hand. With a loud shatter it smashed against the floor, spilling fire and oil amid pieces of glass. The smell of smoke quickly filled the air.

"How *dare* you call yourself his mother!" Kara screamed, lunging at her. In shock, Gabriella could only stare in the face of her assailant.

. . .

Never before had Kara felt such fury toward another human being. As she stared down at Gabriella, her heart raced while adrenal surged through her body. In an instant Kara reached down and grabbed Gabriella's cloak, pulling her to her feet. "You are evil, the daughter of Satan himself," Kara yelled in her face. "And I am God's Child! And that makes *you* the loser!"

Suddenly, a demon yell came from Gabriella as her face contorted and her eyes narrowed. "You won't win! I'm stronger than your God," she hissed in a raspy reply. Although the words came from Gabriella's lips, Kara suddenly realized a demon spoke from within the woman.

She's possessed! I've scoffed at such notions, but it's true! Kara thought when hearing the demon's wail. In the next instant, Gabriella grabbed for Kara's throat. With surprising strength, Kara broke her grip.

Stepping back, Gabriella then lowered her head and glared at Kara. In the glow of the flickering flames, the woman's face appeared more animal than human. With a heinous scream she charged, knocking Kara to the floor. Instantly, Gabriella again had her hands at Kara's throat.

Amid the lantern's debris the two fought. Trying hard to break the choke hold, Kara clawed and pulled at Gabriella's face and hair, but nothing helped. "I'm going to kill you," the demon growled once more.

"Jesus help me!" Kara could barely gasp. Suddenly, she remembered the hidden screwdriver. With trembling fingers she reached up and found the small device. Although fighting for breath, Kara managed to grab hold and pull it free of it hiding place. With her strength waning, she gripped the handle and drove it hard into Gabriella's face.

Screams echoed throughout the dismal confines as the woman grabbed her face, releasing her hold on Kara. While Gabriella lay writhing in pain, Kara coughed and gasped for air amid the lingering smoke. *It's not over, but I can't leave Lorenzo!*

With great effort, she crawled to the wall for support. Although her hands still shook, Kara was able to loosen her braid. However, when trying to retrieve the rope from her hair, she realized tying Gabriella hands would not be easy. In a fetal position, the woman lay moaning, her face buried in her hands as blood ran through her fingers.

Gathering her strength, Kara crawled toward Gabriella, hoping to retrieve the key. *I can't let her lock us up again, I must stop her!* she reasoned as she inched closer. Remnants of the burning oil flickered, casting an eerie glow inside the chamber.

Just as Kara reached for the white cord dangling from Gabriella's cloak pocket, the woman's hand shot out, catching Kara's arm in an iron grip. "Stupid! Now I have you!" the same hideous voice taunted. In one quick motion, Kara was flung to the floor.

The knife! It's my only chance, Kara thought, realizing she battled more than just Gabriella. *Lord, help me do it right this time!* she pleaded, knowing the chance she missed earlier.

Despite the crushing pain in her arm, Kara was able to reach her boot and find the knife. With surprising calm, she began yelling. "In the name of Jesus, take your hands off me! Demons, you have no power over me! Loose this woman and return to the pits of hell where you belong!" she blared.

As she spoke the order again and again, Kara felt the pulverizing grip finally loosen on her arm. Suddenly, Gabriella got to her feet and with screams of torment, ran from the enclosure and into the dark.

Relief washed over Kara. Somehow, within her soul, she knew Gabriella was no longer a threat. "Thank you Jesus! Oh, what *Power* is in your name! Thank you *Jesus!*" Kara shouted, getting to her feet.

Just then she was startled to hear. "Kara? Are you all right?"

Quickly she hurried to Lorenzo's side. "Yes, oh *yes,* I'm fine," she said, taking hold of his hand. Then, as she placed her hand on his forehead, relief surged through her. "Your fever broke," Kara raved, feeling clammy wetness instead of heat. "Soon we'll be out of this place, Lorenzo, as soon as I can find some help," she told him.

"I heard you praying," Lorenzo said. "Thank you, thank you."

"Oh Lorenzo, I didn't use to believe in prayer, but I *do* now," Kara replied. "I'll be back as soon as I can." Just as she started to leave, she heard voices. *They sound excited, and somehow familiar,* Kara thought. "Someone is coming!" she told Lorenzo. Stepping from the cell, Kara waited.

Seconds later, she saw Mitchell carrying a lantern. Then she saw the others. "Mother? Jock? Is it really you?" Kara cried in disbelief.

"Kara, my darling girl, we were so afraid we'd never arrive in time," Emma blurted, holding out her arms. Instantly, mother and daughter were wrapped in a tearful embrace.

"Oh, Mom, it's so good to see you! It's a *miracle* that I'm standing here," Kara said. "I never thought I'd see any of you again!" Then, giving Jock a hug, she continued. "Thank you for coming, what a *wonderful* surprise."

"After your last call, Emma insisted we leave right away," Jock told Kara. "I brought Pierre so he could fly the Lear back and we'll have the Citation to go home in. We asked directions to this place and here we are. Where *is* Lorenzo?" Jock then asked, glancing around.

"Oh, I'm so sorry, I was just about to go for help when I heard you coming," Kara explained. "Lorenzo is right inside. He's been so sick, but I think he'll make it now."

"Miss, we've called fer the ambulance, they'll be takin' Lorenzo back to the hospital," Mitchell informed Kara. "Come this way," he then told Jock, leading the way with the lantern.

"Mother, did you see Gabriella?" Kara had to know.

"No dear, Gabriella is dead," Emma told Kara. "No one knows why, but she apparently climbed up to the tower and jumped off. It's all quite strange."

"No, Mother, it *isn't*, not really," Kara replied. "The woman was demon possessed, I know first hand, because they tried to kill me not an hour ago. As horrible as it was, I've learned a great lesson."

When hearing the news, Emma once more threw her arms around Kara and held her tight. "*Praise* you, God, for keeping my precious girl safe!" she raved with obvious emotion. For the next few minutes, both Kara and Emma cried tears of joy amid their words of thanksgiving.

In her heart, Kara suddenly knew her life would never be the same. Not only because she had found the love of her life in Lorenzo, but first hand, she had witnessed the power from on high that she had so often doubted.

. . .

Upon their arrival at the hospital, Lorenzo was examined by Dr. Lennox and Kara was looked after by a young woman resident. Although she had spent nearly twenty-four hours in Gabriella's prison, Kara claimed no ill affects, except some bruising to her neck. "You've been through quite an ordeal, Miss Westin," the doctor told her. "However, I see nothing wrong that food and rest won't cure."

"Thank you, doctor," Kara replied. "Please tell Dr. Lennox I'll be in the waiting area with my family." With a nod and smile, the dark-haired woman left the room. *Certainly, after I know Lorenzo is okay, I'll sleep for a week,* Kara thought, seeing the dark circles under her eyes.

As she studied her image in the mirror, she no longer saw the vain, self centered young woman she had once been. "You've grown up, the hard way," Kara uttered. *I've learned so much, but it nearly cost me everything,* she thought sadly. After dressing, she left the examining room to join the others.

"We have much celebrating to do when we get back home," Emma said, taking hold of her daughter's hand.

With a nod and smile, Kara leaned her head back and closed her eyes. "I've never been so tired, yet, I've never felt such peace," she said softy.

. . .

An hour later, cheers of thanksgiving erupted when Kara, Emma and Jock heard the good news regarding Lorenzo. "He should be able to travel in a couple days," doctor Lennox told them. "I must commend you, Miss Westin, there's no doubt this happy ending is because you were willing to sacrifice your freedom or your very life, if need be, to save Lorenzo. And you *did* save that young man's life, my dear. Certainly, there *is* no greater love than giving your life for someone else," the man concluded.

"Here, here," someone cheered nearby. "I'll second that," Ben told Kara as he stopped beside her. "It's all good. I just heard the news about Gabriella."

Just then, a loud noise was heard. The windows rattled and the floor shook, causing everyone to stop what they were doing. "That *sounded* like a huge explosion," Jock commented.

Seconds later, a man rushed through the front entrance. "Twas the castle! It blew clean away!" he announced excitedly. In shock, everyone looked around but said nothing.

"Well, it wasn't much of a house anyway," Emma said, shaking her head.

· · ·

Once more, the Highland Inn was a haven of comfort. This time however, Jock made sure Rowan was paid for his generous hospitality. After eating the delicious meal Edwina had prepared, Emma and Kara went upstairs.

"I doubted I would ever see another hot bath or warm bed," Kara remarked climbing under the covers. "How easily we take things for granted, Mother."

"Yes, I'm afraid *none* of us count our blessings often enough," Emma replied, tucking Kara in. "I love you, my dear girl, and I'm so *very* proud of you for what you did," she added, kissing Kara's cheek.

"I love you too, Mom, and I'm glad you're my mother," Kara said softly. "I'm *sorry* I was so pigheaded about things you told me. I guess it took all this to finally wake me up to how *blessed* I truly am."

"Don't be too hard on yourself, dear. We all have to go through these maturing stages in our lives. Often it takes tragedy, or extreme heartache before we see the light," Emma offered in her usual kind manner.

"Mother, tell me about everyone back home," Kara said, yawning. "How is Kelly, and Charles. And how's Ryan?"

"Let me see, Charles is wonderful, but I'm afraid his sister isn't, so he flew to Florida to see her. I told him I'd be fine, and he knows Jock will take good care of me," Emma began. "Kelly is doing wonderfully well, since her kidneys are working again and Abby is looking forward to summer. Aunt Gina is returning to Alaska this spring and Ryan, well, I guess he realizes you are making a new life without him. Now, I hear he's seeing Rebecca North again," she informed Kara. "I feel sure their relationship will blossom into something special this time."

As she talked, Emma saw Kara's eyelids close and soon heard the restful sound as she slept. Quietly, she left the bedroom and rejoined Rowan and Jock downstairs.

"Since you're entitled to the Carlyle estate, when are you planning to return?" Rowan asked Emma.

"Oh, I have no plans to move here," Emma quickly replied. "I have a wonderful new husband and a great life. After all the legal matters are settled, I know *exactly* what I'll be doing with it."

. . .

That night as she lay in bed, Emma couldn't sleep as she thought about her own dear mother and the searing heartache she had suffered at the hands of the Carlyle family. *In that horrible castle, that's where they planned their evil schemes against everyone,* Emma thought. *I'm glad it was blown up. There is no use for such a place!*

Then, word for word, Emma remembered the shocking entry in her mother's journal she had read just days before.

Henry confessed to me that Sabrina is a practicing witch and has vowed to destroy anyone who defies her. Her rituals of voodoo dolls and séances are well known. Although Henry scoffs at such nonsense, I feel he is more concerned than he is letting on.

Certainly, Mother knew they murdered Henry, and it drove her to church where she sought prayer for protection from Sabrina's curse, Emma thought, feeling thankful for God's intervention. "I *know* that's why they didn't come after you, too, Mother," she uttered in the dark.

It all fits, Emma reasoned, recalling Kara's description of Gabriella's demon. *They both were into hellish practices, doing evil of all kinds! How sad, when Jesus would have forgiven all their sins and delivered them from death into life, but now they're dead and it's eternally too late. . . .*

While Lorenzo fully recovered, Emma took care of her business matters. Because of her mother's diaries, Emma knew of legal papers filed in Scotland as to her true identity, proving she was Henry Carlyle's heir. However, despite her Carlyle lineage, the authorities assured Emma she had no right to the estate, that is, until she showed them the diamond necklace she brought with her.

"Oh, I beg your pardon, Madam, this is all the proof you need," the Commissioner told her, seeing the legendary collar of diamonds.

With that, Gabriella's name was removed and after a quick swipe of the gentleman's pen, Emma was handed the deed to the vast Carlyle estate. Later that day, she acquired Gabriella's bank accounts and security boxes containing an array of valuables, from gold coins, precious gems and cash.

That night, with future plans tumbling through her mind, Emma pulled the covers up around her ears as she thought about the day's events. *Who'd ever think that I would come into such riches? Thank you, dear Lord, for all the awesome things you do for me. I have all this* and *the mansion waiting for me up there,* Emma sighed, before falling asleep.

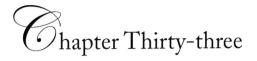# Chapter Thirty-three

Three Months Later

From their place on the hill, the newlyweds stood arm in arm, letting their eyes drift across the landscape; in the distance, the Loch glistened under the bright morning sun. Now, with the gloom of winter faded, new life burst forth in all its splendor. Yellow wildflowers dotted the blanket of green and in the pastures, baby lambs and newborn calves were seen tagging close behind their mothers.

Overhead, small cotton puff clouds meandered lazily across the azure blue sky. "Nothing could be more perfect," Kara sighed, looking at her husband.

"It's perfect because of you, my sweet darling," Lorenzo replied, facing his wife. "I never dreamed I could be this happy, not ever."

"Life can certainly be one big surprise, just look at all this," Kara remarked as her eyes swept the surrounding vista. "I had no idea Mother would sign all this over to us, did you?"

"Certainly not, but then, I had no idea about many things," Lorenzo said, again taking Kara in his arms. "It took all this misery to discover the truth."

"Yes, and I'm so sorry you never knew Carlotta was your mother, for certainly she loved you very much," Kara told him.

"Yes, I loved her too. She was always so attentive and kind to me. I only wish I had known the truth, perhaps I could have helped my father more. His sadness was evident, but I never knew why," Lorenzo replied.

For the next few moments, they stood holding each other, basking in the fresh clean air and the beauty around them. "It's a glorious day, let's drive into Glasgow, have our lunch and then visit the architect to see how he's coming along with the plans for our new house," Lorenzo said, surprising Kara.

"That sounds wonderful," Kara said. "I can't wait till its finished!"

"Nor can I, then we'll start building that family to fill up all those bedrooms," Lorenzo said teasingly.

"That sounds even more wonderful," Kara told her husband, smiling.

Epilogue

Just as Emma predicted, Ryan and Rebecca North's relationship quickly escalated into a deep mutual love. They would be married at the Morning Star Ranch in Montana the following summer.

When she met Ryan's mother, Cora, Rebecca was again told about the One who could heal all her guilt and comfort her sorrows. This time she was ready and at Cora's kitchen table, Rebecca prayed and was born anew, finding joy she had never known.

Leaving her job at Beaumont Computer, Rebecca found her calling when she began working at a Women's Clinic. Here, young girls, scared and alone came looking for answers. But, unlike the clinic Rebecca had found, here they were introduced to Jesus and shown love and support they so vitally needed.

Ned's construction business continued to prosper. Finding no time for dating, he remained a confirmed bachelor while many young women did their best to grab his attention.

Although they failed to conceive, Samantha and Jared's home was filled with the sounds of children when they adopted twin girls from Kiev, Russia.

Aunt Gina returned to Alaska and to everyone's delight, was married to a longtime friend, Gary, now widowed. While visiting Emma and Charles in Arizona, the newlyweds decided they, too, preferred sunshine to snow. Within a week of their arrival, they had bought a Condo. Soon, the two couples were playing golf in shorts and teasingly taunted those still living in the cold-country.

Before their home in Scotland was finished, Kara and Lorenzo were expecting their first child and their family grew steadily for the next four years. Kelly and Jock had their long awaited babies: twins, a boy and a girl.

Now grown, Abby was the object of many young men's attention. Not surprisingly, Tom and Eric North, too, were mesmerized by her beauty and charm. Would one of them win her heart?

On her sixtieth birthday, Emma looked at her family gathered around her. "I am so blessed," she said, fighting tears of joy. "To you, my darling grandchildren, please hear me. You may not understand it now, but one day you will come to know this truth: whether turmoil, heartache, or sorrow of any kind, nothing can stop you if you have and give, love. For love is not boastful or proud, but rather, is patient, kind, and pleasing to God."

When the birthday cake was brought out, Kelly and Kara led the others in singing Happy Birthday to their mother. As she watched the candles burn, Emma smiled and her eyes glistened. "Make your wish, Mother," Kara told her.

"Why would I wish for anything, dear?" Emma replied. "I have everything I want right here," she said, winking at Charles who sat nearby smiling at her.

Contact author Doris Christian
or order more copies of this book at

&

TATE PUBLISHING, LLC

127 East Trade Center Terrace
Mustang, Oklahoma 73064

(888) 361 - 9473

Tate Publishing, LLC

www.tatepublishing.com